UPSIDE DOWN

INSIDE OUT

Deadly Pleasures
Best Mystery Crime Novel of 2005
BARRY Award nominee for
Best Paperback Novel of the Year

"John Ramsey Miller's *Inside Out* needs to come with a warning label. To start the story is to put the rest of your life on hold as you obsessively turn one page after the other. With a story this taut, and characters this vivid, there's no putting the book down before you've consumed the final word. A thrilling read."
—John Gilstrap, author of *Scott Free*

"*Inside Out* is a great read! John Ramsey Miller's tale of big-city mobsters, brilliant killers, and a compellingly real U.S. marshal has as many twists and turns as running serpentine through a field of fire and keeps us turning pages as fast as a Blackhawk helicopter's rotors! Set aside an uninterrupted day for this one; you won't want to put it down."
—Jeffery Deaver, author of *The Cold Moon*

"[Full of] complications and surprises . . . Miller gifts [his characters] with an illuminating idiosyncrasy. This gives us great hope for future books as well as delight in this one."
—*Drood Review of Mystery*

THE LAST FAMILY

Too Far Gone

John Ramsey Miller

A DELL BOOK

TOO FAR GONE
A Dell Book / September 2006

Published by Bantam Dell
A Division of Random House, Inc.
New York, New York

This is a work of fiction. Names, characters, places, and incidents
either are the product of the author's imagination or are used
fictitiously. Any resemblance to actual persons, living or dead, events,
or locales is entirely coincidental.

Book design by Lynn Newmark

Dell is a registered trademark of Random House, Inc., and the
colophon is a trademark of Random House, Inc.

ISBN-13: 978-0-440-24309-0
ISBN-10: 0-440-24309-2

Printed in the United States of America
Published simultaneously in Canada

www.bantamdell.com

OPM 10 9 8 7 6 5 4 3 2 1

This book is dedicated to the heroes of Hurricane Katrina, and to all of those who gave of themselves to help ease the suffering of the thousands upon thousands of victims.

Acknowledgments

I watched, along with everybody else, in quiet horror as a real hurricane destroyed two of my favorite places, New Orleans and the Mississippi Gulf Coast. I had completed the final draft of *Too Far Gone* a month before Hurricane Katrina roared into the Gulf. As it happened, I had written a major storm into the story, which hit New Orleans in the closing chapters. I decided to rewrite the book in order to use the actual hurricane in this novel.

This book is a work of fiction, but in using Katrina, I hoped to recreate the mood in New Orleans in the days before the storm hit to hopefully allow readers to get a sense of the tension the residents of that area felt. I've taken some license with actual events to suit my plot and timetable.

As always I want to thank my family, my friends, and the professionals whose support and talents make my books possible.

1

New Orleans, Louisiana
The Garden District
September 1979

Crashing thunder woke the child.

Casey lay still, taking deep breaths, huddling with the teddy bear as the storm's fury assaulted her ears. Running bolts of lightning slashed the black sky.

Wind blasted the rain hard against the window's panes.

The massive oak tree outside flailed its branches—like furious arms reaching out for the lace curtains.

She clenched shut her eyes.

"There's nothing to fear," her mother had said on other stormy nights. *"You're perfectly safe in your bed, Casey."*

Each dazzling flash made the familiar objects in her room both strange and malevolent. The stuffed animals perched on the window box instantly became monsters on the shadowy wall.

She listened for some sound to let her know if her parents were awake and perhaps moving around somewhere in the house. *They will come tell me it's all right.*

The bedroom door was cracked open, the hallway a dark and endless tunnel.

Bam! A shutter on a nearby window, suddenly unhooked, slapped at the side of the house like an angry fist against a door. *Bam! Bam! Bam!*

The four-year-old pushed back the covers, slid off the mattress, and shot to the door, thinking of the safe, warm nest between her parents in their bed.

Throwing open her door Casey ran across the hallway to her parents' bedroom, clutching the bear to her chest. *They won't be mad.* She turned the knob and slowly crept into the bedroom, where lightning illuminated the crumpled bedding.

They're not here!

The bathroom was dark.

They have to be downstairs.

Casey hurried to find them. On the stairs, between the peals of thunder, she could hear loud noises below, like dogs barking, or seals at the zoo.

One hand on the banister, the other clutching the soft animal to her, the child slipped down the wide staircase one step at a time. The noises stopped before she reached the first floor, and the sudden silence scared her more than the sounds.

In the den, flashes formed into trapezoidal slivers by the windows lit the room eerily. The chair her father always sat in when he was in the room—it was vacant. *Not in here.*

She padded off down the hallway toward the rear of the house. *Mommy? Daddy?*

Casey saw a yellow band of light at the far end of the hallway under the swinging door to the kitchen and she ducked her head and ran for it. She imagined that something large was rushing at her in the darkness—something that would pounce at any second and sweep her up in its jaws like the lion on the television always did to the deer.

"Mommy!" she yelled out. "Mommy!"

Reaching the door, she pushed at it, and because it didn't swing open but a tiny bit, her chest and her forehead struck it hard, and she whimpered in pain. She fought to push the door open, but it wouldn't budge. In her panic she dropped the bear and slammed her hands against the wood, beating, beating, beating, and hollering for her mother.

Little by little, as whatever was making it stay shut moved, it opened just a bit. The kitchen lights poured out into the hallway through the growing crack.

Casey heard an odd sucking sound and a loud grunting.

Something warm and wet touched her toes and she looked down to see a pool spreading from under the door, and her bear was lying there on the floor, his black eyes staring up at her as the puddle swallowed his head and arms.

Casey pushed again, hard.

The door swung in abruptly. Casey pitched headlong into the brilliantly lit kitchen.

She was lying facedown in the warm red liquid that was everywhere.

She looked around and found herself staring into

her mother's face, and it was not at all the right face. So many boo-boos. She knew her father was there, too, but she wouldn't look at him. She squeezed her eyes shut and screamed and screamed.

"STOP IT!" a voice boomed. "STOP IT RIGHT THIS MINUTE!"

Casey quit screaming, turned, and saw two bare feet inches from her face, and let her eyes follow the legs to the hem of a dress. Casey sat bolt upright and looked up into the eyes of a witch wearing a wet dress. The witch's blond and crimson hair stuck out from her head like twisted garden vines. The unfamiliar face, smeared with red, smiled down at her. Two of her front teeth were missing. The witch knelt and put the cook's meat-chopping thing down on the floor.

Casey couldn't move. She stared at the gory hands that reached out for her and she squeezed her eyes shut tight as the witch embraced her, pressing Casey's cheek—wet with tears she didn't even know she was shedding—against her heaving chest.

"What a good baby girl you are to find me," the husky voice told her. "I was just getting ready to come get you."

2

Saturday, August 27, 2005

Using her SureFire flashlight in the dark to prevent tripping over tree limbs, FBI Special Agent Alexa Keen followed the string of Day-Glo plastic that had been run tree to tree by responding officers to lead the way to, then to form a bordered trapezoid around, the crime scene. Carefully, she entered the crime scene, illuminated by portable quartz floodlights. The corpse appeared to be wrapped tightly in a rust-colored blanket—a covering Alexa realized was comprised of tens of thousands of fire ants. As she squatted for a better look, the dead man's lids suddenly opened and he stared at her through eyes of wet obsidian. His mouth formed a silent, screaming circle.

Alexa jerked awake and lay in the darkness, piecing the shards of reality together. *Hotel room. New Orleans. Law-enforcement seminar.* A real siren outside had clawed its way through the gossamer walls of her dream about a dead man she had seen only in photographs until his naked corpse had been discovered in the Tennessee woods two days after his family had paid a quarter-million-dollar ransom. Charles Tarlton had been her first case—involving the murder of an abducted individual—and it played in the theater of her dreams with some frequency. As Alexa's nightmares went, this one was hardly a two—a ten was being awakened by labored wheezing and lying frozen in terror as a pair of clammy hands explored her prepubescent body. Alexa shuddered.

The bedside clock had the time at five past twelve. Alexa slid her hand beneath the pillow beside her to feel the knife. It was always there in case she was ever again surprised by anyone climbing into her bed. The knife's edge was razor sharp, and Alexa Keen knew how to use it.

Except for her shoes placed beside the bed, Alexa was still dressed in the clothes she'd worn to dinner with two other agents, who she'd never met before. They'd all checked into the Marriott—each presenting the "new and more user-friendly" FBI to the law enforcement seminar. Alexa always slept in her clothes when she was away from her own bed. She lay awake for several more minutes with her eyes closed—her mind speeding through a dark forest of troubling thoughts. The most disturbing were of her sister, who was sitting in a military safe house, waiting to testify at a string of court-martial proceedings, which involved several high-ranking members of U.S. Army intelligence, all facing disgrace and terms in military prison, and in one case possible execution. Some of them also faced federal and state charges when the Army was done with them.

Beyond that stack of mind manure, Alexa's brain started going through the cases she'd worked that had ended badly, wondering what she'd missed, how she should have done things differently. Everybody made mistakes, but when Alexa Keen made one, the consequences could be devastating for a family and deadly for the victim.

Alexa's professional life was one long-running stress test. She thrived on edge living—consuming gallons of coffee and running headlong through nights and days without meaningful sleep. She loved the atmospheric highs that success brought, and she somehow slogged her way out from the pit that failures dug. The job was her life. She read inside politics expertly, for doing so was a necessary evil: it often meant the difference between being relevant and sitting behind a desk in some dismal Bureau FO— or field office—in the windswept boonies. Alexa walked the walk—navigating the spiderweb red-tape bureaucracy—and talked the requisite Bureau-jabber. This was the life she had freely chosen, and the other agents were almost the only family she had left. Alexa's was a family headed by inflexible, often paranoid, and generally disapproving parent figures who were slow to reward and eager to punish—and the Bureau was a family where sibling rivalry was unrelenting and pitiless.

With the agility of a panther, Alexa rose from the bed and crossed to the window. Opening the heavy curtains, she peered down through the dark glass at a wide-awake city. Twenty floors below, an ambulance attendant slammed the door of the vehicle whose siren had awakened her and she listened to its scream as it made its way toward Charity Hospital, which had the best trauma care unit in the city. And New Orleans did its dead-level best to make sure the ER remained the busiest venue in town.

Alexa Keen sometimes wondered if there was a place she could call home. All through her adult life she had moved from city to city, settled in superficially, learned the relevant streets in those cities, developed preferences in stores and restaurants, but invariably they all felt cold to her.

Alexa's apartments were interchangeable. She hung the same art on the walls, shifted the same modern furniture in her space. There was no extraneous clutter, plants to be watered, pets to anchor her, and Alexa's telephone seldom rang since the advent of the do-not-call list. Her residence mailboxes collected only spiderwebs and generic adver-junk. Due to the amount of time she was away on-site, all of her bills were automatically subtracted from her checking account or paid electronically. Her television set was only a means to monitor the flowing river of news and the local weather.

Her sound system played Billie Holiday, Wes Montgomery, the Gipsy Kings, R.E.M., The Beatles, the Stones, or Elmore James, depending on her mood. Alexa kept a library card, and she read fiction for entertainment, nonfiction for information.

She was five feet seven inches tall and maintained her weight between 125 and 130. She worked out at the FBI gym before daybreak, and in the evenings she ran several miles. For days when the weather was bad, she had a treadmill in her apartment. When she was on the road she did push-ups, sit-ups, and squats. And over the years she had taken both karate and kickboxing lessons to keep up her self-defense skills. She was strong, agile, had good stamina, was fast on her feet, had remarkable balance, and knew how to defend herself. She went to the firing range monthly to stay sharp, but she would never be more than adequate with a handgun.

Alexa looked down at the pedestrians on the sidewalks. Most were tourists—which was a polite way of saying they were marks whose wallets held the blood that powered the city's real heart—the French Quarter, the casinos, the restaurants and bars.

Alexa had only visited the Crescent City on FBI business. It wasn't her nature to spend her vacation time in tourist magnets like New Orleans, San Francisco, Las Vegas, or Miami. When she took her required vacations, she hiked obscure trails, floated down rivers, camped where few other people wanted to be. She liked the salt air and the solitude of beaches in the winter.

Alexa had mixed feelings where New Orleans was concerned. She loved the jazz, but didn't drink. She enjoyed the restaurants, but she only ate rich foods on remarkable occasions. She appreciated antiques, but wouldn't spend the money on them because she had no desire to own things she might worry about. She enjoyed the architecture and the art. She appreciated the way most of the locals accepted eccentrics and misfits and how they took everyday life with a grain of salt.

New Orleans was a cautionary illustration of what could happen to the entire country as it descended from its golden age. Alexa knew that the things residents and most nonresidents loved about the city were hardly more than smoke and mirrors that hid the real New Orleans, which was a collapsing sump, crippled by rampant ignorance, grinding poverty, shameless nepotism, an inadequate tax base, a crumbling infrastructure, a long-ignored levee system, a generational welfare system, wholesale crime, underpaid and overworked city employees, decaying structures, morally bankrupt leaders who propagated a third-world-style corruption—and it was all gathering speed in a downhill direction.

Some years earlier, she'd been hunting down a sexual predator who had abducted a girl and, in the process, killed two Chicago policemen. She had tracked him to New Orleans. The man had been staying in a motel, using the abducted sixteen-year-old girl to satisfy his sadistic sexual desires. Alexa had found him, and, when he'd run, he ended up abandoning the girl in his car, and Alexa had found herself chasing him through the French Quarter. Alexa wasn't religious, but she had decided that if there was a hell, it must look and feel like Bourbon Street on Fat Tuesday. After catching him he'd wanted to fight with his much smaller adversary, so she'd used her fists and feet on him while the crowd had cheered wildly. As he'd begged for mercy, she handcuffed and arrested him.

Despite the fact that she was wide-awake, the ringing telephone startled her. The red numerals on the clock said 12:22.

"Yes," she said.

"Special Agent Keen?" a male voice asked.

"Speaking."

"This is Michael Manseur. I'm a detective with NOPD Homicide."

"Winter Massey's friend," she said, smiling. Six months earlier, she and ex–Deputy U.S. Marshal Winter Massey, a close friend of hers since childhood, had worked together on a kidnapping case in North Carolina. Massey had spoken very highly of Michael Manseur, the man who had helped him locate and save a young girl's life. The child, whose mother had been murdered by a professional killer, had become a member of Winter Massey's family.

"Well," Manseur responded, "I expect *friend* might be a stretch. *Acquaintance* is closer to it. I have nothing but respect for Winter, that's for sure. He is one memorable individual."

"I spoke to him last week, and he told me I should call you. I really did mean to."

"He called me a few days ago to tell me I should call you while you were in town. I intended to ask you to join my family for dinner while you're here, but I've been up to my belt loops in alligators. And this hurricane track is looking bad."

"I'm leaving first thing in the morning," she told him truthfully.

"I'm sorry to hear it," Manseur replied.

What Alexa couldn't imagine was why Manseur was calling her after midnight. Maybe the detective had been working late shift in a windowless room and lost track of time. It had happened to her enough.

"Maybe the next time I'm in town . . ." she suggested.

"Kyler Kennedy, our Missing Persons detective, sat in on your talk today." His heavy Southern accent was warm and comforting. Alexa liked the way he stretched his vowels out like soft taffy.

"Well, maybe we can get together next time I'm here. It was nice talking to you, Detective Manseur."

"That isn't why I called you, Agent Keen. I'm thoughtless to a fault, but I sure wouldn't bother you at this hour just to chat. I was wondering if I could impose on you a little bit."

"Please do." Perhaps he had a pressing question on a case he thought she might have an answer to.

"We've got ourselves a potential situation. I was hoping you could spare me a couple of hours."

"My flight leaves just after nine."

"I mean right now. This deal is what you do, and Winter said you're one of the best there is at it."

"An abduction?" She straightened and let the curtains drop shut, closing out the night.

"Possibly. Going missing in New Orleans is hardly unusual. Ninety-nine times out of ten, the case solves itself pretty quick. I hope you might be able to help us assess a situation. Tell us what you think we've got. It's a pretty delicate deal."

"You're the head of Homicide, aren't you?"

"Missing Persons is understaffed, and, like in most places, we work hand in hand a lot. I hoped I could get your opinion on this since you're here and have the reputation you do. That's all."

"I see." She was flattered.

"And then I can tell Massey truthfully that we got together. Are you free to go to a location with me?"

This wasn't going to be a question or two over the phone. "How soon?"

"I'm in the lobby now," he told her. "Standing by the elevators. I'm wearing a green suit."

If he hadn't been the only man in a dark green suit watching the elevators, Alexa would have kept scanning the lobby until the detective approached her. Michael Manseur's voice had thoroughly misrepresented him. He sounded like Tommy Lee Jones but looked more like a chronically unsuccessful door-to-door salesman. Even with the thickness of the soles of his scuffed brown wingtips, Manseur was no more than five-seven and, except for the laurel of short pale hair anchored by small ears, he was bald. His pasty round face featured intelligent but sad eyes with large bags beneath them, a razor-thin nose, acne scars, and a smile like that of a child with a secret. The loosened knot on his predominantly yellow tie rested between stiff shirt collars, one of them bent up at the end like a hand waving.

"Agent Keen?" he said, uncertainly.

"Alexa," she said, smiling. "Michael, please call me Alexa." She realized that he had expected her to be a white woman—and not a light-skinned black woman. She knew there was nothing in her voice that gave away her ethnicity.

"Certainly," he replied, nodding. He swept his arm to indicate the direction she should travel to get to his car, which turned out to be a large white sedan waiting at the curb.

Manseur opened the passenger door for Alexa, and closed it gently before hurrying around to get in behind the wheel. He checked the rearview, pulled out, and headed away from the Mississippi River, flipping on the blue light centered on the dash to cut a path through the traffic as the vehicle gathered speed.

"Where are we going?" she asked him.

"Uptown a little way," he replied, as if that answered her question.

Alexa sat back and watched the Big Easy rush by.

3

Detective Manseur drummed his fingers absently on the steering wheel as he sped along streets Alexa wasn't familiar with. Policemen, firemen, and ambulance drivers were required to learn the streets of their cities and towns until they were human GPS devices. If cabbies and delivery people didn't do the same, they were less effective at their jobs, but people didn't usually die on account of it.

Alexa's understanding of the layout of New Orleans was sketchy. She knew that the streetcar ran from Uptown, through the Garden District, and made a loop at Canal Street. She knew the Mississippi River curved around the city, which was why it was called the "Crescent City." She knew that Lake Pontchartrain was north and that the twin-span across it was the longest bridge in the world. She knew where the French Quarter, the Central Business District, the Federal Court Building, and FBI Headquarters were located.

"You ever heard of the LePointe family?" Manseur asked her.

"Can't say I have," Alexa replied. "Sounds French."

"They're the most influential family there is around here. They're socially prominent, wealthy, and as generous as people get. The LePointes don't usually give out in the open."

He stopped talking to make a left turn.

"Any questions so far?" he asked.

"These LePointes make the social page wearing tuxedos more than most people and throw around money and are fairly discreet about it," Alexa said. "But not so discreet so that everybody isn't aware of it."

Manseur sat as silent as might a nun who has just heard someone accuse the Pope of using money sent to the Vatican from poor boxes to buy lap dances.

"So, I assume your missing person is a LePointe," she said.

"Gary West. He married Casey LePointe."

"So Gary West would be a valuable target for a kidnapper?"

Manseur nodded.

"What were the circumstances of his disappearance?"

"He didn't come home for dinner."

"Missed dinner? Obviously a kidnapping."

"Oh, you're being sarcastic. I'm sorry if I'm not doing this briefing right. I just want you to know we're dealing with people who are important to powerful people."

Alexa laughed. "Forgive me. It's late, and being a smart-ass is part of my FBI training. Go ahead."

"I don't mind." Manseur had slowed the car, so Alexa figured they must be getting close to wherever they were heading. "Dr. William LePointe is presently the last male LePointe. His brother, Curry, has been dead for twenty-six years. The Wests have a kid, I think a young daughter."

"The family's influence explains why an out-of-place LePointe by marriage rates the commander of Homicide." *And an FBI agent who specializes in abductions.*

"Kyler Kennedy, our Missing Persons detective who was at your lecture, is meeting us there. It should be Kennedy's case—at least at first—but not this time. I was hoping you could watch how we handle it, suggest things we miss, or whatever. My superiors don't want a big fuss made about this until it's established that there's a need for a big fuss. They'd like to keep everything low-key."

"Like keeping it a secret that one of these LePointes is missing?"

"Alexa, you don't see a LePointe in the newspaper except on the society or business page. Dr. William LePointe was Rex before he was thirty-five years old."

"Rex?"

Manseur smiled. "You're not familiar with Rex?"

"I only know from experience that it's the number-one name for German shepherds."

"King of Carnival. It's about the biggest deal there is in this city. Well, being Momus is probably bigger, but Momus is always masked, so nobody but a few people in that secret society have any idea who the king of Momus is. See, Rex brings in Mardi Gras—Fat Tuesday—and Momus bids adieu to Mardi Gras."

"The festive alpha and omega, or yin and yang. How did I miss that?" Alexa said. Manseur talked about Rex and Momus like a Catholic might speak of the Virgin Mary. He probably was Catholic.

"By the way, I didn't mention to anybody that I was bringing you along."

"You didn't mention the FBI coming in?"

"Just to advise, if that's okay. Unofficially."

"Wouldn't have it any other way."

"I'll be ranking officer at the scene. We have this new superintendent of police. He told me to make sure this went right. You understand, nobody wants to involve the FBI unless it turns out to be an FBI matter—"

"Of course not."

"Which nobody thinks it is. I'm just . . ." Manseur hesitated.

"Covering your bases."

"Covering my something. The LePointes give millions every year to all sorts of things, like schools, libraries, the zoo, museums, scholarships, after-school programs, homeless and battered women shelters, summer camps, and hospitals. They've donated firefighting equipment, ballistic vests, and service weapons to the police. The LePointes are extremely generous to New Orleans."

"I don't suppose their generosity extends to political campaigns?" Alexa asked.

"Local, state, and national."

"Say no more," Alexa said.

4

The West house was a looming thunder-gray brick palatial structure with wood shutters and a steep slate roof. It was protected from prying eyes by a wall of impenetrable privets. The lower floor of the home was visible from the street only where the hedge ended on either side of the ornate wrought-iron-gated driveway and where a matching pedestrian gate protected the walkway. The cobblestone driveway was empty except for a sleek new Bentley.

Manseur parked on the street at the end of a row of identical four-door sedans, each with cheaper-by-the-million hubcaps and short radio antennas centered on their trunks. There was not a single marked police car in evidence.

Alexa followed Manseur through the gate and toward the covered front porch, which was thirty feet wide. Men in casual attire stood in a cluster off to one side, giving the impression of a wake in progress. Alexa had to suppress a smile when she recognized one of two men standing together on the opposite side of the porch from the larger group.

"Dagnabbit," Manseur murmured as he opened the gate. "My superintendent is here."

Alexa wore khaki slacks, a button-down shirt under a navy blazer. Her .40-caliber Glock and a pair of loaded magazines resided in an armory section of her shoulder bag. As Alexa and Manseur closed on the porch, the men grew silent and watched intently. A couple of the plainclothes cops, both looking like desk-bound administrators, nodded at Manseur as he led Alexa to the pair of men standing alone. Superintendent of Police Jackson Evans was a tall, distinguished-looking man whose skin was the color of maple syrup. The top cop's intense nut-colored eyes slowly covered the distance between Alexa's shoes and her eyes.

The older man Evans was standing with reached into his coat pocket for his ringing cell phone, glanced carelessly at the readout, then stepped away for privacy.

"Superintendent Evans, may I introduce—"

"Alexa," Evans interrupted, smiling broadly. "Your presence here is quite an *unexpected* pleasure."

"Well, Jackson. I heard you had taken over down here. If you don't slow down, you're going to run out of distressed cities to rescue." Alexa allowed her accent to slow and flow below the Mason-Dixon Line. Being a native of the Mississippi Delta, her accent had a distinctly Southern edge anyway, but she had worked hard to lessen its dominance. Even so, when she was around other Southern accents, hers came back to the fore in all of its glory. In truth, a slightly exaggerated drawl tended to disarm hostility among practitioners of that accent, and it made a lot of non-Southerners think they had the upper hand intellectually. She had said on more than a few occasions that while she might talk slow, she thought really fast.

"I didn't know you were coming," Jackson said, turning his eyes on Manseur for a split second to let the detective know he was addressing his comment to him more than to Alexa. He obviously felt blind-sided, and Jackson Evans had never appreciated be-ing taken by surprise. He was a political weatherman. When the wind blew from the right direction and his nostrils caught the scent of success, he strutted and crowed like a barnyard rooster. When it shifted and brought ill odors his way, a trapdoor would open for him to drop through.

It amazed Alexa how much the "brass" of the law enforcement world had in common. In the four cities where Evans had been the superintendent of police over the past nine years, crime had gone down, and the citizenry knew it was due to Jackson Evans be-cause he told them so every chance he got. In every department he ran, the police public relations depart-ment was run by the very same dedicated profession-als. They were a troupe of talented fact-spinners who followed their leader from city to city in the same manner a pack of jackals will shadow a lion pride.

"I wasn't aware you two knew each other," Manseur said.

"Alexa and I go back ten years."

"More like six," Alexa corrected. "But who's counting?"

"Last time I saw you was year before last in San Francisco at the Fairmont." Jackson Evans tapped his forehead as though he were remembering. "A gather-ing of police chiefs from around the country."

"Which reminds me," Alexa said, "you never did send me a dry-cleaning bill for your slacks."

Jackson Evans smiled, possibly amused, but more likely just part of his act. "Nonsense. That unfortunate accident was my fault. I can be clumsy."

Alexa probably should have mentioned to Manseur that she and Evans knew each other, but she hadn't expected to run into him. The superintendent had been extremely charming when they'd first met, and the fact that he was married hadn't kept him from hitting on her shamelessly until she had made it perfectly clear his chances of bedding her were nil. On their last encounter in the Fairmont's bar in San Francisco, he had put his hand on her leg. If Evans hadn't become belligerent when she asked him to remove his hand, she would not have poured a glass of house Merlot into his lap, destroying a pair of wheat-colored linen slacks and embarrassing him in public.

Alexa said, "How is your lovely wife?"

The superintendent showed her a smile filled with teeth bleached to a Hollywood standard of perfection. His eyes flickered, the smile shifting slightly. "Sandra is fine. Thank you for asking."

The white-haired gentleman closed his phone and returned, smiling absently.

"Hello, I am William LePointe," he said, fixing watery blue eyes on Alexa. LePointe looked to be in his mid-sixties, had bushy eyebrows, and was dressed in a black polo shirt beneath a dark sports jacket. His black-and-white-checked trousers broke above low-profile loafers.

"I'm sorry," Evans said. "Dr. LePointe, may I present FBI Special Agent Alexa Keen. Alexa's an old friend of mine."

Alexa was relieved that Dr. LePointe merely nodded to acknowledge her presence. She wasn't big on shaking hands.

"What is it you do with the FBI?" Dr. LePointe asked her.

"Agent Keen," Manseur said, "is—"

"An abduction specialist with CIRG," Evans interrupted again. "She is in town as part of a program the FBI is presenting to—"

Alexa took over from Evans. "To promote the ever-expanding assistance opportunities the FBI's departments have to offer local law enforcement in fighting crime. To educate and discuss the latest equipment, and how to apply our techniques to their problems."

"It's part of the FBI's *new* spirit of cooperation," Evans tossed in. "CIRG stands for the Crisis Immediate Response Group."

"I know what the CIRG is, Superintendent Evans," LePointe said mildly. "My question is, why is Agent Keen standing with us on my niece's porch?"

"Well," Evans said, turning his gaze on Manseur, "I'm sure Detective Manseur can clarify that for both of us."

"Allow me," Alexa said. "Detective Manseur and I have a mutual friend who suggested we get together while I was in town. When Detective Manseur called to beg off our breakfast meeting, he said he couldn't make it because an important friend of the department, who I assume is you, Dr. LePointe, had a relative who was unaccounted for. I suggested we could talk on the way. Now that I'm here, I would like to offer any assistance I can give. Perhaps I could observe Detective Manseur and offer my impressions, if he doesn't see it as an intrusion. I'm sure I'd learn a great deal from observing his techniques."

"Unofficially," Evans said. "I expect we could all learn a great deal from Agent Keen."

"Absolutely," Manseur agreed. "To have someone with Agent Keen's experience on hand to share her thoughts in a confidential context might help us save time and better focus our efforts."

LePointe's eyes softened. "I doubt we require FBI involvement, but thank you for coming out at this late hour to help, Agent Keen. Hopefully my niece overreacted by calling the authorities in so soon, but I sincerely appreciate the immediate attention on the part of the police, and I welcome your interest." LePointe's smile seemed genuine.

"Best not to take any chances," Evans said. "It's always a relief when these things turn out to be nothing."

LePointe shrugged. "We are all concerned about the fact that Gary is out of pocket. However, I want you to understand that I am extremely concerned about exposing my niece to possible humiliation, a risk that becomes exponentially greater with increased official involvement. My niece is an emotionally delicate woman."

"A minimum of hubbub. Our main job will be to put Mrs. West's mind at ease," Evans said.

And if we happen to run across her missing husband while we're at it . . . Alexa mused.

LePointe cocked his head slightly. "I expect you know my dear friend Alfred Bender, Agent Keen?"

"I haven't met the new director yet," Alexa said.

She had been in the same room with the director along with a hundred other agents, but she was fairly certain he had no idea who she was. Director Bender was also a close friend of both Presidents Bush and every other individual worth knowing in Washington. The director was widely rumored to be chronically uninterested in the day-to-day operations of any organization he was associated with except his golf club in Augusta, Georgia. It was common knowledge inside the Beltway that FBI Director Alfred Bender elevated delegation of authority to levels that would have stunned Senator Strom Thurmond senior aides.

"I've had occasion to make limited contributions to your Behavioral Science people over the years," LePointe told Alexa.

She didn't bother to tell him that the Behavioral Science Unit he was referring to was now the Behavioral Analysis Unit, or BAU, the profiling unit one subdivision of BSU.

"Contributions?" she asked.

"I have some insight into the abnormal mind," LePointe said. "Especially the criminally abnormal mind."

"Dr. LePointe is a psychiatrist," Manseur told her.

"We can safely say an internationally respected psychiatrist," Evans interposed.

"Is that a fact?" Alexa said, feigning genuine interest. She met the eyes of a red-haired man standing in the cluster of policemen ten feet away. The staring man's features were hard as rock and blade-sharp and his sky-blue eyes were locked on hers. In her job Alexa ran across hard-core individuals who radiated a skepticism that bordered on disease, or transmitted a soul-staining hatred, or possessed a festering sense of superiority. Such people, usually criminals but often cops, chilled her to the marrow.

The sound of a car racing up the street shattered the quiet.

"Well," Manseur said, "Detective Kennedy has arrived."

Everyone on the porch turned to watch the approaching detective, who reminded Alexa of someone who should be fleeing a headless horseman.

5

The monster outboard growled as the seventeen-foot-long boat shot between the soft grassy banks at thirty miles per hour. Standing at the center console, a tall, muscular man with a buzz cut swung the wheel hard at the intersections, casting walls of water when he turned the vessel sharply. Like a dog with his nose out in a car's slipstream, the boat's pilot, Leland Ticholet, luxuriated as the slipstream caressed his face.

Using the powerful searchlight to illuminate the scummy surface, Leland checked his intended path for any floating debris that could puncture the fiberglass hull. On the trip into the swamp, he had seen dozens of pairs of alligators' eyes and enough nutria to fill a truck bed. If he'd had the time, he would have killed a few of the furry critters with his Remington Nylon 66, a .22 carbine made using as much nylon and as little steel as had been possible forty years before. The weather-resistant gun, a dependable and accurate weapon, had been his father's favorite. Shooting was easier than trapping and if you made head shots, the skins and the meat were undamaged. The state paid a four-dollar bounty on each nutria skin. Leland had been told that nutria had been imported to Louisiana from South America for their pelts or some happy crap and then had bred there to beat the band, and started wreaking havoc on the ecosystem, destroying the vegetation that helped keep salt water out of the marshes. Since there were so many of the pesky critters in Louisiana, the state had encouraged chefs to prepare their meat in creative ways so they might become as close to extinct as redfish had become when a famous chef had the world eating pan-blackened carp until only emergency legislation instituting strict limits kept the poor things from being enjoyed off the face of the earth.

The network of interconnected bayous and canals in the snake-infested swamp was a maze navigable only to the few people who traversed it daily in order to scrape out an existence by fishing, crabbing, poaching, and trapping. Leland had spent his life running the light-green-algae-coated highway and he loved the solitude—a life of total freedom and self-sufficiency. The people who lived in the swamp knew better than to stick their noses in another man's business or mess with his things. In the swamps, nobody called the cops, bullets were plentiful, and something hungry would always eat red meat before it raised a stink.

After rounding a familiar bend, Leland turned into his cove—its throat invisible because of tall grass that formed a solid-looking wall—cut the motor's power back, then drifted toward the sagging pier connected to his floating fishing cabin, a twelve-by-sixteen-foot room set on a floating foundation of rusted steel barrels. He killed the motor and the night filled instantly with insects, frogs, and alligators sending warnings or invitations to others who spoke their language.

Mosquitoes swarmed around his head. After he tied the boat to the pier, Leland climbed onto the deck and played the flashlight over his small cabin. He didn't think anything about the fact that one side of the building was closer to the waterline than the other, because it had been that way for as long as he could remember.

Leland reached down and lifted the hog-tied man into the air like he was made of feathers and draped him over his solid right shoulder. Stepping onto the pier, he walked to the cabin door, which he kneed open. He stepped over the first four floorboards, then used the toe of his sneaker to drop a section of plywood over those rotten boards, which were about as substantial as cigar ash.

"Once you get used to the skeeters you're gone to really like it here," he told the man he carried over his shoulder. "They's nobody going to poke needles in you, and try and measure out your brain chemicals so they can control you." Leland dumped his rope-bound guest onto the cot, grabbed a section of rope off the floor, and looped it around the man to bind him to the cot.

Leland went back outside to the boat and fished the new cell phone from underneath the back seat. Dialing the number he had learned by heart, he waited for the person to answer, but nothing happened. He shook the phone gently, assuming some crucial part must be loose, listened to it, then shook it harder. It was lit up like it was when Doc used it, but it wasn't ringing and nobody was talking to him.

"Hello, Doc. I'm at my camp," Leland said. He listened for a few seconds and repeated the message like Doc had told him to do when he got there. "HELLO!" he hollered. "ARE YOU THERE, DOC? ANSWER ME! ANSWER ME, DAMN IT!"

Leland didn't know he had thrown the phone until he realized he was no longer holding it, and he had no idea which direction he had throw it in. Might be Doc would be mad about the stupid little phone. Leland didn't give a damn. He was supposed to watch over the man in the cabin, but he knew Doc wouldn't know it if he went out and checked on his catfish lines. It wasn't like the man in the cabin was going anywhere.

6

When Manseur's cell phone rang, Jackson Evans frowned. After a few seconds spent listening, Manseur held the phone aside and said, "Sorry, I have to deal with this. Detective Kennedy, if you could take Agent Keen inside to get the ball rolling with Mrs. West, I'm right behind you."

Jackson Evans nodded his approval. "Dr. LePointe, please call me if you need anything. And I mean *anything* at all. Detective Manseur will be keeping me up to speed on the investigation. Feel free to call me anytime you feel the need."

"That's very thoughtful of you, Superintendent Evans."

Evans reached into his pocket and took out a card case made of brass. Opening it, he reached behind the front cards to remove one that was clearly different from the ones in front. It was printed on an expensive parchment and looked to be engraved, not offset-printed. He handed it to LePointe. "My private numbers."

Dr. LePointe pocketed the card and, without saying anything further to the superintendent of police, led Alexa and Detective Kennedy through the house's wide hallway back to an open kitchen where two women, one with dark hair and the other a blonde, sat at a table. The blonde held a fair-skinned towheaded child whose eyes were exact replicas of her mother's—except the mother's showed evidence of tears.

Casey West possessed the sort of classical beauty that inspired artists, allowed peasants to end in royal beds, and started wars. Her features, framed by curtains of perfectly straight white-blond hair that was gathered into a wide ponytail, were perfectly balanced. Her almond-shaped green eyes were tinted pink from crying.

"This is Casey, my niece," LePointe told them. "Casey, this is Detective Kennedy of Missing Persons, and FBI Special Agent Alexa Keen, who has kindly consented to give the local authorities her expert assistance."

Casey West managed a worried half smile. "FBI? So you think Gary was kidnapped?" She locked eyes with Alexa. "Is he all right? You know something, don't you?"

"No, Casey," LePointe said firmly. "Agent Keen is merely a friend of Detective Manseur's. The man Jackson Evans told us was handling this."

"What sort of FBI agent are you?"

"The regular sort, I'm afraid," Alexa answered.

"She's here for a law enforcement seminar," Kennedy said. "She gave a lecture on techniques for identifying and resolving abductions."

Alexa saw LePointe roll his eyes toward the ceiling.

"Abductions?" Casey asked, fear in her eyes.

"Nobody has suggested that your husband was abducted. I'm just here to observe and advise if it becomes necessary. You are in very capable hands," Alexa said. "It's purely by coincidence that I'm here."

The other woman, whom Dr. LePointe had failed to introduce, had pasty skin that stood in stark contrast to her sculpted black pageboy and pencil-thin eyebrows. The turtleneck sweater, her shimmering lipstick, and the smears of rouge on each of her round cheeks were identical shades of red. The brown irises of her eyes were almost as dark as her hair and her fingernails. A row of pearl-shaped gold studs curved up the edge of her left ear from its heavy lobe to the crest. She watched them with the wide-eyed intensity of a child having her first trip to the circus.

"I not yew-ah fren," the blond child said.

"You're not my friend?" Kennedy replied, feigning disappointment.

The child shook her head violently.

"She doesn't mean she isn't your friend," the dark-haired woman said, smiling. "Deana picked the expression up from an older child at school."

"Well, that's good," Detective Kennedy said. "I hate to make enemies of pretty young girls."

Deana stuck out her tongue. She was at that age where it was hard to tell whether or not she understood the impact of her words, or was repeating some phrase or action that earned a reaction from adults.

Detective Kennedy, who was all elbows and knees, took a seat across from Casey and immediately worried with the precise position of his eyeglasses.

"I not yew-ah fren," Deana said again, poking out her lower lip.

Casey hugged the child to her. "Okay, Deana. That's enough of that."

Dr. LePointe looked at the woman beside his niece, waved his hand, and said, "Grace, please take Deana to her room."

The woman turned to look at LePointe, her eyes filled with disappointment.

"Grace," Casey said, "would you please get Deana ready for bed?"

"I'd be delighted, Casey," the still unintroduced Grace said. She stood, opened her arms, and the little girl transferred herself easily into the other woman's arms, clinging to her. Alexa saw for the first time that the child was naked. Alexa wondered if Grace was the child's nanny.

As they left the room, LePointe said, frowning, "Put a diaper on the child."

Casey smiled and looked at Alexa. "She takes them off. Sometimes Gary and I let it ride. We're only firm with the important things. Discipline is a tricky issue. Clothing is sometimes optional. Gary and I want Deana to feel free to express herself."

Alexa sat down beside Kennedy, diagonally across the table from Casey. Alexa's view through the wall of French doors was of a large formal garden, which formed a protective horseshoe around a swimming pool. A pool house with a slate roof stood at the far end of the pool, connected by a glassed-in corridor. A ten-foot-tall wall of brick appeared to enclose the entire property.

"Coffee?" Casey offered.

"None for me," Kennedy said immediately.

Alexa shook her head. She wanted to fade into the background and take in the reactions of Casey and her uncle to Kennedy's questions.

"So, Mrs. West," Kennedy said, opening his notebook, "I was told only that your husband failed to show up for dinner?"

"Our family has dinner at six," Dr. LePointe said. He stood with his back to the counter, watching.

"Routine is especially important for children," Casey said.

"Important for everybody in a civilized society," LePointe added.

"We try to always eat as a family," Casey told them. "Most times we manage to do so."

"Does the entire LePointe family eat together here?" Kennedy asked, smiling up at the doctor.

"My wife and I eat together in *our* home."

"Dinner at six," Kennedy said as he wrote it down. "Your house is on St. Charles, isn't it, Dr. LePointe?"

"Our *family* home has been there since the street was put in," LePointe answered. "The original structure burned to the ground in 1855. The one there now was completed just in time, as the War Between the States made stonemasons and detail craftsmen a rarity. It wasn't adequately furnished until after that conflict, as the furniture was imported and there were far more profitable cargoes to be shipped than chairs and tables."

In Alexa's mind, where Dr. LePointe lived seemed totally irrelevant to the case at hand.

"It isn't at all like Gary to be late," Casey said.

"Casey, he's missed dinners before," Dr. LePointe corrected. He took a seat at the head of the table, with Casey on his right, Kennedy on his left.

"He always calls to tell me if he's not going to make it on time," she countered, defensively. "I've called his cell phone for hours, but it went straight to message. He rarely turns it on anyway. He carries it for emergencies. Anyway, I found it in our bedroom. Gary hadn't even taken it with him."

LePointe frowned.

"When did you see him last?" Kennedy asked.

"We had lunch at R&O's."

"Arnaud's?" Kennedy said, starting to write that down.

"R *and* O's, out on the Lakefront. We eat lunch there together every Friday. Except when we're out of town," Casey said.

"Or when Christmas falls on Friday?" Kennedy asked, seemingly serious.

"It's where we had our first meal in New Orleans together. That was five years ago. We usually have the seafood gumbo and a beer. I guess it's a ritual."

"Gumbo's very good there," Kennedy said, straightening his glasses. "Best in the city for the money. Good chopped salad too."

Casey nodded absently.

"You left the restaurant together?" Kennedy asked.

"Well, we were in separate vehicles. I'd been working all morning, so Gary had Deana. She came with him. Gary left a few minutes before I did. I had to go by my studio to do some paperwork on a show I'm shipping out of the country next week," Casey said. "I had Deana with me. I met Grace there."

"Grace is your nanny?" Kennedy halted his note-scribbling.

"Nanny?" Casey smiled. "No. Grace is my personal assistant. We don't have a nanny. I have sitters who come when I need them. Grace has been my dearest friend since elementary school."

"Where is your studio?" Kennedy asked.

"On Magazine Street."

"I saw some of your snapshots at the Contemporary Arts Center one time," he added.

"Formal portraits," LePointe corrected.

"It's like a hobby for you?" Kennedy persisted. "Taking pictures. Or are you a professional?"

"The photography keeps me occupied," Casey said, "but I don't think I'm a professional, because I don't make money at it."

LePointe said, "Casey's portrait work is in every museum collection worth mentioning. We're extremely proud of Casey's artistic accomplishments—her body of work. Can we please get back on point?"

"I meant no offense," Kennedy said.

"Portrait *series*?" Alexa said. "Would that be similar to Richard Avedon's portraits? Subjects with some common association?"

Casey nodded, her eyes springing to life. "I'm hardly

in Avedon's class. I work in color. Longshoremen, homeless people, veterans, racists, midwives, artists, evangelists, carpenters . . ."

"Senators, cabinet members, ex-presidents and their wives," LePointe added.

Alexa was fascinated by LePointe's incessant need to elevate his niece's importance.

Casey's face flushed. Alexa wondered if Dr. LePointe's friends accommodated his niece as a favor to him. Perhaps he used his influence to make sure her work made the right private and museum collections, and the right galleries. Unless she really was that good, and Alexa had seen nothing to indicate she was, his patronage could certainly account for her success. Wouldn't it be something, Alexa thought, if a woman as attractive, wealthy, seemingly intelligent had real artistic talent as well?

"So R&O's at lunch was the last time you saw your husband? Or spoke to him?" Kennedy asked.

Casey nodded. "And nobody's seen him. I've called everybody I could think of. Sometimes he gets with friends and loses track of the time."

"How much did he have to drink at lunch?"

Dr. LePointe looked down at his hands, twisted his heavy gold signet ring.

"One beer," Casey said.

"And before you met him at the restaurant?" Kennedy asked.

"Gary never drinks before five."

"Except at lunch," Kennedy said.

"On Fridays. It's part of the tradition."

"Do you have a recent picture of him?" Kennedy asked. "A physical description?"

"I have hundreds of recent pictures. Gary's five-ten. He weighs one fifty. Blond hair in a ponytail. A patch of hair beneath his lower lip. I have a picture I took a week ago."

"What do *you* think happened to your husband?" Alexa asked Casey.

"I don't know," she said, looking up. "Maybe he's in a hospital with amnesia."

"Have you called the hospitals?" Kyler Kennedy asked.

"Grace and I called all of them before I contacted the police. We found no one matching his description," Casey said, her eyes showing pain. "Please, you have to find him. He'd come home or call if he could, I know he would."

LePointe reached over and put his hand on Casey's shoulder.

"Mrs. West," Kennedy started, "I know this may be a bad time to ask this, but do you know if your husband may have been seeing anyone?"

"What?" Casey snapped immediately. "You mean another woman? Of course not! We love each other."

"You can forget that line of questioning," Dr. LePointe said. "It's inappropriate."

"Sorry, it's just that sometimes men—" Kennedy started.

"Gary isn't like most men," Casey said.

"I believe that's more than enough information to get you started," Dr. LePointe interrupted.

"There are more questions that need to be asked," Kennedy said.

"Perhaps later when Casey is stronger. It's very

late and she's upset and tired. I don't think you'll learn anything else of value here tonight."

"I'm fine, Unko," Casey protested.

Alexa caught Dr. LePointe's reaction to his niece's use of *Unko,* which had to be a pet name he didn't care for.

"Ask whatever you like," Casey said. "We have nothing to hide. If my husband were seeing anybody, I'd know. He is usually right here with Deana and me. He doesn't spend enough time away from us for that sort of thing. And he's incapable of subterfuge or deceit."

LePointe said, "It's likely Gary will come in or call any moment."

Kyler Kennedy closed his notebook and stood abruptly. "Of course," he said. "More than enough to get started. Thanks for your time, Mrs. LePointe."

"West," Casey corrected.

"We need the make and model of the car he was driving and the license number," Alexa said.

Casey handed Alexa a sheet of paper she'd made up with that information on it, as well as Gary's description.

"We'll show ourselves to the door," Kennedy said. "If you think of anything . . ." He placed his card on the table. "Twenty-four hours a day."

"I want to go on, if you need more information," Casey said.

"The picture," Kennedy said as he stood.

"I'll send it in the morning," LePointe said. "Now, my niece needs to get some rest."

"But—" Casey protested.

"It's settled," LePointe said authoritatively. "I'm

the doctor. I'll have the picture dropped off at your office, Detective. If that's acceptable?"

"Certainly, sir," Kennedy said.

"Will you be working on finding Gary, Agent Keen?" Casey asked.

"I'm due to leave in the morning," Alexa said. "Actually, I should get back to the Marriott."

Casey crossed the room, took a framed picture from the shelves, slipped it out of the frame, and handed Kennedy the picture, at an angle that precluded Alexa from seeing it.

"You are in good hands, Mrs. West," Alexa said, and left Casey, LePointe, and Kennedy in the kitchen. As she strode up the hallway toward the front door, her footsteps muted by the Oriental runners, she looked at the art on the walls for the first time. She loved art and had taken an advanced art appreciation class in college, so she knew that the paintings she saw were very valuable. Out of the ten paintings she saw on her way out, she recognized a Joan Miró oil she had seen in a book of his work, and a Marc Chagall. There was a large Rothko oil in the dining room. In a den she saw several framed Avedon photographs, including an incredibly large picture of Andy Warhol's wounded torso. The mantel in that room held dozens of framed pictures, most of which included Gary West. He was a strikingly handsome man.

When Alexa exited the house, Manseur was walking back from the street. The superintendent and the other detectives had left or were driving away.

"So, what you think?" he asked her.

"I think I need to go back to the hotel."

"So, you think there's anything to this?" he asked

her as they walked toward the gate. "Do you think he could have been abducted?"

"I think you have a D11 on your hands."

"That FBI jargon for something?"

"It's a model of a bulldozer," Alexa said. "I'm referring to Dr. LePointe. I suspect he's right that Gary West will come home. If not, maybe Dr. LePointe will allow your Detective Kennedy to start some sort of investigation. Two things I can tell you for certain."

"What's that?"

"Casey West worships her husband, and Dr. LePointe is accustomed to calling the tunes."

7

Elliot Parnell, as a Louisiana Wildlife and Fisheries enforcement officer, was keeping his eye on the hurricane because it could affect his beat adversely. If there was a mandatory evacuation, he would have to run all over the lakes and channels making residents leave. Most of the people who lived in his district were dumb as snakes, and he'd have his work cut out for him. He hoped the storm turned: he had a lot more important job to do than shooing cow-brained swampers from their hovels.

Parnell was a patient man. He had been employed as an enforcement officer for the Louisiana Wildlife and Fisheries Commission for eighteen years. For each of those years—night and day in every kind of weather condition—he had been outrunning scofflaws when necessary, outsmarting them when possible. His job was to catch offenders who dared to take more game or fish than the laws of Louisiana allowed, hunt or fish without procuring the proper licenses, hunt or fish out of season, hunt or fish in restricted areas, sell game or fish, or poach protected animals.

Elliot Parnell never let a transgressor off with only a warning, unless he knew he couldn't make a case, and the perp didn't know it. If he had a man, woman, or child dead to rights, he would issue the citation, do whatever confiscating the law allowed, and testify against them if the case went to court. Parnell had no patience with any type of violator, but he had a special hard-on for people who killed alligators without the proper permits. Leland Ticholet was one of the worst offenders in the state. Any game and fish regulation that a man could break, Ticholet broke. Parnell had caught him on several occasions, and had written him numerous summonses, but mostly the judges let him go. Ticholet was as smart as instincts and criminal genetics could make a man. Parnell had joked that Ticholet's whole family had been thumbing their noses at the law for so many generations that evolution had them emerging from the womb with the ends of their noses and their thumbs already calloused.

Parnell preferred to work alone, unless he was after poachers. A poacher could be dangerous. Although Parnell carried a Colt .38, it was best to have someone watching your back. Lawbreakers could get testy or desperate, and sometimes wardens got shot, cut up, or just plain vanished. With people in the swamps killing deer, ducks, and gators out of season and cooking their methamphetamine, getting shot was a very real prospect.

Parnell looked over at the rookie-in-training, Wildlife and Fisheries Enforcement Officer Betty Crocker. She was asleep, snoring with her mouth open. Betty swore she didn't mind people making jokes about her name, because she'd heard them all in her twenty-one years, and claimed she liked having a name people remembered easily. Some would have changed their names, but not her. She wasn't right for the job, and not just because she was a black woman from the projects. Elliot wasn't prejudiced. He'd had sex with black prostitutes when he was drunk. Probably he'd have sex with Crocker given the right circumstances.

A week earlier Elliot Parnell had spotted Ticholet driving a new boat across the lake. People like Leland couldn't purchase such valuable items unless they were doing something very profitable, and such people could only make that sort of money illegally. Two days after that, Parnell had set up a digital video camera on a tree pointed so's to capture activity on Leland's camp house and dock. Triggered by motion of a boat or someone on the dock, the camera would record, and whatever the subject unloaded or skinned would be captured by the digital video camera, and Elliot would play it in court, and Leland would regret it. The expensive new boat would become property of the Wildlife and Fisheries Commission.

All Elliot needed was an image of Leland Ticholet pulling one gator carcass out of his boat onto the dock—just one.

8

Manseur had driven a good two miles before he spoke. "Would have been nice if you'd mentioned you and Jackson Evans knew each other," he said.

"He had only praise for me, right?"

"He didn't go into any detail. But if he was ever in love with you, he's gotten over it."

Alexa laughed.

"He wasn't happy about seeing you at the scene."

"What was he telling you on the porch?"

"Just that Mr. Gary West married up. There's a prenuptial agreement. He gets nothing but a small allowance to live on, which he wastes. He's something of an embarrassment to the family. He is verbal about his extremely liberal points of view, which are not always in line with those LePointe thinks are constructive. He's also frivolous, and has Casey pouring money into causes like the ACLU, the Southern Poverty Law Center, and the like. The LePointes have their own bylaws and Gary West is never going to get his hands on any of the LePointe fortune. The impression I got is that LePointe hopes his niece will come to her senses and end the relationship. He thinks this abduction is just Gary West playing some game for sympathy or to get attention."

"And yet Gary's wife seems genuinely distraught," Alexa pointed out. "It's possible she agrees with her husband's politics, or at least respects his idealism."

"Either way, Evans wants this deal handled as quickly as possible. It looks like Katrina is going to kick our ass. This storm keeps coming our way, we're likely to have a lot of wind damage, electricity out, a little looting, and maybe some flooding. We've been waiting for the big one for years."

"The big one?"

"The whole city is below sea level, surrounded by levees and pumps. Someday some mean-ass hurricane is going to push the Mississippi River down her throat and Lake Pontchartrain up her butt."

9

Back in her hotel room, Alexa decided to take a hot bath and get a couple of hours' sleep before she left. After she got out of the tub, she put on her robe and switched on the TV, changing channels until she found the weather channel.

"*Now for the latest on Hurricane Katrina,*" the weatherwoman anchor was saying. "*Katrina entered the Gulf of Mexico yesterday after leaving a path of destruction in South Florida. She has been gathering strength due to the extremely warm waters. Katrina is now a category three, with measured winds in excess of 130 miles per hour. The National Weather Service's Hurricane Center is predicting this storm will keep gathering strength and will be a category four by late tonight. It could well be a category five before it makes landfall on Sunday night.*

"*For reference, Hurricane Camille, which decimated the Mississippi Gulf Coast in 1969, was a category four when it made landfall. Two hundred and fifty six people died due to the storm surge.*"

Alexa turned off the set. She would be long gone before the storm was within five hundred miles of the coast. She was towel-drying her short hair when she heard a light, but persistent, tapping at her door. Stopping at her purse for her Glock, she put her eye to the peep lens and was met by the sight of Casey West nervously chewing on her bottom lip.

Alexa returned the gun to her purse, slipped the bolt, and opened the door.

Casey smiled uncertainly. "Please forgive my intrusion. I know it's really late . . . but I was hoping I could talk to you in private."

"How did you find me?"

"I heard you say you were staying here."

"I didn't say which room." Alexa hadn't moved an inch or changed her facial expression since opening the door. This was a complication she didn't need, and guests' room numbers were not supposed to be given out to anybody.

"I know my uncle well enough to know that he probably told everybody that Gary is a gold digger. Probably said that if there was a kidnapping, Gary staged it himself, or something equally absurd. I know nobody's looking very hard, or as hard as they should be, and I have to change that."

"I understand there was a prenuptial agreement," Alexa said.

"There was. But if Gary is alive on Tuesday, he will be presented with a check for twenty-five million dollars."

"Come in," Alexa said.

10

When it came to reading people, Alexa Keen's instincts were like radar. Hard-learned lessons about human behavior had left deep scars on her psyche. She and her younger sister, both products of her dark-skinned mother's liaisons with white men of dubious reputation, had resided in a series of foster homes in Mississippi. Those many residential assignations had been homes with every sort of person imaginable—some decent, some interested in the accompanying state funds, and a couple of them inhabited by predatory beasts.

"First off," Casey said, "Gary did not marry me for my money."

Alexa said nothing.

"When I met Gary, I was staying in New York doing a photography internship with Richard Avedon. That's when I saw Gary's play, *Trailer Park Tales,* which was off-off-Broadway. It was both funny and poignant—a comedy, but tragic, and showed a sensitivity that floored me. Gary is a highly intelligent, very funny, gloriously handsome—a complex individual who tolerates no bullshit. He isn't impressed by wealth or the people who have and hoard it. He's into justice for all, culture for the masses, food for the hungry, and affordable health care for the sick. He cries when he sees starving children on television.

"Despite the differences in our backgrounds, we hit it off. For the first time in my life I felt important—and appreciated for who I really am, on the inside. We talked for hours and hours on the phone and we fell in love like normal people do. With other men I dated, I was never sure it wasn't my money that interested them—or I was convinced it was. He didn't even know about my ties to money until after he'd proposed and I'd accepted. He was shocked by it and he actually tried to back out of the commitment because of it. He is a proud man, and he has never once taken advantage of the fact that he can have whatever he desires that my money can buy. He's never even let me finance a play, even though I've begged him to allow me to. He doesn't spend any of my money on himself. He goes out of his way to ground Deana and me, which is an uphill battle, because I've been spoiled rotten since birth. Gary is the best of me. Without him I am just another miserable, shallow rich girl."

"Tell me about the prenup," Alexa said.

"That's standard with all marriages in the family. Only a blood LePointe can inherit more than a spousal allowance, sit in control of the foundations, direct the dispersal of interest, or make decisions on grants and investments. Did my uncle imply that if I divorce him, Gary gets nothing?"

"I got a short-form version. But yes, I got that impression."

"What my uncle told you was probably a half-truth to make his personal opinion of Gary valid. It is fact that Gary can't ever get his hands on any of the LePointe holdings because he isn't a blood heir. His allowance is two hundred thousand a year, which is only meant to cover his personal expenses. Most of that Gary gives away. The trust pays our household bills, pays the help, all expenses related to the vehicles and insurances, food, et cetera. There are two separate

prenuptial agreements, both of which Gary signed.
One never changes. The other runs out on our fifth anniversary and isn't connected to the LePointes. Five
years ago, when I decided to marry Gary against my
uncle's wishes, I had my lawyers draw up a prenup to
cover my personal assets. On Tuesday, Gary will get
one quarter of everything I have—twenty-five million.
It will be his with no strings attached, to do with as he
sees fit. Period."

"A quarter of your assets."

"I had a trust from my maternal grandfather that I
could draw living expenses from until I was twenty-
five. When I turned twenty-five I inherited half of my
mother's estate. When Deana was born I inherited the
remainder. My great-grandfather was Ben McLintock
from Houston, Texas. He was one of the early oil
wildcatters and buyers of mineral rights in what
turned out to be big oil country. He built a real estate
empire that spread his oil holdings into shopping
centers, office buildings, and housing developments
around the country.

"My mother was one of three children, and her
marriage to Curry LePointe was a merger of sorts,
but her prenuptial agreement ensured that her inheritance
would pass directly to me. Upon the birth of my
first child, the rest was transferred to me. When our
prenup expires, Gary gets ten percent or twenty-five
million dollars. On Tuesday, Gary West will be twice
as personally wealthy as my uncle. In the event of my
death, Deana and any other of my children will share
my estate equally, but Deana alone, being the first-
born, will be entitled to head the LePointe legacy.

Barring a total collapse in the world markets, she will someday control a multibillion-dollar fortune."

"What about your father?"

"He's dead," Casey said, averting her eyes. "I was four when my parents passed away."

Alexa didn't know what to say. Her mind was running in several directions at once. Based on what Casey had told her, Gary West had no reason to make any waves. In fact, he had twenty-five-million reasons not to do so.

"Gary's far too good for me. I try every single day to deserve his love and trust," Casey continued. "He worships Deana. He's never been unfaithful to me, and while he does drink more than he should on occasion, it's very rare. He's unbelievably thoughtful to everybody. He hates it when I give him extravagant gifts. He dresses in inexpensive clothes and buys me gifts with his money from royalties. He is a wonderful human being."

"He has no close friends?"

"His best friends are theater people or people from his life before he started writing plays. Gary tolerates my friends, and is always polite to everybody. He is the only man I have ever loved. If I don't get him back, I don't know what I'll do."

Alexa found herself being far more jealous of Casey's good fortune in love than her fortune in dollars.

"Gary really does love us." Casey started crying and Alexa got a tissue for her and waited in silence for the younger woman to gain control of herself. "I don't really remember my parents," Casey sobbed. "What I do remember about them is that they loved me unconditionally. For twenty years I didn't have that."

"What about your uncle? Your pet name for him is Unko. I got the impression he isn't crazy about being called that."

Casey offered a weak smile. "He hates it when I call him that around other people, because he thinks it somehow minimizes him, but despite his infuriating aloofness, he loves me truly and dearly. His concern for us—me and Deana—is out of affection."

"Your uncle raised you?"

"My grandmother was in control of my upbringing. She was in control of everything else, too, including my uncle. We—my uncle and Aunt Sarah and me—lived with her because Grandmother wanted it that way. My father lived away from her, but what my father wanted, he got. She doted on him and accepted my mother like she accepted few others. After my parents died, servants actually raised me until I was old enough to be some sort of company worthy of her attention. I had nannies, maids, a driver, tutors, and the right playmates. Grandmother said often that I reminded her of my father. She wasn't exactly the warm and fuzzy type." Casey smiled, her eyes becoming misty. "But she loved me . . . in her own way. She was my protector and she was the person who taught me what was expected of me. She drilled into me what duties I had been born to assume and how to comport myself properly. I wasn't always an attentive student and she was often angry with me."

"Did she like Gary?"

"She passed before we met. But I think she would have absolutely hated him. Our relationship could never have been possible had she lived. She would have made short work of him, the way she did of any threats to the way she believed things were supposed to be. And I couldn't have stood up to her the way I did to Unko. You'd have to have known her to understand. Nobody said no to my grandmother without regretting having done so."

"Do your aunt and uncle have children?"

"Uncle William and Aunt Sarah had a son. He died when he was an infant. Sarah couldn't have another child, and she was very kind to me. She has Alzheimer's now and lives totally in the past. She doesn't even know my uncle's name, or who he is. It's been hard on him."

Alexa imagined that *hard on him* was a relative term, since Dr. LePointe had the ability to pay others to do any necessary caretaking.

"Could your uncle dislike Gary enough to do something about him?" Alexa asked.

Casey smiled. "Unko wouldn't harm anyone. He tried to buy Gary off at the beginning, and failed. The only way Unko could understand a man refusing a great deal of money is he wants a lot more. The idea that anyone could be uninterested in wealth makes wealthy people suspicious. Gary doesn't like my uncle, and he doesn't like for Deana to be around Unko, because he thinks Unko will warp her somehow, and my uncle resents that. Not that Unko is comfortable around a child, but he hates it that Gary makes it obvious he isn't welcome in her life, or mine, in any meaningful way—or in the way he chooses to be."

"Who would have a motive to harm Gary?"

"Nobody."

"Obviously Gary would be an attractive target for a kidnapper looking for a big score. Unless there's a motive I'm not aware of. Except . . ." Casey started to say something, but stopped.

"What is it?"

"Gary is not a threat to my uncle, but it's possible others might not know that. . . ."

"What does that mean?"

"Well, someone else might take it upon themselves to do something that they thought would please Unko. Especially before Tuesday."

"Before the prenuptial agreement expires. Who else knows about the prenup?"

"Very few people. Aside from Grace, just lawyers for the trusts, bankers, people running the companies I own who might be affected by Gary's participation—if he ever chose to become involved in any of those businesses, which I seriously doubt. And there's Unko, of course, and maybe whoever he's told, but he would never hang family laundry in the open. His investigator, Kenneth Decell, is the closest thing to a confidant Unko has, but I don't know what he tells him. Unko compartmentalizes every aspect of his life. Sometimes people do things because they think they will be rewarded for it one way or another. It's possible, isn't it? If Gary was kidnapped for a ransom, that's federal, isn't it? You could become actively involved, couldn't you? Please?" Casey's moist eyes—the eyes of a child in pain—plucked at Alexa's heartstrings.

"Yes," Alexa answered. "In the case of a kidnapping, the locals could ask for our involvement, but they don't usually do so if they can avoid it. And in the event they do, I might or might not be assigned to the case. There are a lot of variables and politics at work within the Bureau, and the friction between federal and local authorities is often the least of it. If you think of law enforcement as parts of a large complex corporation with all the red tape, rules, competition between employees, and cliques, you begin to see it as it is."

"You would be assigned to us," Casey said, beaming. "I know you would. I mean, you're an expert and you're here already, so you've got a head start. And you have a wonderful track record."

She stood, extended her hand, holding Alexa's hand for what seemed to Alexa a very long time. "It will work out, I know it will. You are our only hope."

"I truly want to help you, Casey. If this does turn out to be an abduction, I'll do whatever I can."

"I have to go. I don't want Deana to wake up and not find me there. She's already upset that Gary isn't home, and the excitement and strangers in the house has her terribly confused. Please try to help us, Alexa. Without Gary, my daughter doesn't have a chance. As deeply as I love her, I think without Gary I can't stand up to Unko. I simply don't have it in me to give her all that Gary can. We need him in our lives."

11

When the phone rang, Michael Manseur had been asleep less than forty minutes. His wife, Emily, rolled over to face him as he put the receiver to his ear. The clock read 5:12. Manseur repressed a groan.

"Hello?"

"Detective Manseur, Jackson Evans."

Manseur sat up. "Yes, sir."

"I'll see you in my office in one hour."

Manseur started to say something, then realized that his superintendent had already hung up.

"Is everything all right?" Emily asked.

"Cover your eyes, doll. I need to turn on the light for a second."

"You're not getting enough sleep, Michael," she scolded gently. "You need to take a few days off."

"That isn't going to happen any time soon." He settled back into the pillows with a soft sigh. "With authority comes sacrifice."

"You didn't sleep a night through when you *weren't* head of Homicide."

"I didn't?" he said, smiling. "No, I guess not. Shouldn't miss what I never had."

"Who was that on the phone?"

"The super."

"What did he want?"

"He wants you and the girls to evacuate to Birmingham."

"The hurricane isn't definitely coming here, Michael. If it becomes obvious that it is, we'll go."

"Get everything packed this morning. I filled the Toyota last night. I want you and the girls gone while the going's good. No arguing, please, Emily. I can't get my work done if I'm worried about y'all."

"Okay. We'll leave this afternoon. Now, what did Evans really want?"

"I think he wants to give me a lesson on how gravity

affects stinky objects that have been set into motion down an incline."

Emily laughed, placed her hand on his arm. "You need to learn to step out of the way of trouble, Michael."

"Darling, I try. But sometimes the trouble that gets in my way comes at me faster than I can jump clear."

12

As much as Alexa wanted to help Casey, it wasn't going to happen unless Jackson Evans asked her to help, and that was no more likely to happen than the moon was likely to deflate. She had packed her bag, was dressed and watching the latest hurricane news on the Weather Channel, glad she was leaving before the tempest came roaring in from the Gulf of Mexico. She had made arrangements to have a cab pick her up at the lobby entrance in thirty minutes, which gave her three hours before her nine-twelve flight, plenty of time even if traffic was heavy, or an accident stopped traffic. The room phone rang twice before she picked it up.

"Yes?" she answered.

"Special Agent Keen?" a stern female voice asked.

"Yes."

"Please hold for the director."

FBI Director Bender? Alexa waited with the phone frozen to her ear, a hollow churning in her stomach. It was a feeling she was familiar with. She had experienced it on the occasions when she was waiting to be disciplined.

After a long pause, during which time the weatherman on her television set droned on about Katrina, there was a click and a man's voice filled the earpiece.

"Agent Keen, I've heard a lot of good things about you. I need for you to do me a big favor."

"If I can, sir."

"It's just come to my attention that a fellow named . . ." he paused, Alexa assumed so he could check a note, "Gary Alexander West has gone missing. I was informed that you are already familiar with this incident."

"I am."

"Gary West is married to the niece of a valuable friend of the Bureau, a man I have known for some time. I understand you have met Dr. LePointe and his niece."

"Casey West. Yes, sir."

"What is your assessment of the situation?"

"I'm not sure what the situation actually is. It's sort of hard to read at this point. Gary West is missing, and the authorities are looking for him."

"What is your personal impression, Agent Keen?"

The director of the FBI wants me to tell him what my gut feeling is? "At the moment there's no evidence it's an abduction. While there's no indication that this *is* a kidnapping, I don't think it can be ruled out, sir. There are circumstances that make me think abduction is very likely, but at this time there's no request from the locals for us to become involved. I believe the situation warrants close monitoring though."

"Is it, in your opinion, beyond NOPD's capabilities?"

"Detective Manseur is in charge here, and he's a

good and competent man. That said, there's a political angle that could potentially lead to a tragedy. It's complicated, and I'm not sure I have enough information or understanding of the precise politics to make a thorough judgment at present."

"Meaning what exactly, Agent?"

"Dr. LePointe appears to be *the* VIP here. The locals are not going to do much that the doctor doesn't support. The family fortune he heads makes him an indispensable asset to the community. I think the concerns he has for his niece's best interests, for his family's reputation, and his nephew-in-law's best interests may be in that order. I think he sees this incident more as an intrusion by the authorities and a potential embarrassment to his niece than a danger for Gary West."

"New Orleans is a political cesspool. And when I say that, I could be sued by cesspools for slander."

"Sir . . ."

"Everybody knows it, Agent. Dr. LePointe is the closest thing to a god in that particular kingdom, and this Detective Manseur's ability aside, the whole bunch has got to be already tripping over one another to kiss LePointe's ring. Here's what we're going to do: You're going to be my eyes and ears on this. I want you to interface with Chief Jackson Evans. I want you to play the role of adviser to NOPD and be our liaison. If this isn't an abduction, you can back off, the NOPD will appreciate whatever help we gave them, and I won't forget your help. If it turns out to be a kidnapping, you'll be right there on top of things. If you have to hurt some feelings, do it. I know you'll do the Bureau proud, Agent Keen. I'm counting on you to help keep this low-profile, because the family deserves our discretion. If necessary, you request a Bureau team. Call on the New Orleans field office if you need to. The lab is yours as needed. We'll give your evidence top priority. You are representing me personally as well as the Bureau. Make us look good. Find Gary West. That's a direct order."

"Yes, sir."

"Be as gentle with Evans as possible, but don't let him block you. We don't want the locals to think we're working at cross-purposes or trying to steal their thunder. This is a new day for the Bureau, and all that. If we're going to build bridges of trust and cooperation between ourselves and other law enforcement departments, we have to do whatever it takes. But if the locals get in your way, don't hesitate to break a few heads. We are the Federal Bureau of Investigation after all."

Bender hung up.

Alexa set the phone in its cradle, sat down on the edge of the bed, and stared at the wall trying to figure out just what the hell had happened in the hours since Casey West had walked out of her hotel room. She glanced up at her image in the mirror and was surprised by the smile she was wearing.

13

Alexa took a taxi from the Marriott. The radio was tuned to a local station so the driver could keep up with the hurricane. The driver wore a bowling shirt, a herringbone wedge cap, and a patch over one eye. A short, thick cigar jutted out of the side of his mouth like a rotten oak limb.

"... *joining the governor of Louisiana, Kathleen Blanco,*" the announcer said.

"Governess a' Loosana, Katie Blanko," the driver corrected. "She good somewhat, and perty decent-lookin', but she ain't no Edwin Edwards. He was a man knew what this state needed—specially N'awlins. Rest of the state hate N'awlins, always has, even though this where the money flows out to the rest of the state."

"I understand he was more concerned with what *he* needed," Alexa offered, since the moon-faced flamboyant white-haired Cajun Edwin Edwards was spending his golden years in a federal stir for taking bribes as fast as people wanting state favors could offer them up. His corruption seemed to have been a secret the entire state was in on.

"He was a great man, that man. Lived large like a king."

"He had sticky fingers," Alexa pointed out.

"Now, of course he took a little taste here and there, but if he don't take the money the rich companies and all them that's payin' for something they need, somebody else will. Man be crazy not to get his own piece 'fore the rest of the dogs run in."

"The old finite-amount-of-graft argument," Alexa said, reaching into her purse for cash. "I've heard that one before. It rarely works."

The governor went on with her message, "... *so, since it is certain that Hurricane Katrina will make landfall on the Louisiana Coast late tomorrow night, and based on predictions of her strengthening into a category five, I am declaring that a state of emergency now exists and, as governor, I am ordering the National Guard to mobilize in Baton Rouge. People living in low-lying areas should evacuate to safer ground far inland immediately. I . . ."*

"That storm gone turn toward Texas, she gone turn west an' leave us alone. You gone see it fo' yo' self."

"You aren't evacuating?"

"Where I'm go'n go? I got a wife likes it right here. I got four cats that's all old and crotchety. We go'n be safe enough in Chalmette. Even if the wind comes, by the time it gets up here, we blow back at it from the front porch." He laughed.

"I'll need a receipt," she told the driver.

He handed her a printed receipt and winked at her. "This police headquarters. You in trouble with the law, little girl?"

"Perpetually," she replied, laughing as she slid out on the sidewalk side.

Alexa looked up at the New Orleans Police Department and took a deep breath. She passed the eternal flame monument dedicated to officers killed in the line of duty and walked into the glass-fronted reception area. After she showed the disinterested policewoman behind the counter her FBI credentials, the woman made a call, handed Alexa a visitor's pass, and told her, "Someone will be right down for you."

Fifty seconds later, a woman in a business suit exited the elevator, strode over the composite-stone flooring to Alexa, and ordered her to follow her upstairs. They rode up in silence with an assortment of police detectives and office workers. The escort stepped out and, walking fast down the wide corridor, led Alexa through a waiting room, an outer office, and to a door marked SUPERINTENDENT OF POLICE. The woman tapped twice and swung open the door, stepping aside to let Alexa pass into an expansive room where framed photographs, awards, and newspaper and magazine articles pertaining—and flattering—to Jackson Evans covered the walls like scales on a carp.

Jackson Evans sat regally behind his desk in his uniform. Michael Manseur was slumped in the chair opposite. Both men stood when she entered.

"Come in, Alexa," Evans boomed in his finest microphone-ready voice. "We've been expecting you."

"Detective Manseur," Alexa said, nodding, "Superintendent Evans."

"Please, in this room, it's Michael and Jackson," Evans corrected. "Can I get you a cup of coffee, Alexa?"

"No, thank you . . . Jackson," she said, cordially, trying not to smile at how the men's names fit together into what some would see as a comical arrangement. She took the chair beside Manseur. "Nice to see you again, Detective."

"My pleasure, Agent Keen," Manseur said, suddenly yawning into his hand. "Excuse me."

"So I guess we all know why we're here, Alexa." Evans sat down and rocked back in his chair, crossing his legs. "I had a brief conversation a little while ago with your director. He asked me if it might be advantageous if the FBI were to maintain a presence in the form of one Special Agent Alexa Keen. He also offered expedited lab service and whatever additional manpower support we should require, which Agent

Keen would coordinate. I must say that having the Bureau's resources at our disposal is a plus. Let's hope that Mr. West comes home with a hangover and his tail tucked between his legs and that we won't need the FBI's gracious assistance."

Alexa nodded. Manseur sat in silence.

"If he's going to return under his own steam, he'll likely do it by noon," Evans said. "Can we all agree on that? Hell, maybe he evacuated ahead of his wife and daughter."

"I suspect that's correct," Manseur said. "Not that he evacuated. That he'll come in by noon if he can do so."

"Let's hope so," Alexa said.

Evans went on, smiling, "Alexa, I've been talking to Michael and this is how we both think this should work. Michael will be handling this as his case along with Kennedy of Missing Persons. I know this is a missing persons case and should be Kennedy's baby until such time as the situation changes, but I believe that, due to Detective Kennedy's lack of experience with high-profile, high-pressure cases, Michael should head the team. I hope you can work alongside them, Alexa, to monitor the situation as things develop and not seize the case."

"If there even is a case," Alexa replied. "Might just be premature evacuation."

Evans nodded, his smile drying up.

"Michael has agreed to work on this case exclusively until it's successfully resolved."

Alexa nodded slowly. Evans wanted only to come out of this with applause from the right people, and hopefully a nice award for his wall. She heard herself say, "Of course." *As long as you don't put up any walls I have to knock down.*

"I hope it won't take too long," Manseur said, sadly.

"It shouldn't take long," Jackson Evans said. His words contained equal parts of optimism and threat.

If Gary West didn't come back, Alexa wondered, how long would it be before she'd have to shove everybody to one side so she could do what needed to be done?

14

The rising sun turned the eastern windows of the listing cabin a brilliant hot-fire orange. Standing shirtless on the plywood trap-floor, Leland Ticholet stood in the doorway studying the murky surface of the still water in the channel and eating instant coffee granules out of the jar with a spoon.

His guest was still exactly where he'd laid him out on the cot. Bringing the guy out for Doc had cost Leland a day of taking care of his own business, but since he would own the boat moored to his dock for one job of work, it did sort of balance out. He was thinking about all the nutria that were, at that moment, swimming around in his water, eating his vegetation into extinction, pooping floating black pellets by the hundreds, screwing like rabbits, and just plain asking for it while he stood there with his thumb up his ass babysitting some worthless shit-hole, long-haired city boy.

Leland was not comfortable sharing his cabin

with anyone, asleep or awake. He couldn't remember anybody but his daddy, and some of his 'shine customers, ever being inside it. Not one visitor since his daddy passed, and Leland hadn't ever wanted another one. He didn't have any conversations he could avoid. In his world, he could go weeks without saying a word out loud, or seeing another human being except in a passing boat.

Leland didn't own the waterways or any of the land that touched it, yet it was his to use as he saw fit, just as it had been his father's, and his father's father's before him. Leland was like a female alligator that tolerated the presence of others as long as they didn't get too close to her nest or she wasn't hungry enough to go after them.

15

Using an electric trolling motor so's not to be heard by their quarry, Wildlife and Fisheries Enforcement Officer Elliot Parnell and rookie Betty Crocker pulled up on the eastern finger of dry land, one of two thinly forested and weed-choked tracts that sheltered Ticholet's shallow bay. The sixty-yard-long bay ranged from a width of twenty-five yards at its mouth to fifteen at the back, where a U-shaped dock, which was anchored on both ends, held the floating cabin in place.

Crouching and moving slowly, Betty followed Parnell to the hidden camera and watched as her superior removed it from the tree with the giddy enthusiasm of a child on Christmas sneaking downstairs ahead of the family to get a surreptitious look at his presents.

The new boat was gone, so their subject was off, presumably doing something illegal. As a kneeling Parnell was opening the viewing screen, Betty realized she was sweating to the point where her uniform was sticking to her skin. The still August air was muggy. She wished the hurricane would come on and push some wind through the swamps. They were supposed to be riding around the camps making sure everybody that lived around the area knew a monster-ass storm was coming right at them, and would most likely deroof and maybe remove any trace of the rickety-ass buildings that dotted the swamps. They were supposed to be helping the Sheriff's office by making sure all these poor sons of bitches knew staying was dumb as shit. Like the rat-faced inbred scamps that lived back in here ever came upon a smart idea. Everyone they had told said something like: "She'll turn." "This camp's been here through ten big hurricanes." "If my dog runs for it, I'll be right behind her." Most of them were dumb, paranoid, suspicious, and as quick to pull a gun as crack dealers. Maybe no hurricane would be more apt to kill them than it would a snapping turtle. Parnell had been told that the investigation into Leland Ticholet was not a priority, but he had a hard-on for Leland, and that was it. And she didn't like the way Parnell was always looking at her out of the corner of his piggy eyes. First time he tried to mess with her, she'd be filing one of those sex harassment lawsuits on his fat ass.

Leland Ticholet made Betty nervous. He had a reputation for being erratic and violent, and she doubted he took more than a few alligators here and there. Why risk your butt for critters that were dumb as rocks, mean as pimps, and as plentiful as cigarette butts? Elliot Parnell was the biggest by-the-rule-book asshole on earth and everybody hated his ass. She got stuck with him because the other agents all hated blacks—especially black women who weren't mopping their floors—and they thought she'd quit on account of being with Parnell. "We have important warning to be doing," she said.

"This *is* important," Elliot told her.

"Whatever," Betty said.

"We can't have everybody around here thinking they can treat our valuable wildlife resources any way they like." As he spoke he was watching the screen, which was reflected in his beady little eyes. Elliot had a handgun, but Betty wasn't done with her probationary period, so she wasn't packing. In an emergency Parnell had said she could use the shotgun. Although her father and brothers were too familiar with guns, Betty had never fired one in her life, and didn't know one Wildlife and Fisheries officer who had ever had to use deadly force. Parnell had pulled his gun on several people, but everybody said it was because he got scared and overreacted.

"Oh, my God!" Elliot whispered excitedly. "We got the son of a bitch!"

He rewound and turned the tiny screen so Betty could share the view. The teeny boat entered the frame and a bald, shirtless man who had yard-wide shoulders, a narrow waist, and muscles that would make an ox jealous tied off the boat and carried, on one shoulder, something rolled up in a sheet.

"See the alligator he's got?" Parnell said.

"It's so dark in that I can't see shit. But it might be I can sort of see something rolled up in something looks like a bedsheet. Why would the fool roll a alligator up in a bedsheet?"

"So nobody can see what it is."

"Who in the Sam Hill would be out here looking at *him*? I'm new at this, but wouldn't a gator's tail be hanging way out?"

Parnell glared at her disapprovingly. He had a bitch-on because she had never been in the great outdoors before and had just studied how to be an enforcement officer at the community college. Parnell and the others were rednecks and they resented her for not doing it the way they did. She knew they blamed affirmative action for making it so they couldn't just hire one of their inbred potbellied brothers-in-law.

"You ready?" he asked her suddenly.

"Ready for what?"

"To take a look-see in that cabin."

"I'm new at this, but didn't I hear the captain say you need a warrant or something to go searching in people's cabins? I seem to recall something about it."

"This tape gives me probable cause."

"Maybe he's a Klansman and that was his outfit he had over his shoulder," Betty said.

"And maybe that's an alligator, or a roll of gator skins he plans to sell."

Betty looked at the viewfinder again. She saw Leland getting into the boat and holding something against his head, then throwing it like a baseball and going back inside. In the next few minutes of video he came out carrying a gun, got into the boat, and untied it. As the big man drove the boat out of frame, Betty could have sworn Leland looked right at the hidden secret camera.

"Let's do this," Parnell said, as he held out the camera to her.

Betty took the camera and watched as Parnell stood, took his big-ass revolver out of the holster, and opened it up like he was afraid the bullets might have escaped from the cylinder since he'd last checked on them—twenty minutes earlier.

16

After leaving Superintendent Evans's office, Alexa accompanied Manseur down the stairwell, through the Homicide bull pen, which was a hive of activity, past the interrogation rooms—marked "interview" rooms probably because it appeared to suspects and witnesses as being kinder and gentler—to his office. Several detectives waved and one asked Manseur if he could meet to review a case, to which Manseur said, "I hope so."

"Please sit," he told Alexa, lifting a huge stack of files from one of the two chairs facing his desk so she could. He put the files on the conference table, one more stack among many, and went behind the desk after stepping over two boxes in his path. To say Manseur's office was cluttered would have been as soft as describing Little Richard as being odd.

Alexa, who kept her own office as neat and organized as she did her apartment, sat and took in the piles of manila folders, the boxes containing case files. The last-painted-a-decade-ago beige walls were bare of decoration. A single picture containing three people Alexa assumed were Michael's wife and daughters was not quite yet lost in the disorder on the credenza that held it. That lone image containing contented females was it as far as personal items were concerned.

"I'm sorry you didn't make good your escape from New Orleans," he said cheerfully.

"Truth is, after Casey West came to my hotel room to talk to me, I didn't want to leave."

"She did what?" Manseur sat up. "Nobody told me she ever left her house. I have people posted to watch over her."

Manseur picked up his phone and punched in a number. He asked someone named Walker about Casey West's trip out of the house, listened, then hung up without saying good-bye.

"Dr. LePointe put a private security detail in charge of the house, inside and out, soon as we left. My watch was called off. LePointe's people are going to handle monitoring the phones for any ransom demands privately."

"I thought LePointe was a psychiatrist."

"Maybe he is technically, but Evans told me he retired from his state position a year or so ago. He's always officially been the chairman of the LePointe trusts, and I was told he's giving the family's holdings his full energies. I wish to hell my own people would tell me what's happening with my number-one—and presently only—case. Woman's husband is missing and she is out at all hours running around town and—for all anybody knows—might be in danger herself.

Anything happens to her, you know damned well I'm going to get blamed for it."

"I imagine I'll get my fair share," Alexa said. "I hope you know that I'm here to help any way I can."

"Okay, solve all the cases I have open, give the city enough money to pay my squad to work the overtime we need, keep anybody from killing anybody for a few days, and call off the hurricane while I look for Gary West."

"How about I just help you find Gary West really fast?"

"And I'll live with the rest as usual. It's a deal. So what did Mrs. West tell you that made you want to stick around?"

It took less than five minutes for Alexa to tell Manseur everything Casey West had told her. When she was done, Manseur sat back and rubbed his face. "That's a bit different than what Dr. LePointe told Evans."

"I thought the same thing."

"Dr. LePointe said he knew Director Bender. I guess he pulled in a favor," Manseur said.

"That's a possibility. I'd bet Casey put pressure on him because I doubt he did it on his own. Dr. LePointe doesn't strike me as the kind of person who easily admits he's wrong."

"He's got the sway to make things happen. I prefer to imagine he's showing his niece he cares about getting her husband back."

"Alive." Alexa raised an eyebrow. "How can I help?"

"Let's get this said and out in the open. Evans hates the fact that he has to let you come in, but he's got no choice, so he's pissed off about it, and although he wants this resolved, he wants you—the FBI—to fail, but for us—the NOPD—to succeed. You're an FBI agent, so, new spirit of cooperation or not, my experience tells me it's naïve of me to think I can open up to you, since somebody always gets burned when we work together with the FBI and the somebody that gets the short end is us. I've had trouble with FBI agents sticking with their assurances and promises, especially when they're faced with pressure from their brass hats. Sometimes I get the old 'I'm sorry, but' for my efforts. Usually I don't even get that."

"I understand that very well," Alexa replied. "I run into that roadblock every day from local authorities. All I can tell you is that you've never worked with me."

"Can you give me your word that it won't be the case here?"

"I go by the old adage that there is no limit to what can be accomplished as long as it doesn't matter who gets the credit."

"Winter Massey told me you were especially good people, so I'm going to level with you, and I'm asking that you remember I depend on this job to support my family and I'm too old to start a new career feeding the animals at the zoo. I'm aware that everybody from Evans up to Dr. LePointe have my proverbial balls under their heels, and I don't want any of them to decide to jump up and down."

"Michael, I can't control your superiors, but I give you my word that I won't do anything to burn you. If my superiors attempt to hog the credit at the expense of your department, misrepresent facts, or spin things in such a way as to be harmful or deny your department the credit you deserve, I will tell the truth whether or not my superiors like it. I love my job, but I can do other work if I have to. Also, I should tell you that you can't depend on me to lie or to otherwise cover up criminal behavior by anybody, cop or civilian.

"In certain instances, my back may be turned at a crucial moment or my memory may fuzz. But I take my oath seriously. If you abuse my trust, you'll regret it. I'm just a little Mississippi gal, but I can be very large and unpleasant when I'm pissed off or peed on. If Evans or anybody else tries to block us from doing our jobs, I'll handle it with a federal hammer. My orders from Director Bender are clear."

Manseur stared at Alexa, seemed to consider her words for a few long seconds, then nodded. "Evans wants me to report to him what you're thinking and doing. Although I don't know for sure, I expect he's asked Kyler Kennedy to do the same. He told me to keep Kennedy meaningfully involved, and I doubt it's because he cares about hurt feelings. Jackson is most likely reporting to the mayor, the governor, congressmen, judges . . ."

Alexa yawned into her hand. "Jackson Evans's instincts for survival are perfectly pitched. His MO is that he gets as close as possible to the most powerful people that he can ally himself with in whatever city he's running the department in. His staff builds a bulletproof cocoon around his image. As soon as his rising star has hit its zenith, or the real stats are about to be released, and while the perception of other troubled cities is that he has vanquished crime from the city he's in, he gets offers from one or several municipalities in need of a savior. He takes the most attractive offer, and he's off—lock, stock, and super-staff road show."

Manseur shrugged. "I don't have any reason to think Jackson Evans would sabotage this case. There's nothing criminal about having ambition. I used to have a little myself."

"Let he who is without sin . . . ?"

Manseur opened his hands in resignation, reminding Alexa of a beleaguered Mexican border official.

"It turns out this Gary West thing is nothing, we'll say good-bye and it'll all be over. He turns up dead, body's going to be in my front yard and not in front of the Hoover Building. Kidnapping, and it's all yours to deal with as you see fit."

Alexa nodded.

"My job is just to sort out facts, solve crimes, and arrest the guilty parties. I don't get my back-hairs up over things I can't do anything about. I resent people who think there's only equal laws for equal people, but that's how rich people think." He shrugged sadly and looked very tired as he let his eyes wander over the boxes of files. "Kennedy has over three hundred missing-persons files open at any given time, and he wants to be a Homicide detective, not spend a minute longer than he has to running down kids who ran off from home to go on a smoke-up in the Quarter. This case looks like his shortcut to Homicide. I'll let him do some busy work for us until he shows me I can't trust him."

"What about Dr. LePointe?"

"You think he's behind this, jealousy or whatever the motive might be, and I have to tell you I don't think that for a minute. Too much to lose for too little gain. Mrs. West herself told you he wouldn't harm anybody. She knows him better than we do."

Alexa looked out the window. "A man like that, if he were involved in something unsavory, might believe he can't be tied to anything. He probably wouldn't think anybody is smart enough to get him cornered, or brave enough to take it to the next step."

"He'd be about right on that," Manseur said.

When the phone buzzed, Manseur reached for it. "Manseur."

He listened intently for a few seconds. "When did the call come in? What did you tell them? Hurricane coming and they got time to dig into this? Tell them you'll have to locate those files in the morgue, and tell them about how it's a mess to find anything on account of the constant lack of a budget and how we're trying to put the taxpayers' money toward fighting crime. Mention all our manpower is trying to protect the citizens while trying to figure out how we can clear the citizens safely out of the city, and keep looters from cleaning out their property. In the meantime, you get the files to me and misplace the reporter's request form for a couple of days, and she'll probably forget all about it." He hung up. "Crap."

"What?" Alexa asked.

"What are the odds? A TV reporter up and decides out of the blue to look into a twenty-six-year-old homicide case before eight o'clock on the morning after Gary West vanishes?"

"What case?"

"Casey's parents. I better look and see what's in

those files before we let the press have access to them. This I *will* have to pass by Evans."

"Casey's parents' deaths? You said homicide?"

"Didn't I tell you Curry and Rebecca LePointe were murdered? I must have mentioned it when I was telling you about the family."

"I think I'd remember."

"Twenty-six years back, a psychopath broke into the LePointes' house and chopped up Curry and Rebecca LePointe in their kitchen with a meat cleaver."

"Casey told me they were dead, but she didn't mention they were murdered."

"Probably doesn't like talking about it. She was there and saw it happen. Patrol got there in time to save Casey. I expect she was four or five at the time." He shrugged. "Was very big news around here. It's a stretch there'd be anything from those murders that would help on the West case. But it's possible they found out about Gary and they're just digging through whatever they can find. Reporters pay cops for hot leads. It's possible one of the responding officers or someone there last night when we arrived sold it."

"You think one of the people in the loop clued the media?"

"Possible. Money makes the world go around, but it spins New Orleans like a two-dollar top."

There was a rapping on the office door. "Yeah?" Manseur called out.

Missing Persons Detective Kyler Kennedy stuck his head in, looked at Alexa, then Manseur, and nodded uncertainly.

"Detective," Manseur said, cheerfully. "Can I help you with something?"

"I need to speak to you privately for a second," Kennedy said.

"I'm busy. Tell me what it's about."

"The West case," Kennedy said.

"Then you can say it in front of Agent Keen," Manseur told him. "She's involved in this."

"Patrol just located Gary West's car," Kennedy answered. "And West wasn't in it."

17

Leland Ticholet tied his boat to the pier beside Moody's store and lifted the wooden crate he'd brought from his cabin. Balanced on his haunches atop a pier post, a gawky young man of indeterminable age who did odd jobs around the dock watched Leland. Without the overalls, ratty T-shirt, and unlaced work boots, Grub might have passed for a very large version of one of the pelicans that often perched in that exact spot, resting and watching for a meal of opportunity between flights.

"What's in yur box, Lee-lund?" the boy asked.

"Rusty old cottonmouth," Leland said. " 'Bout big around as your empty head."

"Naw it ain't, Lee-lund. Tell me what's really in it."

"Tails."

"Whut kind of tails is it?"

"Nutria," Leland answered just gruffly enough to

discourage further conversation. "What else would it be—catfish tails?"

Grub snorted. "State gives four bucks a tail on swamp rats. How many is it in your box, you reckon?"

"I reckon forty-one," Leland said.

"How much that add up to in money?"

"Four dollars times forty-one. Figure it up."

"Ninety-one dollars," the boy said, a worried look on his face.

"I'm lucky they ain't paying me by your calculations."

"How's that, Lee-lund?"

"Because you're a idiot and I'd starve to death on account of it, you scrawny little dog fucker."

"Big as you are, you ain't missed any meals, you . . . you. Ijit your own self," Grub hissed, spreading his legs wide apart and freeing his eel-like penis through a ragged hole in his crotch with hands that looked like he'd been working on diesel engines. "Tickle this, Lee-lund Tickle-ay."

"It's Ticholet, you wormy retard."

"Lee-lund Teesh-o-lay this, goober-puller."

Leland climbed from the boat slowly, lifted up the crate, and lurched suddenly sideways right at the boy, who sprang off the perch and ran guffawing toward the gasoline pumps outside the store.

"Somebody should gut that little idiot and bait gator hooks with his meat."

As he walked up the dock toward the store, Leland Ticholet threw back his head and barked his laughter at the sky.

18

New Orleans, like most cities, had far more vehicles on the roads daily than the roads were designed to handle, and New Orleans had far less money than was necessary to maintain them. Even at eight A.M. on a Saturday, the interstate resembled a parking lot. The outbound lanes were packed, the inbound lanes flowed. Manseur explained that normally there was less traffic going east toward the Lakefront, their destination, than into New Orleans. Hurricane Katrina was making a beeline toward a city normally known for its open, welcoming arms. Sometimes open invitations came back to bite you on the ass.

Manseur drove as fast as he could—moving in and out of the traffic, using the shoulder when necessary, and using his dash light sparingly. He didn't want to attract any attention to the fact that a plainclothes car was racing to an emergency. Alexa knew that news producers, camera operators, and reporters snooping for stories to fill the airwaves monitored the police, fire, and emergency frequencies, including the restricted tactical ones, which they hacked into. They also encouraged motorists to call in tips, like when they saw blue lights on dashboards. One of the benefits of cellular phones was that any motorist could call the cops from anywhere—and the downside of that was that they allowed any motorist to ring up any of the newsrooms to report police activity. People were helpers or hinderers, depending on whom it was that was dialed and about what.

Detective Kennedy followed Manseur's Crown Vic in a nondescript Chevrolet sedan.

"We should involve Kennedy in a meaningful way," Manseur told Alexa. "Or appear to be doing so. I don't want him throwing a wrench in the works, accidentally or intentionally."

Manseur turned off Robert E. Lee Boulevard and onto a narrow street where neatly kept houses on small lawns faced one another across the pavement. Two squad cars had sealed off the block and a third waited in front of a Volvo SUV, while a policeman stood at the rear bumper. Manseur stopped thirty feet behind the Volvo, reached over to the glove box, and pressed the trunk release. Alexa stepped out into the gathering early-morning heat as Manseur went back to the open trunk. Kennedy walked over from his car and stood watching silently.

A uniformed officer built like a pigeon strolled up to Manseur.

"Sergeant Walker," Manseur said, "this is Agent Keen with the FBI."

"We sealed the scene and left it just like we found it. I called it in over the phone, like we were told to. Looks like it got rear-ended. Doors were unlocked and the keys were in the ignition. I can't believe shit-birds haven't found it and taken it for a joyride, or to a strip shop."

Manseur reached into his car trunk and removed four surgical gloves from an open box. He handed Alexa a pair, then shoved several evidence bags into the pocket of his suit jacket. He lifted out a 35mm camera and put the strap around his neck.

"Since it was rear-ended," Sergeant Walker said, "it's likely a road-rage incident."

"Never know, till you know," Manseur said. "That's all, Sergeant. We'll take it from here. Detective Kennedy, take notes for me?"

"Yes, sir." Kennedy took out his notepad, slipped off the rubber band, and flipped the pad open.

The dismissed policeman walked back to his cruiser, leaned against the trunk, and crossed his arms to watch the process like there wasn't any other thing in the city needing his attention.

Manseur lifted the camera to his eye and took a picture of the ground behind the Volvo. "Subject vehicle damage consists of a dented rear door, skinned bumper, and a broken left rear and clear plastic and red turn-lens covers."

Alexa noticed shards of broken clear glass before Manseur knelt to take a close-up shot. Using a pair of long tweezers, he collected a half-dozen larger pieces, which he dropped into a clear evidence bag. "Broken headlight fragments," he said for the record. "Glass, not plastic, and heavy glass."

"Taillight lens cover?" Kennedy asked.

Manseur moved closer to the rear of the Volvo and inspected the damage. "No. I'd say a sealed-beam headlight. It's real glass. Older vehicle, most likely."

Taking out a pocketknife, Manseur used it to scrape flecks of green paint into a clear bag. "Green paint transfer from second vehicle."

Alexa took each of the evidence bags from Manseur after he sealed them, and followed him around the Volvo to the driver's-side door.

He opened the door carefully so he wouldn't destroy any print evidence that might be on the handle, and looked inside, using the camera to document the state of the cabin.

"Air bag's deployed. Wallet's on the console." Manseur leaned in and lifted the open billfold. "Sixty-two dollars, American Express, Shell, Visa, and a MasterCard, all in West's name. Three pictures of his wife and daughter. Receipts for meals and gasoline, looks like. One blank check, folded." After dropping the wallet and contents into a bag, he knelt and looked at the floorboard. Lifting something by its edges, he held it so Alexa could see it. "License on the floorboard next to the accelerator pedal."

"He took it out of the wallet to exchange information with the other driver," Alexa said. Of course it could be a road-rage incident, but Alexa doubted it, for a couple of reasons, the most obvious being that Gary West wasn't there and hadn't called anybody or turned up.

In the console and glove box, Manseur found a flashlight, a box of tissues, an owner's manual, an insurance card, the car registration, maps, and a few receipts.

Manseur took three pictures of the interior. "Take a look inside, Agent Keen," he said, stepping back.

Alexa leaned in without touching anything. She saw the brown specks that dotted the headliner, the passenger seat, the passenger-side window, and the dashboard. They looked like tiny comets. "Blood spatter. Might have happened while he had the license in his hand. That's most likely why he dropped it."

"Gunshot?" Kennedy asked.

"No," Alexa said. "Low-velocity impact."

"Like he was punched in the nose?"

"Could be, but I doubt it," Alexa replied. "More likely a sap of some sort. Something short and heavy."

"Why short, or heavy?"

"Because the apex of the door would have negated use of a long object like a baseball bat or golf club to inflict the injuries that produced the blood spatter." Alexa turned to inspect the inside of the driver's door, studying the damaged panel. "This gash in the door is round. A pipe or a wooden club could make a mark like that, but it might be something else that's round. I'm no expert on blood spatter, but I know enough to say that whatever he was hit with left castoff on the windshield when the perp drew it back, making the scratch on the door panel. Struck at least twice, because there's splatter in two distinct directions. First one when his head was in one position, the second when it was in a slightly different position. Seat belt probably held him upright."

Manseur nodded his agreement. "Air bag must have stunned him. He recovers enough to get his wallet, and then he opens the door, or it was opened for him, and zot. Out of the frying pan and into the fire. Make a note for the crime-lab boys to check the patterns real close and see how many times he was struck. Tell them to type the blood in case there's more than one donor. Perp might have left some of his. Probably not, but you never know until you know. That's about all we can do out here. Get this vehicle under a tarp, then get it on a flatbed and to the lab. I want it gone over with everything we got to go over it."

"And make sure your lab knows we'll expedite anything they need from my lab," Alexa added.

Alexa and Manseur spent several minutes checking around and under the Volvo, while Kennedy followed with his pen's point hovering over his open notepad.

Manseur started heading for his car, then turned. "Kyler, I need you to canvass these houses to see if anybody saw anything relevant to the incident. After you do that, go back to HQ and write it all up. And remember, you are to talk to *nobody* but me about this."

After making notes on each evidence bag with a Sharpie marker, Manseur put them all into one large paper bag, which he sealed, labeled with a case number, signed, and dated. Taking a screwdriver from his toolbox, Manseur went back to the Volvo and removed the license plate. Back at his car, he slipped the plate into a paper bag, tossed it in the trunk, and slammed it.

"This looks bad," Alexa said.

"Well, it sure doesn't look good," Manseur muttered.

19

R&O's Italian Seafood Restaurant faced shallow Lake Pontchartrain's sloping levee, a tall earthen wall covered with grass whose job it was to keep the lake's brackish water in its assigned area. Alexa tried to imagine a wall of water high enough to breach it, and failed.

Manseur parked on the oyster-shell-covered parking strip, and she followed him into the entrance vestibule. The sky was clear as a bell and the air was beginning to get hot and humid. It was hard to believe a hurricane was hours away.

"So, you think taking the license plate will keep anybody from knowing who's missing and likely the victim of foul play?" Alexa asked.

"I can only hope it gives us a few hours to get a running start on this before the media begins the circus. Looks like he's definitely been attacked. Kidnapped, you think?"

"I hope he was kidnapped. If he wasn't a target because he's about to be worth more than a Mexican drug lord, he's probably starting a worm farm about now. Until we know for sure, it's still your butt against the fire," she said, smiling.

"I'm ready to make some room for you next to the heat whenever you're ready."

"Any ideas on how you're going to conduct interviews without letting on what the deal is?" Alexa said.

"How would the FBI handle it?"

"The FBI would say that Gary West reported his wallet gone and that you're here just backtracking to see if he left it here, thinking he could have been pickpocketed by someone in the restaurant. That way the FBI could ask if any strangers were lurking outside or came or went at about the same time and get the answers without giving up anything. And the FBI wouldn't introduce me if you were us, since the Bureau doesn't normally look for missing personal items."

"You reckon these guys would know that?"

"One would hope so." She winked at him, and she could have sworn he blushed. Alexa had been told for most of her adult life that she was attractive, even desirable to a lot of men, but ninety percent of the time it was a handicap, because it got in the way of her being taken seriously. Being sexually alluring wasn't something she had ever consciously desired. In fact, the opposite was true. When men, or sometimes women, came on to her, she shriveled inside and felt threatened. The only time she made an exception was when she was interrogating a person who was attracted to her and didn't see her so much as a threat to them as a potential bed partner. People with sex on their minds often paid less attention to their constructed lies than they might otherwise.

The restaurant was surprisingly busy considering that everybody should have been heading out of the city. On the television set there was a satellite view of the storm, which looked like a plate of cotton candy. Alexa couldn't hear the report, but by reading the word *parade* at the bottom of the screen she was informed that Katrina was now a category four storm whose winds were roughly the speed of a rail dragster. The projected path had Katrina making her entrance along a line from Alabama to Texas, with the strongest probability of strike being Louisiana. Being a natural cynic, she found it hard to imagine the city actually flooding, given the levees and the massive number of pumping stations. She wondered if it wasn't some sort of fairy tale dreamed up by authorities, perhaps the

Corps of Engineers, to get their hands on a big chunk of federal money to spend to justify their existence. She was sure about one thing: If the city did get hit and the doomsday scenario proved true, only the drunkest, the most uninformed, the dumbest of the dumb, or the poorest and most infirm would be there to make up the casualty figures.

The restaurant's tables held a remarkably varied assortment of customers. Alexa's eyes rested briefly on four men wearing expensive suits mere feet from a group of commercial fishermen wearing filthy coveralls and greasy-looking baseball caps. Their hands, with fingernails that looked like peanut hulls, gripped cans of cold beer like they were afraid their beverages would flee the table if they didn't hold them tightly.

Manseur opened his NOPD shield case so the receptionist alone could see it. While she went to get the waitress who had worked the Wests' table at lunch the previous day, Manseur and Alexa took a seat at a table near the front.

The waitress who came to their table wore a name tag that said CINDY. Cindy was a foot too short for her weight and was saved from being homely by the effervescent smile she wore. The uniform consisted of a carpenter's apron for her pens, tickets, and cash, plus a black T-shirt, dark jeans, and aged running shoes. Alexa noticed that her fingernails were coated in red polish that had been reapplied several times in the way a peeling house might be painted several times without sanding between applications. After the introduction and the obligatory viewing of Manseur's shield, Cindy's big brown eyes darted around as if the answer to any questions he might ask her were printed on cue cards scattered about the restaurant.

"I understand you waited on Gary and Casey West yesterday at lunch. Are you familiar with them?"

"Sure," she said. "They don't ask for me, but if I'm lucky they sit at one of my tables. Their kid's name is Deana. Mrs. West's some kind of rich photographer, and he's like a writer or something. What'd they do?" she asked suspiciously.

"Nothing," Manseur said. "Mr. West reported losing a valuable wristwatch and we're retracing his routine from yesterday." Alexa had to fight back a smile at the way Manseur changed the lost article from the wallet she had suggested. It was subtle, but told her he felt a need to put his initials on her suggestion to make it his. He was a man after all.

"Oh, that's terrible. They're regulars, every Friday. Yesterday they sat at a table up by the front door, but they don't have a regular place or anything. They're really nice ...d super-good tippers. I didn't see a watch after they left. I didn't see him take it off, but it seems to me he usually wears an inexpensive watch. Like a Timex or a Citizen, because we've discussed the way, you know, they're rich, but not flashy. No bling for him." A look of quiet terror crossed her features. "They don't think I took it, do they? I would never do something like that."

"They didn't suggest you took it. We think a pickpocket might have. Did the Wests leave together?" Manseur asked.

Cindy's brow creased as she contemplated the new question. "No, he left a few minutes before she and their kid did. I'm pretty sure Deana was still eating when he left. You wouldn't believe how much that little girl eats. Mr. West paid the bill with cash. I know because he tipped me seven dollars and a nickel, which was their change. He always does that—tips the entire amount like that. I remember because it wasn't very busy around that time, which it usually is on Fridays. But not like Saturdays. The hurricane thing has people jumpy, and I guess most people are putting wood on their windows, gassing up their cars, and stuff."

"How did they seem?"

"Like usual, pretty much. They're always laughing and joking around and like." She looked off across the restaurant. "Happy. I mean, why not? They're good-looking, young, and rich."

"Nothing about them yesterday was different?" Alexa asked.

The waitress looked at her, surprised.

"You said 'like usual, pretty much.' So something was different. What was it?"

"Well, when I took their orders, she made some comment like, 'I want to look at the menu,' and he said, 'As though there's some mystery. She wants the gumbo.' She said, 'I can order my own food,' and he said, 'Excuse me,' or something like that. Snippy. And anyway, she ended up ordering the gumbo, and they laughed about that. He was right. She always orders a bowl of gumbo and eats only half of it."

"After that things were normal?"

Cindy nodded. "Like always."

"So she wasn't upset when he left?"

"Not at all," she answered, glad to be on the positive side of her clients again. "They were talking and laughing like always. I remember thinking what nice people they were. He stood up, they kissed—I remember wishing my husband kissed me like that—and she touched his cheek and watched him all the way out the door. Oh, and he tried to kiss the baby, but she didn't let him. Gosh, I hope he finds his watch. Anything else?"

"Thank you, no, Cindy," Manseur said. "You've been very helpful."

"Oh," she said, laughing, "my name's not Cindy, it's Nancy. I wear the tag because I don't want people to know my real name on account of some men can be *too* friendly and bug me, but I don't wear my wedding ring because it really cuts down the tips. How skitzed is that? Plus, my husband is the jealous type. Men tip more if they think you're single. Do you guys want to order anything?"

"Coffees," Manseur said, closing the notebook. "Black for me. Alexa? And we'll be eating breakfast."

"Black is fine," Alexa said, lifting a menu.

"Right up," Cindy, who was really Nancy, told them.

"By the way, Nancy," Alexa said, "did you notice any odd people in here yesterday? Maybe hanging around outside while the Wests were in here?"

"Odd people . . . in here? Throw a rock." Nancy walked away laughing.

A minute later, she returned with two mugs of hot coffee and two menus. "I don't think most people even know who the Wests are. Sometimes people who know them are here and they visit and like that. But not yesterday that I noticed."

"Did you see any older green vehicles?" Alexa asked.

"No. Well, there was a beat-up SUV that I saw drive by about five or six times."

"Wouldn't be an SUV," Alexa said. SUVs didn't have glass headlights.

"Thanks, Nancy." Manseur smiled. "You've been a big help. If you remember anything, please call me." He gave her one of his cards. Unlike his boss, he only had one kind, with his office phone, fax, and cellular printed on them.

Nancy tucked the NOPD card into the back pocket of her jeans after reading it. "Is there a reward for this missing watch?"

"I wouldn't be surprised," Manseur told her.

Nancy turned and went back to work.

"So it sounds like there was serious trouble in paradise," Alexa said, opening the menu.

Manseur looked at her with a puzzled expression.

Alexa laughed. "I doubt their marriage could have survived the gumbo incident."

Manseur smiled and shook his head. "Obviously they love each other."

"He was abducted," Alexa said. "There's not a doubt in my mind. So there'll be a ransom demand, or he's dead."

"See anything you want to eat?" Manseur asked, opening his menu.

"Detective Kennedy mentioned the seafood gumbo," Alexa said. "Best on the Lakefront, he said."

Manseur said, "Breakfast of champions."

20

Betty Crocker felt like an idiot as she followed Parnell's wide backside through the weeds and around the stunted trees and bushes. She had to fight laughing out loud, because the fool kept waving his hand around in the air, gesturing commands. The trouble was Parnell hadn't told her what his signals meant. As far as she could tell, he could have been saying anything from "Follow me" to "Gal, I've got me some itchy-ass hemorrhoids."

She was carrying the video camera and was tempted to film him from behind, but she was afraid she'd erase the hulk toting up into his private dwelling that sheet-wrapped object Parnell said was probably a gator with its tail chopped off.

Wildlife and Fisheries Officer-in-Training Betty Crocker followed the wide-ass fool Elliot Parnell onto the blistered-wood dock that anchored the floating-on-rusting-oil-drums, crooked little shack. Betty was careful to avoid the pool of crusted blood that looked like a pizza-sized scab that had flies scrambling over it and buzzing in the warm still air. On the dock, just underneath the tin porch roof, bowls of rusted fishing hooks and all manner of spring-loaded traps and empty-halfway-up scum-coated milk jugs were stacked helter-skelter on chicken-wire crab traps. The shack's windows were covered inside with burlap sheets.

Parnell was sweating, so his shirt looked like he'd been juicing oranges using his armpits. The gun, a

Smith & Wesson .38, in his hand was rock-steady. He reached out and slowly turned the shack's doorknob.

"It's not locked." Officer Parnell's voice creaked just like the hinges on the door.

Pushing it open, Parnell looked inside. He took a step into the shack and his right foot crashed through rotten boards to his left knee. His right leg folded, causing him to bang his knee.

"Sheee-IT!" he bellowed.

Betty stared at him, trying not to laugh at what felt like a pratfall, but wasn't.

"My damn leg's caught in something. Shit! What was that!?"

Betty set the camera down and grabbed his left arm and pulled him up while he used his bent leg for additional leverage. When his leg came out of the hole, there was a large band of something wrapped around his boot. To Betty's horror, it flopped and writhed hideously, then fell back into the hole. "Moccasin! It was a cottonmouth!" he screamed.

"You git bit?" she asked.

"Can't bite through my boots. It was sliding all over my foot. If I hadn't been wearing my snake-proofs, I'd be good as dead." Parnell sat back in the doorway, pulling off his boot. Using his fingers as well as his eyes, he explored his naked fish-belly-white ankle with veins in it looking like blue lightning strikes.

"It was a damned booby trap!" He leaned forward and looked down. "Two of the biggest cottonmouth bastards I ever saw! Christ almighty." He laughed nervously as he stood and, holding on to the doorjamb, tested the floor beyond the rotten spot.

When he found solid flooring, he moved into the room. "Careful, Betty. Wait a second."

"I don't want none of them snakes," she said, watching him lift a hinged plywood panel that he flipped over to cover the trap. She walked in and let her eyes grow accustomed to the dim interior and her nose to the remarkable stench comprised of God knew what all. The room was as cluttered as a junkyard storeroom and she knew she would have to be careful in case there were more booby traps, or snakes.

"Smells like a crack house," she muttered.

"You been in a crack house?" Parnell smarted off.

Her eyes found a cot with a sheet covering something that appeared to be hiding a more human than alligator form beneath.

"Careful," Parnell warned as she approached the cot. He was aiming his revolver at the still form.

"Your alligator's breathing," Betty said. She leaned out, reached down, and threw back the sheet.

"Good God!" she said as air rushed from her lungs. "It's a man. He's been beat to shit."

"You sure he's alive?" Parnell said.

"Put that gun away," Betty said after noticing Parnell was still aiming his gun at the poor man. She felt the guy's neck. "He's got a pulse."

"We need to call this in to the sheriff." Parnell was looking around, probably hoping to find a fresh alligator skin or two in the mess, because that was the kind of prick Parnell was. A half-dead man and he's still looking for some evidence on Leland Ticholet, Betty thought. Just itching to write a damn citation, like he was paid by the piece.

"I need something to wash off his face," she said. "Call for help."

As she started looking for some water, she noticed Parnell slapping at his belt. "My radio," he said.

"You must have left it on the boat."

"No, I think I set it down when I was looking at the video out there. Go get it."

"What?"

"I'm in charge, Officer Crocker. Go get the radio."

"You going to help this man while I'm gone, or search for alligator skins? He's your responsibility. He got to be cleaned up—top to bottom."

"Okay," Parnell said, "I'll go."

"And bring the first-aid kit," she said. She would have bet that Parnell had never changed a baby diaper, much less cleaned up a grown man.

Betty found a mason jar and filled it with questionable water from the faucet—rainwater that came from the cistern beside the cabin. For several minutes, she worked to clean the man's head wound and soften the dried blood so she could wipe it off. He was in his thirties, she figured. His long blond hair was matted with blood. He opened his mouth and said something that sounded to Betty like "Ca . . . zah?"

"I'm here to help you, sir." She lifted his head, put the jar to his lips, and poured some water in, which he managed to swallow. He opened his eyes and she saw that the right pupil was a tight pinpoint set in a bright blue iris; the other was fully dilated. Her mother was a nurse's aide and she had told Betty what different-sized eyes meant. "You going to be just good as new. Betty gone get you to the hospital, and they'll fix your concussion."

Finally she heard the door open and Parnell's lazy ass coming back. He stopped just behind her.

"He's going to be all right, I think. He's breathing, and took some water. He got himself a concussion. Did you bring the first-aid kit?"

When Parnell didn't say anything, she turned and looked up. Betty's eyes went first to the face—the features covered with tiny red droplets, the forehead filled with crisscrossed scars. She let her gaze shift downward to take in the gore-streaked length of pipe clenched tightly in Leland Ticholet's large hand, inches from her face. Betty felt her bladder give and the warm wetness as it flowed between her legs and pooled around her knees.

She opened her mouth to scream, but no sound came out.

21

Despite the number of other boxes in Manseur's office, he pointed to the one that had arrived while they'd been out of the office. "The LePointe files."

Alexa was closest, so she picked it up. The cardboard box was roughly the size typing paper came in, but with flaps that were secured with thin cord wrapped under hard plastic disks the size of quarters. On the end and top someone had used a permanent marker to write the subjects' names, a pair of consecutive case numbers, and the date of the crime. A bright orange sticker that said CLOSED had been added. As she lifted the box to the conference table, Alexa was struck by how remarkably light it was.

While Manseur looked on, she unwound the cording and opened the flaps. Inside there were file folders, one tabbed with the name Curry LePointe and the second with the name Rebecca LePointe. There were no more than ten sheets of paper in each file, which consisted of the medical examiner's report on the cause of the deaths; a sketch of the crime scene by homicide detectives, indicating the locations of the bodies; and photocopied pages of the detectives' spiral case notebooks.

"This is a very thin case file," Alexa said. "Where are the autopsy pictures, the crime-scene photos?"

"Should all be in there," Manseur said.

"Well, they aren't. So where would the rest be?"

"No idea. Maybe it got misfiled in another case box, lost, or stolen. Taken as a souvenir or something. Those were different days for the department, to say the least."

Alexa was familiar enough with the New Orleans PD's reputation for corruption and criminality that came to a head in the early nineties, when the FBI came in and arrested a large number of cops, a lot of whom went to jail, two ending up on death row. The FBI had almost taken over the department, and state troopers had been used to patrol the streets alongside the cops who hadn't been arrested in the initial days of the crackdown. It was one of the reasons New Orleans cops didn't care for the FBI—like they needed more reasons than the cops in most other cities had collected in their own day-to-day dealings with the Bureau.

Alexa held up the detectives' report. "Investigating detectives were a Harvey Suggs and Robert Bryce. They still around?"

"Both are dead," Manseur said.

"Wasn't Suggs your predecessor? Wasn't he murdered when Winter Massey . . ."

Manseur nodded. "Suggs was beaten to death with an aluminum baseball bat by a crooked businessman named Jerry Bennett, who murdered a judge and his wife. Bryce was dead before I got here—killed by Suggs—and totally crooked."

"So, the files could have been sanitized by those two detectives for some reason."

Manseur nodded, took some of the papers from her, and thumbed through them, reading. "Reason would be money."

Alexa said, "The patrolman who answered the alarm that night was named Kenneth Decell. He suffered an injury when he disarmed the perpetrator, Sibby Danielson. The name *Decell* seems familiar to me."

"Decell was at the Wests' house last night when we got there. Red-haired fellow in his early fifties. Been a private detective since he retired about ten years ago. Mostly rich people uptown call him when they have family that get themselves entangled with issues of the unpleasant type. Police problems, runaway or out-of-control kids or spouses, extortion threats, cheating husbands or wives, background checks on people they are curious about. Security issues."

"He bent?"

"Bent? Oh." Manseur shrugged. "More than some, less than others. He was a detective and . . ."

Manseur turned his sad eyes to hers. "New Orleans has all kinds of people in it. Some rich."

"Expensive, is he?"

"People Decell works for don't complain about price when the work gets the results they want. He's got a pretty big operation, with lots of licensed investigators. Some were cops, some weren't. He's well connected."

"As in, to the mob?"

Manseur shrugged. "As in, to lawyers, prosecutors, police officials, politicians, and the like. Around here more people go to prison for doing other people favors than for stealing cars. 'Do me one' is a way of life. A friend will help you move across town today, and in return he might ask you to help him move a body across town."

Alexa laughed. Then she said, "The murderer was a twenty-one-year-old woman. Why did she kill them?"

"She was crazy. It was a long time ago. The reasons for things that happen here aren't always written down accurately. Most people on the job in New Orleans could teach a creative writing course. Back when that report was written, our detectives wrote more fiction than Anne Rice."

"That still the case?"

"I wouldn't know for sure, naturally."

Alexa went over to Manseur's computer, and within seconds she had the LePointe murders' media coverage on the screen. "Says here that Sibhon Danielson was a paranoid schizophrenic. Committed to a state facility for the criminally insane."

"She went by 'Sibby,' " Manseur said.

"Maybe it's just me, but I find it an odd coincidence that Dr. LePointe, the brother and brother-in-law of the victims, is a psychiatrist who's an expert on *criminal* psychology. Don't you find that strange?"

"I find it an interesting coincidence," Manseur said. "But in New Orleans, painting your privates blue and dancing in the street with a bottle in your hand while people file past isn't considered noteworthy. Curry LePointe was the star of that family. William was smart, but without the charisma and personality his big brother Curry had."

Alexa said, "I wonder if there was any connection between our psychopath and Dr. LePointe *before* the murders. But I guess, however interesting all this is, the question for us is whether we waste valuable time chasing down twenty-six-year-old murder information."

"I doubt this has anything to do with finding Gary West. It's a sidetrack of the investigation at best. And I'm not writing a book or investigating for some cold-case television show," Manseur said.

"Seeing that we're talking about Dr. LePointe—the number-one philanthropist and authority on mental defectives—the LePointe murders are best left to historians?"

"You're catching on," Manseur said, chuckling. "Let the big sleeping dogs lie if and when possible."

"You're not going to be any fun," Alexa said.

At that moment Manseur's office door flew open and Jackson Evans strode in stiffly with a grim expression on his face.

"I need a progress report," he said, crossing his arms.

Manseur gave him a quick rundown of the physical evidence they'd collected. He explained that neither the canvass of the area near the Volvo nor the wait-ress's interview had produced anything helpful.

"You're the big-deal expert, Alexa," Evans said. "Is Gary West dead or alive?"

"I'd say the odds that he is alive depend directly on who has him—"

"If anyone *does* have him," Evans interrupted.

"And why they have him. If Gary was the victim of a road-rage incident, he could be dead or seriously injured and lying in a backyard or a ditch nearby. If it was a murder for hire or some other reason, like re-venge, he'd have likely been left in the Volvo."

"Unless they didn't want a body found," Manseur added.

"If he was taken out of the car alive, it means there was a reason to go to the trouble and risk being seen grabbing him. Hopefully he's still alive. If so, the most likely reason for that is because he's been kid-napped for ransom. In that case, he might live through it, depending on several factors."

"Like?" Evans demanded.

"The odds of us retrieving him alive—if he doesn't know his kidnappers' identities, and if a ransom is de-manded and paid—may be as high as eighty percent."

"It's still possible he staged it," Evans said.

"It took some concerted effort if he did," Manseur said.

Alexa said, "In my experience, people rarely beat themselves in the head. Maybe fingerprint evidence from the Volvo will give us a perp, but I don't think it will. If West was kidnapped, I seriously doubt the person who did it was some disorganized, naked-fingered, liquored-up, or cracked-out thug."

"Naked-fingered? Is that FBI terminology?" Evans asked sarcastically.

"It's the latest in hot Bureau-speak," she said without missing a beat.

Jackson Evans looked down at the open evidence box on the table beside him and turned his head so he could read the writing on the flap. "The LePointe murders? What's this, Michael?"

"First thing this morning the media requested the LePointe homicides' file from seventy-nine," Manseur said. "So I had them delivered here so I could see what was in them the press might be interested in."

"The twenty-fifth anniversary of the murders," Evans said, quickly, "so maybe they're just looking into it for some prurient media reason."

"Could be," Manseur agreed.

"My math sucks," Alexa said, "but the twenty-fifth anniversary was last year. And it occurred in July, not August. Timing's wrong."

"Good move, grabbing the files. You find anything interesting?" Evans asked Manseur, ignoring Alexa.

"No, but the media sure will," Alexa said.

"Like . . . ?"

"Like what isn't there," she said. "That box is like an Egyptian tomb that has been pilfered until all that's left inside is a few old bones scattered about. The media gets their hands on that box, there's a bigger story in the missing items than there would have been if it were complete."

"What happened to the rest of it?" Evans asked.

"Your guess is as good as mine," Manseur said.

"Who had access to it last?" Evans asked.

Manseur picked up the phone and dialed the evidence morgue.

"Percy, did you inventory the contents of that evidence box you sent me? Read me the sheet." Manseur took out a pen and made notes as he listened. "Okay, and can you check and see who checked out the box last and what the inventory sheet said was in it when it was last checked out? You find that out for me?" He covered the receiver with a hand. "We got what was in it when he sent it to me."

Thirty seconds later Manseur grew alert as Percy found the list. "Yes. Okay." Manseur scribbled as he listened, thanked the evidence clerk, and hung up. "File was last checked out by Harvey Suggs, nine years ago. According to the paperwork, it was inventoried by the clerk last time it was checked out. The original list had a meat cleaver, fingerprint cards on Danielson, the interviews conducted, Sibby Danielson's psychiatric evaluation, the autopsy report, and transcripts from the sanity hearing, as well Kenneth Decell's incident report."

"Okay," Evans said, sourly. "Let's concentrate on locating Gary West. I spoke to Dr. LePointe thirty minutes ago and there's been no ransom demand." He focused on Alexa. "I mentioned your assistance was continuing and he seemed genuinely surprised."

"He had to have called Director Bender to get me on board," Alexa said.

"I don't think so," Evans replied. "Anyway, you two keep me posted. I don't want to get blindsided here. Not like I don't have other things to keep me occupied. They expect me to deal with evacuation plans, scheduling officers, and making sure of a million things key to survival of thousands and thousands, not just one rich brat who's probably on a bender. If West was beat up, it was probably by some crackhead or pimp. We're facing a potential disaster of biblical proportions if this hurricane does what the experts say. You find Gary West and I'll handle everything else."

"Gary West is no substance abuser," Alexa said, her anger rising. "From everything we've learned, he has never shown any side but that of loving and dedicated husband and father."

Manseur nodded. "That's a fact, sir."

Evans ignored their words, flipped open his cell phone, and swept from the room as suddenly as he had come in, not bothering to close the door behind him. Alexa saw a phalanx of his staff clustered out in the open area, awaiting their leader.

"Sisyphus," Alexa muttered.

"What?" Manseur asked.

"Mythology. Evans is pushing a giant ball of crap up the mountain so he can roll it down on us."

"If Dr. LePointe didn't call your director, who the hell did?" Manseur asked.

"The only other person I know of who has the clout," Alexa said, smiling to herself. She took her cell phone from her purse and, after consulting the slip of paper Casey had given her in her hotel room, started to dial the private number that was on the card, but stopped. "It's time to talk to Casey West again. Face-to-face, I think."

"You want to handle that end? I'll go see what the evidence lab staff has got, and meet you later," Manseur told her. "I'll have Kennedy drop you off and I can pick you up myself when you're done. Why didn't you mention the twenty-five million?"

"It isn't my job to keep Evans informed about every little thing, knowing he'll pass it up the chain. Besides, he has too much on his mind already. What with saving the city from God's plan and all."

22

The black warden woman had pissed herself in the cabin, but she did what Leland said to do and even grabbed one of the fat warden's ankles to help Leland move the heavy bastard through the brush over to the boat they'd come to his camp in. The man he'd brought to the camp ought to be dead, but he wasn't. His head was smashed in where Leland had taken the pipe to him, but he was still breathing, taking in water, and making rattle sounds and gurgling to beat the band.

"You give your promise you'll wait here without running off while I load this bastard in y'all's boat?" Leland asked her.

"I won't run off. I promise."

Leland knelt, grabbed the warden's wrists, and lifted him up over his shoulder like a burlap bag filled with grain. Standing, Leland steadied himself under the dead weight.

"Are you going to . . . kill me?" the woman asked, her voice breaking, tears running down her cheeks.

"Of course," Leland told her. He sure wasn't going to let her go and tell people how easy it was to sneak into his camp house. Telling lies to people wasn't something he did if he could help it.

She started blubbering and shaking. "P-please, p-please. Noooo."

"It's all right. My daddy used to say that dying is just the tail end of living. You do what I tell you and you won't suffer none. I'm good at making it so it don't hurt."

Leland stepped onto the boat, causing it to rock, and dropped the dead warden's sorry ass onto the floor. When he turned around, he saw the warden woman had run off. Leland hated liars worse than gar. He shook his head, grabbed his pipe out from inside his belt, and trotted off to catch her.

"I don't want to die!" she hollered into the swamp.

"If you don't want people to kill you," he hollered as he ran after her, "stay outta their personal places!"

23

Other than saying he'd learned a lot from her talk at the Marriott, Kyler Kennedy didn't speak to Alexa during most of the long ride to Casey's house from HQ. She knew the young detective felt slighted because Manseur hadn't shared what was happening inside the investigation, which he almost certainly had to believe should have been his to run. Alexa was actually thankful he wasn't making small talk, because she used the heavy silence to think about the case.

She had requested a Bucar, an official FBI vehicle,

from the local FO, and had been assured that one (complete with a GPS mapping system) would be delivered to her at the West residence within the hour. Alexa was also told that the Bureau's office was being readied for a move out, because the hurricane probably wasn't going to change course enough to spare New Orleans some serious damage. The decision had been made that nonessential staff and the families of agents were being evacuated from the city the next morning. The office in Baton Rouge would become their temporary HQ until it was safe to return to their offices at the Lakefront in New Orleans.

Alexa trusted Michael Manseur because Winter Massey vouched for him—not something the ex–U.S. deputy marshal, and Alexa's dearest friend, did often or lightly. If Massey recommended she trust somebody, she would do so without reservation—but she would also verify periodically just to make sure that trust wasn't misplaced. It wasn't that Alexa couldn't trust people—not exactly. Some people were such good liars and manipulators, though, that you either never knew the truth of them, or didn't learn their agendas until it was too late. She was 99.9 percent certain that Michael Manseur was every bit as trustworthy as he appeared to be—as Massey believed him to be—but having the GPS would free her to travel independently, so they could work the case much more effectively and require fewer bodies. She certainly didn't trust anyone else in the New Orleans Police Department.

As an FBI agent in the field, Alexa sometimes had to ignore her instincts and go in whatever directions her superiors pointed her. Cases she'd worked on had turned out badly because she'd had to follow orders instead of her own instincts. But, as importantly, she had been wrong on a few occasions and had paid a price for letting her opinions or impressions color an investigation. Her superiors didn't care that nine times out of ten her initial read on people and situations was right. For instance, in child abductions, she could spend ten minutes with the family and know which, if any, of them were lying and therefore hiding something they were ashamed of, or might even be involved in the crime. She wasn't psychic—didn't believe in the ability to see through the eyes of dead people or talk to spirits—but sometimes she could stand at a crime scene and see how things had happened with the clarity of a film.

It is scientific fact that some people have an instinctive ability to detect lies. People can learn to read others with amazing accuracy, because there are scores of facial expressions, eye motions, and facial muscles that act independently and denote a person's truthfulness in responding to a question with far greater accuracy than either a lie detector or voice-stress analysis. Professors at Duke University who were studying human ability to detect deceit agreed that Alexa Keen was very talented when it came to spotting liars. After she took an advanced course in reading evasion techniques and standard facial tics, she was even better.

Knowing when people are lying is a blessing and a curse. In any event, hunches were not admissible in court, or valid cause for a search warrant.

Kyler Kennedy pulled up out front of the Wests' home. "You want me to come in with you?" he asked, violating his silence. "Mrs. West knows me, feels comfortable with me since I've interviewed her already."

"Thanks, but this needs to be a girl-to-girl thing," Alexa said as she climbed from the car, taking her shoulder bag with her.

She closed the door and Kennedy roared off down the street like a teenager who'd just been jilted. Alexa walked to the gate, which was opened by a man built like a professional boxer. He locked his intense eyes on her. "May I help you?" he asked, but his body language said that being accommodating was dead last on his list of things he wanted to do.

Alexa reached into her purse, which caused the man to slip his hand deeper inside his jacket, until she pulled out her badge case. He scrutinized her FBI identification and stepped aside, saying, "Mrs. West is expecting you." Alexa wondered what the man would have done if she had come out with her Glock instead of her badge. There was no way he could have drawn his gun before Alexa had blown his heart out. Standing so close, he should have kept his right hand free so he could use it to disarm her, were she so inclined to pull a weapon.

Grace, Casey's assistant and best friend from childhood, opened the front door. "Casey's taking a shower. She didn't sleep at all. She thought she looked terrible. Like that's possible."

Deana trotted up the hall, hugged Grace's leg, and, sticking out her bottom lip, peered up at Alexa.

"Hello, Deana," Alexa said, smiling.

"She's acting out because of the *thing*. Come on back to the den," Grace said, leading the way. Deana took off, running ahead of them, but Grace scooped her up and held her to her side as the child squealed and kicked violently to free herself.

"Me-do-ee!" she protested.

"No, Aunt Grace will help you, Deans. She's at the age where she wants to do everything herself, like she's capable. It slows everything to a crawl. Gary spoils her by caving in to her whims. But who am I to say that isn't how I'd do it?" As they passed by the dining room, Alexa saw a man seated at the table with a tape-recording device in front of him. Grace said, "He's monitoring the phone in case there's a ransom demand." The man looked up from the magazine he was reading and stared at Alexa as she went by. "Casey told me she went to see you at your hotel. We are absolutely thrilled you're on the case. Casey says she can't live without Gary, and if anything has happened to him, I'm afraid of what she'll do to herself."

Alexa sat on the sleek Italian leather sofa. The coffee table was a long slab of rose-colored hardwood with several lighter wood butterflies to keep the cracks from enlarging. Alexa couldn't remember the maker's Japanese name, but she knew he had worked in a studio in the Pacific Northwest and his work was very collectable and valuable. Alexa was familiar with the Avedon image of Andy Warhol's scarred torso. In the picture Warhol's hand held up his black leather jacket to allow Richard Avedon's view camera to capture the damage to his chest that a psychotic woman inflicted by shooting him several times point-blank for not making her a movie star, or some imagined slight. The Frankenstein-like stitching on the lily-white torso—this one enlarged to four-by-five feet, and framed by black lacquered wood—was a visual jackhammer that dominated the warm, sunlit room like a rogue elephant.

Deana went straight to a box of her toys and started lifting them out one by one and throwing them behind her without seeming to care where they landed.

"Casey tells me you two have known each other for a long time."

"We've been thick as thieves since second grade," Grace said. "Casey is the kindest, most generous person who ever lived, and the most thoughtful. I hung out with her—of course, everybody wanted to, but most of the time it was just us two. Mrs. LePointe, Casey's grandmother, started taking me with them all over the world when we were twelve—Casey insisted because she was always bored to death when she was with her family by herself. We got in our share of girlish mischief. We were as close as twins." Grace smiled. "Casey could do no wrong, of course. When she went to boarding school, she begged to take me along, but my parents wouldn't hear of it. Mrs. LePointe would have paid for it, but my parents wanted me at Blessed Heart because it's a family tradition." At that, Grace's eyes seemed to lose their focus for a split second and her facial muscles shifted. Alexa read her last statement for an exaggeration maybe the woman almost believed.

"We wanted to go to college together, but I went to LSU and she went to Harvard, like everybody in her family does. Then about six years ago, Casey was getting so much interest in her work, she needed someone to organize her life, so I left my job—I was an executive assistant buyer at Bloomie's—and started working with her full time. Like she needs anyone to organize anything. She's brilliant and totally focused. Always has been. Oddly enough, I'm the disorganized one, but for her I somehow organize the organized."

"So you're Casey's employee."

"Technically speaking, you can say I am, but she treats me like her sister. I get a generous salary, but I do work hard and I'm totally dedicated to Casey and her career. Loyalty is something you can't buy. I'd do what I do for nothing, but unfortunately I can't devote my life to anything without financial compensation. I'm not independently wealthy."

"You keep regular hours?"

"I don't punch a time clock or anything. It's not set up as an hourly arrangement. I liken coming to work every day to what a priest must feel upon entering the Sistine Chapel and looking up. You've seen Casey's art?" Grace's eyes brightened.

"No. Are you a fan of Gary's plays?"

"I guess I'm his biggest fan after Casey. Casey's art is in a class of its own."

"I thought she was a photographer?"

Grace frowned. "Her photography elevates the medium to art."

"I haven't had the pleasure." Alexa looked around hoping she might see a portrait that Casey had done hanging in the large room. Counting the torso, there were seven Avedons on the walls—all were Avedon's portraits that Alexa was familiar with from his books.

"She doesn't have any of her own work hanging here. She doesn't have an ego. My apartment is completely done in her portraits. Another advantage of my position is that she gives me whatever prints I want. The frame shop that does her framing does them for me for practically nothing, because Casey uses only one frame stock—which she designed, and has it manufactured exclusively for her photographs. They keep a ton of it in stock for her work only. Nobody else gets any of it but me unless they buy a portrait. Would you like to see?" Grace's excited eyes were lit up like Christmas bulbs.

Deana had gone to the window and was beating on the glass with a rubber dog toy that emitted a sharp squeak with each blow. This seemed to fascinate her, because she kept doing it. "Eeep, eeep, eeep, eeep."

"Didn't you just say there wasn't any of her work here?"

"Not on the walls," Grace said softly. She went to the bookshelf and took out a large book and, after removing it from its cloth slipcover, handed it to Alexa. "She owns the most extensive collection there is of the most important photographers, from Brady to Avedon. She has most of it out on loan or donated to museums, or in a climate-controlled storage facility in Manhattan. This volume of her own work just came out two weeks ago, in a very limited edition of five hundred copies. One thousand dollars per. I don't have one, but I will, because it's being reprinted in a larger and less expensive edition next month. Casey only got three of these for her own use, because it was completely presold. Gary has one, of course. And Casey has two—one locked up for Deana, and this one."

"The small edition means she won't be signing very many copies."

"She doesn't ever sign them, because she just doesn't feel comfortable doing so. She doesn't think the book is about her, but her subjects. But I expect she'll pen a note to me in one of the mass-produced ones if I pester her."

The book, which Grace placed on the coffee table, was roughly ten-by-fourteen, and an inch thick. On it, what appeared to be a photographic print of a young woman had been mounted on the off-white linen binding. An acetate sleeve protected the cloth and the image. The child-woman portrayed in the shot had enormous, almond-shaped eyes that stared into Casey's lens with the sort of mixture of intensity and revulsion of someone who was studying a spider in the process of capturing a luckless butterfly. The title of the volume was *All Together/All Alone: Portraits by Casey West*. Not Casey LePointe West, Alexa noted.

Grace said, "This is a show catalog published by the museum in Zurich that hosted the exhibition. The show is going next to the Corcoran in D.C., and then to the Metropolitan Museum in New York. She spent six months working as an intern for Avedon, but everybody thinks she's far better than he was."

"I'll make a point to see it at the Corcoran." Alexa opened the book and turned the pages gently. Grace put her hands together as if praying and studied Alexa intently as she scanned the introduction penned by Casey's husband. *"A better husband and father never drew a breath."* Alexa had heard a dozen times in investigations. *"They broke the mold."*

The foreword was an affectionate critique, obviously penned by a fan.

Medium format camera somehow captures her subjects' essence—their hopes, dreams, illusions,

*and fears laid bare for the viewer in equal mea-
sure. They say the eyes are mirrors to the soul, and
Casey's art seems proof that the soul exists, and
that we—despite our differences—are all varia-
tions of a single being. To experience Casey West's
work is to not just see, but to experience our most
basic and complex connections to one another.*

*How one person among millions is touched by
the magic so they are able to show us so much
about ourselves in others is a question that has
puzzled man since the dawn. Art is most often created out of painful experience. Despite her amazing complexity, Casey is somehow able to see
simple truths in those around her, and to capture
those truths in such a way as to say, through light
and photographic dyes, what Leonardo da Vinci
said in oils, William Faulkner said with words,
and Michelangelo said in marble. As her husband,
I have been blessed and privileged . . . Casey is following a divine calling, following her inner vision
armed only with a camera. . . .*

If Casey really lacked an ego, Alexa reflected,
Gary's words of praise must have made her squirm.
Only love for him could have allowed his worshipful
foreword to be connected to her work.

The first portraits hit Alexa with the force of open-
hand slaps, each one more powerful than the one before it. The expressions on the subjects in the static
and crisp images were like the unblinking eyes of
cocked handguns, remarkable in their emotional
power. The eyes of each subject—vulnerable in one,
sad in another, and furious in yet another—had a

hypnotic effect on Alexa. She was awed by Casey's work. Most photographers would have been lucky to get even one picture the equal of these in the course of a long career, but here were scores of photographic masterpieces, gathered in one collection.

"That one says it all, and then some."

Grace was referring to a portrait entitled "Husband and Daughter—2003, Monaco," showing a shirtless and strikingly handsome man holding a small child against his chest, his hand positioned in such a way as to hide her features behind his fingers. Gary West stared into the lens with the naked emotion of a lioness protecting her cub from a gathering of starving hyenas.

"He looks protective," Alexa said. It wasn't the smiling man she'd seen in the snapshots of him she'd seen before.

"He didn't even want *that* picture of Deana in the book. He lives for Deana and Casey. Protecting Deana is an obsession with him."

"Does he have any flaws?"

"Well," Grace said, frowning. "An obsession with anything might be a flaw, don't you think so? Every person has flaws—only some people can't see them."

"Give me that!" Casey demanded as she entered the room—hand outstretched to Alexa. Her cheeks were bright red, and Alexa couldn't tell if she was embarrassed or angry. Her eyes were red from crying or lack of rest, and the fingers of her outstretched hand trembled.

"This is amazing—" Alexa began.

Deana ran over and held up her arms to her mother, hoping to be lifted. Casey looked at her, placed her free hand on Deana's head gently. "Just a sec, darling. Mommy has to do something."

"Uh-uuuuh," Deana protested. "Ut."

Alexa closed the volume gently and handed it to Casey, who sat beside her. "Grace, my pen."

Grace went to a writing desk across the room and brought Casey back a lacquered fountain pen. Casey uncapped it, opened the book to the flyleaf, and carefully wrote something in the page's center. After Casey capped the pen, she blew gently on the wet ink for a few seconds until she was certain it was dry. Returning the volume to its slipcover, she handed it to Alexa and smiled uncertainly. "This is for you."

"I can't accept it," Alexa protested, honestly. Taking a gift from a subject in these circumstances—which might have been misinterpreted as an agent taking a gratuity from a vulnerable woman—could easily come back to haunt her. And a one-thousand-dollar gift at that.

"It's just a book," Casey insisted. "Are you resisting because you're an FBI agent? Is it against some federal law?"

"That's not it. I just know how dear this book is—how few copies you have," Alexa said. Of course she wanted the book. Who wouldn't?

"Well, I've already inscribed it, so unless someone named Alexa Keen comes along, it won't be of any use to anybody else. I do hope you'll enjoy it."

Grace stood near the couch, looking as though someone had just told her they'd run over her kitten.

Alexa said, "It's far too generous."

"So you will accept it?"

"I guess you've left me no choice. Thank you. Thank you very much."

Deana was trying to climb onto the couch. With her eyes on the book in Alexa's lap, Casey pulled Deana onto her lap. The child started pulling at the gold chain her mother was wearing. Casey allowed her to tug to her little heart's content.

"Casey, Director Bender asked me to assist the police. I thought your uncle was responsible for talking to him, but I'm not sure he was."

Grace looked away, her body language a blast of super-chilled air.

"Alexa, your director's daughter, Alicia Bender, went to school with me. A portrait I did of her was in my first book. I don't accept commercial assignments because what I do, I do because something I can't explain about a subject attracts me. When people ask me to do their portraits, the pictures rarely ever work nearly as well, so usually they're just technically pleasant likenesses. Alicia's mother wants me to do her husband's official FBI portrait. I've avoided doing it, and somehow I doubt he'd open himself up. I called Alicia early this morning, and I mentioned our desire that your expertise and assistance be made available to us, and I think I told her how much it would mean to me personally. She called her mother in Aspen."

"I'm amazed," Alexa said. She tried to imagine how the director's wife felt about being called hours before the sun came up.

Casey seemed to read her thoughts.

"I didn't wake Felicity. I awoke Alicia, who assured me her mother was wide-awake in Aspen.

Perhaps after this is over," Casey said, "you'll allow me to photograph you."

"Why me?"

"You have a remarkable presence and you are beautiful, have amazing eyes, exotic features, remarkable hands. Strength and depth."

Alexa was embarrassed, not merely because she chewed her fingernails and was ashamed of that compulsive habit, but because she had never felt comfortable receiving praise unassociated with her job. She felt herself blushing and was powerless to stop it.

"I'm embarrassing you." Casey smiled at Alexa and patted her hand. "We'll talk about it later."

"I came because I have some news," Alexa said.

"My uncle told me you found my Volvo. What did you learn from it?"

"Your Volvo?" Alexa asked.

"The Volvo is technically my car. Gary took it yesterday because Deana's car seat was in his Pontiac, since he brought her to the lake. It was easier than changing it out. I went there from the studio to meet them. We have one baby seat for each car, but I'd taken mine out the day before to make room for some framed prints Grace had to ship out."

"What kind of Pontiac does he drive?" Alexa asked.

"A white 1965 GTO convertible with a red top that I bought for him as an anniversary present a few years ago. That's what he was driving yesterday. He also has a Rover, which he sometimes drives to spare wear and tear on the GTO."

"The GTO is his only toy," Grace added.

"Gary always wanted one because it was something his father had when Gary was a child."

"And you didn't see the Volvo after you left the restaurant?"

"No."

"I guess you didn't head in the same direction," Alexa said.

Casey shook her head slowly and wiped away a tear. "I wish we'd left together. I assumed he was long gone, so I didn't even look for him."

"We don't have the results from the crime-scene technicians yet. Detective Manseur is handling that as we speak."

"Shouldn't your people be doing that?"

"The local crime techs are fine for the prelims. All we know so far, or what we think happened based on what we saw, is that it appears that an unsub ran into the Volvo, approached Gary's door, opened it—or maybe Gary did—and the unsub—"

"Unsub?" Casey asked.

"It's FBI jargon for unknown subject," Grace chirped in.

"He struck Gary while he was still inside the Volvo."

"A violent attack?" Grace asked.

"Yes, it was."

"Could it have been fatal?" Grace asked.

Casey's eyes widened. She clenched her daughter tightly to her chest.

"No, I don't think so," Alexa said.

"What did he use?"

"The object used was probably some short, cylindrical club."

"A golf club?" Grace asked.

"We don't know exactly what it was. May have been a weapon of convenience—something the unsub picked up at the scene. Or perhaps he had the weapon with him already."

"Weren't there any witnesses?" Grace asked.

"Not that we've located," Alexa said.

"Then how do you know he was attacked?" Grace asked. "What evidence is there?"

"I'd rather not go into that." Alexa had already told them much more than she normally would have, and she didn't want to upset Casey any more than she had already.

"Please, Alexa," Casey said. "I need to know."

"Okay. There was low-velocity blood spatter inside the Volvo and a mark on the door that seems to have been made during the course of the event."

"How do you know it was his blood in the car?" Grace asked.

"The blood was human and O negative, which is the same as Gary's. He was driving the vehicle, so I think we can assume it's his."

"How did you know his blood type?" Casey asked. "I didn't tell anybody that."

"The identification card in his wallet listed his blood type," Alexa told her.

"You found his wallet in the Volvo?" Casey asked.

Alexa nodded. "He was most likely struck while getting his license out because he'd been rear-ended and was expecting to exchange information. The wallet, containing cash and credit cards, was on the console, so I figure it was already in his hand when the event occurred."

"Event?" Tears ran down Casey's cheeks. Grace fetched her a tissue. Deana looked at her mother curiously and reached up to touch the tears.

Alexa felt a catch in her throat and fought the urge to show any emotion. FBI agents did not let anyone see their softer side. They were not supposed to become emotionally invested with victims, because emotion clouded objectivity.

"Excuse my choice of terminology. We don't have enough facts to draw many conclusions. I'm just telling you what evidence we do have, which is very preliminary and may give us an inaccurate picture. We can't afford to jump to any conclusions at this stage. The early evidence is often misinterpreted."

"Do you think he could be dead?" Grace asked.

"Grace!" Casey snapped angrily. "Gary isn't dead! If he were, I'd know it. He's *alive*! Don't you dare say he's dead!"

"I'm sorry," Grace said immediately. "Of course he isn't, Casey. I didn't mean . . ." She let the apology dangle unfinished—lingering in the silence like an unpleasant odor.

Alexa didn't particularly care for Grace, but she admonished herself for that judgment. Grace may have been trying to comfort Casey in her own misguided way, or trying to control the situation in her capacity as Casey's closest friend and an employee whose job was to make herself useful in whatever way she could.

"On the positive side," Alexa told them, "there wasn't the amount of blood to indicate a fatal wound. The blows, based on the weapon's mark in the door panel, would seem to indicate that the door's proximity to Gary's position means the area necessary to draw back was shortened and lacked enough inertia to inflict a fatal injury."

"But he still might have been very seriously injured?" Casey asked.

Alexa nodded. "That's possible."

"It isn't a probability?" Grace asked.

Casey fixed her with a warning glare.

"Forgive my intrusion, Casey, but if someone killed Gary, they'd probably have left the body there, right?" Grace asked.

Alexa nodded.

"I mean, why would they drag a body from one vehicle to another in a residential neighborhood, where they could be seen by anybody looking out the window? They abducted him, and chances are, he's going to be alive in case Casey wants proof of life, right? Isn't that how it goes? Abductors usually release the people after they get the ransom, don't they?"

"Well, taking him could be a positive thing," Alexa said, fighting to control her urge to ask Grace how she knew where the Volvo had been found. Instead, she turned to Casey and said, "Casey, could I have some water?"

Grace left the room without waiting to be sent for the requested water.

Deana slipped down from the couch, went back to her toy box, and began looting it again, squealing with delight.

"My poor baby," Casey said. "Deana knows only that her father isn't here. I'm thankful for that. I know she's picking up on my fear and anxiety. I should try not to be so emotional, but I can't help it.

I know you'll find Gary and he'll be all right. I know that."

"We're doing everything we can," Alexa said. "Look, I'll keep you apprised as best I can as the investigation goes forward, but I'm asking you not to share anything I tell you from here on out with anybody else."

"You mean Unko? Ken Decell?"

"I mean *anybody*. I know it's going to be hard, but can you do that for me?"

"Anything you say, but . . . You can't mean even Grace?"

Alexa nodded solemnly. "Normally I wouldn't be sharing as much as I have, but since you're responsible for my involvement, I'm breaking protocol a lot more than I should. Protocols are in place for good reason. It dictates we share almost no information with a possible suspect, or anyone who might share our information with someone who might be involved, and giving you premature information that could change has obvious drawbacks and risks, putting you through needless emotional turmoil, or might give you unrealistic expectations. I'm making an exception here because I think you need to know certain things so you might see something we don't or make some connection we wouldn't that's useful in locating your husband."

"Okay," Casey said softly. "Nobody. I promise."

"You should also understand I'm not warm and fuzzy when it comes to my work, and what I tell you may seem blunt or harsh. I hope you'll understand that it isn't because I don't empathize with you. Empathy can be detrimental. Casey, I promise you I'm going to do everything I can possibly do to find Gary, but you have to understand that I might not succeed. As much as I hate to say so, there are no guarantees. I'm not in control of this, and may not ever be. But I will do everything in my power to resolve this satisfactorily."

"I'm really much tougher than I look," Casey said.

"I'm sure you are. I need Grace's social, phone numbers, and her current address," Alexa said, taking out her notebook.

24

A fly landed on Leland's top lip and crawled right into his nose like it lived there. He turned, pinched his nostril to pin it, closed his mouth, pressed his index finger to close the clear nostril, and expelled the stunned fly out into the shallows, where a minnow ate it right off the surface, then vanished into the murk. What he was doing wasn't hard work, but it was time-consuming, and he had things to get done.

Overhead, a line of honking geese churned the air as they rose from the bayou. Turning from his task, Leland watched the flowing line of geese start to straighten, and he smiled at how the birds formed up into a flying V. How could they learn such precision, know a letter of the alphabet like that, with brains no bigger than a rat turd.

After field-dressing them—removing their innards so they couldn't float up—Leland had filled the empty cavities of the corpses with chunks of concrete, then tied up their torsos with nylon rope. Blood had made the deck so slippery, he had to move carefully to keep from falling. He had decided to bait some gator hooks on the way back to camp so he wouldn't waste time. He didn't want the warden's boat, because the twin engines were smaller than his one, and it was too sloppy in the turns for his taste. Before he'd got the better boat from Doc, he mighta kept it and painted it and used it to work out of, but his boat was a lot, so he didn't mind scuttling theirs.

As he approached the last gator hook, hanging over the water from a tree limb, he slowed and let the vessel coast in under the tree. A fat cottonmouth swam across the water, sitting up so high it didn't appear to be getting wet as it made for the shore, vanishing into the reeds. Leland wished he could catch it and put it in with the others, but he didn't have time just then, and he'd find one just as big when he did.

Leland took the last piece of meat off the bone and baited the hook with it. After he was satisfied that the tendon would make the meat difficult for the gators to steal off the hook, he looked at the way the sock was rolled down under the ankle before throwing the leg bone, socked foot and all, up into the weeds on-shore.

25

"Grace isn't involved," Casey insisted. "I know her like I know myself. Better even."

"I have to check out everybody who's involved with

you and Gary on a regular basis. It's standard operating procedure to look first at everyone close and work our way out. Make me a list as soon as you can. For the time being, I'm assuming that whoever did this knew yours and Gary's schedule—when he'd be where."

"Grace Smythe. One twenty-three Durban Place. I'll make up a list of our other friends and close associates and their addresses and phone numbers."

"Okay," Alexa said.

The phone rang.

"Grace'll get that," Casey said. "Every time it rings I pray it's a kidnapper just asking for some money. If they ask, I can pay the ransom. You wouldn't interfere with that, would you, Alexa? If an exchange got messed up and Gary suffered for it, I couldn't live with myself."

"It's totally your decision, Casey. I'll make suggestions based on my experience, though, and you'd be smart to take them. If you get a demand, you should let me know immediately."

"They usually say not to tell the police, don't they?"

"Yes, but they won't know you did."

After a few seconds spent in silence, Grace Smythe, wearing a worried expression, came back with a chilled bottle of water in her hand and gave it to Alexa absently and unopened. "It's Lucille Burch. The bottle blonde with the sharp nose and whiny voice. The reporter, or whatever she calls herself."

"What does she want?" Casey asked.

"She told me she wants to get your reaction to something."

"Gary?"

"No. She says that she's been told that the

Danielson woman is out of the hospital. She's trying to confirm the story before she puts it on the air."

Casey gasped.

Alexa knew who Sibby Danielson was, but not that she had been released from the hospital she'd been committed to after murdering Casey's parents twenty-six years before.

"Don't talk to her," Alexa advised. "Grace, tell her Casey has no comment."

"No comment always looks worse than anything people say," Grace insisted.

"I know Lucille Burch," Casey said. "She'll never give up."

"She's likely just looking to get her facts in line and spice up a story by getting you to tell her something she doesn't yet know is true," Alexa said. "She probably doesn't know about Gary's disappearance yet, or she wants to get confirmation if she has caught wind of it. You shouldn't talk to the press until the time is right, and I don't think it is."

"I'd think you'd want people calling in tips," Grace told Alexa.

"We need good tips, but we don't have the manpower to run down hundreds. So far we're lucky not to have to deal with the complications the media would provide. When the time is right, we'll fill them in and ask for their help if we think it's in Gary's best interest. I've been here before. Trust me. With the hurricane heading this way, and nothing from you to fuel chasing after Sibby rumors or looking into a tip about Gary, she'll probably put it on a back burner. When and if we decide to announce that Gary has been abducted, we'll get maximum exposure. Let's give it a few hours before we make that call. If this is a kidnapping, the perps probably will be watching the news, and the media will make any coming and going unobserved very difficult."

"You could say she doesn't concern you," Grace told Casey. "You could say if she's cured, it's cool, or something like that."

Casey's eyes went from Alexa to Grace and back. "Tell Burch I said this is the first I've heard about it. Tell her I won't involve myself in speculation."

Alexa nodded. "Grace, tell her Casey has no knowledge about Ms. Danielson nor any comment at this time."

Grace left the room, headed for the kitchen.

"I didn't know that woman could ever get out," Casey murmured. "How could Sibhon Danielson be let out and me not know about it?"

"If she was insane when she committed the offense, she could be released as long as she was no longer a danger to herself or others. They don't set specific sentences for those adjudicated insane."

Alexa figured the anniversary could explain why the media was snooping around after information on a twenty-six-year-old case. The date had drawn media interest, and with a few phone calls a researcher could easily discover whether or not the perpetrator was still incarcerated. Alexa wondered how long it would be before some cop clued them in on Gary's disappearance. She was amazed it hadn't happened yet. That could only be due to the threat of the storm and the fact that most people in the area, including the police, had more pressing things to be concerned with at the moment. It appeared that the hurricane might actually be beneficial to the investigation.

She knew that she had to find out where Sibby Danielson was. It seemed unlikely, but if the murderer was really out in the world, she might be somehow involved—especially if the person, or persons, who took Gary might have been after his wife. Casey was the lone witness to a twenty-six-year-old double homicide. It was remotely possible that, in a psychotic mind, Casey West might fall under the heading of unfinished business.

26

A very tired Michael Manseur sat at a desk in the office of the evidence labs just around the corner from headquarters. CSI Chief Sergeant Mickey Wayne Cooley put a piece of paper in front of his guest, along with a cup of strong coffee. The head of Homicide merely nodded once in appreciation.

"The glass shards are from a sealed-beam headlight manufactured for older vehicles—which makes sense, given the height of the bumper strike on the Volvo and the green paint sample," Cooley said. "Used to be a fairly common stock lens that fit hundreds of vehicles."

"Great," Manseur replied.

"The transferred paint in the sample isn't as common. There are two layers showing two paint jobs. The outer layer is more recent and was sold by auto-paint suppliers. But the undermost layer is a factory color from an early-sixties GMC truck."

"A truck," Manseur said.

"It wasn't used on just any trucks. You're looking for one of these in a sun-faded goose-shit green, Michael." Cooley set a photocopy of an old advertisement for the vehicle in front of Manseur. "Panel truck—forerunner to the commercial van."

"That's great. Won't be many still registered."

"Not a single one in that color is registered in the state of Louisiana. We're querying adjacent states now. The scratch on the Volvo's inside driver's door was made by a pipe that's three-quarter inches in diameter that was cut off clean. No thread mark in the impression. Pipe is no more than about sixteen to eighteen inches long, based on angle of the strike and the distance that the door opens."

"Great," Manseur grumbled before carefully sipping his hot coffee. "Pipe."

"According to trace, it's a pipe with high lead content. What's commonly referred to as a 'lead pipe,' as in Colonel Plum did it in the conservatory with a lead pipe."

"So that's rare?"

"Lead is toxic. Lead pipes haven't been commercially available since the early sixties, and you only find them in old structures or scrap yards."

"Lucky thing for us there's no old buildings in New Orleans."

"True, it's around. If it helps, there was trace water with a high salt content transferred along with the blood, so the pipe's been immersed in water recently and there are other blood types. One human."

"One human?"

"O negative only on the human side. The other is

animal blood. Also found a hair that looked like rodent hair, but not rat."

"That leaves, what, gerbils, hamsters, squirrels, and muskrats?"

"It's closer related to South American tapirs than muskrats."

"Tapirs?"

"Nutria cousin the size of a pig. There's one out at the zoo. The hair might have been there before the attack."

"I doubt Gary West had any dealings with swimming rodents."

"Amount of human blood was negligible and there were two blows."

"That's what Keen said," Manseur said to himself.

"Keen?" Cooley asked.

"FBI Special Agent Keen," Manseur said.

"Not *Alexa* Keen?" Cooley asked.

"You know her?"

"I know of her. Tech I work with at the FBI lab told me about her. He said she reads crime scenes better than he can. Said she has a gift for thinking twisted, reading people, and interpreting scenes accurately. I've sort of kept up a little with her career since. Last year she was involved with that Army Intelligence shake-up around that judge's daughter's kidnap deal in the Carolinas."

"With Winter Massey," Manseur said, nodding.

"Winter 'hell-comes-to-breakfast' Massey. He's another one I try to keep up with. Seems whenever he's anywhere around here, I get almost as busy as the medical examiner. Next time I hear he's in town, I'm going on sabbatical till the smoke clears. You know him from that Manelli firefight out near St. Rose?"

Manseur shook his head. "The Porter homicide. I was out on vacation for the Manelli thing."

"Man's a human tornado," Cooley said. "You know how lightning never strikes twice in the same place? If Massey was here, wouldn't be any point in another hurricane coming."

"Yeah." Manseur smiled. "He's a very good man."

"I'm sure. We're processing the Volvo prints, and there's a bunch to go through. I need reference prints from the people who use it. How'd Alexa Keen get involved?"

"She was here in town and agreed to help out." Manseur stood and picked up the report. "For practice, I guess."

"You picked out a dry spot to get your girls to, Michael?"

"They're going to stay with my wife's sister in Birmingham. Leaving later today."

"You might want to go with them before leaves are canceled."

"All leaves are already canceled. Everybody's reporting in. You didn't know?"

"I haven't heard anything on account of what I've been doing on your *secret* case. This Katrina might be the big one," Cooley said. "You thought about that? It happens, there won't be much left of this place."

"They always turn," Manseur said. "Most of the citizens won't stop their normal business until they're sipping their drinks underwater."

"So where's the plate?" Cooley asked.

"Sorry?"

"The license tag from the Volvo?"

"Why you want to know that?"

"I was wondering why all the hush-hush was afoot on an obvious red ball case without anybody saying so. Must be a big one. I could run the VIN to find out," Mickey said.

"You could, but I don't think you want to."

"Why's that?"

"Because, if word of that name were to happen to leak out prematurely, everybody who knows is going to have to bend over so the super can shine a great big spotlight up their hidey-holes. Curiosity killed the cat, Mickey."

"One thing I always wondered," Cooley said.

"What's that?"

"What was it that cat wanted to know?" He laughed at his own joke.

"Wasn't what he wanted to know that killed him," Manseur said, walking to the door. "Was the answer did that."

27

Manseur was moving up on the sidewalk toward his office when his cell rang. It looked like every cruiser in town was parked on the street outside HQ. Uniformed officers and detectives were gathered in groups, shooting the breeze. He fished the phone from his coat pocket, looked at the caller ID, and answered.

"Agent Keen," he said. "Looks like we're looking for an old GMC or Chevrolet panel truck. CSI says it was a pipe, just like you thought. Lead, with a nutria hair and salt water on it. Nutria's a pesky swimming rodent the size of a house cat that lives in the swamps and marshes. Two blows. They're running the Volvo prints now. You get anything new?"

"Michael, I think it's possible the woman who killed the LePointes, Sibby Danielson, is out," she told him. "That may explain the media's sudden interest in those files."

The implication of that possibility didn't escape the seasoned detective.

"Can you find out where she was being held and if she's out?" she asked. "We need to do it quietly so we don't set off any alarms and have the hospital calling the media."

Manseur's heart rate sped up as his gait increased.

"I'll check on her place of incarceration, and I'm on my way," he told her. "Sit tight and I'll come get you."

One call and he found out Sibby Danielson had been sent to River Run, ten miles north of the city, facing the Mississippi River levee. He picked up Alexa at a strip mall parking lot and drove out River Road, which more or less hugged the Mississippi River levee. The highway started at Canal Street at the river and ran, under a variety of highway numbers and street names, clear to Minnesota, or someplace up north. Despite what the weather people said, the crystal-clear sky and the dry air seemed to belie the fact that a storm was swallowing up almost the entire Gulf of Mexico, making its way toward them.

"Sibby aside for the moment, you think Gary got grabbed because he was in Casey's car?"

"Since the Volvo's windows are tinted dark, it's a possibility the assailant didn't see that Gary was driving her car," Alexa said.

"If the Danielson woman did do it, she had to have had some help. I suppose the perps could have thought Casey was still in the car if they hadn't been watching closely and seen him leave in it," Manseur said.

"If they saw him drive there in the GTO with the baby, they could have waited down the road for the Volvo and followed it, assuming Casey was in it," Alexa said. "The perps could have waited down the road so they wouldn't be seen lurking, and followed the car. But . . ."

"But?"

"It's also possible that someone on the inside knew they'd switch cars and told the perps."

Manseur absently tapped the steering wheel. "So you like the assistant, Smythe, for it," Manseur said.

"Well, Grace talked about the Volvo being found in a residential neighborhood. I never said where the Volvo was found."

"You sure?"

"Location never came up. I suppose Evans could have told Dr. LePointe and he mentioned it to Casey."

Manseur said, "Grace could have assumed that since the Volvo wasn't found immediately, it was because in a residential area parked cars wouldn't attract police attention. She's been a close friend of Casey West's forever, so why would she be involved? What would she have to gain . . . besides cash?"

How could she relate the feelings she had about Grace Smythe's hero worship? With Gary out of the way, Grace might think she'd be closer to Casey. That Casey, in her grief, might cling to Grace as a convenient life raft.

"Maybe Grace has another motive," Alexa said. "My impression of Grace is that she is the sort of person who was born into a respected family but without any money left to go with the name. She told me the LePointes took her around the world, implying she couldn't have gone on such trips otherwise. Given her history as Casey's friend, she can't enjoy being a salaried employee and fetch-it girl, which is exactly what she is. Dr. LePointe treats her like a servant, and to a lesser extent so does Casey. I suspect that Grace went on those trips because she was an acceptable traveling companion for Casey, and a paid pal was how the LePointes saw her, and that's how William still sees her. I think Grace knows it deep down, and is in denial over it."

"So Casey isn't her friend?" Manseur asked.

"Yes, a close friend, but she's also her employer. Grace is a remote second banana to Gary with Casey, and maybe that's a hard wire to walk. Grace is basically expendable, and maybe Gary sees her that way. He's fiercely into Casey and Deana, but it's possible he doesn't care much for Grace. She's sort of clingy and self-important."

"I don't see her best friend doing it, but she's on the inside, and I'm open to anything. But lots of people not connected to the Wests could have gotten this every-Friday meal pattern by watching them, or maybe a waitress, like Cindy/Nancy, or another waitress, said something to a husband, or a hundred somebody else's."

Alexa shrugged. It was true and possible. But it didn't feel right to her.

"You think Casey West could be in any danger?" Manseur ventured. "Say, if Sibby Danielson is out and is after revenge or something, a crazy person obsessing on it for twenty-six years might act on it as soon as she can swing an exit from the nut hatch."

"I think Casey's well-enough protected from an axe-swinging middle-aged woman," Alexa said. "Even if Casey were the original target and somebody'd planned to get LePointe to pay a ransom for her, they'd certainly know Gary was a valuable enough commodity to make their effort pay just as much."

"Not a crazy woman's thinking," he said. "More likely revenge."

"Someone acting with her might have changed the focus for her. If they took Gary by an unanticipated turn in events, they could be flexible enough to adapt from revenge to profit."

"You have a point or three," Manseur agreed.

"And something Casey said needs to be considered. It's also possible that someone who thinks it would please Dr. LePointe is behind this."

"Like who?"

"I don't know. Why not Decell? He sure could have pulled it off."

"He wouldn't have targeted Casey. If that's the case, Gary West is dead. If Decell's behind it, he'll have covered his tracks and wouldn't have any reason to keep Gary alive. You can take that to the bank. And if that's the case, it means we're wasting our time."

"Pollyanna Manseur," Alexa said, laughing.

28

"This is where the hospital property starts," Manseur said, pointing out through the windshield.

The corner of the perimeter fence started a quarter of a mile before the driveway into River Run. The buildings were set back from River Road on a field of green grass that looked like a fairway. The manicured grounds were dotted with stately oaks. A green tractor towed a mowing platform, doing a job that probably never had an ending place. The hospital's main structure was a two-story brick monster with massive columns spaced its entire width to support the extended roof. The building might have passed for a monastery or a junior college, except for the steel wire grates covering some of the windows.

"Tara," Alexa said.

"Place was built during Governor Huey P. Long's administration," Manseur explained. "In order to steal big, old Huey had to spend big. He built roads and bridges and hospitals and got millions back from the contractors. The Long administration designed the snatch-and-grab model for the political structure of the State of Louisiana that lives on today."

"Stephen King would love this place," Alexa said dryly.

"If Sibby isn't here," Manseur said, "she was let out. She might have been moved to another hospital, or released to a halfway-house situation or something. She sure didn't escape, I can tell you that for fact. They even have their own graveyard out back."

The sign on the grounds read RIVER RUN PSYCHI-ATRIC HOSPITAL. The fence was topped with razor wire and the concrete guard shack added what the sign failed to spell out—*For the criminally insane.*

Manseur pulled up to the gate and showed his badge to the guard seated in a kiosk, peering out at him through a sheet of extremely thick glass. Alexa imagined the designers of the kiosk had an image of the guardhouse being attacked by an armed gang of the insane who desired to break out one of their members, or gain entrance without going through the appropriate steps—like using meat cleavers to chop up people in their kitchens.

"I'm Detective Manseur, NOPD," Manseur called out through his open window, holding out his badge case.

"What's the nature of your business, Detective?" an electronic voice asked through a speaker. Clearly opening the kiosk's bulletproof window was done only as a last resort.

"We're here to see the director, on official business."

"Do you have an appointment?"

"I do not."

"I'll announce you," the guard said. He lifted the phone and made a call before hanging up and press-ing the push-to-talk switch so Manseur and Alexa could hear him. "Administration is in the center of the main building. Follow the signs and park in the visitors' area. You are required to leave any weapons secured in your vehicle." The heavy steel gate behind the car closed loudly before the one in front of the car rolled slowly aside to allow them to enter the facility. "Have a nice day," the guard said.

"So far it's been a peach," Alexa said in a low voice.

29

When it came to controlling its guests and visitors, Fort Leavenworth, the maximum-security federal prison located on the stark windswept plains of Kansas, had nothing on the River Run mental facility. After locking their weapons in the Crown Victoria's trunk, Alexa and Manseur walked together up the wide stone stairs, stopping before a wide wood door with a thick glass panel that allowed them to see into a short hallway that ended at another security door. A buzzer sounded and the front door swung open to allow them to enter the hallway—the sides of which were floor-to-ceiling glass panels that, once they were inside, allowed them to be viewed like fish in an aquarium. They entered into the mantrap, whereupon the door behind them locked electronically with a loud snap. As the pair approached the second door, it unlocked and slid open to allow them into a vast lobby.

The hospital's security was both comforting and mildly disturbing. Despite its pastoral setting and the antebellum architecture, it was obvious that River Run was not a country-club facility that pandered to the nervous conditions of the general populace.

Across the expanse of the lobby a man the size of a refrigerator, dressed in a white shirt and blue tie, waited for them with his meaty hands flat on a long, granite-topped counter in the manner of a store clerk awaiting customers. Alexa half expected to hear the screams of the insane echoing from the wards, but the space was silent, save the sounds made by Manseur and Alexa's shoes on the polished stone floor and a radio playing a national public radio broadcast. As they approached, the receptionist smiled down at them and nodded.

"May I help you?" he said in a high-pitched voice that Alexa decided made Mike Tyson sound like Paul Robeson.

"NOPD Detective Manseur and FBI Special Agent Keen. We're here to see the director."

As the receptionist read their credentials, his lips actually moved. "The administrative director of the facility or the director of psychiatry?" he asked, smiling like a man eager to make a sale.

"The director who would control who is released from the facility," Manseur told him.

"That would be Dr. Whitfield," the receptionist said, lifting the telephone receiver. He said, "I have an NOPD Detective Manseur and an FBI Agent Keen here to see Dr. Whitfield."

He replaced the receiver and told them, "Please have a seat. Ms. Malouf will be right out to show you to the director's office."

Alexa and Manseur sat in chairs that may have been original to the building. They had the appearance of furniture made of oak and leather in a time when quarter-sawn oak and cowhide were inexpensive and craftsmanship—perhaps from prison laborers—was in long supply. The mission-style side tables were barren of reading matter.

A young woman, no more substantial than a child of twelve, wearing a blazer over a cotton dress and running shoes that chirped when she walked, came out through a heavy wood door and tuned in a smile as she approached. Her dark hair was gathered into a tight bun and her heavy eyebrows looked as though they had once been united to form a protective hood over her prominent nose. The nose, when added to a weak chin, gave the woman's profile a shape that suggested an arrowhead.

"I'm Veronica Malouf, Dr. Whitfield's executive assistant. Sorry to have kept you waiting, but we didn't have you on the director's schedule."

"I'm sorry for any inconvenience. We had no idea we were coming until a little while ago and we were close by." Manseur's Southern voice added a honey-flavored edge to his apology.

"May I inquire as to the purpose of your visit?" Ms. Malouf asked.

"It's an official matter best kept between us and the director for the moment," Manseur replied.

"Might I ask if it pertains to a resident inmate?" she persisted. "The director is an extremely busy man."

Manseur nodded. "Yes, it does. If you don't mind, we're very short on time."

Ms. Malouf's smile froze in place. "Please follow me."

30

In the administration section of the hospital, burgundy linoleum tiles covered the floor, and the walls were an institutional green. Framed black-and-white photographs of plantation manses viewed through parted curtains of Spanish moss adorned the walls. In the offices they passed, Alexa noted, the modern telephones and computers seemed totally out of place in spaces that could have been sets in a movie about the Great Depression.

Dr. Whitfield's office, in marked contrast, was modern and opulently furnished. Floor-to-ceiling windows, visible through open curtains, were spaced along the far wall. Three matching carpets defined the distinct areas in the huge space. The director's desk was comprised of a slab of granite two inches thick resting on stainless steel legs.

In the center of the room four black-leather chairs faced each other across a square coffee table. The conference area at the far end of the room held a larger granite and steel table surrounded by eight ebony leather chairs on stainless castors. Built-in cabinets and bookshelves ran along the wall opposite the windows.

Dr. Whitfield, a lanky man in his fifties with salt-and-pepper hair combed carefully back, entered the room through a door behind his desk that appeared to lead to a private bathroom. He smiled as he shook his guests' hands. "Thad Whitfield," he said. "Detective Manseur and Agent Keen, it's a pleasure to meet you. Please, do sit down." He motioned to the lounge chairs. Alexa and Manseur declined refreshment.

After Alexa sat, Manseur followed suit. Whitfield sat with his back to the window, crossed his legs, and put his hands together in his lap.

"So, what brings you to my office on this fine day?" the director asked.

"We're checking into what may just be a rumor," Alexa told him.

"What rumor is that?" Whitfield asked, still smiling.

"That a patient named Sibhon Danielson was released from this hospital recently. We were curious to find out if that information is correct and, if so, where we might find her now," Manseur said.

"She was committed twenty-six years ago—a double homicide," Alexa added.

Whitfield said, "I'm not familiar with that particular patient. I've only been here for a few months and we currently have two hundred and sixty-three patients in residence. The majority of our patients, or inmates, in most cases are either violent sexual predators or dangerously unstable offenders deemed not to have been legally responsible for their actions at the time they were committed. We have fourteen wards here, each designated for inmates categorized by threat levels. Number one houses the healthiest, or most improved of our wards, up to number fourteen, which houses the most volatile and violent of our inmates."

"I don't know where she'd be on the number system now, but in 1979 she would have been a full-blown fourteen," Manseur said.

"If she responded to treatment to the point where she could function, she may have been reassigned or released."

"If she could refrain from acting on the impulse to chop people up," Manseur offered.

Whitfield flinched. "Detective, the insane are truly no more able to control their behavior—to conform to accepted norms—than a goose can control where it drops its offal."

"Usually on the golf course greens," Manseur said. "On in regulation, then they turn a perfect lie into a putt-putt course."

"All too often," Whitfield agreed, chuckling. "So you're a fellow devotee of the old anger sticks. I have a six handicap at present. Yours?"

"I'm afraid I'm up there in the double digits," Manseur said, smiling. "Maybe if I played more and worked less."

Alexa was certain, based strictly on his lack of reaction to hearing her name, that Dr. Whitfield had no idea who Sibby Danielson was.

"What exactly is the process for releasing a patient?" she asked, bored by the golf talk and the time it was wasting.

"Release of a patient inmate requires a unanimous vote of the psychiatric review board, and sometimes a prerelease hearing has been stipulated by the courts. Releasing a patient who was formerly violent is not something done lightly. But patients have well-defined rights and ours is not a punishment facility, but a maximum-security treatment hospital whose goal is curing the inmates so they can rejoin society as productive members."

"You can cure chronic violent sexual predators?" Manseur asked, stiffening.

Alexa knew Whitfield was thinking how he—a

man who probably had released untold numbers of rapists he had believed were cured—should respond to a Homicide cop who had probably seen the results of recidivism enough times to doubt such people could ever change or be changed. Most cops believed that any rapist who was released had only managed to con the doctors into believing they could work miracles.

"A board made up of whom?" Alexa asked.

"The staff doctors and clinical psychologists who have treated and evaluated the patient, a nurse, and myself, the director. The committee has at least six individuals, who have to agree before an inmate can safely be released. The liability is too great to leave it to the flip of a coin," Dr. Whitfield said, laughing at his joke.

"Can we find out if she was released?"

"Our patients enjoy patient-doctor confidentiality, much like those of private medical patients, but whether or not an inmate is in the facility is nonprivileged information."

To Alexa, the idea that a multiple murderess who had been committed to a maximum-security asylum in lieu of the electric chair or life in prison had the same rights to confidentiality that a citizen undergoing private psychotherapy enjoyed seemed idiotic. She nodded anyway and added a smile of reassurance.

"We just need to locate her," Alexa said, looking at her watch, not because she didn't know the time, but to telegraph a sense of urgency. Sibby probably wasn't going to be a key to locating Gary West. While a freed Sibby Danielson might have attacked him— Alexa knew that a woman in her late forties alone could probably accomplish the assault—she wouldn't be able to muscle a semiconscious or unconscious man from one vehicle into another. And what would her motive be for such an action? Sibby couldn't possibly know Gary West. Also, since she had been incarcerated for over a quarter of a century, how likely was it she could enlist someone to help her? Unlikely or not, Alexa knew that if the murderess was out, somebody would have to find out everything they could about Sibby Danielson and eliminate her as a suspect, because anything and everything was possible.

Dr. Whitfield pressed a button on an intercom on the table beside him. "Veronica, could you please come in when you have a moment?"

Veronica came in immediately, holding a pad and pen. "Yes, Dr. Whitfield?"

"Would you please check on the status of a patient for me?"

"Of course," she said, raising the pad.

"It's Ms. . . . ?" Eyebrows raised, the doctor looked at Alexa, waiting for her to give him the name again.

"Danielson, Sibhon Danielson," Alexa said, watching Veronica closely when she said it.

Veronica's expression told Alexa that the assistant was very familiar with Sibby Danielson, but she took the time to write the name carefully on the pad, as though she might forget it. "I'll check the patient's status for you, Dr. Whitfield. It should only take me a few minutes."

"This is a nice office," Alexa said, making conversation. "For a state facility."

"Indeed," the director said. "I can thank my predecessor for the fancy digs. He paid for them himself."

"Really? A state-paid doctor?"

"Well, he was technically a salaried employee of the state, but he hardly depended on that for his bread and butter."

"Independent means?"

The director laughed. "Dr. LePointe was never a devotee of Sparta."

"Dr. William LePointe?" Alexa said. She looked at Manseur and saw that he hadn't known either.

"When?" Manseur asked.

"From the late seventies until last year. Do you know him?"

"I didn't know he was the director here," Manseur said. "Or if I did, I'd forgotten."

"Veronica was Dr. LePointe's assistant before I took over."

Alexa felt as though she'd been poleaxed. Her mind swarmed with implications of the knowledge, and she only waited a few seconds while they sank in before standing. "Excuse me for a second. I need to ask your assistant something."

Veronica sat at her desk with her back to Alexa, a cell phone to her ear. When the sounds of Manseur and Whitfield's conversation registered and she realized the door was open, Veronica pressed the END button, put down the phone without saying good-bye. She placed her hands on the keyboard of her computer terminal as though she hadn't been on the telephone at all, but diligently searching for the whereabouts of the axe princess of the Garden District. Alexa suppressed the urge to lift the phone to look at the number Veronica had just called.

"When did Sibby Danielson leave, Veronica?" Alexa asked.

Veronica turned her chair around to face her. "I was just about to check that for you."

"Cut the act. We both know she's gone. Lying to an FBI agent in the course of an investigation is a felony punishable by three to five years in prison. You can ask Martha Stewart."

"What Sibby did is familiar to anybody from New Orleans. I used to jump rope to 'Chop-Shop Sibby took an axe to give old Curry ninety whacks; when Becky LePointe saw what she'd done, Sibby gave her a hundred and one.' "

"Very original. Where is Sibby?"

"I've never even seen her, because I've never been in the wards. The only patients I ever see are when they're brought into these offices, and it's never violent-ward patients."

"You know she's gone, though. Tell me how."

Veronica nodded. "The TV reporter, Lucille Burch, called this morning. She said she had it on good authority Sibby was out. I told her I was sure she couldn't be. I looked her up and her name was on the master patient list." Veronica pointed at the screen, where Alexa saw Sibby Danielson's name on a long list. "I told her Sibby Danielson was indeed here in maximum-security ward fourteen, but Burch said, 'We'll see about that.' Later I asked someone who works in the violent wards, and he told me he hasn't seen her in almost a year. He figured she'd been transferred, since she wasn't 'outside' material. I checked, and there's no transfer or release information on her in the computer. The person who told me could be wrong. It isn't unusual for inmates to change wards and even move to other facilities, and often the records are late being updated because we're so badly understaffed."

"Why didn't you mention the media inquiry, or this possible discrepancy, to Dr. Whitfield?"

"I intended to, but I got busy. I was afraid that was why you were here."

"Who were you calling just then?"

Veronica's eyes were suddenly filled with what looked very much like terror. "My mother."

Alexa snatched Veronica's phone off the desk. "Then you won't mind if I check the readout."

"I don't think you can legally make me show you my personal information like that!"

"If you're telling the truth and the last call was to Mama Malouf, why does it matter? Will you nod if I guess right?"

Veronica nodded once, slowly.

"Dr. LePointe?"

Veronica shook her head.

"Who, then?"

"You said I could just nod."

"You got your last nod *here,*" Alexa said, reaching behind her, freeing the handcuffs from the case on her belt. "You can play Little Miss Bobble-head all you like before a federal grand jury."

"No," Veronica said. "Just a minute."

"Talk, or I'll take you to FBI headquarters and let interrogators ask you in a way you won't enjoy. These days a person can literally vanish into the federal system for a very long time while we investigate

them for ties to terrorist organizations. I'm not nearly
as nice as I appear to be."

"Mr. Decell."

"Kenneth Decell?"

Veronica nodded slowly.

"Why?"

"A few months ago he said I should let him know
immediately if anybody ever asked questions about
her. Sibby."

"You told Decell that Lucille Burch called?"

"Yes. He said I'd be rewarded for reporting anything that popped up about Dr. LePointe or Sibby
Danielson or Dorothy Fugate."

"Who is Dorothy Fugate? An inmate?"

"Ms. Fugate was the ex–chief nurse here."

"How long did you work for Dr. LePointe?"

"Almost six years."

"Did you like him?"

"Like?" Veronica nodded. "He's a good man."

"Do you know where Danielson is?"

"According to the records, she's still in ward fourteen. That's all I know."

"You know the records are incorrect. She's gone.
From ward fourteen straight to the front gate, right?"

"I'm only a secretary."

"An executive assistant," Alexa corrected. "This
could spell very serious trouble."

"I didn't know," Veronica said, quickly. "I assumed
she was maybe moved based on her state, but . . ."

"Her state?"

"Everybody who has been around her says Sibby's
in the stratosphere. All she ever did was sit and rock
back and forth in her chair."

"So she's that sick? Or she's kept heavily med icated?"

"I'm not authorized to see her treatment record and I wouldn't know what I was looking at if I did."

"Are there paper records in addition to computer ized records on the patients?"

Veronica nodded. "I suppose they'd be in th locked file cabinets."

"Who would know where she is? Best guess, Alexa said, her cuffs tapping a steady surgical stee rhythm against her thigh.

"I suppose Nurse Fugate."

"Why would she know?"

"She was in charge of the nursing staff and the or derlies and janitors on all the wards. She left her around the same time Sibby did. She didn't just spenc a lot of time in that ward, she had her office there."

"Left about the same time? So you do know wher Sibby left. One more lie and you can kiss your swee butt good-bye."

"Around a year ago," Veronica said hastily.

"How do I find this nurse?"

"I can give you her address. But if anybody finds out I told you, I'll be fired."

Hands shaking, Veronica Malouf flipped through the Rolodex on her desk and copied down an addres and phone number.

"Keep helping me and I'll do my best to keep it be tween us. In the meanwhile, if that reporter call back, tell her Sibby Danielson is still in the hospital because you checked and saw her. Now, how coulc she get out through security without having receivec a release form?"

"She couldn't. There had to be a release form or she'd never get out the gate, but it isn't where it should be."

"Unless she maybe went out in a car trunk?"

"The staff parks in a fenced-in lot to the rear of the building, and it's under constant surveillance. Standing policy is that every vehicle is searched when it leaves. No exceptions. They'll search your car when you go out. You'll see," Veronica said.

"They searched Dr. LePointe's car?"

"I'm not sure. Maybe. Not always."

"How much power did LePointe exercise here?"

"His mental health foundation gives a lot of research grant money to most of the doctors as well as the clinical psychologists, and it pays for continuing ed for nurses and orderlies. He's Doctor Emeritus of River Run, and he's the past chairman of the state's mental health board. Half the people on the payroll get some form of financial subsidy from Dr. LePointe. He doesn't have an office here anymore, but truth is, Dr. Whitfield only runs the place on paper, and he knows it. When Dr. LePointe calls, Whitfield trips over himself to put down his putter and grab the phone."

"Do you think Dr. LePointe has reason to stay on top of what's happening here?"

She shrugged. "He checks in with me like I'm still his secretary. Before he retired, he gave me a new Honda Accord Coupe. I think he worked here so long, he can't let go—hates not knowing everything that's up. What do I tell Dr. Whitfield about Sibby?"

"I'll tell Dr. Whitfield that Sibby Danielson can't have been released. We'll leave satisfied."

"He might check."

"He obviously doesn't know who she is. But you're going to search until you find her records for me."

Veronica's eyes lost their focus.

"Twenty-six years means there's an awful lot of paperwork on her. If you want this to go away, you'll find and deliver that paperwork to me at NOPD HQ. It isn't a suggestion, Veronica. The alternative to compliance will be catastrophic for you. You have my word on that."

"Take official records out of here?" Veronica looked stunned, and afraid. "It's against the law."

"I'm the only law you need concern yourself with. A word to the wise," Alexa said, "I know a *lot* more about all this than I'm telling you. If you cross me, whatever you imagine anybody else might do to you is nothing in comparison to what I *will* do. Dig for those records like your very freedom and future ability to find meaningful employment depend on it." Alexa smiled at Veronica. "When you find them . . . straight to me. Now, when you call Decell back, say we were satisfied that she was here, because there was no release form."

Veronica nodded slowly.

"And," Alexa added, "I want the names and pertinent info on all of the staff that worked on Danielson's ward in the year before she vanished."

"I don't know . . . that's kept—"

"I have all the confidence on earth that you'll find those things for me," Alexa said firmly. "When there's no choice, there's always a way."

31

Alexa returned to the hospital director's office after her visit with Veronica Malouf, to find Dr. Whitfield expounding on the hospital and the role it played in not merely protecting society from the anti-social actions of the hospital's residents, but, just as importantly, in protecting the residents from an ill-informed and suspicious society.

"Patient inmates are re-evaluated on a yearly basis. If Danielson was judged to be of less danger to herself or others, she would certainly have been moved progressively into less restrictive wards and eventually—as a result of successful therapies—she might have been released into a halfway house, or to her family if certain criteria were met, or into some other appropriate, and authorized, living situation. Do you know her original diagnosis?"

"Paranoid schizophrenia," Alexa said. She didn't want Dr. Whitfield getting curious and starting to dig into this patient the FBI found of interest. "Voices commanding her to kill. Standard diagnosis."

"Ah, if she was delusional, it is generally accepted that she was not responsible for her actions," Whitfield said.

"She's here, by the way. Safe and sound," Alexa said.

"That's the end to our little mystery," Whitfield announced.

"Looks that way," Manseur said. When he looked at Alexa, she tilted her head to signal him that it was time to go. Dr. Whitfield stood when Manseur did.

"I'd love to pick your brain sometime," Dr. Whitfield said. "I'm fascinated with police procedure as it relates to homicide cases and I'm sure you must have a plethora of tales in your grab bag. I've thought about writing a novel—more or less a fictionalized version of my own experiences with the criminally insane. We have to get together soon."

"It would be my pleasure, Dr. Whitfield," Manseur said, handing him one of his cards.

"Maybe we could schedule a round of golf," Dr. Whitfield said.

"Absolutely. The frustration of chasing the ball around and making numerous attempts to steer it into a small hole relaxes me."

"Frustration relaxes you? Now, that is interesting."

"It's great, since my life is nothing but frustration," Manseur said, smiling. "Stress kills more cops than bullets. Me? I'm always loose as a goose."

"And a sense of humor helps, I bet," Whitfield said. "Doctors use humor in stressful situations, just like members of the Detective Bureau."

"Thank you for your cooperation and insights into mental health," Alexa said, shaking Dr. Whitfield's hand.

"It's what I know," Whitfield replied. "Anytime. Let's get together next week, Detective Manseur. You'll join me at the Metarie Country Club for a round of golf?"

"Depending on what the hurricane does," Manseur said.

"They'll have any downed trees cleared from the fairways next day. Mark my word."

After they left the building, Alexa said, "There's a common theme in this case."

"What?"

"Missing files."

"The release form, you mean?"

"That, and there are no treatment records. I inspired Veronica to find them for us. She's scared to death of crossing LePointe, but I think she's more afraid of me at the moment. She told me that LePointe is still exerting influence over the place."

After retrieving their weapons, they got in the car and Manseur started it. "At least we know Sibby Danielson is locked up."

"She may indeed be locked up, but not here," Alexa said.

"You just said . . ."

"Veronica was calling Decell. I interrogated her. She assured me Sibby isn't here, despite what the lack of a release form indicates. I lied to Dr. Whitfield. I'm praying your brain-picking, future golfing partner doesn't decide to check on her for himself."

"How is Decell involved?"

Alexa explained what she'd learned from Veronica Malouf.

"That doesn't mean the one thing has anything at all to do with the other. Sibby and Gary West."

"Dr. LePointe was the director of the hospital just after his brother's murderess was sent here. I can't believe the obvious conflict of interest."

"This is New Orleans. Conflict of interest has a different meaning here than most places."

"I keep forgetting that the rules that govern the rest of us mortals don't apply to Dr. LePointe," she said, tasting acid in her throat. She fished an antacid from her purse and chewed it.

At the gate, a waiting guard asked them to open the car's trunk. Manseur hit the button and the lid rose. They sat in silence while the guard looked inside, using a flashlight to illuminate the shadowy corners. After looking through the windows to make sure there were no inmates hiding in the car, he signaled for the gate to be opened and waved them on.

"It doesn't mean anything," Manseur told Alexa, "but Sibby was here while he was running the facility. We have to eliminate her as a possible participant in the abduction. I admit it's somewhat strange on its face. He does have a degree in psychiatry and a well-documented social conscience."

"I find it somewhat strange on *any* face that a wealthy physician like LePointe, who probably has a medical school degree from a no-doubt impressive medical school and an ego the size of the Great Pyramid would take on running an ancient, crumbling mental asylum out in the middle of nowhere. Social conscience or not, it's odd."

"I seriously doubt Dr. LePointe would commit a crime or otherwise risk his reputation. He's a dedicated physician."

"You might just think what he wants people to think. You don't know him."

"Neither do you," Manseur said, bristling. "Let's do some investigating before we get our panties in a bunch."

"Michael, are you wearing panties?"

"I don't believe Sibby Danielson is connected to Gary's disappearance. She's a side issue, and LePointe's connection is better suited to investigation by the state medical ethics board than by the NOPD . . . or the FBI."

"So you suggesting we drop Sibby?" Alexa asked.

"I didn't say that," Manseur said, defensively.

"We have to compile a list of individuals involved and run their phone records to look for call patterns that tie them to each other and the Gary West event."

"That could be tricky for me," Manseur said. "Soon as I ask for LePointe's phone records, red flags are going to wave all through City Hall."

"I wouldn't dream of involving anybody local," Alexa told him.

Manseur frowned.

"Anybody else, I mean."

32

Because of the headache, Leland Ticholet was chewing up one aspirin tablet after another as he piloted the boat toward Doc's place. He needed his good headache pills and a dark space until the lights in his brain stopped flashing. He was tempted to pull over and lie down on the bench with a burlap bag over his head, but he needed his pills bad. It had been a while since he'd had a migraine, because he had pills to take every day to keep them away. They had worked until he forgot to take one due to all the excitement of thumping that man for Doc and all.

As he turned into the channel toward the little house, he could barely focus his eyes ahead because the sunlight hitting the water shot right into his brain like a nail.

He spotted the car Doc drove parked alongside Leland's father's old panel truck. He hoped Doc didn't yell at him or make fun of him in that smart-ass way, because Leland didn't want to hurt him. But if he did holler, then what happened to him was not going to be Leland's fault. Most of the time he didn't even remember the stuff happening that brought the sheriff's men. He was going along just fine as you please, then somebody did something and the infuriation blast happened and Leland was as surprised as anybody else about it.

Doc was waiting at the back door, looking mad, as usual. "Why didn't you answer the telephone?" he demanded. "It's what I gave it to you for. Where is it?"

"I didn't hear it ring," Leland said as he pushed easily by the smaller man.

"What the hell do you mean?"

"Battery might have died. Little as it is," Leland said, going through the kitchen cabinet drawers looking for his pill bottle. "And I got a headache on me. Feels like my brain is on fire."

"You haven't been taking these, have you, Lee?" Doc asked. Leland looked up and had to squint to see that Doc was holding his brown bottle of headache pills.

"Give me 'em," Leland said, reaching for the bottle and snatching it out of the little guy's hand.

"Where is the cellular phone I gave you?" Doc asked.

Leland remembered hurling it into the water, but he wasn't about to tell Doc that. He threw six capsules into his mouth and chewed before he answered, his teeth slimy from the plastic casings. "I guess maybe it's in the boat."

"Well, go get it."

"I will when I go back to it," Leland said. "Right now I'm gonna shut my eyes."

"Unacceptable," Doc said. "Totally un-ac-cept-able behavior, even for a man without any social filters whatsoever."

"Who gives a hoot," Leland said, going into the closet. He slammed the door behind him, which made his vision go bright white and the pain almost put him on his knees. He curled up on the pine floor like a nesting rat. He heard Doc walking around in the kitchen, but he was smart enough not to say anything else. He sure as hell couldn't go get the man staying at Leland's camp, because he didn't even know where it was. And Leland knew Doc wanted that man brought here. He wasn't sure why he wanted him moved here, and whatever the sombitch was thinking didn't matter to Leland one little bit.

33

Kenneth Decell hung up and slipped his cell phone into the pocket of his sports jacket. He looked at his employer, who had been staring at him anxiously while he talked to Veronica Malouf. LePointe raised a bushy white eyebrow, waiting.

"Manseur and Keen left satisfied after Malouf told them Danielson was still in the hospital."

"Took her word?" LePointe asked.

"They didn't ask to see for themselves. How the media got on this bothers me. Somebody set them up to it; I just can't imagine who, or why."

"Pressure," LePointe said. "It's obvious that whoever is behind all of this wants to keep pressure on me until I pay them off."

"I'm not sure that's the smartest way to deal with them."

"It's your job to deal with this, Ken," LePointe snapped.

"Keen makes it a lot more complicated. She's not local. I can't close her down like I could if it was just Manseur."

"Casey went behind my back to ask for Keen to be on this because she didn't trust the police here to be competent."

"Casey—"

"I don't blame her, Ken," LePointe interrupted.

Decell was glad he hadn't finished his thought because, true or not, it wasn't a good idea to criticize Casey West in front of her uncle. "He is her husband," Decell said.

"She loves that little hippie. This Keen person is adept at what she does?"

"Extremely. An almost perfect record of successful case closures. When they're solvable, her rate rises higher. She doesn't miss much."

"Which means what here?"

"For starters, what Veronica thinks Agent Keen believes and what she does believe may be vastly different."

"If Casey had just left this alone, we wouldn't

have your second front to deal with, but there it is,"
Dr. LePointe said. "If she had just left this alone. No
second front." Dr. LePointe had the annoying habit
of repeating himself, perhaps just to hear the sound
of his own voice, but maybe because he doubted an
ex-cop could keep his mind wrapped around the facts
LePointe thought worth remembering. "You're a miracle worker and I need a miracle right about now."

"I won't let you down, Dr. LePointe," Decell
promised. "You can count on that."

"I believe it's time to let the authorities know
about this letter." LePointe lifted an envelope and
then tossed it onto the desk in front of Decell, who removed the letter and read it slowly.

Refolding it, Decell said, "It's probably better to
let Manseur and Keen chase their tails for a few
hours, until I can put things in order."

"Inarguably you are expert at what you do,
Decell. Cop-think works well enough situation-by-
situation as in working with individual criminal
cases. But this game is far bigger than the simple ele-
ments you're concerned with. Dealing with complex
situations and looking far into the future is something I have to do with accuracy every day. I intend to
hold on to what my ancestors built brick-by-brick
over three hundred years of hard work, learning from
mistakes, and strategic planning. Naturally they suffered the occasional setback, but without receiving a
lethal blow. That's not going to change on my watch.
During my tenure, the worth of the family's assets has
increased dramatically, and not merely due, as some
might claim, to the economy's performance.

"What I do," LePointe said, opening his hands

expansively, "is like playing several chess games at once. It's a blessing that you don't have to think on the level I do, Ken." LePointe spoke in the manner of a patient parent explaining something to his child. "Failure is not an option, whatever the cost. Do we understand each other here?"

Decell stared across the desk at LePointe, knowing the man was just starting his Mr. Superior song and dance. Decell was accustomed to having to sit and be lectured to while trying to seem impressed, interested, and in agreement.

"Naturally, you are the only person I trust to handle this, Ken. And for doing so in a satisfactory manner, you will be rewarded most handsomely."

"You've always been more than generous, Dr. LePointe."

LePointe took a slip of paper from his desk, for a long ten seconds seemed to be considering what he was going to write down, then scribbled a figure on the paper before pushing it across the desktop.

Decell made a show of leaning forward to read the figure and prepared himself to act astounded by LePointe's beneficence. LePointe had always paid him well, which considering the mundane nature and low effort level that most of LePointe's requests required was indeed generous. But the figure Decell saw written there stunned him, because it represented the kind of money you'd expect to pay to have a senator killed.

"Is the amount adequate to ensure that this problem is going to be solved to my satisfaction?"

"I guarantee it."

"That figure will be paid to you upon completion. Wherever and however you choose."

Decell nodded, and realized he was holding his breath.

LePointe snatched the paper and put it into his desk drawer, stood up, and walked Decell all the way to the front door, which was unusual and—although Decell seriously doubted it was more than a ploy to make him feel appreciated—seemed to signify a change in Decell's status from servant to trusted associate. It wasn't the first time, but it was rare. LePointe didn't want to know details, and Decell wouldn't spell out the particulars of his mission.

If violent means were required, such measures would be forthcoming, with animal swiftness and absolute certainty. When it came to conducting the symphony of ending threats to his clients, Decell was willing, if not eager, to get his hands dirty.

For what LePointe was paying, ex-detective Kenneth Decell would have dressed up in the vestments of a cardinal, pulled a hammer from underneath his robe, and beat the Pope to death as he addressed the faithful gathered below the papal balcony.

34

Deep in thought, Alexa stared out the passenger window. She was thinking about how things appeared, and wondering how those things might be connected to Gary West's vanishing. As director of psychiatry, LePointe had been in the perfect position to influence what treatment Sibby received, how that treatment was applied, and probably who administered it. Although it was hard to imagine him doing so, it certainly appeared that he could have been torturing Sibby for years. Unless something untoward had been going on, why would Decell, most likely acting on LePointe's behalf, have offered Veronica a reward for warning him if anybody came asking after Sibby, LePointe, or this Nurse Fugate. How Fugate fit in with LePointe and Danielson was a mystery Alexa needed to solve. That anybody could imagine they could make a notorious inmate vanish without someone discovering it and reporting it was a mystery worthy of New Orleans.

"Didn't Sibby have a family?" Alexa asked Manseur.

"Her family was so scandalized that she'd killed the LePointes that they left New Orleans shortly after the killings. I believe her father was some kind of big dog with the Whitney Bank and they lived Uptown in a nice house on Napoleon. Her mother killed herself, I heard. I went to school with her brother at St. Barts. He was a squirrelly little kid who dressed in starched shirts and pressed slacks and had his belt so tight that he looked like he was wearing a lace-up corset from one of those Storyville portraits. He was redheaded and pretty as a girl and held his hand up so it sort of flopped off his wrist, so we all thought he was a little light in the loafers. His name was something odd like Cyrus, or Cecil, which didn't help." Manseur shook his head slowly, remembering. "He had a hard time *before* his sister chopped up the LePointes. I think there was another brother, who was sort of nutty and mean as a snake if you pissed him off, but it's fuzzy. Not like I hung with him or anything. He didn't fit in and I didn't care. Hell, I didn't fit in either, but I didn't fit in with a better crowd. So, how do we

talk to this nurse without setting off dynamite? I
don't imagine Dr. LePointe is going to sit still when
she calls Decell, or him, and you know damn well she
will."

"I won't know until we talk to her. We'll just tell
her we're following up on our visit to the hospital,
and since she knew Sibby Danielson, we're wondering what she can tell us about her."

"Sounds lame," Manseur said.

"That's only because it is. I'll know when I see her
and can watch her reactions to our presence and questions. We don't have to tell her why we're asking questions. We only need to know where Sibby is and that
she isn't connected to West's disappearance. Maybe
Gary found out about Sibby's vanishing act. Somebody
out at the hospital might have ratted LePointe out to
Gary because there was no love lost between them.
That could be a connection. Decell could see any threat
against LePointe as marching orders."

"If that's the case, Dr. LePointe may not even be
aware of it. Maybe Decell just does what he thinks
needs doing. Maybe he spirited Sibby out and
LePointe doesn't even know it. Decell is capable of
who knows what. He could do whatever he thinks is
in his employer's best interest."

"A spin doctor who carries a gun instead of a
pen," Alexa said. "His relationship with LePointe
might go back to Sibby's murders. And she cut him
pretty good. I suppose LePointe may be unaware of
Decell's work on his behalf, but I doubt it."

Manseur said, "Makes perfect sense to me."

"In that New Orleans sort of way?"

Alexa was not sure how to take the fact that

Manseur hadn't seemed outraged or even particularly surprised by the LePointe/River Run bombshell. Alexa wondered, if she hadn't taken him to the hospital, would he have even gone, or just called the director and been told Sibby was there and let it go at that. And it seemed to her that Manseur considered *This is New Orleans* a phrase that explained anything that was out of line, bordering on illegal behavior in the same way that *After all, this is Mars* might.

Maybe he was burned-out by the grinding down the job did to a man, the terrible pay, the complex political minefield, the embedded corruption of the city, the endless line of corpses, the guilty being set free in astounding numbers by juries who actually were peers of the accused or just anti-cop enough to ignore the truth, ignorant enough not to get the evidence, or nullify the charges because they didn't like prosecutors. She couldn't know that he wouldn't fold up on her if his career were to be in jeopardy. She still wanted to trust him, but she wondered if trust was something he hadn't earned, something that shouldn't be given out like a door prize. True, Winter liked him, admired him, and trusted him based on one situation that had elevated Manseur to his present position. But any way you cut it, Manseur was no Winter Massey.

She tried to picture all of the people she trusted as much as she did Winter, and the gallery walls of her mind were as painfully bare as those of a museum between exhibitions.

There was a lot to admire about Manseur. He seemed to be a good enough detective in a town—to put it kindly—not known for having a gentle, good, or honest police department. He was a family man, who had a picture of his wife and daughters banded to the visor of his vehicle and in his office.

Manseur's cell phone played "The Star-Spangled Banner," breaking Alexa's train of thought. They drove into the parking lot of the strip mall where she'd left the Bucar.

"Manseur," he said, pulling to a stop beside the dark green Ford Taurus owned and maintained by the FBI.

"Okay, I'll tell her," Manseur finished, closing his phone. "That was Evans. Said to tell you Dr. LePointe heard from Gary West, so thank you for your help."

"Heard how?"

"Letter in the morning mail. West said he's coming back tomorrow morning from a little trip he took to go off and commune with nature or some other happy crap."

"You're serious?" Alexa said.

"It's what my boss told me. You think he's lying?"

"Somebody is."

"Why?"

"You're joking, right?" Alexa retorted.

"What makes you so sure it isn't true?" Manseur asked.

"Well, for one thing, when a person is taking a trip to commune or whatever, would he get somebody to crash into his car and hit him in the head with a pipe? LePointe or somebody close to him wants to shut us down. You're a *detective*, Michael. What do you really think?"

"I think maybe you're being a bit paranoid," Manseur answered. "You're convinced there's a conspiracy."

"Well, why would I imagine such an odd thing? Let me see . . . Dr. LePointe most likely had the ability to exercise his will over the woman who savagely murdered his only brother and sister-in-law, leaving their young daughter, who witnessed the horrific scene, orphaned and emotionally devastated. He certainly doesn't want that known, even in New Orleans. Even a plumber's assistant in any other city in the country would see that as less than a normal circumstance."

"Maybe he's a dedicated professional who can set his personal emotions aside in order to help a very sick woman, who isn't responsible for her actions, regain her sanity. Look, if I were the superintendent of police, and if one of the beat cops gave my wife a ticket, I wouldn't have to leave the department because his sergeant, a man under my command and control, put him on a foot beat in the projects to teach him a lesson."

"What if the patrolman had been on drugs and he murdered your wife, and your daughters saw it happen?"

"In that case, he'd be in prison," Manseur reasoned. "Hopefully on death row. Would I want to kill him? You're damned straight I would. But I'm a detective and a professional and I do not take the law into my own hands. And I would have the responsibility to my girls not to end up in jail myself."

"Right. So you are a professional and you could, if not forgive, let the system deal with him. How would it look if you left the department to become the warden of the prison where the man who murdered your wife was doing time? Say he can be paroled whenever the guards agreed he wasn't a threat to anybody because he had the drug thing kicked?"

"Saddled with two fashion-conscious young girls and the expenses associated with a deceased wife, like a burial and having to hire babysitters, I could never take the pay cut," Manseur countered, smiling.

"Don't you feel a burning *need* to know the truth?"

"About LePointe's job and if he gave butcher-girl a few extra shock treatments? Most people would say the more shocks the murderess got, the merrier."

"In the homicide report, it says that Sibby was Dr. LePointe's patient before the murders. I can't help but wonder if a psychiatrist could manipulate a mentally unbalanced person to commit a brutal double homicide. Why, you may ask. Because that would make him guilty of double homicide."

"Motive?"

"Gee, I don't know. Maybe his brother beat him at backgammon and said, 'nanny-nanny boo-boo.' Look, if Dr. LePointe did, how could he make sure the truth never came to light? Me, I might do something like make sure she could never rat me out by keeping her drugged stupid in my own private hospital. And if I were retiring and someone else were taking over her care, I could make certain the ugly truth would remain buried by making her vanish. I might bribe or blackmail someone to help me pull it off. Maybe I would turn to a nurse who would agree to help me."

"Why would a nurse agree to do such a thing? The man is a multimillionaire! You'd never convince a jury he could or would do such a thing. You couldn't convince me."

"A box of chocolates. A lot more money, which he has access to. But I suspect it is worth looking into. Since we haven't found a shortcut to Gary West, we actually could take a few minutes to check it out. Especially since it could lead us to his abductors."

"Dr. LePointe did it in the kitchen with a lunatic." He turned his basset hound eyes to Alexa. "You might make sure your potential witness, who is insane and couldn't get anybody to believe her if she said Christmas was in December, remains under your control?" Manseur asked, sarcastically. "At the risk of his freedom?"

"Exactly," Alexa said. "Say she's where he can still do that. And it's not too much of a stretch that it's connected to Gary West's disappearance. Suppose we can find and use Sibby to pressure LePointe or Decell to come clean, and maybe that gets us Gary West."

"Evans called it off."

"Fine. Let him think you're off it. This hurricane has him with plenty more to think about than what you're actually doing. In the meanwhile, we keep following the evidence off his radar."

"If you are right and this does involve them spiriting Sibby away somewhere, like LePointe's private torture chamber in his basement—"

"Or another hospital," Alexa offered.

"Okay, another hospital. The nurse will tell Decell immediately and Decell will tell LePointe and LePointe will tell Jackson Evans and then, best case here, he'll come down on me with a ten-pound hammer and I'll be ticketing parked cars for the rest of my career. If I'm lucky."

"Fine. I'll go talk to Nurse Fugate myself."

"It's a free country. I expect you can defend yourself if anybody wants some answers why you kept going on this after it was over and done. The fact is, I've been ordered to report to HQ as soon as I've dropped you off. The West case is officially closed until something shows up that merits reopening it."

"So you're going to HQ?"

"I have no choice in the matter unless I choose to ignore my superintendent's direct orders," Manseur said. "It isn't like I don't have pressing cases that I'm ignoring to hunt for escaped lunatics and Baby Big Bucks. If I disobey Evans, he'll cut me a new you-know-what. This is our stopping place. Go home, Alexa."

"I'm not leaving," Alexa said, angry. "Not until Gary West is home with his wife and child. I don't care how much sway LePointe has or even that we *are* in New Orleans. If he or Decell are in any way involved in Gary West's abduction, they're in my sights. If and when I'm sure they've committed a federal crime, I'll push for an indictment with everything I have. If my director calls me off because he is LePointe's pal, he'll have to face the consequences of this pissed-off Mississippi gal who can take whatever punishment his Harvard-going ass can devise, and more, because I know firsthand what real meanness is all about."

"Men like LePointe don't go to jail," Manseur pointed out. "Will not happen."

"The prisons are full of rich people like him who thought the very same thing," Alexa snapped.

She threw open her door and slid out, slamming the door behind her. Before she got her keys out of her purse, however, Manseur rolled down his window. "Hey, Keen!"

Alexa turned.

Manseur had a smile on his face. "You're serious about this?"

Alexa raised an eyebrow.

"While you're running around stirring up a Mississippi shit-storm, I'll see if I can get Cooley to work faster on identifying those prints, and I'll go through the phone records if they're in yet. You call me if you have anything to tell me. We need prints on Casey and Gary West for comparisons."

"You're going to keep working this?"

"You can bet that frown I am. I just wanted to see exactly how serious you were. If I go and get my ass fired, I want to know somebody is going to be standing beside me in the unemployment line."

He winked at her.

She smiled, wanting to slap and hug him at the same time.

"You find out anything, call me and fill me in," he said. "And if you need my help at any point, you'll get it. You need a map to that Fugate nurse's house?"

Alexa found the keys to her car in her purse, and said, "If the GPS fails, I can probably smell my way to it."

35

The car.
Wind and rain.
It is dark in my eyes.
The dark talks.

I am dark.
You do the chop now.
Cut here and there and everywhere.
Why the winds?
Cuts everywhere.
Look they lie here.
My belly.
Not the baby.
No chops.
Yes chops.
The cop.
Chop a cop.
Sibhon! . . . Sibhon! . . . Sibhon!
I am Dibbly, dubbly, do-do Sibby Dibby.
Mommy love you, yes she do.
For the fucker man says to do.
I am Sibhon . . . what?
You are the bloody one.
You are twenty-one.
He says to fuck.
Fuck yes.
Fuck is good.
Fuck is right.
Fuck at night.
Fuzzy Wuzzy is the bear.
Fuzzy Wuzzy put it there.
What? What? What?
Blood. Blood. Blood.
You are the bloodmaker.
They make it so.
I am bloody.
All the blood.
I am here.

We are there.
There is much blood everywhere.
I don't want to be here.
Take me away.
Get the baby.
Lies. Lies. Lies.
The blood?
To say the truth.
I have to remember.
Hack Chop, hack chop, hack chop.
Find her, find her, why?
Take me back.
Don't like it.
You go back, when you
Hack, hack, hack.
I will not forget.
I am not done.
They lie.
They die.
Not I.
Not I.
It is dark in my eyes.
I am inside a whale.
Remember the chop, chop, chop.
They say lies.
Where my eyes?
What's that sound in my ears?
Is someone coming?
A cop to chop?

36

Miraculously, the GPS knew exactly where Nurse Fugate's house was located and, in a pleasant lady voice, told Alexa which streets to take, where she was to turn, and in what direction, and even gave her the exact distances between those turns. It was a thirty-minute trip, which was longer than it should have taken, due to the heavy traffic on the bridge over the river caused by a wave of citizens who'd decided to flee the hurricane, which the radio announcer explained was gathering frightening strength over the warm Gulf waters.

If the hurricane did turn from its projected course, didn't force water over the levees, or lost focus on the way there, and didn't have the wind left to blow down houses, no one in the city would ever again lend the weatherman their ears. Since the skies were clear and it was hot, humid, and still, it was hard to believe the latest reports predicting an end-time hurricane. The announcer mentioned that there would almost certainly be a mandatory evacuation. What Alexa noticed he didn't say was that the city would be making modes of transportation available to those residents who had no cars or other vehicles to carry them to safety. He did interview a resident of a housing project who said she would stay because her "check" wasn't going to arrive before the storm, so she had no choice. That made Alexa feel both sad and angry. She wondered why the President didn't get the Air Force to send a fleet of C-5As to haul out all the poor and helpless.

Seconds before she arrived, Alexa called the nurse's number to see if anyone was home, and was disappointed when a machine answered—using a generic message, in what sounded like an electronic voice that came with the unit. She didn't leave a message, in case the nurse was monitoring the calls—not answering the ones she wasn't in a mood to take or when the caller ID showed a name and number she didn't recognize.

Dorothy Fugate's address corresponded to a single-story, vinyl-sided Victorian on a quiet street in Algiers Pointe near the Mississippi River. Alexa studied the gingerbread facade as she cut off her engine. She had the uneasy sensation of being watched, and when she turned to look at the house across the street, a curtain seemed to be moving gently—as if someone had drawn it back in order to peer out and then released it. But maybe it was a trick of light, a gust of wind moving through the interior of the brick home.

Its sharp points like piranha teeth, a picket fence whose white paint was chalking defended the Fugate yard from potential invasions. Behind the fence, the sheltering oak trees had leeched nutrients from the soil, leaving large areas of the grounds bare.

All Alexa knew about Nurse Fugate was that she had been the top nurse in the ward where Sibby Danielson had been last kept. Alexa wasn't sure how she was going to find out what the nurse knew. She decided that she would play it by ear, hoping to surprise Fugate, and that her badge would work the magic it had in similar situations. Alexa would push some buttons, read the woman's body language, interpret facial expressions, and look for tells while she interviewed her, to see if she could figure out what

Fugate was afraid of, using her fears to get her to tell what she knew about Sibby Danielson's exodus from the violent ward.

Alexa gathered her will, buttoned her blazer, strode to the gate, and, opening it, let herself into the yard, the gate slamming shut behind her with a loud metallic *click*. Climbing the front steps, she looked at the wicker swing hanging from the ceiling at one end of the porch. She twisted the knob to ring the antique doorbell that was built into the door. Taking a deep breath, she rang it again.

No one answered.

Forming a makeshift visor with her hands, Alexa peered through the beveled glass panel set in the door. Judging by what little she could see, it appeared there was no one at home. She knocked harder, using her knuckles against the wood. Then, when that still didn't raise anybody, she tapped at the glass, using the tip of her car key for a sharper noise and listened for footsteps.

Maybe Nurse Fugate had joined the trek of refugees from the approaching hurricane. Were it not for Gary West, Alexa herself would certainly have been back in D.C. by now, monitoring the storm from the safety of her apartment.

She tried the doorknob and, finding it unlocked, opened it a few inches. One thing was certain: The nurse wouldn't have left the city with her home unlocked.

The shade from the oak trees made the interior gloomy, and Alexa immediately noticed the weak antiseptic odor of bleach and the smell of something decaying. A fly that must have come in with her buzzed past her and headed down the hallway toward the rear of the house.

"Hello? Anybody home?" Her voice echoed through the house. "Ms. Fugate, your front door is open."

Several styles of antique furniture were arranged to view the fireplace, which held an arrangement of fifty or sixty long-stem silk roses spraying out from a low Chinese vase in the unfortunate shape of a spittoon.

A lifeless oil painting of a sunrise on a bayou hung over the mantel, and prints Alexa thought were titled *Pinky* and *Blue Boy*, by a painter named Gainsborough, in golden frilly frames were positioned with prominence over a marble-topped side table.

Bills and catalogs, lying on the floor in front of the mail slot, were positioned in such a way that no two pieces were facedown or overlapping each other. It was as though someone had moved them around in order to read the envelopes without lifting them. Not wanting to surprise anyone, Alexa slammed the door loudly enough to be heard in the rear of the house.

A mantel clock trapped within a glass globe chimed twice.

From the rear of the house there was the distinctive creaking of floorboards. Alexa's unease surged and her empty stomach growled. Old houses made settling noises, she reminded herself, but she doubted that was what she'd heard.

What if Sibby was here—in this house? The thought of coming face-to-face with a murderous psychopath was a sobering one. Alexa was capable of defending herself against conventional attacks, but she'd never dealt with a cleaver-swinging lunatic, and she wished she had backup.

"Ms. Fugate?" she called loudly. "Ms. Fugate? Is anybody home? FBI." Part of her was tempted to open the door and go back outside. The dusky house seemed to hold a malevolent presence, but she was determined, and not about to turn tail. Besides, she was armed with a Glock .40, more than a match for any man or woman. A bullet doesn't distinguish between whether its target is sane or bubble-blowing crazy.

Alexa unbuttoned her purse, removed her Glock, pulled the slide back firmly, and slid it forward slowly so the shell went silently into the chamber, before returning it to her purse, leaving the flap open so she could get to it rapidly. Though technically the Glock couldn't fire a chambered round unless the trigger was pulled, she always left her chamber empty unless she needed it armed. Arming the weapon was a pull of the receiver and a release away. And besides, when sobering was required, the sound of that receiver slamming shut had the same effect as the warning buzz of a rattlesnake.

"Hello," Alexa called again, easing toward the hallway, which was painted Granny Smith green. She flipped the light switch, which chased away the gloom.

"Ms. Fugate? Are you home?"

The smell of decomposition was stronger. Alexa didn't relish the prospect of opening a door and finding Fugate lying dead and decomposing. If the nurse wasn't dead, Alexa dreaded the awkward conversation that would follow if the woman came in from out back and caught a strange and uninvited FBI agent—sans warrant—deep inside her home.

"Ms. Fugate!" she called out, convinced now that it was a waste of effort. Alexa was just snooping now.

Alexa paused at the first door and pushed it open. Light made entrance into the bedroom through the curtains. There was no corpse. Centered on the bed's coverlet was an open steel security box with four brown pill bottles inside it.

Alexa picked up one of the bottles by the top and bottom edges. The prescription for a strong tranquilizer was filled for Dorothy Fugate. The prescribing physician was William LePointe, MD. The label dated the issuing of that prescription in July, just a month earlier.

The security box had been opened with a key that was still in the lock; a beaded neck chain similar to those used for military dog tags ran through it. Alexa could see several long blond hairs caught in the links.

Personal items lined the dressing table. Nurse Fugate had stacked magazines and books in the precise pyramids that indicated an anal-compulsive personality. In the open closet, several neatly pressed, heavily starched white uniforms sealed in plastic cleaner bags had fallen to the floor. All of the other hanging clothes had been parted and shoved to the sides.

One of the drawers in the chest had trapped a pair of panties, an edge sticking out like a handkerchief accenting the pocket of a gentleman's suit.

Alexa left the bedroom and peered into the bathroom across the hall. There was a toothpaste tube on the sink, beneath a rack that held a pair of dry toothbrushes. The faucet dripped onto a brown stain in the porcelain sink bowl. A nightgown hung on a hook on the door, and the toilet seat was up. Veronica Malouf had called Nurse Fugate a spinster, but, as far as Alexa knew, only men lifted toilet seats.

The sliding bolt that could be thrown to secure the last door on the right side of the hallway was engaged. Alexa drew the bolt and gently pushed the door open, to reveal a bedroom in the sort of thoughtless disarray you'd expect from a teenager. Flickering light from a television set on a TV tray pulsed over the narrow, unmade bed. *Why is the set on, with the sound off?* She quickly scanned the room, which also contained a rocking chair on an oval braided rug, and a small dresser. Steel security bars were mounted on the inside of the window frames, probably to prevent anyone from leaving that way, as opposed to preventing someone from breaking in. This was Sibby's room.

Alexa left Sibby's new cell without searching.

Maybe Veronica's call to Decell had caused him to warn Fugate to vacate, to move her prisoner. The house sure felt abandoned. As if in answer to the question, Alexa heard, from the back of the house, the loud creaking of a floorboard, followed by the unmistakable sound of a door snapping closed. She pulled out her Glock and held it aimed at the ceiling. "FBI! Come out, I have a gun!"

Getting no response, Alexa lowered the barrel and moved to the swinging kitchen door. Heart pounding from an adrenaline rush, her mouth dry. Breathing slowly, Alexa steadied herself. *If she's armed and it's between the two of us, I'm the one going home and she's the one going to the morgue zipped in a bag.*

Taking a position of cover behind the jamb, Alexa pushed the door open with her left foot and followed her gun into the kitchen, pivoting and taking in the entire room. The putrid stench of decomposition hit her like the wave of heat from an oven door.

The kitchen and dining room were combined in one large space. There were two partially open doors—a pantry and a broom closet—as well as a third door, this one closed, beside the refrigerator, and a back door with glass panels. Buzzing black flies performed acrobatic maneuvers in the still air over the garbage can.

A bucket filled with rose-colored bleach water rested against the back door, which was locked; the dead bolt was missing the key required to open it. The window over the sink was cracked open, its screen missing, which was obviously how the flies got in.

The flies were gathering on the garbage can. Thanks to its partly open lid, flies crawled in and out freely. Pressing her foot on the pedal to fully open it, Alexa saw a paper sack filled with shrimp husks, the source of the stench.

Stiff spaghettilike strands of a cloth mop filled the sink, its handle resting on the counter. The message machine—also on the counter, beside the telephone—was blinking the number eighteen; the open trapdoors showed her that both its cassettes had been removed. From the time she had called and gotten Nurse Fugate's outgoing message, someone had removed the tapes in the ten minutes since.

Alexa kept her attention focused on the one door that was closed. Whoever was in the house had to have pulled that door shut from inside, and was hiding behind it.

The floor creaked as she moved carefully to the

side of the door. "Nurse Fugate! FBI! I have a gun, come out now!"

Using her left hand, Alexa twisted the knob, pulled the door open, and was surprised to find a set of steep stairs leading down into the darkness. She knew that basements were rare in New Orleans because of the water table. Bodies were buried aboveground in crypts or inside concrete vaults, because a casket buried belowground would, with the first rain, pop up out of the ground like a surfacing submarine.

"Ms. Fugate! You need to come up here. I need to ask you some questions." *Like why you're running a private insane asylum.*

She didn't see a light switch where it should have been located, so Alexa figured the switch for the light must be downstairs. There wasn't one good reason to go downstairs alone, and a hundred reasons not to. Even if Fugate was down there with Sibby Danielson, how would Alexa justify coming into the woman's home and pointing a gun at her? That she'd sweat over later. *Alexa, you've got some 'splainin' to do!*

She reached her left hand into her purse for the small SureFire flashlight. "I said *come on up!*"

Alexa took a tentative step down, turned on the flashlight, and aimed it down the steep stairs. She was assailed by flies swarming up into the kitchen, and put her hand up to protect her face. There was a creaking noise behind her, and before she could turn, someone shouldered the door hard, slamming it against her and knocking her down the staircase— her left side, her hip, and her arm hitting the edges. She saw a flash of light when her head struck the floor. The flashlight and the Glock landed noisily on the concrete floor.

She blinked her eyes slowly, stunned. She knew, lying there, unsure whether she was seriously injured, that Fugate or Sibby must have been hiding in the pantry or broom closet, and she cursed herself for not looking inside them. She had driven that person to the kitchen, where there was no escape without the back door key, so they had shut the basement door and had hidden in one of the tiny spaces.

Lying there dazed, Alexa distinctly heard the skeleton key turning—the door into the basement being locked.

She listened to footsteps moving out of the kitchen and down the hallway. When the front door slammed shut, it sounded a million miles away.

Alexa rolled her head and saw the flashlight a few feet away from her, illuminating a circle of brick wall next to the base of an old furnace. Flies swarmed in the beam. There was an odor of blood and decomposition down here that wasn't coming from a pile of shrimp.

Lying still for a few seconds taking inventory, Alexa moved her arm at the shoulder, then the elbow, the wrist, and finished by wiggling her fingers and making a fist. It was painful, but nothing was broken except her self-respect.

She sat up slowly, wincing. Her head was sore, bruised, but not wet, so she wasn't bleeding. Her hip felt numb and she knew that she was going to be bruised from her ankle to her shoulder.

Alexa crawled over to the flashlight, and picking it up, she swung the circle of light around to locate her handgun, illuminating as she did a shelf where ancient spiderwebs covered dust-caked jars of canned fruit and pickles so old the tin lids were painted with the white powder of oxidation.

She shifted the light and saw a single, unlaced white orthopedic shoe with a brick-colored sole, and beyond it the foot it belonged to, looking like an overstuffed sausage. The skin on the leg looked like sundried earth. The other shoe was still on its owner's other foot.

Alexa steeled herself before raising the circle of light.

A female corpse sat on the concrete floor, her shoulders against the wall, legs splayed open. Her open left hand rested beside her leg as though positioned to catch a flipped coin. Her right hand gripped an unusually large aluminum meat-tenderizing hammer that was caked with dried blood, bone chips, hairs, and blackened brain tissue.

Alexa had seen all manner of dead bodies in various stages of mutilation and decomposition, but nothing more horrific than what she was sharing the small basement with.

She raised the beam, whimpered involuntarily, as tears filled her eyes.

The woman's head had been smashed in with such force that the top of her skull was indented in the way of a rotten rubber doll's head that some child had pushed her thumbs into and peeled open like an orange. The froglike eyes appeared to be coming out of her cheeks. The open mouth was so completely filled with blackened tongue and animated larvae that the jaw was resting against her chest.

Alexa scooted back against the furnace and, using it for support, made it to her feet.

Based on the shoes, Alexa assumed that this horror was what remained of Dorothy Fugate, since the alternative was that the nurse had gone crazy and beat Sibby to death with a meat hammer, which seemed highly unlikely. Although why Sibby would have positioned the corpse that way was a mystery best left to psychiatrists. Maybe it was some sort of humor springing from an insane brain.

Using the flashlight, Alexa located and tugged on the string to turn on the overhead bulb. Flies reacting to the sudden light filled the room like a cloud. Alexa located her gun and stuck it into her purse's holster compartment.

Alexa was trembling. She wanted only to get out of there, into breathable air, away from the corpse. She heard a noise and realized that it was the sound of her own whimpering as she moved as quickly as she could up the narrow stairs. Peering into the keyhole, she saw that the key was no longer in the lock. Her flashlight caught a glint of the skeleton key, which had been pushed under the door.

Sibby knocks me down into hell and then is thoughtful enough to leave me the key before she flees the house?

Alexa opened the door and after she slammed it shut she leaned with her back against it and took her first deep breaths since she'd been pitched down the steps. Then she started crying, overwhelmed by the embarrassment of being taken by surprise, the pain of the fall, what she had seen. Her whole body was racked by the sobs as she fought to regain her composure.

Her crying turned into the hysterical laughter of someone who understood, at a whole new level, what a blessing life was. She wiped her eyes and headed for the front door.

37

If she had been a smoker, Alexa would have lit up and gone through an entire pack. At the gate, she looked in both directions down the still street. Sibby Danielson was gone.

Reaching into her purse, Alexa found her cell phone.

"Yeah," Manseur answered.

"I'm at Fugate's."

"She know where Sibby is?"

"I couldn't ask. She's dead."

"You sure it's her?"

"Reasonably. I mean, the corpse is a bottle blonde, and I don't have the slightest idea what Sibby looks like."

"How did she die?"

"Somebody played patty-whack on her skull. Best I can tell from looking at her and based on the odor and the insects' labors, she's been dead a few days. But Sibby was here until a few minutes ago."

"Danielson did it?"

"She didn't type out a confession, but based on the fact that it's pretty clear she's been staying here in the house, and given her track record for anti-social and impulsive behavior, it's a good bet it wasn't the mailman."

"Don't do anything. I'm on my way."

"I think I've done quite enough for the time being," Alexa said after she hung up.

It appeared to Alexa that Sibby Danielson had killed her jailer and then stayed in the house. Maybe, Alexa thought, the woman hadn't had any place to go. Most people, even insane ones, would have left the scene of their crime before now, especially considering the smell.

Alexa decided that while she was waiting for Manseur, she would take a look around and see what she could discover about Sibby. She was no longer worried about not having a search warrant to enter—the odor of decaying flesh wafting through the open front door had given her enough probable cause. Manseur could collect evidence since it was a homicide.

The pill bottles that had been with the steel box on the bed were gone, but the box was where it had been earlier. Had Sibby stopped escaping long enough to pick up the bottles because she needed to take the medication? If she'd been medicated, would she have killed Fugate?

In the drawer in Fugate's bedside table, Alexa found a polished wooden box with delicate ivory inlay work on its lid, which she opened, to discover a stack of snapshots. She flipped up the prints by their edges so she wouldn't disturb the existing fingerprints, or make new ones. Despite the very heavy makeup and teased blond hair, the buxom Dorothy Fugate had been attractive in her younger years. In a picture probably taken at her graduation from nursing school, she looked more like Jayne Mansfield playing a nurse than a real one. As time had passed she had become somewhat pudgy, and, though still attractive, her features had softened with age, her body rounding itself off. The hellish effigy in the basement bore no resemblance to the woman in the pictures, but Alexa had no doubt this was Sibby Danielson's keeper.

Alexa lifted the mattress and found nothing. There was nothing of interest in the drawers but a few pieces of fairly expensive-looking gold jewelry.

Looking into Fugate's closet, she lifted the fallen nurse uniforms and noticed that one of the wide floorboards wasn't flush. She raised it, to find a secret compartment, within which was a lone wooden cigar box. Inside, there were more pictures. Again being careful in handling them, she flipped through them one by one.

There was a snapshot of a small boy and a young girl attempting to pull a red wagon with an adult laughing man seated in it. Another seemed to be a fairly recent shot of Dorothy and the same grown man, whose hair had turned gray. There was such a marked similarity in their features, Alexa thought he was a relative of Fugate's.

Another picture showed a stern-faced Dorothy standing beside a short male teenager dressed in a military school's uniform who stared blankly at the camera. The young man could be a relative or a friend's child and he might even be the wagon-pulling child. He had a round face, which matched his body, small eyes, and his fat lips added to the smirk he wore.

The other snapshots were of Nurse Fugate with

hospital staff or civilians, taken at various times over the years. There were several shots of small groups that included Dorothy, some of which also contained Dr. William LePointe. The next-to-last photo in the stack was of Dorothy in her starched uniform standing alone with LePointe at a party. It was a recent photo, and Alexa thought it might have been her or his going-away party, because there was a partially disassembled slab cake on a table in the background. Dorothy was smiling broadly, while Dr. LePointe looked like he was about to have a tooth extracted instead of his picture taken. In the background, Veronica Malouf was in profile and was obviously talking to someone out of frame.

The final shot was the stunner. It was a Polaroid taken from the hallway into the bedroom through a partly opened door. The image showed a naked man with wet and carefully combed silver hair standing in front of a full-length mirror, obviously admiring his body, which was nothing to write home about. Well, he was naked but for the black socks held up by elastic bands. "Jesus," Alexa murmured. Dr. William LePointe's appearance, aside from being naked in Dorothy Fugate's bedroom, might be the key to some answers. Unless he had been showering at Fugate's house for some innocent reason, Fugate and LePointe appeared to be more than coworkers.

Alexa put the cigar box on the dresser and replaced the board in the closet floor. She noticed that there was a smudge on the outside of the box, and it appeared to have been made by a bloody finger.

She sat in the living room to wait for Manseur. She had no physical description of Sibby nor any idea how she was dressed. *Let Manseur's locals handle this.* She pictured LePointe's smug face and felt a flush of anger. *Controlled through modern medicine,* she thought to herself. *You really flubbed this one, Doctor. Now Dorothy Fugate is dead and Sibby killed her for some reason we'll probably never know. I guess they'll round her up and send her back to River Run.*

When Manseur came in, Alexa led him back to the kitchen, letting him stamp alone down the stairs. She'd already seen more than enough of the basement.

Manseur spent five minutes downstairs, and when he re-emerged he was holding a handkerchief to his nose.

"I'll never get used to that smell," he declared. "You okay?"

"Sibby shoved me down those stairs," Alexa snapped. "Can we go outside before I faint?"

"Tell me everything," he said as they walked.

"I knocked and got no answer. I tried the door and it opened. I smelled decomposition and entered to investigate. While searching for the source of the odor, I heard a door closing. I came into the kitchen, and the basement door was the only one that was closed. While I was shining my light down there, somebody—whom I assume was Sibby—knocked me down the steps."

"Solid statement. Did you get a good look at her?"

"No. The basement door was between us."

"How do you know it was her?"

"I'm just assuming it, based on the fact that she's been staying in Nurse Fugate's guest cell," Alexa said.

"Christ," Manseur said. "This is a grand mess."

"There's a cigar box with a bloody fingerprint on

it that was under the closet floor in Fugate's room. Sibby might have taken something of hers out of it at some point. There's a metal lockbox on Fugate's bed that was full of tranquilizers and anti-psychotic drugs prescribed to Fugate by Dr. LePointe. Sibby took them when she split."

"Alexa. Only you saw them, but she took them. Maybe she'll have them with her when we find her and we can use them somehow to question LePointe. We have to be damn sure of something before we accuse him of anything. Very, very damn sure."

Alexa nodded.

"You're lucky she just pushed you down the stairs," he said. "That sure isn't the worst she's capable of."

"Obviously not."

Manseur said, "Here's the deal. I'll handle this as an anonymous-reported death and keep you out of it. So, how do you think it went down?"

"I think Fugate was attacked in the kitchen probably with that meat hammer and dragged down to the basement, because the kitchen and the stairs were cleaned up. You know, something about Sibby doing this doesn't quite make sense," Alexa said.

"Since when do crazy people make sense?" he asked.

"Okay, she loses it, beats Fugate to death, then drags the body down there to keep it from being found, which means she knew killing her was wrong. I wouldn't imagine an inner-voice-minding psychopath would bother to mop up. And there's no blood spatter on the walls and ceiling. That would seem to indicate Fugate was first assaulted upstairs, maybe was struck just hard enough to knock her out. Sibby calmly drags her down the stairs, props her against the wall, and then does the real damage with the mallet and puts it in her hand for some reason."

"Maybe her rage grew as it went on," Manseur conjectured. "Or she was staging it as a suicide."

"Funny. To be released by the committee, Sibby had to be cured. Twenty-six years rocking away and suddenly she does this. It doesn't feel right. And why would she mop up?" Alexa asked.

"Maybe she *was* crazy enough to kill her, but cured enough to realize she screwed up and, filled with remorse, cleaned up as best she could. Or maybe she just straightened up because she planned to stay here and didn't want to stumble over the corpse every day when she was cooking her breakfast."

Alexa was silent.

"So, where's Danielson now? I have to get an updated description of her." Manseur nodded solemnly. "I'll see if that young woman at the hospital can give me one. You suppose Fugate's tied into the West thing?" he asked. "I didn't see a car in the driveway. Maybe Sibby took her car and went after Gary West?"

Alexa shrugged, which made her shoulder ache. "I only know that the only common thread in both is Dr. LePointe," she said.

"I'll assign two of my detectives to this scene. Find anything on Fugate's next of kin?"

"I found papers and pictures. If she has kin, I don't know who they are or where. Somebody took the answering machine's outgoing and incoming voice tapes out. The machine showed there were eighteen new messages, though. We need her phone records."

"I spoke to Jackson Evans about the letter from Gary West. I asked to see it and Evans thanked us for trying to help. I'm not sure how to handle it to get a look at the letter. He's made it clear the case is closed."

"You could push it," Alexa said.

"How?"

"You'd have to bring in this murder."

"Not unless I have cause," Manseur said. "I don't think this is enough as it stands."

"Maybe when you process this place, you'll get something. Check the toilet for prints. I think a man was here recently. He might have left something of himself. Fingerprint, DNA in the bowl."

"I'll tell Cooley to check."

"Come take a look at something I found," she said, leading Manseur to the cigar box. Carefully she sifted through the pictures until she got to the money shot of LePointe.

He whistled softly. "I could have gone the rest of my life without seeing that. I think I should take that one out."

"Send it to *Playgirl* magazine," Alexa said. "It's evidence."

"Maybe. I'm not sure of anything other than the doctor's obvious suntan deficiency," Manseur said.

"I'll figure it out." Alexa picked up her purse, wincing. "First thing I'm going to do is run by the hotel and take a hot shower and change clothes. Then I'm going to have a talk with Casey West."

"Remember that the letter means it's not a kidnapping," Manseur reminded her, shrugging.

"Even if Gary West did send LePointe a letter, it

doesn't mean he wasn't abducted after that. Gary West was the victim of foul play. Only question is who's behind it and what the reason was. Maybe West will show up, but he'll have a bad knot on his head and hopefully he'll tell us what happened and who abducted him."

"This is your field, but if he knows who abducted him, will they let him live?"

"That's not how it normally goes, unless the abductor used a third party, or Gary has a reason *not* to tell anybody. I'm going."

"Like they know if he tells he'll have more to explain. Maybe Gary West has a secret he doesn't want anybody to know. Think Gary has secrets he doesn't want Casey to know? West could have staged this."

"Why?"

"To get his wife wet for him. I don't know. The way this is shaking out, nothing would surprise me. Rich people like them live in a different universe than we do."

"And *who* makes that possible?" Alexa asked, waving good-bye as she left.

38

When Leland's head stopped hurting, he was in the closet, his body drawn up into a tight fist, drenched in sweat. One second pain was all there was in the world and then it was gone, leaving him totally spent. He knew the weakness would pass momentarily and he could step back into the light-filled world. He wouldn't soon forget to take the medicine Doc had gotten for him.

After a few minutes, Leland climbed out from the stuffy space, to discover that Doc sat on the edge of the bed reading a red notebook he carried everywhere he went.

"Feeling better?" Doc asked without looking up, or meaning it either.

"Hate headaches," Leland said.

"I agree," Doc said. "Nothing worse than a migraine. Unless it's having an abscessed tooth, your fingers flattened by a hammer while a furious big dog is chewing on your balls and you're having to hit him with your broken hand." Doc chuckled to himself.

"You say awful things, you know that?" Leland said.

"Medical knowledge warps the innocent. I can't help it."

"What's it say in that there book that's so interesting you have to keep reading it all the time?" Leland had never learned to read, but he knew some of the alphabet, and recognized his name when he saw it written out. And he could write it down by rote, having learned to re-create the specific letters.

"Aside from wealth beyond imagination?" Doc closed the book with a *pop*. "Nothing to speak of, my fine cretinous companion."

"What you need me to do now?"

"You may go out into yon murk and mire to get the nice young man who's presently residing within the four walls of your lovely floating hovel and bring him back here."

"What if he's already dead? Then do I have to?"

"Regardless of his vitals, you definitely have to do that for me. Best if he is, of course, but what is, will be."

Leland shrugged. "I need to go get in my boat and check on my traps, because you stay off for long and just anybody can mess with your traps and lines. You know it?"

"*Your* boat?" Doc said in his high-pitched voice. "*Whose* boat is it, Leland?"

"You said I could have it for the jobs I've done did already," Leland said, feeling the heat building in his head. People that lied and did take-backs got hurt and deserved it. Leland couldn't change the way he saw that, and none of the doctors at the old hospital that smelled of pine resin and Clorox could either. The medicine they gave him made his arms feel heavy as wet oak logs, and he didn't plan to ever take it again, on account of he didn't like the way it made him feel like he was living in an underwater dream.

Doc wagged his finger at Leland. "Don't go ribbity-rabid on me, Lee baby. It's going to be your boat after tonight's activities. The vessel will be a gift to you from me as soon as this is all over. The job isn't over till the fat lady sings."

Leland hadn't heard a fat lady sing since he was in the hospital, and her voice hadn't been worth listening to either. Maybe Doc liked bad singing, which wouldn't surprise Leland. Anything Doc said or did wouldn't surprise Leland one bit. "With owning papers saying it's so, right?"

"Of course with a proper bill of sale turning the immaculate vessel over to one Leland Ticholet, Superman of the swampy glade. Don't I always tell you the truth? Who was it that furnished you with copious quantities of Juicy Fruit during your unfortunate incarceration?"

Leland searched his memory, and it was true that, so far, Doc had always done just that. But Doc was a little bitty smarty-ass fool who seemed to like to get Leland just on start-up mad and then cool him back down with his flowery promises. Leland nodded and felt the heat in his face cooling. The mention of Juicy Fruit sent his mouth to watering. Leland smiled at the memory of the explosion of flavor he experienced when he chewed the magnificent little slabs of chewing gum that came wrapped in yellow. He kept forgetting to get some when he bought supplies.

"That's better," Doc said, putting the red book into a paper bag. Leland wondered why Doc was always wearing those gloves that made his hands look like he painted them blue.

"I need to get back out to my camp," Leland said. "You got any Juicy Fruit?"

Doc reached into his pocket and threw Leland a jumbo brand-new pack of the gum, which hadn't even been opened yet.

"Keep it," Doc said.

"I have to go now."

"Yes, so you've said. Go and fetch forth our guest. There's lots to do before tonight's big bang-bang. Don't tell me you aren't excited."

"About what?" Leland asked, suspiciously.

39

After a hot shower to remove the smell of death she imagined was on her skin, Alexa dried off and looked at herself in the mirror, shaking her head at the dark splotches, scratches, and welts she'd acquired in her tumble. She was extremely lucky that she hadn't broken any bones. Or her neck. Sibby Danielson was a local matter, unless it involved the abduction of Gary West. Truthfully, LePointe wasn't the only man with power who used it to abuse weaker people, or who believed the rules of conduct and law that applied to everyone else carried a clause exempting him because of an accident of birth.

Alexa opened her suitcase for a change of clothes. She looked at a stack of postcards in there bound together with a rubber band. Lifting them, she flipped through them so she could see the bottom one. It was addressed to her, care of her D.C. apartment. There was no return address. The note consisted of carefully printed words, written by a hand she knew very well. *You are dead, kitty cat. I will hate you forever.*

Alexa's throat closed as though being gripped by powerful hands, and she threw the stack of postcards into the suitcase, closed the lid, and zipped it up. She knew she should tear them into confetti, but it was as if she didn't have the strength, so she merely collected them, and had brought them with her to New Orleans. There were ten of the picture postcards, each postmarked from a city in a different state or foreign country, even though the author was under arrest, being held in Virginia. The picturesque correspondence had arrived at the rate of one a month for the past ten consecutive months. Some were promising violence: *You will die soon;* some just said something like *Thinking only of you . . . bitch.* Threats or not, Alexa hadn't brought them to the FBI's attention, because she knew who the author was, and knew there was nothing anyone could do to stop her.

The person who had penned them might or might not actually mean her physical harm; the harm they did wasn't visible. Overwhelmed with grief and the pain of failure where it most mattered, Alexa had cried while reading each of them. Every time she read them, the wound was torn open again. *Hate me if it makes you feel better about who and what you became. I did what I had to do, what was right. I would do nothing differently. Nothing, but go back to our childhood and try to make sure you had turned out differently, or at least more right than you did. I did the best I could for us both.*

Saddened beyond words, Alexa turned and saw the book Casey had given her earlier. She picked it up and opened it to the inscription Casey had penned, which she hadn't read in the author's presence. *For the Patron Saint of the Lost. Kindest thoughts & warmest regards. Always, Casey.*

Casey had appealed to her for help, and Alexa was going to help. Casey was a woman who had learned that enormous wealth was no guarantee that pain couldn't find you just like it did the less fortunate. That beautiful woman, who seemed to have everything, stood to lose the only thing that made having everything matter to her. She trusted Alexa, a woman she had just met, to make her life whole. How could you not feel for a small girl who had seen her parents horribly murdered? How could anyone not empathize with a child who had been raised by people who measured life by a heavily weighted balance sheet or placement on the social register?

Alexa had known real physical and emotional pain in her own life, but she felt lucky not to have felt the kind Casey LePointe West had.

She thumbed through the pages of Casey's book. Alexa felt as though she should be wearing cotton gloves to keep from soiling the page corners. Casey's work had an intensity to it, an edge that held Alexa in its thrall. Each of her subjects seemed to have been stripped of pretension, their souls reflected in their expressions, their eyes.

The photos weren't captioned with the subjects' names, but with dates and geographic locations where the images were taken, or perhaps where the subject lived. "10/09/04—West Virginia" was a man whose face was so blackened with coal soot that his eyes seemed to be twin pools of turquoise water surrounded by a fire-scorched, heat-cracked wasteland. Alexa went from each image to the next, pausing a few seconds to study the people depicted. "5/27/03—Georgia Coast" showed an elegant, elderly, seated woman regally posed, her ancient skin glistening like wet bronze. She wore a starched servant's uniform, her rheumatoid hands folded together on her knee. She possessed a raw pride and peered through rheumy eyes that seemed to convey that she had lived her life at peace with the universe.

Alexa's cell phone rang and she opened it and saw that Casey West was calling her. "Hello."

"Hello, Alexa. I thought I should call to tell you something wonderful."

"I heard Gary sent a letter to your uncle."

"I'm just now driving over to see it," Casey said. "Of course, I'm going to be pissed off at Gary for all of five minutes. I can't believe it! What was he thinking? I should be furious for what he's put us through, but I'm not."

"I'm happy for you and Deana," Alexa said, not wanting to throw a wet blanket over Casey's elation by saying that she'd believe it when she saw Gary with her own eyes.

"Listen, if you aren't too busy, could you come to Unko's?"

"I suppose. Why?"

"I could use a friend along for moral support. It's not necessary if you're busy. I wouldn't ask, but Unko has a way of sort of intimidating me. Honestly, I wouldn't ask, but if you're there, maybe it won't be so one-sided."

"Where's Grace?"

"She had some errands to do for her parents to get them ready to leave the city. We'll all be leaving for Manhattan as soon as Gary gets back. We're sure not going to stay here. A couple of weeks away will be like a second honeymoon."

"Give me the address." *I need to see the letter for myself anyway,* Alexa decided.

Alexa scribbled down the address on St. Charles Avenue. Before she left, she slid the book back in its slipcover and started to put it into her suitcase, remembered the postcards, and decided against it, putting the volume instead into her briefcase with her laptop. She dressed quickly, and before leaving the room took the folding knife from under her pillow and slipped it into the bottom of her purse.

40

Alexa drove up St. Charles Avenue, following the GPS lady's unemotional directions, and when the helpful lady informed Alexa that she was at the destination, Alexa turned into the driveway of a monstrous, two-story stone mansion surrounded by a tall wrought-iron fence. The sturdy man standing inside the gate opened it just enough to come out. He asked her if she was expected and, even though she said that she was—and what reason would the FBI have to lie about it?—used his radio to call someone to ask if the FBI agent could enter the grounds.

The gate swung open and Alexa drove into the enclosure. Lush foliage grew on a swale that was strategically placed to hide the LePointes from the street. She passed beneath a portico that would protect people from the rain while they got in and out of vehicles. Alexa drove to the courtyard, where LePointe's dark Bentley Continental and a Range Rover were parked beside each other. Alexa parked beside Casey's Rover and strode to the front door, passing through open gates to a cage of decorative wrought iron. The downstairs windows also had the same elegant filigree work—attractive, and effective security. The security measure must have been expensive. And she wasn't surprised that the construction of the home had taken five years. The Civil War–era structure was so pristine that it looked as if it might have been completed six months ago.

A thin, dark-skinned woman wearing an apron over a starched uniform opened the door. Deana was beside her, and the little girl smiled at Alexa. "Hello, Deana," Alexa said.

Deana spun around and ran down the hall, laughing.

"Stay with me, baby girl," the woman called out to her.

In the vestibule behind, a vase holding an enormous spray of exotic flowers stood on a table crafted entirely of cut glass. Alexa entered and looked up at a dome that crested thirty feet above the table. The dome was made entirely of elaborate stained glass—a garden scene with greenery and multicolored flowers made brilliant by sunlight. A wide stone staircase floated up to a mezzanine with the same filigree motif in bronze railing as outside. From an arched throat in the foyer, a hallway punctuated on either side by several doorways extended deep into the home.

Alexa saw Deana and a female figure in a flowing silken gown at the far end of the hallway. The woman began waving her arms and striding in a series of exaggerated movements as she made her way toward the front. Deana stood against the wall laughing melodiously as the bizarre ballerina came toward her. Alexa saw that she was elderly, her long gray hair cascading to her shoulders. She appeared to be attempting an interpretative dance, but her joints and muscles could no longer produce fluid movements. Well before she arrived at the foyer, the woman turned abruptly, bowed with her extended and intertwined arms aimed at a doorway, and, raising her right leg awkwardly, lurched, vanishing through it, with Deana following her.

"That's Mrs. Sarah," the servant told Alexa.

"Dr. LePointe's wife?" Alexa asked.

"She have the Alzheimer's," the woman said in a soft voice. "She believes she's a dancer up in New York City, and it's nineteen-whatever-it-was when she was up there."

"Sorry to hear it."

"Dr. LePointe and Ms. West are in his study. I'll show you back."

As Alexa and the maid passed the doorway Sarah LePointe had chosen, Alexa turned and saw Mrs. LePointe—arms waving as though she were drowning—prancing energetically around the furniture in a large formal sitting room. The maid lifted Deana up onto her hip. Sarah LePointe's eyes were hidden behind large sunglasses—her mind generating music she moved to, her face illuminated with a smile of pure pleasure. Alexa envied the woman her beautiful delusion, and hoped she didn't stumble over something and snap her hip.

Alexa heard Casey's raised voice through the heavy door as she approached it. The servant knocked and Casey fell silent. LePointe called, "Come in."

Alexa was first struck by the Jackson Pollock painting that took up the entire wall behind the desk. There was a sharp contrast between that oil and the likewise massive oil seascape on the wall to its right— a painting that Alexa was sure she had seen before in a book. She pulled her eyes away and looked at Casey, whose face was flushed.

LePointe motioned to a chair. "Please sit down, Agent Keen. You know art?"

"I know the difference between a Pollock and a Turner," she said, bringing a smug smile to his lips with her accuracy—and perhaps the fact that she would appreciate the value of both. "Usually I see paintings of this quality only in books or museums."

"Quite so," LePointe said. "Where they usually belong. This house is climate-controlled and the light is regulated carefully. If the hurricane comes and breaches the levees, all of the art here will be high, dry, and secure. The Turner is one my father purchased for next to nothing that was owned by a collector who fell victim to unfortunate circumstances. The Pollock is one my mother bought in the fifties from the artist himself. She was quite taken with the Moderns."

Casey said suddenly, "The letter from Gary is a fraud, Alexa."

"How can you be so sure?" LePointe asked, turning his eyes on his niece.

"Gary never types. He only writes letters with fountain pens. He thinks typing is impersonal. He never even uses e-mail."

"That's hardly proof," LePointe scoffed. "I imagine he knows how to type."

"Secondly, he wouldn't send it to you, of all people."

"Why not?" Alexa asked.

"He hates Unko. He thinks he's—let me quote: 'a pompous, controlling, egocentric, self-important windbag.' Which he is. God, I should have known!"

LePointe stiffened. "Gary's a man in crisis. I've

seen this a thousand times. Self-destruction due to the fact that he's standing at the verge of something life-altering that he knows he doesn't deserve. He can't handle the prospect. He's crying out for 'poor me saddled with all of this attention'. Anxiety. Self-loathing. Inferiority complex. Mania. Insecurity. Round peg in a square hole, et cetera, ad nauseam."

"You are so full of it," Casey snapped. "If that were the case, Gary would have told me yesterday at lunch, or before. I'd have known if he was having problems. Unlike you, I pay attention to those around me. And that letter isn't in his voice at all. Emotional turmoil? Inner feelings? *My* future? Never could Gary be so selfish. He would never let me worry like this or leave Deana without her knowing he was coming back soon."

"So, if he didn't send it, who did?" LePointe asked.

"Gee, I don't know," Casey said. "Maybe it was some pompous ass-bite windbag who wanted to get the authorities off the case. Better to die because nobody's searching for you than cast a shadow on the immaculate LePointe name," Casey said, raising her voice. "Obviously it was someone who thinks I'm dumb enough to accept such an obvious crock."

"May I see the letter?" Alexa asked.

LePointe tossed a folded sheet of typing paper across the desk. Alexa used her ballpoint to open the letter, then read the single-spaced paragraph.

Dr. LePointe,
    Please tell my wife that I am sorry if I've caused her any emotional turmoil, but I needed a few days alone in order to evaluate my position in this life

and contemplate my future. Please do not involve
the authorities, as I am fine and should be home on
Saturday, or Sunday at the latest. Give my wife and
daughter my love.

Gary

" 'My wife and daughter'? It's clinically imper
sonal," Alexa said.

"He didn't use our names! Impossible," Casey
said sourly.

"The envelope?" Alexa asked.

LePointe looked in the trash can beside his desk
pulled out an envelope, and placed it beside the lette
It was a plain security envelope, available by the hun
dred anywhere office supplies were sold. It had beer
opened using a sharp blade. The flap was one tha
used peel-off tape instead of needing to be moistene
to activate the adhesive. The stamp was also a pee
and stick. Obviously there would be no DNA to ex
tract.

"Do you have an envelope?" she asked LePointe
"An unused one."

LePointe opened a drawer and handed Alexa a
large envelope made of expensive white paper. Alexa
opened the envelope and slid the letter and its envelope
into the larger one before she folded it closed. "I'd lik
to take the letter, if you don't mind," Alexa said.

"What is the point of taking the letter?" LePoint
asked.

"I'm going to have it analyzed for Gary West's fin
gerprints to see if he ever had it in his hands. If he
didn't, I want to know who did. Casey, I'll need to
have something Gary has handled."

"His prints should be on file," Casey said. "He was arrested for protesting in New York when he was at NYU."

LePointe raised an eyebrow, as if Gary West had been arrested for a serious felony.

"Giving me something he's handled recently might actually be faster than going through AFIS."

"AFIS?"

"Automated Fingerprint Identification System. I imagine the crime-scene lab needs them anyway in processing the prints found in and on the Volvo."

"No problem," Casey said. "Gary has silver accent pieces on his desk—a letter opener, cigarette holder, and lighter. He plays with the cigarette holder when he's at his desk."

"What about my fingerprints?" LePointe said. "I handled that letter."

"Have you ever been arrested?" Alexa asked.

"Of course not! I've never even been fingerprinted," LePointe snapped.

"I would have thought maybe the Secret Service or the Bureau might have printed you for security clearances," Alexa said.

"They didn't print me. I suppose I am well-enough known to make that unnecessary," he said, having missed the point of her barbed comment.

"Another one of your envelopes, please, Dr. LePointe?" While he got another envelope, Alexa opened her purse and took out a spare magazine for her Glock. Using a handkerchief, she carefully wiped the magazine clean and set it on the desk.

"Rub your fingers on your nose. The oil transferred to the pads of your fingers will help make your prints stand out. Just grip that magazine by placing your thumb on one side of it and your fingers firmly on the other, then lift and release it," Alexa told the doctor.

"You're not serious." LePointe acted as though Alexa had asked him to provide her with a stool specimen.

"Uncle William," Casey said. "It's important."

"This is absurd," LePointe sputtered.

"I'm sure you want to know, as badly as I do, who wrote this if Gary West didn't," Alexa told him.

He wiped his nose, reached out, and squeezed the loaded magazine, then took his hand away.

Alexa gripped the magazine by its base, looked at the sharp prints on the polished steel, then dropped the heavy magazine into the fresh envelope.

"I touched the letter and the Volvo," Casey said. "Do you have another magazine?"

Alexa used her second spare magazine to obtain Casey's prints just as she had LePointe's. She placed the second magazine in a separate envelope and wrote Casey's name on it.

"Now the lab will have exemplars for comparisons," Alexa said.

LePointe sat silently, his eyes unfocused. Something was bothering him.

"If you're worried, Dr. LePointe, the lab will be instructed to destroy your print records after they've used them for this."

"It's just that someone else also handled the letter," LePointe said. "My investigator. Kenneth Decell. Naturally he read it."

"I'm sure his prints will be on file with NOPD," Alexa said.

"So, you're going to keep looking for Gary?" Casey asked.

"My initial feeling is that this letter is a fraud, perhaps intended to discourage the police from looking for him. I'm not sure what the motive is, but I'm certain, based on the physical evidence alone, that he was the victim of foul play. Even if he did write and mail that letter, somebody attacked him brutally with a pipe afterward. The good news is that this is obviously an amateur production, and I'm certain we'll be able to figure out who's behind it. You don't have any objections to the NOPD and me continuing to look for Gary, do you, Dr. LePointe?"

"Of course not. Why should I?"

"I'll notify Detective Manseur," Alexa said. "He's in Algiers Pointe investigating the death of a retired psychiatric nurse. A woman named Dorothy Fugate."

LePointe locked his eyes with Alexa's. What he was thinking was impossible to guess, because his face, although draining of color, was devoid of expression.

"Dotty?" Casey asked, locking her eyes on LePointe. "Jesus! I'm sorry, Unko."

"Sorry? Why?" he asked, swallowing. It must have been difficult, since he had to have a dry mouth.

"You two were such close friends," Casey said. "You've known her for thirty years, that's why. You worked together at River Run."

"Nurse Fugate was employed at the hospital and I was the director of psychiatry. We were hardly *friends*. She was an acquaintance, although I suppose we developed a superficial relationship over the years. She was a talented and dedicated professional. Naturally I'm very sorry to hear that she's dead. I haven't spoken to her since she retired last year. We didn't see each other socially."

"Even so, you must be curious to learn how she died," Alexa remarked.

"I assume it was a heart attack, stroke, or something," LePointe said. "She was not a young lady."

"She was murdered," Alexa said.

LePointe shrugged. "That's terrible. Did she live in a bad neighborhood?"

"I'm sorry?" Alexa asked.

"Well, she was a nurse. Perhaps drug addicts knew that. She resisted them and they killed her."

"It appears a mental patient who was living with her most likely committed the crime. So, you've never been to her home?"

"Why on earth would I go to her home?"

Alexa would have loved to show him the Polaroid of him standing naked in Fugate's bedroom preening before her mirror.

"What patient?" It was Casey who asked, and not her uncle.

"I don't think we need to dwell on such unpleasantness at this particular juncture," LePointe said stiffly.

"If you haven't spoken to her, I guess you didn't know that she was such a *dedicated* professional that she kept a mental patient locked away in her home?" Alexa asked him. "A mental patient who was supposed to be in ward fourteen at River Run."

"Nurse Fugate was a career psychiatric nurse and a compassionate human being," LePointe said. "And she's retired and capable of helping a patient."

"A patient who vanished from ward fourteen about the time Nurse Fugate retired."

"What are you talking about?" Casey asked, bewildered.

"The patient was Sibhon Danielson," Alexa said. "And Fugate kept her in a padlocked bedroom with bars on the windows and a bolt on the outside of the door."

There was an audible gasp from Casey, and despite the fact that he'd been doing a good job holding his feelings back till that point, LePointe's eyes flashed surprise for the briefest instant.

"Her?" Casey whispered, her eyes fevered. Openmouthed, she sat down in an armchair. "Dear God . . ."

"Oddly, it appears there's no record at River Run that she isn't still locked up."

"You're sure?" Casey asked. "Oh my God! Lucille Burch was right."

"Beyond any shadow of a doubt, Burch doesn't know it for certain, but someone must have told her about it. You didn't know that Sibby was living with Nurse Fugate, Dr. LePointe?"

"Of course not!" LePointe snapped. "How would I know that?"

"No reason, besides the fact that you've been writing Nurse Fugate prescriptions for anti-psychotic medications used for treating schizophrenia. Along with some heavy sedatives. You didn't prescribe them for Nurse Fugate's personal medical conditions, did you?"

"I assume, if what you say is accurate, the prescriptions were forged," LePointe said. "I never prescribed anything for Dotty. I'd like to see them."

"Nurse Fugate, you mean," Alexa said. She wondered if he knew the pill bottles were gone. But what would that mean? Either Sibby had told him she'd taken them from the house, which seemed very unlikely, or someone else had told him. *But who?*

"What?" he asked.

"You said you always called her Nurse Fugate, but just now you called her Dotty," Alexa said.

"Sibhon Danielson was at River Run and you never told me?" Casey asked her uncle.

LePointe stood, and Alexa could tell he wanted to throw things at her—chase her out of the house swinging the poker that leaned against the fireplace. But he came around the desk and stood beside Casey's chair. "Agent Keen, you've upset my niece with your insinuations. Please leave us and get on about your business. My niece is not emotionally able to withstand this sort of pressure. I am warning you: you are stepping on very dangerous ground."

Casey was sobbing. When her uncle put his hand on her shoulder, she shot from the chair and fixed him with an icy look of rage. "What is going on here? My God, Unko! What the hell is going on here?"

"I have no idea," LePointe said. "I don't know anything about Sibhon Danielson. I'm as stunned as you are, my dear, but I've yet to see any proof that she is indeed out of the hospital, or was living with Nurse Fugate." The smile Dr. LePointe intended to be reassuring would have looked at home on a Bell's palsy victim. "Let's not jump to conclusions and say things we'll regret."

"That monster *murdered my parents*!" Casey yelled. She turned her eyes to Alexa. "Where is she now?"

"We have no idea."

Alexa decided she had nothing to lose in pushing, to see what happened. "You don't know anything about

Sibby Danielson, Doctor? Odd. If Sibby Danielson was an inmate at River Run for the twenty-six years where you were director of the facility, and were seeing patients on her ward, you must have known she was there."

"Of course I knew she was there," LePointe replied angrily. "So what? I never treated her. I wouldn't know the woman if she walked into this room."

"According to the police files, I understood that she was your patient when she killed your brother and his wife," Alexa said.

Again Casey's eyes widened with obvious disbelief. "Unko? Is that true?"

"She was no longer my patient when she did that!" LePointe roared. "She was upset because I had quit treating her. She was a psychotic mess and she was disturbed, and possibly she imagined that my brother was behind my refusal to treat her. Patient transference. She imagined we were married and Curry was standing between her and some ideal of happiness. She confronted my wife and created a scene at the country club. I tried to get her committed before! Casey, I did not know she was out of the hospital! Sibhon Danielson is an extremely dangerous woman. I don't know, but if she killed Dorothy, it was because poor Dorothy had taken it upon herself to help her, which the hospital was never able to do. Maybe Dorothy aided in her escape in some misguided sense of compassion or sense of duty. It's even possible they may have had some codependent relationship that Dorothy didn't want to have ended."

"I'm sure they're pulling her records at the hospital about now to get a photograph and a physical description. Since we are here together, perhaps you could give me a current description, Dr. LePointe?"

"What? How would I know? I just told you I haven't so much as laid eyes on her in years. I never treated her at River Run, if that's where you're taking this, Agent Keen. I doubt you'll find anybody who will say differently."

"I don't disbelieve that," Alexa said truthfully. "But things can change."

"Maybe I should call Lucille Burch and tell her that Gary's been abducted," Casey said.

"No! The media will just make it into a sideshow!" LePointe snarled.

"They'll jump all over it," Alexa agreed. "The possibility of a Sibby Danielson connection to Gary's disappearance will be one hell of a trigger, especially since they were already looking into Sibby's whereabouts. They'd had a tip that she'd been released from River Run," she said for LePointe's benefit. "I assumed it was because it's an anniversary of the murders. I think we *should* use them to get word out on Gary."

"About time," Casey said.

LePointe's worried eyes shifted back and forth between Alexa and his niece. Alexa was sure he was seeing the horror of film crews camped outside his high gate, the unpleasant questions, scores of investigative reporters rooting around in his business like a pack of wild pigs.

"The police report said that Kenneth Decell rescued Casey from Sibby that night," Alexa said. "Your private investigator, who conveniently was here when the postman delivered this letter."

Alexa felt Casey's eyes on her, but she kept hers on

LePointe, watching every facial tic and eye movement, every gesture.

"Is that some sort of accusation?" LePointe demanded. Clearly Dr. LePointe was a stranger to being accused of anything. "He helps me and the trusts with a variety of matters, and he has been searching for Gary West too. And yes, Sibhon injured him, so perhaps I have felt some degree of responsibility toward him. But he is a good and thorough investigator."

"I'm not accusing anybody of anything, *yet*. I'm just stating what I believe to be the facts, and wondering how things may be connected."

LePointe's eyes shifted as his mind glimpsed solid ground and stepped toward it. "Do I need to remind you that you are a guest, invited in by us, a consultant who is supposed to help *us* find Gary?"

"I am an FBI agent trying to assist the local authorities in finding Gary West, and in the course of that investigation I have uncovered information that may figure into the disappearance of Mr. West."

"And how was it that you ended up at River Run interviewing Dr. Whitfield about Sibhon Danielson?"

Alexa pounced. "I didn't say that I had been at River Run or mention that I spoke to anyone there. How did you know that?"

Dr. LePointe's silence was deafening, so she went on.

"The media asked for the official police files pertaining to the homicides, which Detective Manseur pulled to see if there was something there that might be helpful. I thought the media investigating a rumor that Sibby Danielson had been released was too coincidental. I accompanied Detective Manseur to River Run. Nurse Fugate's name came up, and I discovered, in the course of trying to contact her to discuss Sibhon, that Nurse Fugate had been murdered and that in all likelihood Ms. Danielson had been staying in her home. All that I've been trying to do since early this morning is to find Mr. West, and I intend to do exactly that. Unfortunately, this letter's appearance and your pronouncement of its authenticity to Jackson Evans has cost us precious time. As of now, it appears to me that you may be trying to mislead the authorities and impede their investigation. Now I'm going to kick this into high gear, no matter how the media chooses to deal with it. It appears it may open some personal and professional unpleasantness for you, which I can honestly say doesn't bother me."

"There's a great deal at stake," LePointe said. "A very great deal. The foundations' reputations are paramount. If we are careful about what we say publicly, no—"

"I don't care about that!" Casey snapped. "I don't care about what anybody says or thinks, and why you do is a mystery. All anybody gives a flip about is how much money they can get from you. They couldn't care less about our illustrious reputation. Damn you! I'll give away every penny I own to anybody who will give Gary back to me. If he isn't back today, I'm going to drop to my knees and beg on television. And if he doesn't come home, I'll spend every cent I have to find those responsible and see them punished."

"If Gary can be found, he will be," Alexa said.

"Casey, show some backbone!" LePointe growled. "You will not do any such thing. You will not let anyone see you begging!"

Casey pointed her finger at her uncle. "I never

realized what a horrible and disgusting person you truly are. I wish to God I could hate you. If I find out you or Decell had anything to do with Gary . . . I'll see you in prison." That said, she rushed from the room.

After collecting the envelopes containing the evidence, Alexa followed Casey, who had taken Deana from the maid and was striding for the front door, while her uncle's booming voice—ordering her to come back this very moment—rang hollowly through the house.

41

The name his mother gave him was Elvis Cash Orbison Brown, but nobody had called him that since he was a kid, and so he thought of himself, as everybody else did, as Grub. He wasn't sure how old he was, but he reckoned it at nineteen or twenty years, give or take. He knew his birthday was in the winter, and since it could be Thanksgiving, he had decided on that day. Someone asked him for the exact day he was born, because they said Thanksgiving was always on the third Thursday in November. Grub was still trying to figure out why they'd laughed at him, though he believed it had something to do with him having his birthday on a big holiday.

By the time his mother passed—dying from a cottonmouth bite that she got while walking home along the bayou late one night from the Big Time Tavern—Grub had already been working odd jobs around Moody's Bait & Gas a good while, to earn the pocket change that his mother had taken from him as soon as he got home. Well, she stopped that when she died. He wasn't glad she died, because he'd liked the way she cooked for him and stuff, but it was the first opportunity he'd had to keep what he earned.

Once she had told him that she'd give him a dollar if he could jump over his own shadow, and when the men in the store had laughed at him about the Thanksgiving birth date, he had told them that very thing. It silenced them and they didn't laugh at him for a while. And Grub wondered if any of the men at the store could jump over their own shadows, because he had tried and tried till he was winded, but it was too hard. He could only jump all around it, so he'd given up.

He hadn't gone to school long because of how the other children held their noses and laughed at him and the teachers decided he wasn't able to learn the stupid crap they wanted to teach him. Even though they'd acted like they liked him, he'd known the teachers didn't. His mama didn't care one way or the other, but the few times she'd read the notes they'd sent home pinned to his clothes, she'd gone to the school drunk and raised almighty hell with them. After the last visit, they stopped talking to him, much less pinning notes on his shirt. His mama was most happy walking back and forth from the bar along Bayou Berant where she'd spent her time.

Although he wasn't book smart, Grub knew enough to hide when he saw Leland Ticholet pulling up to the dock. Leland didn't just get mad at you and forget it later. Leland had never given Grub any money, because he didn't look for help from anybody, and you didn't want to talk to him unless he talked to you first. Grub had broken that rule that morning trying to be friendly and make conversation, but it had gone wrong because Leland was a mean shit-head and he had given Grub offense. Leland didn't want any friends and, the way he acted, he wasn't about to get any either.

Grub knew what Mr. Moody had told the game wardens a few days back was a big lie. He'd told them that he didn't know if Leland sold alligators, and nobody with good sense wanted to know bad enough to go near Leland's camp. Mr. Moody told them nobody he was aware of bought alligator meat or skins, but Grub knew Moody bought them—not only from Leland, but off of lots of other people, too, only not at the store. He did that at a shack he used for alligator business.

Leland stole things, and people didn't like it. In these parts a man with more smarts than a tire tool didn't go near another man's traps—nets, crab traps, the floating jugs that marked trotlines, or muskrat or nutria traps. Stealing from the residents out in the swamps was suicidal, unless you were Leland Ticholet. If people knew Leland stole from them, they didn't say it to him.

Grub wondered if the wardens knew what sort of crazy bastard they were messing around with asking after Leland. Grub didn't like Leland, but he didn't like the wardens even more.

Leland didn't have friends, but a week earlier, when he'd come over for some gas, which the new boat used a great deal of, he'd had with him a little soft-handed stranger who was wearing a shirt with the collar turned up like it was cold and a big straw hat with a wide brim and he'd had on sunglasses. Moody wondered if he was a fisherman Leland was guiding, which was what Leland claimed, but Grub didn't see any fishing pole rigs or bait either. The man acted like he might be a movie star trying not to be recognized. One time they had filmed part of a movie around the dock, and Grub heard that some of the actors were famous, but he didn't know much about movies or the people that were in them. They all wore odd hats and sunglasses and talked funny. Grub didn't watch television or go to movies because he couldn't sit still long unless there was a lot of shooting and chasing, and he tended to lose track of what they were all about.

Grub lived in a surplus school bus that Mr. Moody parked in the trees near the bait and gas store, for free so long as he did chores for his keep. Grub got to eat the sandwiches that Mrs. Moody made that didn't get sold. People in the boats sometimes gave him money for helping load and unload their boats. He also cleaned fish for a dime each. He kept all his money in coffee jars that he hid in really good places so nobody could steal them.

That new boat was a puzzle that nobody could figure out. Nobody knew where Leland got the boat from, and nobody dared to ask him anything they could help not to, because he might get crazy and growl in your face, throw you in the water, or break something. Mr. Moody said it was likely he stole it, because there wasn't any way he'd scraped up enough in one piece to get it, and nobody in their right mind would finance a maniac like Leland Ticholet even if God Himself consigned the loan. Mr. Moody allowed as how God had better sense than to do something so stupid as that.

That morning, Grub watched Leland come racing in, pull up to the pier, tie the boat, jump up, get the pump handle, pull it to the gas tanks, and squat down while the tanks filled up. When Leland was done, he put the pump handle back, ran in, and paid Mr. Moody by signing his book for it, which went against what Mr. Moody owed him for the gator hides he didn't actually buy—just traded goods for them.

Grub waited until Leland was inside the store before he ran up the dock to the boat and looked inside it. There was something big wrapped up in a bed-sheet. Grub figured it was a person, on account of the shoes sticking out at one end. It appeared to Grub that the sheet was moving, that whoever it was wrapped up in there was alive. If he'd had time he would have poked the bundle with something to see if it moved, but if Leland was to catch him poking at his sheet deal, he might get crazy.

Grub had quickly jumped up onto the graveled lot above the dock, scampered back to the store, and hidden behind the live-bait well. Leland came back out with a loaf of white bread under his arm and a cola in his hand, and pretty soon he was eating a handful of bread, and was hauling ass away from the dock at full speed, no matter the signs said NO WAKE. Leland wasn't big on minding signs—if he could even read them, which Grub doubted he could.

Grub figured that the little movie star with the sunglasses and the straw hat was likely who was rolled up in the sheet. Grub considered mentioning the man in the sheet to Moody, but the store owner didn't care about what people did as long as they didn't do things that could make trouble for him. Plus, if Leland was to find out that Grub was telling his business, like wrapping up people in things and driving them around the swamps, it might end up being him that was rolled up and lying in the bottom of that fancy new boat.

Grub couldn't swim, and didn't want to have to learn all the sudden either.

42

Alexa followed Casey West's Range Rover, glancing down to find Manseur's number in her phone's directory and press the button to dial him. He answered immediately.

"Yeah, Alexa."

"Michael, the West letter is a fraud, so the hunt for Gary West is back on. I think LePointe or Decell authored it."

"You sure?"

"Casey said Gary writes everything out by hand and it isn't in his voice at all and he wouldn't send it to LePointe because he hates him. I have the letter with me. We won't find West's prints on it, but it gave me an opportunity to get LePointe's print for reference, and I'm on the way to get some of Gary's things."

"Why would the doctor try something so transparent?"

"Desperation," Alexa said. "We're ripping his world apart and he can't do anything about it."

"Where are you now?"

"I'm following Casey to her house for Gary's fingerprints. I'll see you at HQ in half an hour or so. You'll be there?"

"Where else would I be? The mayor's got the press assembling and he's going to get the cops to go door to door to enforce the order. They're going to pull every available cop off whatever else they're working on."

"If I didn't know better, I'd think LePointe had something to do with the hurricane's timing."

"I wouldn't bet any of my money he didn't," Manseur said.

43

Casey sat at the dining table where Alexa had first met her, crying. Grace Smythe, who had finished seeing after her parents' packing, had been there when they'd come in and had taken Deana out in the backyard and was playing with her, which amounted to making sure the child didn't jump into the pool.

"I never thought Uncle William could be so horrible. It makes me wonder if he's behind Gary's disappearance, and that letter is supposed to give Decell the time he needs to get everything cleaned up so nobody can prove anything. Is that possible? Kenneth Decell knows how to cover things up. You're never going to find Gary," Casey sobbed. "Unko knew Dorothy Fugate *very* well. Very, very well. Boy, did he know her well!"

"How do you know that?"

"Because I saw him with her. Once, seven, eight years ago when my grandmother and Aunt Sarah were away in New York and I was supposed to be staying with a girlfriend, I came back home to get something. The servants were all off that day. I used my key, and as I was passing his office—the door was cracked open—Dorothy was bent over on his desk naked except for the nurse hat and he was behind her. His pants were down and he was standing there—you know." Casey smiled. "She was chanting." Casey laughed suddenly. "I can't say it. It's too vulgar."

"Go ahead," Alexa said. "We're adults."

" 'Oh, Dr. Fuckerman! Oh, Docky Big Dick! Oh, pour it to me, Dr. Fuckerman! Dr. Fuckerman. How distinguished!' "

Alexa didn't mean to, but she laughed too.

" 'Oh . . . Docky Dick! Pour . . . it . . . to me! Heeeere I come again, Dr. Fuckerman!' And Unko's bare buns and those socks being held up with those garters and his shoes on. Shirt and tie in place! It was like a . . . a Monty Python skit."

Casey leaned back and laughed harder. Soon, they were both laughing.

"He and Dorothy carried on for years. My aunt Sarah and grandmother knew it and they ignored it the way someone knows their adult child is sneaking a cigarette and they don't mention it. Aunt Sarah was never in love with my uncle. I'm not sure she liked him much or had any respect for him. She stayed gone from our house more than she was there, and Uncle William didn't care."

Casey used the word *house* instead of *home*, Alexa noted.

"As long as Aunt Sarah was in town for the right social events, he couldn't have cared less. The universe revolves around Uncle William."

"Narcissistic personality," Alexa said.

"That's what Gary says," Casey told her. "He told me that Uncle William didn't love me because he didn't know how. Maybe it's true. He's always been so rigid. He sees everything in strict terms of how it will affect him, or the family's reputation.

"He's always thought I'm too soft to take an active part in the family trusts. Since I was very young, he's pecked at my self-esteem instead of building it, and berated me for being emotional and weak. He gives me a compliment and it's a barely concealed dig. He's passive-aggressive, like my grandmother was. My grandmother would say, 'I like your hair short, Casey. It will look so much better when you've lost a few pounds.'

"I don't really remember my parents, but I know they were always holding me, kissing me. I think I can remember their laughter. Grandmother never laughed. Aunt Sarah used to laugh at the dinner table, and Uncle William and my grandmother would scowl at her like she'd passed gas. It was hell growing up in that hideous mausoleum. I know my parents' house wasn't like that. Do you know what it's like to grow up unloved and unappreciated?"

"He seemed very protective and complimentary about your work last night," Alexa said, purposely not answering Casey's question.

"Only because Detective Kennedy called my work snapshots. Unko has called my photography a lot worse things, though. Grandmother said photography was a common pursuit. She wanted me to paint or sculpt as a hobby. 'Why would you want to take pictures when you can hire a professional,' she said. Had I funded a photographic center for underprivileged children, or something that made the family look as though it cared about the poor, that would have been okay. When I started getting outside attention, praise from their social equals, and publicity in the right magazines, it became somewhat bearable. Of course, being a LePointe helped get the right sort of people interested in my work. The right curators, critics, gallery owners, corporate and museum collections . . ."

"Your work is remarkable," Alexa said. "I've seen enough to know that who you are is irrelevant to the work. The accolades are well deserved."

Casey smiled. "That's very kind of you."

"It may be kind, but it's also the truth."

"You grew up unloved," Casey said, studying her. "Neglected."

Alexa looked out at Deana, who was tugging flowers from their stems while Grace looked on passively.

"What makes you think that?" Alexa said. The denial she wanted to convey sounded false to her.

"Alexa, even a cat that's been raised since birth by a dog knows another cat when he sees one. I've felt it since the moment we met. Maybe that's why I know I can trust you. I'm sorry if I've overstepped. Your personal life is none of my business. This is all professional with you, and I understand that."

Alexa knew exactly what it felt like to be unloved and beaten down by passive-aggressive people. But the emotional pain from her past wasn't something she could share with Casey West. She had always told herself that her history never adversely affected or interfered with her job. The idea that this woman and she had something that basic in common had no bearing on the job at hand. Alexa's empathy, while powerful, was irrelevant. Casey must see her only as a professional.

Alexa looked out again and caught Grace Smythe staring in at her from the garden. The assistant averted her gaze immediately. She suspected that Grace wasn't accustomed to being out of Casey's loop, and Alexa was sure she resented it.

"Forgive my prying?" Casey asked.

"It's okay," Alexa said. "No childhood is perfect."

"Please, Alexa. I want to know all about you. You probably know more about me than most people I've known for years."

Alexa didn't want Casey's pity, but she thought it might help Casey to know she wasn't as alone as she felt. "My parents were addicts and low-level criminals feeding their habits. My father was killed by a store owner he was robbing. My mother died of an overdose when I was five. My little sister and I had no relatives, at least none that wanted to deal with two small children from a mixed-race relationship between two thieving junkies.

"We were split up and put into the foster system. We both acted out, so we were shuffled around a lot. When I was thirteen, this wonderful woman and her husband gave me a home, and when I asked, they brought my sister there and adopted us both. After that, life was easier. They were poor, but for the first time I felt loved and appreciated. Those people—and a very special young man who came into my life when I was fifteen—undid most of the emotional damage I sustained, by loving me unconditionally. I was unlucky for thirteen years, but lucky just the same. The way I see it, because of what my life was, I'm better able to relate to other people going through painful experiences."

"Are you and your sister close?"

"We stay in touch. I get postcards from her from all over the place."

Smiling warmly, Casey gripped Alexa's hands in hers. "When I found Gary, I felt truly loved and valuable as a human being for the first time in my life. I mean, after my parents were killed. I never felt loved between the time I lived here with them and here with Gary and Deana."

"Beg your pardon? You mean in different houses."

Casey looked at Alexa, perplexed. "Alexa, this was their house, my house," she said. "My mother owned it. She refused to live in the big house with my grandmother like William and Sarah did. It stayed vacant, except for a caretaker, until I was old enough to move back in. The estate kept it up so it wouldn't lose value, and it was mine when I reached twenty-one. Unko and Sarah didn't think it was a good idea for me to move back in, but it was the only place I'd ever been happy and felt loved. And it's still the place where I am happiest and loved best." She smiled warmly at Alexa. "As soon as you find Gary, it will be perfect again. You'll really like Gary."

Alexa didn't know what to say. She was stunned that she and Casey were sitting in a twenty-six-year-old crime scene—maybe unaltered except for the removal of the mutilated bodies and a professional cleaning.

44

When his cell phone rang, Kenneth Decell was seated
in an office at a bank, closed on Saturday afternoons
to all but the most important customers, watching
the distinguished-looking man across the room carefully count the bearer bonds he'd just placed on the
conference table. Decell frowned when he saw the
name on the phone's caller ID.

"Decell," he said.

"Kenneth," Dr. LePointe said, sounding exhausted.
"Jesus Christ."

"What is it?"

"I need you here now. I . . . well, truth is . . . I
don't know . . . Truth is, this is all getting out of
hand. Keen was here and she got Casey upset by
telling her some things. Keen's a problem."

"I'll be there as soon as I can get out of the bank,"
he said. "I'm picking up your paper now. Relax. You
have nothing to worry about." *So much for playing all
the chess matches at the same time,* Decell thought.

"Good. Kenneth, I don't know what I'd do without you. I depend on your expertise, loyalty, and discretion. Thank you."

"My pleasure." Decell closed the phone and smiled.
I know where you'd be without me. And so do you.

After the banker had finished placing the counted
bonds in the valise, he locked it, placed LePointe's
key on the table beside it, and stepped back, folding
his hands so they covered his sex, posing like a morti-
cian beside an open casket.

"Two and one-half million in ten-thousand-dollar

denominations is the confirmed count," the banker said, opening his fountain pen and placing it beside a document.

Decell crossed the room and lifted the valise.

"Please sign the receipt, Mr. Decell."

Decell looked at the document and shook his head. "Dr. LePointe authorized it, didn't he?"

"Yes," the banker said nervously. "He did. Over the phone."

"Are you satisfied that the man on the phone was Dr. LePointe?"

"I've known William since grade school," the banker replied. "It was he."

"And they're his bonds to do with as he sees fit, right?"

The banker nodded.

"Then you can ask him to sign."

"But I'm turning them over to you—"

"He said to, right?"

"Yes. But you are taking possession."

"Okay. Hit REDIAL on my phone, or call him yourself and tell him he'll have to come sign the receipt. I'm not going to put my name on any piece of official paper."

"Why?"

"Well, for one thing, I can't possibly repay it if anything happens to it. If the FBI comes to you, you'll tumble to the badges and show the receipt to them, and they'll come to me and I'll have to account for it by explaining why I picked it up and what I did with it, which would be problematic. I doubt Dr. LePointe would like having his private business thrown back in his face by the authorities. Dr. LePointe is a major depositor and his family the major stockholder in this institution. You want to go against his wishes, be my guest. Maybe nothing will happen, but maybe the board of directors will suddenly decide this institution could use some fresh blood in your position. Dr. LePointe is under a great deal of stress, and where his family is involved . . ." Decell shrugged. "I'll just leave the bonds here and you can explain it to him. Maybe he'll just get in his car and come get them himself and sign your paper and have no ill feelings about it."

"Take them." The banker wiped the beads of perspiration from his upper lip with a handkerchief he pulled from his suit pocket. "Do you need an escort?"

"I don't," Decell said, patting the gun in his shoulder holster. He lifted the valise and walked casually from the office.

45

The mayor of New Orleans and the governor were making another one of the many announcements that Alexa had heard earlier during the day. *"I have ordered the police to close off inbound traffic to New Orleans. As of four o'clock, all lanes of state roads are designated as outbound lanes only. We are opening the Superdome as an emergency shelter for residents who cannot leave the city. I have directed that city transit buses will carry residents to the shelter. Residents are directed to immediately evacuate Orleans, Jefferson, and St. Bernard parishes, in an orderly manner. Again, I want to stress that this is a mandatory evacuation and all residents in the affected areas must leave or they will be forcibly removed from their property by law enforcement officers."*

Alexa switched off the radio. She could use her identification to go where she needed to. Grace Smythe kept invading her thoughts as she drove to meet Manseur in his office. She would have sent the supposed West letter to the FBI labs, but she didn't want to lose the time it would take to courier a package to D.C. on the next flight out. She gave it to Manseur when she walked in, along with the envelopes containing her Glock magazines and some articles of Gary West's Casey had given to Alexa for collection.

"Tell your lab to hurry it up. We need to check for prints on the West letter. They'll probably find Casey West's, William LePointe's, and Kenneth Decell's. I seriously doubt you'll find Gary West's on either *his* envelope or the letter."

"What about the letter carrier? Whoever picks up the mail and gives it to LePointe?"

"The envelope has a crack-and-peel stamp and a peel-and-stick flap, so forget DNA. And to answer your question, there's no mailman, because there's no cancellation mark."

"So whoever came up with this brilliant subterfuge didn't actually bother to mail it."

Alexa nodded. "Decell maybe, on LePointe's behalf. He told me Kenneth Decell had read it."

"Not Decell's work," Manseur disagreed. "He was too good a detective. He would have either mailed it or had LePointe say the letter was delivered to the gate by courier. I suspect LePointe just showed it to Decell,

ho didn't bother to look at the envelope, or doubted
nyone would ask LePointe for the letter."

"Know what I think?" Alexa asked.

"No man ever knows what a woman is thinking."

Alexa smiled. "This letter was supposed to be mis-
irection, which opens an interesting avenue."

"I'm listening," Manseur said.

"I'm wondering if he knew that by the time any-
ne started snooping, it wouldn't matter."

"Because the hurricane would destroy evidence?"

"No. Because he knew that Gary West was going
o be home before that. The letter might be an im-
romptu ruse designed just to get Evans to call us off."

"So we didn't find out about Sibby?"

"No. What if Gary's abductor contacted LePointe,
nd he's going to pay a ransom to get Gary West back
afely? Doesn't want us in the way. How he accom-
lishes getting Gary back—whatever deception or
use he employs—becomes irrelevant then because
verybody's happy and Gary's back and nobody is
;oing to look too closely at anything else. So Sibby
tays hidden, which has been undone, but he
vouldn't have known that would happen at the time
e was pulling the plan together."

"Makes sense," Manseur said.

"Although I can't prove it yet, Sibby's vanishing act
rom the hospital, Gary's abduction, and the Fugate
nurder are directly related," Alexa said. "The tipping
of the press at this moment is too coincidental. The
ame people are behind the grab and tipping the press
o Sibby's exit from River Run. I have a feeling that
hey knew about Sibby before they grabbed Gary, and
hey may have killed Fugate and framed Sibby. Maybe

she didn't leave earlier because she hadn't done any
thing—didn't know Dorothy was in the basement."

"That's a stretch. I mean, it might be true, bu
there's nothing to support it but your hunch. And th
press might have been snooping on their own."

Alexa nodded. "LePointe and Fugate were muc
more than coworkers. It's just my gut talking, but
think that not only did LePointe know Sibby was a
Fugate's, but he knew Fugate was dead, and was onl
surprised that I brought it up. I'd bet his and Fugate
phone records will tie him to her."

"He'll have plausible denial. You may well be righ
about the ransom," Manseur said. "It would explai
one thing."

"What?"

"Why Kenneth Decell arrived at his office tw
hours ago, picked up a briefcase, and then went to
bank. He left the bank twenty minutes ago carryin
said valise and proceeded directly to Dr. LePointe'
house, arriving there twenty minutes after you an
Casey West left."

"How do you know that?"

"Because my old partner Larry Bond staked ou
Decell's office."

"Your partner's working on this case?" Alex
asked.

"My *former* partner. We worked together for si
years."

"You failed to mention to me that you brough
him in," Alexa said.

"I just told you."

"I'm not always good with time lines, but you

mean to tell me your *ex*-partner wasn't already watching Decell's house when we were at River Run?"

. "You think I'd keep information from you on purpose? I didn't think it was important, I guess. I didn't know for sure how Decell was involved."

"Gosh, Michael, I sure hope not. If I thought I couldn't trust you, I'd be really upset. You *are* the one who pulled me into this mess," she said, anger rising.

"Casey West did that," he protested.

"If I hadn't been in Casey West's kitchen, she would never have asked for me. Who was it that woke me in the middle of the night, and placed me there?"

"Not like you were asleep."

"Is this about who gets the credit?"

"No! Look, I wanted to compile more before we had a meeting to assimilate our separate findings and make a plan for bringing this to a *joint* close. Sometimes I play things close to the chest. Habit. I'm sorry."

"Okay," Alexa said. "Clean slate. So what have you compiled so far from Fugate's?"

46

Leland's mouth was packed with a large wad of Juicy Fruit and he was humming a song his daddy used to sing all the time. Something about me ho my toe down the bayou. Leland's boat pulled the wardens' piece of crap flat-bottom easily. Leland's father had said his son had eyes like razor blades. That morning when he was leaving to check lines and get gas, he had spotted the tree camera because the sun made the

thing cast a shadow where he'd never seen one. H
had searched the bank and found the place where
boat's hull had pressed reeds down and left the im
pression of its bow in the mud, so he followed th
boot prints across the peninsula to the suspect tre
and looked at the camera from the side.

He had known that whoever had put it there woul
come back for it, and when they did, he'd make sur
they paid for invading his place and spying on him. H
remembered now that he had spotted the game war
dens several times in the past two weeks, far more of
ten than he usually saw wardens. One had been th
bastard whose name was something that sounded lik
pump handle. The bastard had ticketed Leland mor
than a few times over the years, so he knew him.

Nobody liked them wardens.

Nobody would miss them.

Even if one was a woman.

He had never made a woman disappear before.

Their boat was aluminum.

Leland truly loved his boat's shallow-draft fiber
glass hull, but he was suspicious that Doc was going
to try to pull a take-back deal. Doc had told Leland
not to tell anybody he owned the boat or where he'd
gotten it. He couldn't see why he should tell a lie
about it, so he'd told Moody it was his on account he
did a job to get it. Leland didn't like liars. Well, you
could lie to wardens, because they were sneaky bas
tards that thought they owned the birds, the fish, and
everything else God put around the world.

Most people couldn't be trusted to do what they
said. They'd say they just wanted to talk to you, then

hey'd handcuff you, lock you up, and stick needles in
ou and say you were crazy.

Leland knew that he was only safe from being
monitored deep in the swamp, because *they* wouldn't
ever dare come in here. He had fixed it so if they ever
did somehow track him to his cabin, they'd never get
a chance to tell any of the others about it.

The boat was his because he had done everything
Doc and the woman with the dark hair told him he
had to do for it. If they kept adding things onto the
list as long as they felt like it, Leland would have no
choice but to fix them both good.

Every time Leland turned around and finished one
thing, they had this next thing that needed to be
done, and Doc went on about how they only trusted
Leland to do it right, and how much the boat was
worth, like he wasn't close to being even.

Doc said an FBI lady was fixing to make trouble,
and what they might need to do about that, which
meant what Leland might need to do. Doc said she
could put Leland back in the hospital for keeps.
Okay, if the FBI lady really had a mind to put Leland
back in there and let them bastards shoot electricity
into his head and all that, he'd knock her in the head.
If need be, he would.

Well, maybe he could do one or two more things.
It was a nice boat.

47

Grace Smythe unlocked her door and entered carrying packages containing clothes and things she'd been needing. She was surprised to see a paper bag and a bottle of wine and a glass on her kitchen table. Inside the sack were several stacks of new currency.

Grace smiled. She had expected the money, but the wine was unexpected lagniappe—a little something extra.

She picked up the stacks of new one-hundred dollar bills. It would be fifty thousand dollars—traveling money.

She went into the bedroom and dropped the bag she'd brought in, as well as the sack of cash. She rushed into the bathroom and started hot water running into the tub.

Back in the kitchen, she opened the wine. Grace took the bottle and the glass with her to the bathroom, where she tested the water. The way to appreciate a good vintage was to open your pores with hot water, and sip the wine slowly, savoring the fragrance, the richness, the variety of flavors.

She poured herself a glass and took a test sip. She rested the glass on the side of the tub, and scooted the bottle to the floor so she wouldn't knock it over accidentally. You didn't waste wine this good. Not this special a Burgundy.

Lowering her pants and sitting on the toilet, she sighed as relief swept through her like a warm wave. After she finished, Grace stepped out of her slacks and underpants and removed her blouse and bra. Standing aked before the door mirror, she admired her body or several long seconds, turning first one way and hen the other, trying to see her buttocks. She could tand to lose a few ounces, perhaps pounds, and nches here and there.

She put in her blue contacts, removed her wig, took ut the hairpins, and shook out her bleached blond hair, vhich reached almost to her shoulders. Using her finger- ails, she scraped the gold studs from her ear. Using cot- on and polish remover, she rubbed the glue residue that eld them on, and slipped on a pair of dark-framed eye- lasses. *You are not Grace Smythe anymore. After onight, Grace Smythe is no longer.*

She turned again to look at herself in the mirror, nd smiled. She looked, if not just like Casey, like her ctual sister. They had always been sisters. Thinking bout Casey made her feel giddy, and she blushed. he hugged herself, closed her eyes, and imagined she vas in Casey's embrace, feeling Casey's beautiful ody against hers, their tongues entwined.

Soon it would all be over, and Casey would be ers alone. Grace understood, far better than Casey, hat Gary had never belonged in their world. He said e loved Casey, but he could never love her like Grace lid. He said he loved Deana, but, despite what he aid, Deana was more Grace's daughter than his. The act that he had given his sperm didn't mean any- hing. There were laboratories that did that without he complications a man brought to a situation. And he lily-hearted asshole had been going to give wenty-five million of Casey's money to a bunch of Africans for drugs and food, and who gives a shit if hey die like they're supposed to anyway.

Grace had taken care of Gary—taken the bull b
the horns. Now, after tonight, Gary would be n
more. Casey would understand once and for all tha
it was Grace alone who loved her—only Grace wh
cared about the real Casey LePointe. Darling Case
the girl whom Grace had been with until she was
woman—a woman who had given her heart to Grac
as children, who had shared all of her pain, insecur
ties, and her sadness with Grace alone.

Gary West didn't know the real Casey, the chil
who had cried on Grace's shoulder a thousand times
and who had professed her undying forever love fo
Grace when they were both mere children. Case
hadn't said it since, but Grace knew it was still tru
No matter what Casey told Gary, she had never love
him. She had only ever loved Grace.

She wet her index finger and massaged hersel
slowly, imagining it was Casey's wet tongue. Soon i
would be more than an imaginary Casey who wa
making love to her. Soon they would be lying to
gether in Casey's large bed, exploring each other'
bodies while listening for Deana's waking cries. I
would be Grace who made Casey forget she'd eve
slept with any man, and Deana that she had ever ha
a father.

She had enough money, both to get to Spain to wai
for the firestorm to go away and for her to become an
other person. She would have reconstructive surgery t
give her a new and sculpted face worthy of Casey
LePointe, have those additional ounces removed, he
buttocks lifted, and wait patiently in Madrid for Casey'
grieving period to end. Then she would be—in a fa

nore acceptable and worthy form—the woman Casey
leserved.

After the bath was drawn, Grace closed the door
and eased slowly, inch by inch, into the hot water. She
reached out and lifted the wine bottle to pour more
into the glass, leaning back so she could see the picture of Casey and herself as teenagers that hung on
the wall over the toilet.

The past weeks had been difficult. Watching Gary,
knowing he was thinking he was about to be a very
wealthy man. Whether he admitted it or not, the
money would have changed him. And it wasn't his
money, it was Casey's and hers. Yes, it had been hard,
but, as her father always said, nothing worthwhile
was easy.

Grace held her glass up to Casey's beautiful face,
toasted the future, and the death of Gary West.

48

"The bloody print from the cigar box was too smudged
to be worth much, but there are three points that could
be used to compare for a match if we have a set to compare to. Not enough to hold up in court, but evidence is
cumulative. The blood type is RH negative, which is a
match to our nurse," Manseur said.

"Any personal papers?" Alexa said.

"All we found were household bills. No Christmas
cards, no letters from friends or family. No computer
for e-mails. Just the pictures you saw. Looks like she
didn't have much of a life outside her work."

"She took her work home. I think her house was sanitized," Alexa added. "Somebody went through and removed things that would lead us somewhere."

"Maybe the perps? I imagine there is more than one person involved."

"Makes sense. Or maybe it wasn't Sibby at the house today. Maybe one of them returned today to make sure the place was really clean—that they hadn't left anything to tie them to the house. They weren't expecting me to show up. When I called just before I went inside, the answering machine picked up, and they knew time was short, and they were already at work. The machine was taping when I called, so the message tape was in the machine then. When I was in the kitchen, the tapes had been removed."

"Doesn't seem like something Sibby would do," Manseur said.

"She might have taken the pill bottles on the bed, but I don't think so."

"Those only tied LePointe to Fugate. You think he did it?"

"I'm sure LePointe knew I had been to Fugate's before I told him. He knew we'd been at the hospital. Maybe Malouf told Decell after she thought it over."

"She could have decided to play both sides against the middle," Manseur said.

Alexa put her hand to her forehead.

"What's wrong?" Manseur asked.

"I just assumed Sibby was in Fugate's house. Whoever was in Fugate's house went out the front door. I need to go back there," Alexa said. "The house across the street. Someone was looking out at me when I drove up. Maybe they saw who went out."

Manseur picked up the phone and dialed a number. "Manseur," he said. "Who interviewed the residents in the houses across the street?"

He listened. "Let me speak to him."

"Jimmy Alexander did the canvass," he told Alexa. "Jimmy, who lives across the street from there?" Pause. "Did she see anything?" Pause. "Okay. Thanks."

Manseur hung up. "Elderly woman named Cline. She didn't see anything. She was watching her TV soaps."

"I have to go talk to her," Alexa said.

"Why?"

"She's lying," Alexa said. "But she won't admit it to your detective."

"How you know that?" Manseur asked.

"Because soaps run on weekdays. Plus I'm a woman, and so is she," she answered, scooping up her purse.

"Let me tie up a couple of things. Take me fifteen minutes—"

"Stay. Get those prints off my mags and the cigarette case going. I'll call you if I need you."

"Alexa," Manseur said. "You carry a forty, right?"

"Yes," she said.

He reached into his pocket and tossed her a full Glock magazine. "Take a spare, just in case. You never know."

"I usually don't accept personal gifts from married men," she said, winking.

49

A crime-scene van and two Crown Vics were parked on the street in front of the Fugate house. A uniformed patrolman stood on the walkway smoking a cigarette. No crowd had gathered, but a couple walking a dog craned their necks as they strolled past. Of course, most of the residents had probably already left town or were packing to do so. Alexa looked at the neighbor's house and saw the window curtain fall back into place.

Alexa was assaulted by the heat and humidity as she climbed from the Bucar. Purse over her shoulder, she approached the Cline house. She rang the bell and flashed a warm smile as she gazed through the sheer curtain behind the glass and saw a figure rapidly approaching the door.

An elderly, slightly stooped, and round-faced woman opened the door and stared at her through little reading glasses. The woman wore a rosy-cheeked smile and had a carefully trimmed helmet of white hair. The smell of cookies baking filtered out onto the porch.

"I'm FBI Special Agent Alexa Keen. Ms. Cline, is it?" Alexa held up her badge.

"Rosemary Cline."

"I'm doing follow-up interviews, Ms. Cline."

"The detective wouldn't tell me what's going on at Miss Fugate's. But I know enough to know that's a crime-scene van. If y'all don't want to tell me what's happened, that's fine. I'm sorry, dear, but I'm very busy. My son is coming to get me in two hours to take me to DeRidder for the hurricane. I've got more packing to do after the cookies are done." Rosemary Cline started to close the door.

"I noticed when I drove up earlier that you looked out the window."

"I occasionally look out my windows," Ms. Cline said. "That's the value of having them. We have a neighborhood watch."

"Did Dorothy Fugate attend watch meetings?"

"Goodness, no! She's lived in that house for over twenty years now and I've spoken to her maybe a dozen times. She isn't the outgoing type, you could say without telling a lie. She made it known as soon as she moved in that she had no interest in making friends or being involved with the neighbors. She was downright unpleasant, even for a Yankee, if you want to know the truth. Seven days a week, dressed in her uniform, going and coming at all hours. Until last year. She stopped going out in her uniform, moved in a roommate, and we all assumed she'd retired."

"Can you describe the roommate?"

Ms. Cline smirked slightly. "She has the fairest complexion you'll ever see and long gray hair. Heavyset, but not obese, by any means. I've only seen her a few times on the porch with Miss Fugate at night, getting fresh air, I suppose. Is she all right?"

"Far as we know."

"She stays inside in the daytime, but when the weather's nice she comes out at night sometimes, like I said, with Miss Fugate, and they sit on the porch swing and rock back and forth. Once I called out to them about how nice a night it was and they went inside like I'd shot at them. I don't think she's quite right. The roommate. Is that right? You know, some people thought she was, you know . . ."—she dropped her voice to a whisper—". . . a lezbin." She resumed a normal tone. "But I say, live and let live and so what if it's true, and I don't have the foggiest idea yes or no. Living alone is lonely sometimes. Especially so when you're cold to your neighbors."

You don't know the half of it. "Did you happen to see the roommate leave this morning?"

"No, I didn't. A few nights back there was an old truck parked there when I went to bed, and the next day her car was gone and hasn't been back."

"Nurse Fugate's?"

"A small black one of some sort. I don't know cars."

"Did Nurse Fugate have any company over? Any friends or relatives?"

"Nobody ever spent the night that I recall. This man with white hair used to come by at night, parked in the back of the driveway. And years ago a young man used to visit her during the summers for a few days. He was a small boy when he started coming. Stayed inside mostly. Odd-looking child. He stopped coming years ago. The last time I saw him he was high-school or college age, and he hadn't changed much. Still odd-looking. Miss Fugate never took a vacation, as far as I know. I don't know which hospital she was affiliated with."

"River Run. It's a mental facility."

"So, when can *we* know what's happened over there?" The older woman crossed her arms under her breasts as though she were suddenly chilled.

"Nurse Fugate passed away," Alexa said.

Ms. Cline shook her head sadly. "Heart attack?"

"We're not sure as to cause of death yet," Alexa replied. "We have to locate next of kin before we make any announcements."

"We get mostly heart attacks, cancers, and strokes in this neighborhood. Mrs. Childs caught her robe on fire once. She has scars all over her legs and arms, poor thing. You were to see it, you'd just cry. All that exercising she has to do, but she never complains."

"Can you remember when you last saw her?"

"Day before yesterday morning. I took her over some sugar cookies. She says I could sell them in grocery stores. I couldn't make enough to do that."

Alexa was confused. "You saw Dorothy Fugate day before yesterday morning?"

"Oh, no. I thought we were discussing Mrs. Childs. She doesn't get out much, she's eighty-one. All of her family's left the area. My son offered to take her out of here, because of the hurricane, you know. She might go, but she's stubborn."

"When was the last time you saw Ms. Fugate?"

"Maybe Sunday. It was a few days back I saw her when she was taking groceries inside. Didn't see her after that." She shook her head. "Most of us are retired. Some young people have started moving in as some started dying or going to nursing homes." Sadness crossed her eyes. "It's not a real official neighborhood watch or anything. I had my lawn mower stolen and Mr. Hamilton saw the man and called the police. That was last summer. No, the summer before. He was a black man with pants falling down so his shorts showed plain as day. The police didn't catch him, said he probably sold it and bought crack to put up his nose. I had a nephew who crushed up his father's medicines and sniffed them. The police that took the report said I probably wouldn't get the mower back and I didn't. Then Mr. Hamilton had a big hanging plant taken right off his porch in broad daylight. A plant, can you imagine that? Why would anyone steal a fern and leave two beefsteak begonias sitting right there. He collects coins. His son's a plumber, but I don't use him because he charges way too much and gets the floor dirty and doesn't clean up behind himself."

Alexa had to let Ms. Cline talk because the woman might tell her something useful, but now she interrupted since she didn't have time for the grand tour of the neighbors. "Nobody else coming or going lately?"

"Just you and the salesman this morning, and I thought how unusual it was to see visitors there in the daytime."

"Salesman?"

"I was waiting on the mailman and I looked out the window and saw the salesman going to the door. That was a little while before you got there."

"How long?"

Ms. Cline looked at Alexa as though she were an idiot. "Well, you two were inside together. He got there twenty minutes or so before you and came out after you were in there a few minutes."

"How do you know he was a salesman?"

"Because he was carrying one of those little suitcases."

"What did he look like?"

"Well, not that I was paying attention or anything, but I noticed the suitcase. He was white. He seemed tall, but I'm not sure. He might have had a sports jacket on, or not. He didn't look suspicious, so I didn't look for specifics. You had to see him in there."

"Did you see his car?" Alexa pressed.

"Come to think of it, he parked down the street. Salesmen do that, going from one house to the next. Like I said, I don't know kinds of cars, but his looked new and was gray, or silver."

"Can you remember anything else about him?"

Ms. Cline gazed at Alexa over her glasses. "I'd guess older than you. Are you sure you're an FBI agent? You're awfully young and pretty to be one." She smiled, trying to please the agent.

"Did you see his hair?"

"Red. Oh! I forgot about my cookies!"

"Thank you," Alexa began, but Ms. Cline had already locked the dead bolt and disappeared. Through the sheers she looked like a body sinking in water.

Kenneth Decell, Alexa thought. *That son of a bitch could have broken my neck.*

She strode to her car, dialing Manseur as she went.

50

Alexa parked on Broad Street and hurried toward the front of the headquarters building. She was approaching the glass front entrance when someone yelled out her name. She turned to see Veronica Malouf carrying a briefcase hugged to her chest as though it were a baby in distress and she was trying to get it to the emergency room.

"Ms. Malouf," Alexa said. "I tried to call you a few minutes ago to see what you'd come up with."

"I couldn't leave because Dr. Whitfield was closing the office early. So nonessential personnel could evacuate and I had to finish up. My phone battery was dead and I forgot my car charger, which I couldn't find when I went home for these. Sorry."

"The files I asked for?"

Veronica ignored the question. "They're the ones you want. Call if you have any questions."

Alexa took the valise and said, "If I have any questions, you're going to answer them in person. After you."

"But I need to get packed."

They rode the elevator up in silence. Manseur looked from the papers he was reading as Alexa and Veronica walked into his office. "Agent Keen. Ms. Malouf," he said.

"Veronica has something for us," Alexa said, hanging her heavy purse on a chair.

"I hope you brought us a recent picture of Sibby Danielson."

Veronica Malouf shook her head. "There isn't one. I looked."

"Let's have a look at what you do have," he said.

51

Alexa was amazed by what she read in the files, but Manseur might have been reading the phone book for all the reaction he showed. Veronica Malouf sat at the end of the conference table, looking into her lap—Marie Antoinette sitting in the ox-drawn cart being delivered to the Place de la Révolution, where a masked executioner with blood-spattered hands awaited her arrival.

"Dr. LePointe seems to have been Sibby Danielson's sole attending physician during her stay," Alexa said. "Might that not rise to the level of unethical, even in New Orleans?"

Manseur shrugged. "He lied about that."

What hasn't he lied about? Alexa thought. "This is a release form for Sibby, so she was released legally."

"She wasn't," Veronica said.

Alexa looked at her. "This is a release form for Sibby Danielson and it's signed by what I assume is an entire committee."

"Dr. LePointe's signature is on it?" Manseur asked.

"No. How do you explain that?" Alexa asked Veronica.

"They're valid signatures," Veronica said, looking nervously into Alexa's eyes, "but not on Sibby Danielson's release form."

"How do you know that?" Manseur asked.

"Because that form was somehow altered. I think one patient's name and number was removed and hers put on. That's how I think they did it."

"I can't see any alteration," Alexa said. "It appears to be an original."

"That form was delivered to Dr. LePointe by Mr. Decell," Veronica said. "He delivered it in an envelope and Dr. LePointe told me to tell him as soon as it arrived. In the fifteen minutes it took the doctor to come to the office, I opened it and looked at it."

"How do you know it was altered?"

"Because one of the psychologists who signed it hadn't worked at River Run for two years before it's dated. He died from liver cancer. I . . ." Veronica stopped.

"Go on," Alexa said.

"I think it might have been sort of illegal for me to do what I did with the files."

"Go on."

"Taking them and, you know, bringing them here. They're hospital property and there's privilege. . . ."

Alexa thought for a moment. Then she said, "The main problem with them is that misappropriated files can't be introduced as evidence in a court of law."

"So they can't be used against Dr. LePointe?" Veronica asked, a little frantically. "And what about me? Not because of the privileged content, but because I took them."

Alexa looked at Manseur, then back at Veronica. "If you tell the absolute truth, there will be no legal repercussions from either Detective Manseur or myself. It will end here." Alexa certainly didn't want anybody knowing she'd intimidated a state employee into stealing confidential hospital files on a hunch.

Manseur nodded for Veronica's benefit. The truth was that the police can lie to suspects with complete impunity. "Just level with us."

Then Alexa saw it clearly. "You had these before we came to the hospital!"

Veronica sat frozen for a few beats, and then nodded once.

"It's time to come clean, Veronica," Manseur told the young woman. "We're not going to judge you. We need to know everything you can tell us. If you're afraid that your motives or intentions might paint you in a less than favorable light, don't sweat it. Let's just get the whole story out in the open."

"We're not interested in when you took them. A man's life may be on the line," Alexa said.

"Whose?" Veronica asked.

"Gary West's," Alexa told her. "He was abducted yesterday."

"You think Dr. LePointe had something to do with it?" Veronica asked, alarmed. "That Mr. West could be dead?"

Alexa shook her head.

"He *might* be dead?" Veronica asked, fear in her pale eyes. "I won't testify against Dr. LePointe or Mr. Decell. You better know that. I don't know anything about any abduction. If Mr. Decell killed him, he could kill me."

"Do you know Mr. West?"

"He came by the hospital a few times with Casey, Dr. LePointe's niece. LePointe talked about him like he was a horrible person, but he wasn't. He'd ask about a person and he was asking because he wanted to know and not just to be polite. He was good-looking, but it was like he didn't know it, or think he was better because he had money. He wrote plays, but I doubt they were as bad as Dr. LePointe said, though I never saw one. Casey is the same way, and she's also a big-deal photographer. Her assistant is a bitch, always throwing her weight around, acting like she's all that, when she just works for Casey West.

She always goes, 'Mrs. LePointe-West wants this,' or 'Mrs. LePointe-West wants that.' "

Alexa said, "That's good. Just tell us what you know about Danielson, Dr. LePointe, and Fugate."

52

Veronica Malouf told Alexa and Manseur that she knew someday the files could be crucial in establishing the truth about Dr. William LePointe and his reign over the patients and staff at River Run. She claimed she'd taken the files home with her months before in the hope that she could someday bring the whole stinking story into the cleansing spotlight of authoritative scrutiny. Veronica told Manseur and Alexa that she began watching and listening soon after she started working for Dr. LePointe as his executive assistant, which Alexa translated to mean poorly paid state employee who worked for one of the wealthiest men in America not named Gates, Buffet, or Walton.

"Dr. LePointe was difficult to work for. I never knew which Dr. LePointe would be my boss. He could be the mean arrogant ass, or he could be the sweetest thing, going out of to be thoughtful and helpful to me," she said. "And he could change from one into the other several times a day sometimes. I'm not saying he used drugs or anything like that, but it sure would explain some one-eighties he subjected me to."

Alexa nodded, content to let Veronica run on to fill the silence while she read through the files.

"About four years ago, Dr. LePointe called from outside and asked me to get a file from his personal file cabinet and read him something. He told me where the key was. I was putting the files back and opened the wrong drawer by accident and I saw her name on all these files. Well, you can just imagine that caused alarm bells to go off in my head. Sibby freaking Danielson! At that point I didn't even know she was there. Not many people did." Veronica sipped water from a bottle she had brought with her. "See, I figured that I might find myself with some legal complications, you know, down the road, so I decided to photocopy the files when the doctor wasn't in the office, which was pretty often."

"To protect yourself if any sort of charges were ever leveled," Manseur said, sympathetically.

"You had a key to his personal files?" Alexa asked.

"Not exactly."

"Not exactly?" Alexa prodded.

"Of course, I knew where he kept it," Veronica said, "from that time."

"These are all originals," Alexa commented.

Veronica tried to act surprised, but her acting was not on par with her skills as a thief.

"That's a mistake. I mean, I guess I was nervous about doing it, don't you see?" Veronica said defensively. "I must have inadvertently swapped the copies I'd made for the originals."

"How did you choose these files of all twenty-six years of her records?" Manseur asked.

Veronica stared silently, surely thinking how she should answer him.

"Why these specifically?" he pressed.

"Well, I couldn't copy all of the files, because there were so many, thousands, like you said."

"These were the most likely to keep you out of any potential accusations of complicity in malpractice suits," Alexa offered. "Or criminal charges, of course," she added.

"Of course," Manseur said. Alexa could imagine Veronica reading through the volumes of accumulated paper to select the most incriminating, and therefore the most valuable, pages. And Alexa doubted she cared that photocopies were nonadmissible in legal proceedings, but she had known that they'd be useless as blackmail leverage.

Not that Manseur or Alexa cared, but it was obvious that Veronica Malouf had planned to trade the life of an underappreciated laborer for one of a moneyed dilettante. The young woman didn't realize that an assault on LePointe's reputation, and perhaps his very freedom, might be worth big money to him, but Alexa doubted Veronica had what it would take to actually collect any while Kenneth Decell was running interference for him.

Alexa was delighted. If Veronica hadn't had a larcenous streak, they'd have no proof to bolster their supposition that LePointe was as nasty a piece of work as they suspected him to be. The basics contained in the papers were proof that Sibby Danielson had not only been under Dr. LePointe's direct care for those years, but that Dorothy Fugate had been responsible for the patient's day-to-day care for the same time period. Dorothy Fugate had been the most powerful nurse in the hospital, moving steadily, and rapidly, up the ladder of authority until she was the head administrative nurse. The nurses, the nurses' aides, the orderlies, and even the janitorial staff on the wards answered to her directly. Sibby Danielson spent her twenty-six-year tour in the same room in the most violent patients' wing. And Nurse Fugate had taken Sibby home with her and had kept her heavily medicated and imprisoned there.

"How did Dr. LePointe keep all of this from the staff?" Alexa asked Veronica.

"Each doctor, psychiatrist or psychologist, has a full contingent of patients. They only discussed the cases the doctors, psychologists, or nurses brought to the attention of the others. Only Dr. LePointe would have brought up his patients if he wanted to discuss one."

"Danielson's nurse never had reason to bring her up?"

"Dorothy Fugate was Sibby's only nurse—or her supervising nurse, at any rate—and she was the nurse who brought up the other nurses' concerns at the staff meetings with the doctors and psychologists."

"So, Dorothy Fugate was where all roads to Sibby intersected?" Alexa asked. "And as director, LePointe controlled these meetings?"

Veronica nodded. "Dr. LePointe personally recruited all of the doctors and psychologists who are working there now. The doctors are real busy and they only worry about their own patients."

"And Dr. Whitfield?" Manseur asked.

"Let me guess," Alexa said. "Whitfield is a William LePointe production."

"He brought him in from a hospital in Richmond," Veronica said.

"So River Run—a state institution—has been without normal checks and balances of any kind for over twenty-five years?"

"Dr. LePointe still exerts control," Veronica said.

"Then why did he feel compelled to spirit out Sibby Danielson?" Alexa asked. "Wouldn't it have been safer if he had left her there? Why not just make sure she remained drugged up?"

"Or died," Manseur offered. "One little mistake with the medication, and there's a natural death. Or overdose her and say she saved up her meds and committed suicide."

"Dr. LePointe wouldn't ever kill anybody. Sibby's no big deal. There's other patients on the maximum-security wards that are well known," Veronica told them. "Serial killers, a woman who poisoned her family, even a transvestite who collected severed penises and made hatbands with them that she sold to tourists."

"We need a picture of Sibby," Manseur said, changing the subject. "So we can find her."

"I don't have access to pictures of the inmates. Staff is HR. Inmates is another department altogether. I got you the names of the staff in the ward like you asked, but no pictures or addresses. They're all there."

"Did you know that Sibby was living with Nurse Fugate?" Alexa asked.

"For real?" Veronica said, appearing genuinely surprised.

"She isn't now," Manseur said. "Somebody murdered Nurse Fugate, and Sibby was no longer around. That's why we need a picture."

"Did Sibby chop her up?" Veronica asked.

"Somebody caved in her skull. Might have been Sibby."

Veronica said, "Was it with a pipe?"

"Why did you say pipe?" Alexa asked.

Veronica shrugged. "Don't know. There was this guy they put into the violent ward who had mega muscles, and scars all over his forehead. I saw them walking him once. One of the girls in Admissions said he caved in somebody's head with a pipe."

"*A pipe?* Do you know what happened to him?"

"I'm not sure. I do know the orderlies said he was the scariest man they'd ever had to deal with. They were saying they would hate to run into him on the outside."

"What did he do for a living?" Manseur asked. "Clubbing people isn't a full-time occupation."

"Some kind of fisherman or trapper. They said that's all he talked about. He used that pipe to kill things like animals he trapped."

"Was he in the same ward as Sibby?" Alexa asked.

Lead pipe . . . nutria hair . . . salty water.

"He was in one of the violent wards."

"Ward fourteen?" Alexa asked.

"Maybe it was."

"Trapper with a pipe," Manseur said, stroking his chin thoughtfully. "Yes, I remember. . . ."

"You know who she's referring to?" Alexa asked him.

"About two years ago some fisherman beat another fisherman half to death in front of a bunch of witnesses. Two other people in the area had been found with crushed skulls, so they figured this guy did all of them. He was strong as an ape. Took half a

dozen deputies and three stun guns to restrain him.
can't remember his name, but the case fell apart be
cause the witnesses got amnesia, and the man he bea
couldn't remember who'd done it. They had to re
lease him."

Veronica shrugged. "People get released all th
time that shouldn't. That's all I know." She looked a
the papers on the table. "I guess Dr. LePointe has t
find out about these?"

Manseur frowned.

"Maybe he won't need to know," Alexa tol
Veronica. "You've been a big help." *Even though yo
are a criminal. Maybe this will straighten you out be
fore you end up in jail . . . or dead.*

"I think that's all for now. Stay near your phone,'
Manseur told her.

"Go home," Alexa said. "Don't even think abou
discussing this with anybody. If you do, we'll fin
out, and we won't be nice about it."

"I'm going to my parents' in Lafayette until nex
week. The hurricane and all . . ."

"Go," Manseur said, waving his fingers at her
"Keep your cell phone hot, and we'll call if there'
anything further."

Veronica grabbed her purse and left the room like
there was a bomb on the table, pulling the door shu
behind her hard enough to rattle the opaque glass
panel.

Manseur went directly to his computer and started
typing. Thirty seconds later, he looked at Alexa.
"Leland Ticholet was twenty-three. The instrument
he was suspected of using to pound the victim's head
in was never recovered, but the medical examiner

speculated that the attack was most likely committed with an instrument consistent with a section of pipe. Lead pipe is a relatively common item among commercial fishermen. Not sure why."

Alexa said, "A lead pipe is both heavier than wood and softer than galvanized, so it does more deep damage without splitting skin against the bone."

"How'd you know that?"

"I spend a lot of time talking to crime techs about cold cases. Or maybe I read it in a novel. Got an address on him?"

"I guess no address could be established. Ticholet was released without any probation or restrictions."

"I guess the swamp is a nonspecific address. He was locked up in River Run's violent ward while Fugate was there. He might have harbored a grudge. Got even with her," Alexa said.

"With a meat-tenderizing hammer, not a pipe," Manseur said.

"Perhaps the hammer was a weapon of convenience. Maybe he knew the pipe would point to him. He could have attacked Gary West with a lead pipe. Maybe he was hired by Fugate to do the West grab and he wanted to up his percentage."

"Money could have been his motive for attacking Gary West?"

Alexa said, "You've never been open to considering that LePointe might be directly involved. A blind spot."

"No. I still can't see it."

"Maybe LePointe knows Leland from the hospital and hired him to kill Fugate."

"Alexa, think about this. Dr. LePointe hired a

retarded giant mental patient to kill Nurse Fugate and abduct Gary West?"

"It's easy for me to imagine Fugate knew far too much about him and Sibby. Maybe he wanted to get rid of Fugate and stuck her with the responsibility of springing Sibby, and he got Leland to get rid of one or both of them. Maybe he worked all of it through Decell. Arm's-length transaction. And if he did that, why is it unimaginable that he grabbed West while they were settling family business. Whoever was in an old green panel truck was in both places. They took Sibby out of Fugate's and they abducted Gary West using it. What are the chances two such trucks were involved?"

Manseur nodded slowly. "I'll concede that point. Somebody did both. I can't picture LePointe risking everything by leading a conspiracy, because he knows enough about people who conspire to know they rat out each other."

Alexa picked up the handwritten list of staff Veronica had furnished and read it.

Ward 14 Staff:
Nurses:
Judi Bodiker
Vicky Lane
Kerry Hamilton
Abbey Dunn
Jamie Smith

Orderlies:
Bunky Bouvier
Bob Waller
Andrew Tinsdale

Terry Fourchet
Jack Warden

Janitorial:
Tommy Dogrel
Raymond Carrouth
Joe Jefferson

"Sometimes very smart people don't think they can be foiled by what fells lesser men. We're not dealing with a man who believes normal rules apply to him. Arrogance, a sense of entitlement, intelligence, and power can make for a deadly combination. No guns or knives—all blunt force. We find Mr. Ticholet, we'll know the truth. What do you suppose Swamp Boy is driving these days?" Alexa asked.

Manseur shrugged. "I can find out easy enough."

"Fifty dollars says it's something old and green."

53

Except for a few fish camps scattered along the bayou—owned by people who didn't live in them—Doc's house was in a very isolated area. There was a seldom-used parish road that ran parallel to the water that made the camps accessible by land or water. Leland thought that made the sites unacceptable to someone like him, who appreciated privacy.

Leland carried Doc's sleeping man over his shoulder up the gentle slope to the house. Once inside, Leland dumped his burden into a chair and, after peeling back the bedsheet he'd wrapped him in, watched while Doc used rolls of duct tape to secure the bastard to the chair, looping the whole deal to a wooden six-by-six post that held up the center roof beam.

"He don't look barely even alive," Leland said. "Ought to put him out his misery."

"Dear boy, he's in acceptable physical condition. Mr. West is a remarkable example of youth and virility," Doc said, his words spilling out like cigarette smoke, all silky and smooth. "He's been cleaned up since I last laid eyes on him. Florence Leland Nightingale now, is it?"

"What?"

"She was a nurse. She bathed the faces of the ill and those put under the weather thanks to the ravages of lead balls and saber slashes."

"She cleaned that old blood off his face."

"She who?"

Doc's face twisted itself up and Leland knew he'd have to tell him about it, even though it was none of his business. Leland didn't like nosy people. But he didn't see that telling would hurt anything.

"Game warden and lady warden came to my camp this morning. They had this camera stuck up on a tree to spy on me. He was going to get his radio to get help, but I caught him, and she was cleaning the blood off this guy's face when I came in."

"Holy shit! Game wardens? And you did what?"

Leland shrugged, taken aback by the dumbness of the question. "They was trespassers. I killed 'em."

"And then?"

"I got shed of them and I sunk their boat where nobody won't never find it. A deep hole I know of."

After thinking for a few seconds, Doc smiled. "Not a problem. Good thinking, Leland. You did the right thing."

"You mean on killing those wardens?"

"You, a specimen endowed with such suspect genetics, take instruction amazingly well for an overly muscular individual blessed with the intelligence usually associated with invertebrates and the inanimate. You actually showed initiative and took what might have been a disastrous situation, and—I have little doubt—handled it with the thoughtful planning of an enraged primate encountering a potential Armageddon. You never fail to astound me with your Kong-like aplomb, your measured directness in solving complex problems with straightforward acts. Leland Ticholet, I am more certain than ever that for you the world holds no mysteries whatsoever."

Leland felt his face flushing. He couldn't help but smile when Doc laid on fancy compliments. "I just do what needs to get did, I reckon. Nothing nobody else like me wouldn't a' did in my place."

"If you could accomplish another complex assignment, get that stepladder out of your old truck for me? We have a lot of work to do in preparation for this evening's festivities. Perhaps you can observe what I do and give me unsolicited, and undoubtedly moronic, advice while I connect up my little *devise du demise*."

Leland went out and brought back the ladder, which was in his father's old truck. Doc had gotten a mechanic to fix the truck up so it worked pretty good and he'd told Leland he would be able to use it after things were settled, and the wheels would come in handy for getting up groceries and like that. All

Leland wanted to do now was get back to the swamp, but since Doc had asked so nicely, he'd stay and watch him put his little contraption together. Doc was a very smart man, and Leland listened to what Doc was saying without being interested in any of it, or caring how rich the man was going to get from this.

Doc didn't talk much about things that Leland cared anything about. He told Leland he knew more about most anything than any man alive, teachers even, and Leland believed him. Doc was the best electrical man, the best plumbing man, the best car driver, the best food cooker, the best wine drinker, the best lover of beautiful women. Hellfire, Doc was about the best there was at whatever the hell it was he decided to tell about.

An hour later, Leland had to admit the deal Doc had built in the little house was something to look at. All those wires that went all over the place through the pulleys and the way it was all hooked up to that bowl. Doc explained it, but it seemed like a bunch of showing off to Leland. Why go to so much work for something so simple to do and be done with?

Why would anybody waste all this time and effort when all he needed was a piece of pipe? Maybe the smarter you were, the more you figured you had to show off. Leland couldn't figure out why Doc was always telling him what he was going to do and exactly how he was going to do it. Leland didn't care if the little man could light a match to his fart and fly up to the moon from the flames shooting out from his ass.

Leland was, as usual, bored enough to bash Doc's head in and go back out to the cabin where he had traps that wouldn't set their own selves.

Thinking about the cabin reminded him that he had done everything he had said he would do on the boat deal. He was tired of thinking about it. If Doc added one more thing Leland had to do to get the owning papers on the boat, Leland was going to kill him. And it wouldn't be nobody's fault but Doc's.

"You want some gum?" Doc asked him.

"You got some?"

The package of Juicy Fruit chased all other thoughts from his mind, and as he opened it, Leland was thinking that Doc was the best guy he'd ever known and that was a fact.

54

At ten minutes past five o'clock, Kenneth Decell arrived at LePointe's, parked beside the Bentley in the courtyard, lifted the valise containing the two and a half million dollars, and strode to the front door, noting a slight breeze. He knew it was at least twenty-four hours before the feeder bands from the hurricane arrived and stirred things up. By then he would be a well-heeled man. He would take a few weeks off and go to Paris for some R&R. After Decell had stood at the front door for thirty seconds, Dr. LePointe opened it, and he shook Decell's hand vigorously. He led Decell back to the office, never once so much as glancing at the valise, which held one man's fortune and another's walking-around money.

"So did Roger give you any trouble?" he asked Decell.

"He expressed mild concern when I refused to sign a release," Decell answered.

"It is a substantial amount," LePointe said.

"I told him he should call you if he needed clarification as to your wishes, or have you come and sign his receipt. He declined to pursue the matter, and here it is."

LePointe nodded. "He's a professional worrier and has my best interests at heart."

"More likely his own."

"I'm sure he's covered, since he has a video recording device in his office, which I'm sure captured the transaction. One can't blame him for being cautious."

Decell said, "Bastards won't get to cash the bonds. They'll be back in the bank's vault Monday morning."

LePointe shrugged. "Ransoms are just forced business transactions, Kenneth. Business arrangements. Someone has something that they want something else in exchange for. In this case, two and a half million dollars. The thing that bothers me is that whoever is behind this has to know the item in question is worth a larger percentage of my holdings than this. If I could pay it and be done with this forever, I'd just pay it and write it off to lessons learned. Just lessons learned. In this case, the extortionists may see this as a down payment. Human nature being what it is ensures that the extortionists see me as a golden goose. Giving me what I'm paying for would be killing the goose. There are people who understand economics, who are comfortable with wealth, and there's everybody else. It's a remarkably small club, Kenneth. So the question is, how do you get the object and keep from rewarding such greed?"

"It's under control," Decell said.

"I suppose you understand the criminal psychology as well as I do, based on your experience with such people. So, fill me in on your day. What did you find at Dorothy's house?"

"Just what I told you earlier."

"I want to hear the details."

"Are you sure?" Decell wondered if LePointe was recording this and his questions were designed to give the doctor a lever.

"I know Dorothy is dead and you tidied up the residence, removing any and all incriminating evidence. There's more, isn't there?"

"I did what you asked." He reached into his pocket and placed a small cassette on the desk, which LePointe merely looked at as though it had no real value.

"I lifted this from the answering machine. Your voice was on it eighteen times. If they pull your phone records, there are calls to the house, but short ones. You can say you wanted to check in on an old and valued friend. Perhaps you wanted her to help take care of your wife."

"Let's leave Sarah out of this. Unless it becomes necessary, I mean. It's a solid reason, and one I overlooked."

Decell nodded. "Of course."

"No other complications?" LePointe asked.

"Like?"

"Like any unexpected complications?"

"I was interrupted in my search by that FBI agent.

Keen." Decell knew she had visited LePointe, and there was no way to avoid telling the doctor about her involvement, since it was unlikely that she'd failed to mention it. "I assume she picked the lock. I had the key you gave me, but I'm sure I locked the door." He told one small lie to cover his failure to lock the door.

"The FBI agent showed up and you did what . . . slipped out the back door?"

Decell contemplated his fingernails for a second. "She was searching the house. She never saw me. When she went into the basement, I locked the door and left."

"Why not escape out the back?"

"The back door was dead-bolted and there was no key in the mechanism. I went out the way I came in."

"You removed all of the evidence tying myself or Sibhon to Dorothy's house, I assume?"

Decell felt heat rising in his chest. "I found a package of correspondence, cards, that sort of thing. But I was interrupted before I had a chance to really search with the sort of thoroughness I would have liked."

LePointe's eyes grew cold, and he stared at Decell.

"I might have missed something," Decell said hastily. "There were a few bottles of pills. Danielson's name wasn't on any of them. Of course, I took those and destroyed them."

"My name, as the prescribing physician, *was* on them. I learned that from Agent Keen, who saw them *before* you took them. I assured her the prescriptions were forged, and I doubt she can prove otherwise, but she knows they were there. She also knows Sibhon was there. The only thing that eludes me is how she knew to go to Dorothy's house in the first place. That had to have come from someone at River Run, and I have to admit it makes me anxious to think there are loose lips out there. Veronica Malouf springs immediately to mind because she was in a position to pick up things, and she told you Keen and Manseur were there. Dr. Whitfield didn't have the information, and wouldn't dare inform on me if he did. Anything else?"

Decell was satisfied that LePointe wasn't recording their conversation, because he couldn't edit it without leaving evidence, and it implicated him.

"As to who at River Run told the agent about Dorothy Fugate, I don't believe it was Malouf or Whitfield. We have to assume there are people out there who might have heard talk of one sort or another."

"I see." LePointe drummed the desktop with his fingers. Decell had never seen LePointe worried about anything before. "There is no evidence remaining pertaining to Sibhon Danielson's release or stay. Those records are ash."

"You burned them personally?"

LePointe nodded.

"I don't believe Agent Keen or the Homicide cops will find anything." Decell tried to maintain an air of confident certainty. "If they do, I'll deal with it."

"How?"

"I have a lot of good friends in the department," Decell said. "And so do you. I can pull in a lot of favors, and nobody in there will be quick to allow anything to happen to you. This city loves and appreciates their saints, and only one's among the living." Decell saw LePointe's eyes light up at the saint reference, just as he had hoped, and he relaxed somewhat. God only knew what kind of shit-storm LePointe might have to weather if the Sibby-in-his-hospital thing found its way into the press. "Right now every cop within a hundred miles is worrying about the hurricane, and it's only going to get worse until Sunday night. We have a clear window."

"With the possible exceptions of Agent Keen and Detective Manseur, I am totally confident that you can keep the lid on this," LePointe said. "Thanks to this FBI agent's meddling, though, Casey is aware that Sibhon Danielson was Dorothy's guest, and that she was also at River Run. I think I can deal with Casey so this doesn't create a schism in the family, but my niece is more upset than I've ever seen her. There was something in her eyes that I never thought I would live to see. She was horrified and crushed, and she could act irrationally until her husband is returned. Once he's home, all of this will be behind us and forgotten. If she's determined to have West in her life, I'm prepared to live with it. I'll explain to her truthfully that I wrote that letter to gain time to pay his ransom without police interference, to ensure West's recovery. She is a LePointe. She will accept my actions once I've explained. Kenneth, you are the only living soul, aside from the perpetrators of this mess, who knows the whole story. You alone I can trust. As long as these extortionists know, this is not over. We can't have that."

Decell knew that if it hadn't been for the fact that he had run headlong into LePointe's secret when he was a street cop, his own life would have been a far,

far poorer one. If Fugate hadn't shared it, too, none of this could have happened. LePointe had needed Fugate's involvement, but Decell knew LePointe only cared that the woman was dead because of what came of it, thanks to the fact that she'd kept a record. Who knew she was capable of such stupidity and disloyalty? LePointe had thought that the nurse's involvement, a gift here and there, his affection in the guise of his erect penis (administered very occasionally), and a few promises—kept or not—would ensure Dorothy Fugate's silence and loyalty. Decell knew better, but LePointe, for all his intelligence and knowledge of the psyches of patients, knew jack-shit about women.

"I can't imagine Sibhon killing Dorothy," LePointe said.

"Who else but Sibby could have?"

"So, where do you think Sibhon is? If she did kill Dorothy, where could she go? Did the extortionist find her? Or she him?"

"Or her. The blackmailer might be female."

"Perhaps. What if the police find Sibhon? I don't believe she could say anything with enough coherence that would matter. But I'm not one hundred percent sure of that. If she isn't medicated, who can be sure? I wouldn't want anything to happen to her, but if she were . . ."

"Possibly the blackmailer has her, or had her . . . if she's even still alive," Decell said. "The fact that she was at River Run is already out. That won't be a problem, because the release form is misfiled, but it is in the files, so I doubt it will amount to anything but speculation. However it breaks, you have deniability and a depth of credibility few other men have. Sticks and stones."

LePointe's eyes grew dark and angry and he slammed his hand down on the desk. "Just speculation? Don't you understand the harm that can do? I treated the woman who murdered my own brother. Do you know how that could make me look? The appearance of impropriety can be as deadly as any gunshot."

"It shows that you are a professional with a heart. You treated her out of a boundless sense of compassion. You wanted her to have the best care, because she was already your patient before the incident and you wanted to help her regain herself, even though she'd killed people you loved." Even as he was saying it, Decell saw how terrible it made LePointe look and regretted saying it out loud.

LePointe was silent for almost a minute. "Yes, Kenneth. What you say is probably true. Of course her mental health was at stake. Yes, I think you're right." LePointe squeezed his eyes shut and massaged his forehead. "It was compassion. Perhaps misguided. God, we all make mistakes out of misguided good intentions."

"No good deed goes unpunished," Decell added. "We can deal with that. Absolutely. Now, we need to talk about *tonight*."

LePointe made a tent out of his hands. "I'm all ears."

55

Alexa and Manseur sat across from each other at the dining table in his Uptown home eating the shrimp po'boys they had picked up en route to his house. They were studying the printouts of the telephone records that Alexa had requested covering persons of interest in the West case.

"How can people talk so much?" Alexa said.

Outside, car doors slammed.

"Sounds like my girls are home," Manseur said.

The kitchen door opened and two young girls Alexa recognized from their pictures in Manseur's office burst into the kitchen, laughing. Upon seeing Alexa, the girls stopped laughing and stared at her. Both had long hair and large expressive eyes. The elder was a head taller than her sister, and thinner. The younger was stocky and resembled her father.

A woman carrying groceries entered the house and closed the door behind her using her foot. She set the bags on the counter and turned.

"Girls, this is Alexa Keen," Manseur said. "Alexa, may I present my daughters, Emma and Madge, and my wife, Emily."

"It's nice to meet you," Alexa said, standing. She extended her hand and greeted each girl with a handshake.

"I'm Emma," the youngest said, pulling her blond hair back and tucking it behind her ears.

"Madge," said the other.

"You a police lady?" Emma asked.

"Alexa is an FBI special agent," Manseur said.

Emily Manseur radiated confidence. She was thin, had olive skin, long black hair, and smiled easily, exposing a slight overbite. "Agent Keen, Michael speaks very highly of you."

"Are you really an FBI lady?" Emma asked Alexa.

"Yes, I am," Alexa said.

"Don't let us interrupt, Agent Keen," Emily said. "Michael, we're packed. There are enough can goods, bread, and bottled water to last you two solid weeks. Everything's in the pantry. There's candles, matches, flashlights, and batteries."

"Then y'all need to get going."

"We could wait until tomorrow to leave. It might turn."

"It isn't going to turn much. You should go now," he said. "I-10's bumper-to-bumper, and it'll be worse in a few hours. The Toyota's gassed up, and don't forget to take the charger for your cell phone. Call me when you get there."

"I wish you'd come with us," Emily said. "Not like you don't have weeks of sick leave and vacation time due you."

"All leaves are canceled. I told you that."

"Do you arrest people?" Emma asked Alexa.

"Of course she does," Madge said. "She's an FBI agent."

"Sometimes I have to," Alexa said.

"I'm going to be an FBI agent when I'm big," Emma said.

"I'm sure the FBI would love to have you, Emma," Alexa said.

"Do you have a gun like Daddy's?" she asked immediately.

"Yes, I have a gun identical to your daddy's," Alexa said.

"Where is it?"

"I keep it in my purse."

"You ever shoot anybody dead with *your* glop?" Emma asked.

"Glock," Madge said, giggling. "Not glop. Glop is an ice cream that falls on the floor."

"I've never had to shoot anybody with it yet," Alexa answered.

"Neither has my daddy," Emma said. "But you could if you wanted to, couldn't you?"

"If she *had* to," Madge corrected, frowning at her little sister.

Emma put her hands flat on the table and tossed her head to get her hair out of her eyes. "Daddy catches murder perks. Did you know that?"

"Yes, I did know he does that," Alexa said, smiling. "You must be very proud of him."

"Girls, let's go see Aunt Janie," Emily interposed.

"My sister was supposed to have her first communion Sunday," Emma told Alexa. "I was going to wear a white dress, too, and watch her eat Jesus in front of everybody. Now I can't because the church might get blown down."

Madge nudged her little sister. "You don't know what you're talking about, Emma."

"I do too," Emma said, nudging her sister playfully. "I'm going to be an FBI lady arrester when I grow up."

"She is not," Madge said to Alexa. "She's just saying that because you're one."

Alexa told Emma, "You can be whatever you like."

"Yesterday she was going to be a gymnast and get a gold medal," Madge said. "And before that it was a nun and a teacher and a doctor and a high diver. . . ."

Emma smiled. "When I'm an FBI, I'm going to arrest Madge and put her in jail for being mean to me."

"That's silly," Madge said. "You can't arrest your own sister."

The words uttered by an innocent child shot through Alexa's heart, and she felt her smile melt.

"Okay, girls," Emily intervened. "Tell Agent Keen good-bye and go get your bags. We'll leave you two to your work." She kissed Michael on the lips before following the girls out.

"Something wrong?" Manseur asked Alexa. "You look like somebody just walked across your grave."

"Nothing," Alexa replied. "Just thinking about something. You have wonderful women around you."

"I do at that," he agreed.

She looked down at the phone numbers in front of her and fought to focus on them.

"They're very competitive, my two. But they sure love each other," Manseur commented.

Swallowing, she murmured, "Sisters can be very competitive."

Alexa felt Manseur's eyes on her, and she wondered if the detective knew what had happened between her and her sister. That she had arrested Antonia and charged her with a dozen serious federal crimes. She had no idea how widespread that particular knowledge was, because cops swapped more gossip than hairstylists.

56

Leland wasn't a happy camper, because Doc had come up with yet another requested task, which was accompanied by a threat that he'd take back the new boat. While Doc was explaining how simple his transportation job was going to be, Leland was considering how he could beat the little jerk to death and let the crabs and gators handle the required disposal of his remains. It was just that simple, and ownership papers or not, he'd just keep the boat. Anybody showing up to take it away would be sorry.

Doc was still fussing with his fancy device, measuring with his roll-up ruler, fussing with this wire and that one and scurrying up and down the ladder here, moving it and climbing up into the rafters like a fussy little rat. He did remind Leland of a rat . . . or a nutria.

The man in the duct-tape suit moved his head once and Leland saw for himself that he was still alive. Leland found it puzzling how some people were so much harder to kill than others. This one was sort of fragile-looking, and he'd been hit hard enough to kill him outright, but here he was not dead.

Doc had been talking on the phone to the woman he was always talking to and making silly sounds and kissing the little phone after he closed it. Leland thought about the pipe he had in the boat that he used to bash critters that he found alive in his traps, and to finish off the garfish he caught before he threw them back in the water for gator food. Gars were useless as balls on a cow. You couldn't eat them because there were so little meat and too many little bitty bones in them. Plus they ate other fish you could sell, their teeth were like straight pins, and they were mean little suckers.

Once, when Leland was a little boy, he had been sitting on the camp's dock with his feet in the water, wiggling his toes, when a two-foot-long gar had taken a good bite on Leland's foot. When Leland jerked his foot to free it, the gar flip-flopped so hard that some of the fish's teeth broke off right in his foot. Worst part was the foot had gotten infected and, before his daddy finally decided to take him to a doctor, it turned black as a moonless night and the doctor almost had to cut it off. His daddy told the doctor to take it off, but the doctor wouldn't do it just so Jacklan Ticholet could get back to his camp sooner.

Leland had hated gars since the day he was bitten. He enjoyed catching them and opening up their jaws and wedging a stick in there so they couldn't ever close their mouths again and they starved on account of it. It was more satisfying than just killing them outright with the pipe. It gave the sneaky mean bastards something to think about while they died—knowing who had done it to them.

Leland sometimes thought about his daddy, who had been a swamper and moonshiner. Leland didn't know anything about his real mama, because his daddy never talked about her but to say she was a slut who'd spread her legs for anybody she saw. His stepmother hadn't been any better, and a drunk too.

Leland's daddy had made him help out with fishing, crabbing, trapping, and making clear liquor from the time he was real little, and he'd learned everything by being hollered at and having the crap knocked out of him as they went about it. His daddy's favorite thing was making, selling, and drinking moonshine. Leland couldn't hardly remember a single time when his daddy wasn't sipping from a jar or a milk jug.

If Leland's daddy had to go to town, he'd leave Leland locked in the cabin while he was gone. Sometimes he came back when he said he would, but other times he would be gone days, till, stinking drunk, he'd come stumbling in, collapse on his bed, and snore like a mill saw. Sometimes when Leland was hungry his daddy would make him drink whiskey to help him forget about his empty stomach, but Leland never liked the taste or how it made him feel.

Leland grew up without going to any schools, but he knew everything there was to know about the swamp, the bayous, and the lakes around there. He knew where to find the things that you could sell and how to catch them, how to clean them, and how to cook what you needed to eat.

When his stepmother killed his daddy, Leland had taken his body to the landing and got Moody the store owner to call the sheriff to come and fetch his body, which was the last Leland had heard about that. The sheriff had gone to visit his stepmother. She told the sheriff truthfully she'd done it and explained it was self-defense. But of course the sheriff, who said he just needed to talk to her, put her right in jail. Leland had gone to her and his daddy's place, picked out the things worth keeping, like the Nylon 66 .22 and some food, then he'd gotten in her hound dogs and a one-eared cat, and set that cabin full of critters on fire. That done, Leland motored out a ways so the heat didn't hurt his skin and drank some moonshine in his daddy's memory while he watched that cabin burn to the ground. He hadn't done it because Alice Fay shot his daddy dead. He knew if she hadn't shot him, he would have done it himself. He burned her cabin because he knew she'd figure out that he had gotten all his father's goods instead of her.

He was fifteen then and he had waited for months, but nobody had come to take him away from his cabin, and so Leland just went on doing what he'd been taught to do, because there wasn't anything else he knew how to do, or wanted to try. His father's boat was one he'd traded liquor for, and when the motor got used up, Leland just went to a fishing camp when there weren't any people around and stole a good one, which he painted black so it looked just like the old one he'd thrown off in the lake. He never got in trouble for doing that, so he figured rich people didn't spend time looking for their missing motors, just bought another one.

Leland looked up, to see Doc studying him from way up on the ladder.

"Penny for your thoughts," Doc said.

"I don't got no penny," Leland told him.

"Leland," Doc started. He opened his hooded sweatshirt, probably so Leland could see the handle of the little lady gun he had stuck in his pants. "I know this must be frustrating for you, that the sirens of the bayou are singing to you. I give you my word that as soon as you do your part this evening, you can head off to whatever scuzzy fishing hole your little heart desires and pull fish out of the scummy water with reckless abandon until you have filled up your boat to the gunwales."

"Gun whales?"

"Fill to the top until you are knee-deep in eels, or whatever it is you collect out of the vast stagnant purgatory you inhabit."

Leland didn't know the words, but he didn't like the whiny tone. He wondered if Doc was mocking him. "When do I get the papers?"

"What papers are you referring to?"

"The owning papers on the boat."

Doc smiled. "You mean the pink slip? The registration?"

"Yeah, the paper saying it's mine and nobody else's."

"Tonight when you drop me at my car, I will give you your just reward. Scout's honor. You'll drop me and I'll drop you . . . the owning papers."

Leland said, "I guess so, but dropping them to me right now would be better."

"If I gave them to you now, you'd go out that door, get in the boat, and haul ass back to your little home in the sticks. For all I know, if you had the papers in your pocket, you might be tempted to keep time on my head with that pipe."

"You give me the pink papers and I won't do nothing but say good-bye-dee-by."

"And I'll never see you again, not even in the funny papers?"

Leland nodded his head slowly.

Doc closed his sweatshirt so the gun was hidden and he clapped his hands together. "Absolutely positively tonight. Cross my heart and hope to die. Stick a needle in my eye. Guaranteed. Signed, sealed, and delivered, I'm yours."

Doc made an X on his chest with his fingers.

"Before the sun comes up in the morning, you will be hotfooting your way home to Valhalla aboard your new vessel. You have my most absolute disingenuous word of honor."

"Okay, then," Leland said, smiling. "Before the sun comes up again."

57

There were so many calls made and received from the requested numbers that it was going to take hours to go through them all and cross-reference them. Alexa had Casey's list of friends and acquaintances for cross-reference.

"How did you get the cellular records so fast? All the different providers—that takes us weeks and we have to raise hell."

"There are advantages in being FBI. Especially when the director is running interference for you."

"The Wests' home phone and cells are clean," Manseur said. "Calls to and from the friends on her list, stores, tradesmen, attorneys, accountants, LePointe, Grace. No surprises."

Alexa was looking for specific calls that pointed to a conspiracy. "We've got Grace and Casey talking before eight and after nine on most days. Talking with Casey takes up the majority of Grace's cell minutes. No surprise she doesn't have much of a life aside from her employer. Through this morning is where the record ends. But in the past two weeks, Grace Smythe has been talking a lot to someone who's using a paid-in-advance disposable unit. The disposable unit called her several times today. I'd love to know who that is. She probably won't tell the truth unless we can confront her with evidence, and I don't want to tip her just yet that we're interested."

"She won't be hard to find," Manseur said.

"Maybe this prepaid-phone owner is her outside man willing to do the heavy lifting. Who's in a better position to plan the grab? Grace knows Gary's schedule. Right after the grab, the prepaid unit calls Grace, and she calls it back a little while later. And several times after we left Casey's last night they talked back and forth. And she called a travel agent three times; once before the grab, twice after."

"Call the travel agency and find out if she bought tickets, how many, where and when they're for. Now, what do you have on LePointe's lines?"

"LePointe has talked to Decell a lot since the grab, but not once in the weeks before. That makes sense. But LePointe called Fugate scores of times: last call was an hour before you arrived at her house. After that call, LePointe called Decell. Decell called LePointe a few minutes after you got clobbered. Talked three minutes. Minutes after that, LePointe called the president of the bank Decell visited an hour later. Looks like maybe LePointe is going to pay somebody for something."

"Could there be a ransom demand the doctor hasn't mentioned?" Alexa asked.

"I don't see Fugate tied in with Grace. Fugate didn't make any calls to anyone else on the list, did she?"

"Fugate didn't call anybody the month before the grab except LePointe. Short-duration calls. She'd been dead two days when Gary was taken. LePointe always called her. A lot of those calls from LePointe were immediate hang-ups. Eighteen ran thirty seconds or longer. It looks like LePointe didn't know about Fugate's death until after it happened. He didn't start frantically calling Fugate until a few hours ago. What was the trigger?" Alexa wondered.

"If LePointe found out the media was hunting for Sibby, he could have started calling Fugate to tell her to circle the wagons. But she doesn't answer. He panics. When LePointe can't reach Fugate, Decell goes over to check on her for LePointe—see why she wasn't taking his calls. Once he gets there he finds her dead and Sibby's gone. He begins to sanitize the house, but you interrupt him. He pushed you down the stairs and ran away with all the evidence he could carry. Bond saw Decell twenty minutes later go to his office to ditch the evidence. It fits."

"And then Decell goes to the bank when it's closed to normal people," Alexa said. "Decell went to the bank because he found something at Fugate's house that LePointe needed money to deal with."

"This is giving me a headache," Manseur said.

"Or because LePointe got a ransom demand."

"How do we find Gary West?"

Manseur's cell phone rang and he answered it.

Alexa watched his face as he listened. "Good work. We need to put out a BOLO on him." Manseur closed the phone. "Got a hit on a partial fingerprint taken from Gary West's Volvo."

"Leland Ticholet?" Alexa guessed.

Manseur nodded and smiled.

"If you can deal with the travel agency, I need to talk to Veronica Malouf."

"Why?"

"After that, you join Bond watching LePointe's. I'll meet you there. We're going to need some help staying with the money. Can you get GPS trackers?"

"I'll see if I can. Finding help to follow money sounds easy enough."

58

When Veronica Malouf answered her door and saw Alexa, her face crumpled.

"This isn't a good time," she said, after looking up and down the street.

Alexa heard the volume of the stereo drop and knew Veronica wasn't alone. "I hope I'm not interrupting anything."

"I have a friend here."

"That's fine. I don't have time to come in."

"What do you want?"

"A favor."

"What kind?" Veronica pulled the door shut behind her.

"I want you to go to the hospital and get me a set of records."

"I gave you everything I had."

"On Sibby. But I need the records on another inmate."

"Who?"

"Leland Ticholet."

"Who?"

"Swamp Boy."

"Now?"

"Yes, now."

"But I never go there after five. The offices are closed except for a skeleton crew. How about early in the morning? I might not be able to come back home. The way back into town is being blocked by highway patrolmen."

"If they won't let you through, call me."

"You're going to get me fired," Veronica said weakly.

"That is the least of your worries," Alexa told her.

59

It was dark when Alexa arrived on St. Charles Avenue, parked, and climbed into Manseur's car. A man she had never seen before was in the back seat.

"Alexa, Larry Bond. Larry, Agent Keen," Manseur said.

"Pleasure," Bond said. Manseur's ex-partner wasn't at all what Alexa expected. He was blond, muscular, and tall. His face was all sharp angles and sunburnt. "Decell's been in the house since he got here from the bank."

"Casey arrived twenty minutes ago," Manseur said.

"Was Grace with her?"

"She was alone, far as I could tell. Might have the little girl with her."

Alexa opened her cell phone and dialed. "Casey, it's Alexa."

"You won't believe this, but I was just about to call you," Casey told her. "I'm conflicted and I'm trusting you to tell me something."

"Shoot," Alexa said.

"I'm at Unko's. He admitted there was a ransom demand for Gary, and that he faked the note to keep you and Manseur from screwing things up. The kidnappers are going to be watching, the note said."

"You saw the ransom demand note?"

"Yes. I threatened to call you, so he and Decell showed it to me. They didn't want to. I want you to promise me you won't interfere in getting Gary back. But I want you involved, Alexa. You're better at this than Unko and Decell. I can't risk Gary getting hurt."

"It's your call, Casey, not your uncle's. Gary is *your* husband."

"They treat me like I shouldn't know anything. If it's my call, I'm making it. Unko's going to pay in bearer bonds. I told him he had to tell you and he and Decell both said that if I did, Gary's death would be on my head. The note says that Unko is to handle the actual swap. It could be dangerous, couldn't it? Decell should do it."

"This is far too dangerous for your uncle to deal with. I doubt even Decell is capable of handling it."

"Why?"

"Because it's possible that the person who has Gary may have killed Nurse Fugate. If it is who I think it is, he's very dangerous and mentally unstable."

"Alexa, there's something else."

"What?"

"I overheard Unko and Decell talking about some item Decell had to make sure he got from the kidnapper, no matter what else happened."

"Gary could be the item he meant," Alexa said.

"I don't think it was a reference to Gary. I know it sounds paranoid, but I think they have more than just Gary to recover in this exchange. I didn't hear it all, but I'm sure Unko said something about a diary."

"That's interesting," Alexa said, remembering the secret stash in Fugate's closet. If Fugate had kept her diary under the floor, there was no telling what she might have written in it that LePointe wanted it back to prevent anyone knowing its contents.

An ambulance raced past, its siren blaring.

"Where are you?" Casey asked.

"I can't say," Alexa said, knowing Casey had heard the siren in stereophonic glory.

"You're right outside!"

"Look, I'll do whatever I can, you know that. Try to trust me a little longer."

"I knew you were good. You already knew there was a ransom demand, didn't you? You're going to follow to the exchange, aren't you?"

"I need to get off the phone, Casey. We'll talk later."

"The note said Unko was to come alone and that they'd know if anybody else was with him or following him."

"Casey, do you know where Grace is?"

"Her phone must be off. I've tried to call her several times, but I get her message. Why?"

"I just wanted to be sure you weren't alone,"

Alexa lied. "The waiting will be excruciating for you until this is over. Where's Deana?"

"I have someone watching her at home."

"Just a sec, Casey." Alexa muted her phone and told Manseur and Bond what Casey had said. "Grace is in the wind," she whispered. "Fugate may have had a diary. That may be the trigger we discussed."

"Grace is going to be involved in the drop," Manseur said.

"If there aren't but a couple of people involved, I suspect she's got a job to do. Since she doesn't know that she's a suspect and was sure she'd learned everything she could from Casey, she's free to help out. What about the GPS tracker?"

"I got a pair of trackers and receivers. How are we going to get them planted?"

"LePointe's security is first-rate," Bond said.

"I have an idea," Alexa said.

She unmuted the phone and put it against her ear. "Casey, I need to ask you if you are willing to do something for me. It's important. It may also be risky."

"Name it, Alexa," Casey said.

60

Thirty minutes later, Casey appeared on the inside of the wrought-iron fence and Alexa handed her two half-dollar-sized disks. "They're magnetized," she said. "One for the Bentley and the other for Decell's car, so we can cover either or both. You think you can attach them without being seen and get back inside without being detected?"

"God, I've sneaked out of that house a million times without getting caught," Casey assured her. "They aren't interested in what I'm doing. They're making plans, or going over their plans. The note said the exchange would begin at nine, so I'm sure Unko will be leaving before then." Casey reached out and took Alexa's hand. Casey's hand was warm and her touch warmed and assured Alexa.

"How will they contact him?" Alexa asked.

"Calling his cell phone. Unko's supposed to come alone."

"Will Decell be following along?"

"I don't know how they're doing it. I'm sorry. But Decell must be planning to go. Unko wouldn't do it alone if it's dangerous."

Unless not doing it is more dangerous. "It doesn't matter," Alexa assured her. "Whichever car they use, we'll be ready."

"Okay. Will you call me as soon as it's over?"

"Word of honor," Alexa said.

Casey squeezed Alexa's hand, released it, then turned and was gone.

61

Casey West threaded her way between the bushes surrounding the courtyard to reach the cars parked there. She moved cautiously, keenly aware of the guard stationed at the gatehouse and of the closed-circuit cameras that covered the grounds. There was a second guard walking the property and she'd have to watch out for him.

Kneeling, she planted the first of the devices under Ken Decell's sedan to the frame, and after making sure it adhered to the steel, she scatted back into the foliage, to wait for the camera to take in the cars and sweep past to scan the portico.

As soon as the camera made its arc, she moved, stopping beside her Rover. Looking over the hood to check the camera's position, she was ready to move to her uncle's Bentley, when sudden light drew her eyes to the second guard, coming directly up the driveway toward her, a lit flashlight in his hand. She crouched down and froze. When the guard drew even with the back bumper of the Bentley, he stopped, and she flattened herself to the ground hastily. She heard a lighter click open and the odor of cigarette smoke reached her. The guard remained against the Bentley smoking, showing no sign of going anywhere any time soon.

As she squatted there she had an idea. Moving slowly to avoid making noise, she pocketed the bug and backed into the bushes. Swiftly she made her way back around the house, avoiding the other cameras, and the sensors that would turn on floodlights as she went. She made it to the door she had come out through, and slipped into the utility room, and from there, through the kitchen.

As she sneaked up the hallway, she noticed that her uncle and Ken Decell were still in the den, sitting together on a couch, Decell busily making diagrams and both men talking in hushed voices—exactly as they had been when she'd gone out to get the bugs.

She moved farther up the hall and slipped into Unko's office, where she went to a cabinet and opened the door to expose her uncle's safe. He hadn't changed the combination since she was a teenager and had found the combination while snooping in his office.

Once the heavy door swung open, she smiled as she saw the briefcase. She had guessed correctly that her uncle would have put the bonds there for safe-keeping until it was time to take them on his errand.

"What are you doing?" a voice asked.

Casey quickly straightened up, her heart pounding. Her aunt stood in the doorway.

"Are you looking for candy?" Sarah asked.

"Yes," Casey lied.

"It will make you fat," Sarah said.

"Dancers have to watch their weight," Casey replied. "You gain one ounce and you're not a ballerina any longer."

"Have you seen me dance?" her aunt asked.

"I love to see you dance," Casey said.

"Watch this," her aunt said, waving her arms wildly and moving her feet in what could only be described as an amazingly poor imitation of a tap routine.

Casey heard footsteps coming up the marble hall, and turned and slipped out the door she had come in through, just as her uncle's voice boomed behind her. She didn't dare close it for fear he'd hear the sound.

"Sarah, what in the world are you doing in my office?"

Casey listened, poised to retreat if she had to.

"Out of bounds," he finished.

"Candy makes you fat," she said. "We weren't looking for candy."

"We?" William asked. "Who's we, Sarah?"

"The lady that comes here wasn't looking for candy either."

"What lady?"

"You know perfectly well. That lady from the audience," Sarah said. "You're being silly, aren't you? You know her as well as I do. Rebecca."

"Rebecca's dead," LePointe said.

"Was somebody really in here?" Decell's voice asked.

"I am not telling you anything, Mister Redhead Man. Or you either, white-haired man!"

"It's all right, darling. You don't have to tell us anything. Where's Angela? Angela!"

Casey heard the night maid's voice. "Sorry, Dr. LePointe. I'm here. Miz LePointe, you best come on with me. She left out of the room while I had my back turned. I'll take her back up to her room."

"No harm done," LePointe said.

Casey fled back to the kitchen, poured herself a cup of coffee, and exhaled for the first time since she left the office. "Mission accomplished," she whispered. Then she smiled.

62

From her vantage point across St. Charles Avenue, Alexa could see the LePointe mansion illuminated by floodlights, the front gate, and, parked beyond the intersection, Manseur's Crown Victoria. She looked down at her passenger's seat, at the scuffed-up NOPD laptop, which was set to the frequency of the trackers. She had turned the brightness down so the glow wouldn't be apparent to the guard in the gatehouse. Alexa felt the familiar sense of excitement and anticipation growing inside her that she always got when the payoff was in sight—like a hunter watching a deer moving in the deep woods, making its way slowly to an exposed space in the trees.

Manseur's computer had the same views of both tracker frequencies, and he and Larry Bond would be able to follow whichever vehicle Decell used. They had lucked out by having Casey plant the trackers, and Alexa just hoped their luck would hold awhile longer. In the event that both vehicles left, Alexa would follow LePointe. Decell would certainly follow LePointe somehow, and would be pissed that the cops were covering the transaction, because there was obviously something going on that his employer wanted to keep quiet. If the police timed their appearance, they'd have unfettered access to a diary, hopefully detailing LePointe's crime—if such a diary indeed existed.

Alexa was startled by a sudden movement and turned to see Casey pulling open the passenger door.

"What's going on?" Alexa asked.

"I sneaked out. I had to talk to you."

"You could have phoned me. What if they miss you?"

"Relax, they won't even know I'm gone. I didn't get to put one of those bugs on the Bentley. A guard came. I had to go back inside."

"Did you get one on Decell's car?"

"I sure did," Casey said, smiling.

"One is a lot better than none. Good work."

"The other one is inside, in a much better place."

Inside is better? Might the house move? Alexa's phone rang and she saw it was a call from Manseur's cell. "Yeah?"

"Is that Casey in your car?"

"It is. She only rigged Decell's car."

"Well, then it's Decell who's on the move. Let's give him thirty seconds and trail him."

Alexa looked at the screen and saw a dot moving on the line. "You have to get out, Casey. I have to go. Decell's car is moving. Probably LePointe's will be leaving soon too."

"What about the other bug? Is it moving?"

Alexa looked at her screen again. She saw that the other dot, denoting the second bug, was stationary. "It's not," she said.

"Just watch it," Casey said.

"Decell's on his way out," Alexa said, pointing at the headlights approaching the front gate.

"He's not taking the bonds. Not unless the second signal shows movement," Casey said.

"How do you know that?"

"Because I planted the other bug in the briefcase containing the ransom bonds," Casey told her. "Unko's going to make the exchange personally. Decell will probably circle around to be there to cover him. That isn't Unko. I'm certain."

Alexa told Manseur what Casey had said.

"Damn it," Manseur growled. "I'm tailing Decell. I'll tell Bond to break off and follow the Bentley."

"No, I'm on LePointe," Alexa said, watching the

gate open and the Bentley pull out onto St. Charles Avenue. "Casey, they must have put the bonds in another valise."

"No, they don't have any reason to do that."

"The other bug is in the valise *with* the bonds," Alexa said to Manseur.

"Both cars are leaving," Manseur said.

"Unko is not in the Bentley," Casey insisted again. "It's got to be that extra guard Decell had come to the house."

"I think you're wrong," Alexa said. "My gut says the bonds are in the Bentley."

"I trust you, why can't you trust me?" Casey demanded, placing her hand on Alexa's wrist. "I know Unko. I think they're making sure they aren't being watched. They're very cunning."

Alexa lifted the phone and told Manseur, "Tell Larry to stick on the Bentley. I'm going to stay here to see if there's something else going on. If the valise doesn't move in ten minutes, I'll catch up."

"Hell, knowing Decell, he might not even have the bonds. He could be planning not to give them anything and take what they have by force. Decell probably thinks he's got the upper hand on a bunch of amateurs."

Alexa looked at her watch and back at the immobile flashing dot positioned inside the mansion. She prayed Casey was right and the caravan was a ruse.

The tracker's range was less than ten miles, and as she watched the tracker in Decell's car moving away, Alexa felt like a child being abandoned in a foreign place. Once the bug was out of range, she'd have to rely on Manseur to give her the location and on her car's GPS to get her to the meeting place. That would be both an inefficient way to navigate and she would certainly arrive late.

"It'll move soon," Casey repeated. "You'll see."

"Go back inside," Alexa told her.

"No way. Gary's my husband. I'm going with you. I'm going to be there when you find him."

"Absolutely not," Alexa said firmly. "This is dangerous, Casey. They've already killed Fugate."

"But I thought Sibby Danielson killed her. Is she in on this?"

"I think someone intended it look that way. I think whoever did it either killed Sibby or maybe has her stashed somewhere."

Casey looked at the computer screen, then crossed her arms stubbornly. "I'm not getting out, and unless you go now you'll never get to the ransom drop."

Alexa glanced at the flashing dot, which was moving toward the rear of the house. "What's out back?"

"The garage and staff parking, among other things. Unko's going to take one of the other cars. Aren't you glad I put the tracer thing in the briefcase?"

"What vehicles are there?" Alexa asked.

"There's a Caprice wagon, a Mercedes 500 sedan that was Sarah's, the servants' cars, and the guards'. If it's Unko, he'll take the Mercedes."

"Out!" Alexa ordered. "I can't worry about your safety and do my job!"

"I can handle myself. I'm a black belt," Casey said, pointing at the screen. "You better get going. Alexa; you can't drive and follow this little dot, and I don't think you know your way around well enough to divide your attention between the road and the screen. Let me stay. I can read you the streets he's on and you can just drive. See, he's already in a car, moving down the service alley."

Alexa knew Casey wasn't going to get out, she couldn't force her to do so, time was running out, and she could certainly use Casey's help. She slammed the Bucar in gear and pressed the accelerator down, pulling onto St. Charles. "Fine. Then put on your seat belt. And you will do what I tell you to do when I tell you to do it."

"Of course," Casey said. "I wouldn't have it any other way."

63

Alexa drove through the streets at forty-five miles an hour, holding a half-mile distance behind LePointe's Mercedes 500 sedan.

"The other tracker," Casey said. "It's off the screen."

"Let's just worry about ours for now," Alexa said. "I suspect they'll converge eventually."

"Left at the next light," Casey said. "I thought you'd have like fifty people covering this."

"In retrospect, I should have added one more person with local geographical knowledge."

"You'll be glad I'm along," Casey told her, resting her hand on Alexa's leg for a second. "You'll see."

Alexa needed Casey's help at the moment, but she was increasingly uneasy having a civilian along on what could be a dangerous operation. Worrying about Casey could keep her from taking chances she might need to take. "Just remember what I said about doing exactly what I say. I'm dead serious."

"It's your call all the way. Do you really think Grace could be involved in Gary's abduction? Left at the light."

"What about her personal life?"

"She spends most of her days with me. She's a very dedicated and hardworking individual. Gary doesn't appreciate her. He thinks . . . Well, it isn't important why."

"It might be," Alexa said.

"He thinks she's *too* dedicated. Jealous of him. I know it's silly." Casey laughed nervously. "He thinks she's in love with me."

"A girl crush?"

"More than a girl crush. It's nonsense. If she were, you know, I'd know. She loves me because we're close friends. Gary was just being . . . Gary. He watches out for me."

"Does Grace ever seem to dislike Gary?"

"Grace seems to like him just fine."

"Does she have a boyfriend?"

"Well, she did mention a while back that she met a man who's in medicine, but she said it wasn't serious. She calls someone and someone calls her, but she never said it was the same man. She'll tell me if it gets serious. Right at the next street. That one."

Alexa glanced at her. "What else do you know about him?"

"Not much. I've never met him. I don't even know his name. I told her to invite him along to a couple of functions, but she always said he was too busy. Wait a minute, she didn't tell me he was a medical professional. I overheard her answer the phone once; she called him Doc."

"Does she spend much time with you socially?"

"Well, she's my friend."

"Does Grace know about Sibby Danielson?"

"She knows she murdered my parents."

"Could she have known Sibby was at River Run?"

"How could she? I didn't know it myself!"

"You've been to River Run."

"Yes, but never on the wards."

"Do you know what Sibby looks like?"

"No idea."

"So you could have seen her and not known who she was?"

"Once I took pictures of some of the mental patients. Grace was with me. But those inmates weren't dangerous or anything. The orderlies brought them in to the cafeteria, stayed while I worked, then took them out again. It wasn't like I was in any danger. Grace assists me, but out there she was less helpful than usual."

"Why? Was she frightened?"

"No. She was sort of flirting with one of the orderlies. Small guy. But I don't really need an assistant for sessions."

Alexa's cell phone rang.

"Manseur," she said, opening it.

"Decell and the Bentley have led us on a wild-goose chase over the twin bridges, out to the English Turn golf course. It looks like we're heading back to the twin spans."

"Decell and the Bentley are red herrings," Alexa told him. "LePointe is going to make the drop. We're tracking his Mercedes out of New Orleans, along River Road. Maybe we're heading toward River Run."

"They're both headed back to LePointe's; we're coming that way. Just keep me posted on your location if you change roads."

Alexa closed the phone.

"I guess it's up to us," Casey said.

"Looks like a definite possibility," Alexa said.

"Unko's turning right," Casey said.

"What's this way?"

"Nothing," Casey said.

64

Leaving River Road, LePointe's Mercedes sped up dramatically. It turned down a series of county roads that Casey said were taking them toward Lake Bourne. By telephone, Alexa fed Manseur each turn. Manseur was racing to intersect them, but evacuation traffic made his route slow going. Alexa could imagine him blasting his horn, using the shoulder like a lane, and using the flashing blue lights like a snowplow.

It appeared that LePointe was carrying the bonds to some remote location. Unless Decell was hidden in the Mercedes, she prayed she could get to the drop before LePointe got himself hurt. If he did get hurt, she and Manseur would catch hell. She would do the best she could, and her first priority was to keep Casey out of harm's way. The potential for what the feds called a cluster-fuck event was too real.

They were on a narrow gravel road that wound along a mossy bayou. They passed several cabins, but saw no one, nor did they pass any other vehicles.

"He's stopped just ahead," Casey reported.

According to the tracker, LePointe had come to a stop or maybe he had reached some predetermined spot and thrown the briefcase from the car. Alexa cut her lights and drove slowly down the gravel road. When the tracker's location was fifty yards away, she pulled off beside some moss-covered trees and cut the engine. She called Manseur and told him where she was.

"I want you to stay here and wait for Detective Manseur," Alexa told Casey. She handed her the cell phone, took her Glock and badge case out of her purse, and slipped the ID and the extra magazines into her jacket pockets, one side of the handcuffs behind her belt, one outside.

"But you might need a hand," Casey protested.

"This is not a negotiation, Casey. You swore to do what I said."

"I rarely ever swear, but I did agree. Please be careful, Alexa. If you get hurt helping us, I'd never forgive myself."

"Just stay in the car."

Casey nodded. "I'm disappointed that you don't believe that I can handle myself, but your command is my order."

Alexa took her Kevlar vest from the back seat and stepped out into the sultry night, leaving Casey sitting alone in the Bucar. Outside the car, the air was filled with the smell of mud and stagnant water. The moon offered just enough illumination so she could make out the road and the trees. She slipped on the vest, cinched it tight, and started walking. Thirty yards down the road she came to a dirt driveway. She could just make out the shape of a cabin in a clearing on the bayou and the low shape of the Mercedes parked outside the shack.

As she moved toward the little wood-frame house, she froze. The interior light of the Mercedes came on as the door swung open. LePointe, wearing a wide-brimmed hat and a trench coat, despite the heat, climbed out, carrying a briefcase. Motionless, Alexa watched as he closed the car door and slowly approached the cabin's porch. She had been within thirty feet of the car when LePointe climbed out, close enough that she heard his cell phone snap shut.

Somebody swung the front door open, the interior light silhouetting his form for a moment before LePointe stepped inside and the door closed again.

Alexa closed on the structure, gun in hand. As she neared the porch, she could hear voices. The windows were covered from the inside with what looked like bedsheets.

Hoping to peer in one of the side windows, she moved quickly and as stealthily as possible around the side of the house, across the weed-covered brick-hard ground. The old panel truck they had been looking for was parked just behind the house, its rear end facing the building. On the bayou, a boat with a center console was tied to a short dock.

At one of the two windows at the cabin's back, a vertical rip in the curtain allowed Alexa to see what appeared to be the main room, lit by a camping lamp hanging from a beam. What she glimpsed through the narrow slit filled her with horror. Gary West, wrapped around with enough duct tape to make him look like a mummy, was bound to a wooden chair, which in turn was taped to a support post. A rucksack lay on the floor at his feet. A man wearing a dark running suit was aiming a handgun at LePointe and rocking back and forth on the balls of his feet. He had a woman's stocking over his face, mashing his features. The briefcase was still in the silver-haired LePointe's right hand, the brim of his hat pulled down over his brow like some gangster in an old film. The man pulled up the stocking, exposing his face, perhaps to see LePointe better, or so LePointe could see him clearly, because he was smiling broadly and brandishing a small revolver as he spoke.

It appeared to Alexa that the man with the gun was an older version of the same young man she'd seen in the pictures in Fugate's house.

The cabin wasn't insulated, so Alexa could hear some of what the man was saying. He was giving LePointe a severe dressing down, gesturing menacingly with the handgun, probably building up his courage to put one in the good doctor, Gary West, or both of them. Alexa was certain that since he had seen the man, LePointe was not going to leave the shack alive. She could see LePointe's right hand slowly reaching into his coat pocket. The armed man was pointing the gun at the ceiling above him and at Gary West, explaining something. Alexa wondered if LePointe was reaching for a weapon.

Alexa moved swiftly to the back door. She'd put her hand on the knob to turn it when two gunshots reverberated inside the building. She shoved open the back door and aimed her Glock inside, her eyes scanning the interior, trying to locate the armed man.

"FBI!" she yelled. The man was gone. LePointe was lying on the floor. She spun, spotted the man aiming at her, and was bringing her gun around when, from behind, a massive hand gripped her neck, a second hand reached around and twisted her Glock from her. He shoved her violently, the force sending her sprawling into the the chair holding Gary West. Whoever had manhandled her had been outside, watching in the darkness. She thought she smelled something familiar from her childhood. *Juicy Fruit gum.*

"I got her, Doc!" the man who'd shoved her yelled. "Hello there, Miss FBI."

The still-warm barrel of a gun pressed against her head. The sharp odor of cordite filled her nostrils. She couldn't take her eyes off the huge figure of Leland Ticholet, his massive hand gripping a section of lead pipe. In his other hand he held her Glock.

"It's futile to struggle," the gunman said. "I'd rather not kill you if I don't have to. Dr. LePointe pulled a gun, so I shot him in self-defense. *His* fault."

It's never the killer's fault. Alexa turned her head and looked at Dr. LePointe. The wall behind him was peppered with blood and brain matter. A compact semiautomatic handgun lay on the floor beside his lifeless body.

The man Leland Ticholet called Doc dropped to his haunches, opened the briefcase to make sure the bonds were in there, closed it, then stood.

"Where's Grace?" Alexa asked.

"It wasn't my turn to watch her." Keeping his gun on Alexa, Doc reached into the rucksack on the floor and took out a spiral notebook. "You should read this. It is highly enlightening and informative reading on the great and powerful Grand Poo-Bob of mumbo-jumbo, the destroyer of lives for the pure hell of it. He was a sadistic bastard who received too light a punishment. You'll see that I've killed a monster."

"He was a bastard," Leland agreed from the door, tapping his leg idly with her Glock.

Doc patted Alexa down, located her handcuffs, and pulled them out. "On your stomach," he commanded. "Hands behind you."

Alexa rolled over and, as he cuffed her using her handcuffs, looked at Gary West. She wasn't sure if he was alive or dead, until he moved his head slightly.

When the masked man rolled her back over, she saw above her a plastic-coated steel cable crisscrossing the rafters between pulleys, and then she saw the shotgun that had been bolted to the rafter. It was aimed down at Gary's chest. This creature had created a complex booby trap designed to end Gary West.

"Do you like my apparatus?" he asked her. "It was a great deal of trouble to put together, but the tinkering was a nice diversion. Leland, put her gun on the counter."

How is it set off? Her eyes ran along the cables until she saw the transfer-of-weight mechanism, a steel bowl connected to a counterweighted lever that would, as sand filled the bowl, tighten the wires running through several pulleys, until the increasing pressure on the trigger fired the shotgun.

"You didn't come out here all by your lonesome, did you?" the man asked. "Leland, is she alone?"

"I ain't seen nobody else."

"You can escape," Alexa said. "If you hurry."

"Tell Mrs. West that had not Dr. LePointe tried to rub me out, he and Mr. West would both still be alive."

"You don't have to do this," Alexa said. "You can take the ransom and get away. I've got backup on the way."

"Detective Manseur? Gary probably sustained some brain damage thanks to my somewhat overzealous assistant, but he might have recovered had it not been for the double-ought buckshot that will go through his lungs by means of my mechanical invention."

"LePointe was self-defense. Murder of a hostage in the course of a kidnapping earns you the death penalty."

"Everybody dies, dear Alexa," he said. "The question is whether it's best to die a pauper or prince." He lifted the briefcase so Alexa could see it. "I think the answer to that lies herein, don't you? Two point five million." He reached up, and taking hold of a thin cable, pulled it. Alexa saw the pin fall as the corner of an overstuffed bag opened and a thin stream of white sand started pouring into the bowl.

"Don't do this!" Alexa yelled at him. "Stop it and go."

"I'll go when—"

The front door flew open and Alexa turned her head to see Casey West standing in the doorway with her hands stretched out before her. Leland Ticholet reacted like he was spring-loaded—whirling and darting out into the night.

At Casey's entrance, Doc turned toward the door. He lifted the briefcase just as Casey fired the gun she was gripping. Bullets slammed into the case and Doc stumbled backwards, using the case as a body shield, moving for the open back door as fast as he could work his legs.

Casey advanced deeper into the house, firing steadily as she came. The reports were earsplitting. Casey ejected the empty magazine, letting it clatter to the floor. She shoved in a new magazine as she moved purposefully toward the kitchen. The man scrambled backward frantically, turned, and ran outside.

Casey fired several more rounds, then stopped.

Outside, a boat motor roared to life.

"Gary!" Casey yelled. She ran to him, dropping the weapon as she reached to hug him.

"Casey, get back!" Alexa yelled. "There's a booby trap. Get the cuff keys from my jacket!"

Kneeling, a fumbling and shaking Casey located the key and unlocked the handcuffs.

Alexa stood. She could see the cables to the apparatus losing their slack—tightening.

Casey was staring at the shotgun in the rafters. "Do something! Alexa, help him!"

Alexa's mind raced. The shotgun was not only bolted to the rafter using U-bolts so it couldn't be moved at all without tools, a steel plate had been placed over the receiver to keep anything from being placed behind the trigger to prevent its discharge. The cables were comprised of plastic-coated, twisted steel strands, which couldn't be cut without bolt cutters, and they were thin enough to make shooting them in half out of the region of normal marksmanship. Shooting the sandbag, perched near the peak, would only add to the speed the sand was flowing into the bowl, and hasten the inevitable.

Casey began clawing at the duct tape, hoping to free the chair from the column. It was clearly a futile effort, given the speed with which the bag was draining. The bastard had designed his device well; disarming it quickly was impossible.

The gun was going to go off.

Gary West was going to be killed by the blast.

Alexa hurriedly removed her ballistic vest and draped it over Gary's chest.

Almost before she got her hands clear, the shotgun exploded, the lead's off-center impact causing the vest to fly off, hitting the floor six feet away. She heard the wind rush out of Gary West's open mouth; smoke curled between the shotgun and its target.

Casey stood frozen, crying hysterically.

The buckshot hadn't penetrated the Kevlar vest. Alexa pressed her hand against Gary's neck and her heart leapt when she felt a weak but steady pulse under her fingers. "He's okay," she said.

Casey wrapped her arms around Gary and kissed him frantically. "Oh, my poor, poor, darling Gary," she sobbed. "We'll get you to the hospital."

Alexa ran to the Bucar for her purse, which held her folding knife. She found her phone on the seat, pressed the CALL button to reach Manseur, and ran back inside the cabin. Quickly, she began cutting away the tape.

"Manseur and Bond are on the way," she told Casey.

"Thank God," the other woman said.

Casey peeled the tape from her husband as Alexa made the incisions. When the tape was removed, they lowered Gary to the floor.

Next, Alexa moved over to LePointe, and as she removed his hat, his hair came off with it. When the wig fell to the floor she saw the bright red hair and the unmistakable features of the dead man.

"Poor Unko," Casey sobbed.

"Your uncle's still alive. It's Decell."

The steady whooping of sirens and bright headlights burned through the window sheets as cars swept into the driveway.

Alexa's eyes came to rest on the notebook on the floor. She picked it up and folded it, putting it into her purse.

"Is that the diary?" Casey asked.

"I won't know until I've read it," she answered. *Pandora's book,* she thought. Technically the notebook was evidence and she was collecting it for the investigation—albeit surreptitiously. She intended to see for herself what Fugate had written before deciding how she was going to proceed.

"I want to make sure it gets read. Just between us, for the time being, okay, Casey? Your uncle can't know I have it."

Casey nodded once and turned her attention back to her husband.

65

Manseur exploded into the cabin, gun in hand, the sirens outside still blasting. "Clear!" he yelled.

Bond came through the back door, holstering his gun. "Back's clear."

"EMS's ETA is thirty minutes," Manseur told Alexa as he squatted beside her, looked at Decell's corpse. "You're all right?"

"Fine. Gary's pulse is steady, but weak," she said.

"Should we take him to the hospital in your car?" Casey asked. "Wouldn't it be faster?"

"No," Manseur said. "There's a life-flight helicopter en route. The techs will get him ready for the ride, and see what he needs. We'd do more harm than good if we moved him, Mrs. West."

"I shot the kidnapper," Casey murmured. "I can't believe I actually shot someone."

"If you hadn't, Gary and I would both be dead," Alexa said. "I saw his and Leland's faces. . . ." Like a villain in some James Bond film, Doc had wanted to make sure Alexa appreciated his genius by setting his killing mechanism in operation before he killed her. Egotistical people were unpredictable criminals, and the smarter they thought they were, the dumber they thought everybody else was.

"So this kidnapper shot Decell for Dr. LePointe? Decell's almost a foot taller than LePointe. Maybe the shooter had never seen Dr. LePointe in person," Manseur said.

Alexa said, "Between the shadows, him expecting LePointe, not Decell, I can see it. And Decell was drawing a gun. We should make sure the rear is secure," Alexa said, standing.

"Larry, could you kill those sirens?" Manseur said.

Manseur followed Alexa out the back door. Flipping on his flashlight, he ran the beam over the truck, the sloping yard, the small dock. "Cooley at the lab sure nailed that truck."

"I have the diary," Alexa said in a low voice.

"What's in it?" he asked her.

"I'd like to examine it in private. Casey saw me pick it up. I told her to forget she did."

"What about fingerprints?"

"Leland took me by complete surprise. I never saw him until he had my gun. The guy Casey shot is the one in the pictures from Fugate's. Doc, Leland called him. He had gloves on, so I bet he didn't leave his prints. I'll wear gloves to preserve any other prints on the book."

"And then you're going to give it to me, right?" he asked. "The diary is part of the Fugate homicide."

"It's also part of the West kidnapping. I'll pass the book to you after I've seen if it is relevant to any federal crimes. I want to know why Dr. LePointe was willing to go to so much trouble to get his hands on it, but I don't want anybody else knowing I have it. Nobody else."

"When can I read it?"

"Tomorrow."

"First thing?" Manseur's expression reflected suspicion.

Alexa smiled. "Relax. You'll get your fair share of the credit."

"It'll be nice, having credit," he said. "Maybe the federal prosecutors won't be as easy for the good doctor to influence."

"You think?" Alexa said, frowning.

Twenty minutes later, sirens announced the arrival of an EMS ambulance. After checking Gary West's vitals, the techs placed him into the vehicle and it raced off to meet a helicopter being sent from New Orleans. Parish deputies had popped flares to guide the life-flight chopper to the closest paved road. After hugging Alexa tightly for a few long seconds, Casey accompanied her husband in the ambulance.

"Michael has to keep your gun for ballistics," Alexa told Casey.

Casey said, "I don't expect I'll be needing it again."

While Alexa and Manseur were standing beside the Mercedes, a Crown Victoria pulled into the driveway. Detective Kyler Kennedy got out.

"I called Detective Kennedy in because we need a warm body," Manseur said.

Without looking at Alexa, Kennedy addressed Manseur. "What do I do first, sir?"

"Ask Agent Keen," Manseur said. "We're out of our jurisdiction. This is a kidnapping case. She's in charge. It's up to her."

Flashing lights announced the arrival of two sheriff's department cruisers, following a Blazer with a light bar on the roof.

A tall, pole-thin man in a starched white shirt climbed from the Blazer and approached them.

"I'm Sheriff Buddy Lee Tolliver," he announced. "Y'all New Orleans PD?"

"I'm Special Agent Alexa Keen with the FBI."

The sheriff nodded at her.

"Sheriff Tolliver, I'm Detective Michael Manseur," Michael said, offering his hand.

The sheriff took Manseur's hand, smiled, and pumped it briskly. "Well, finally we meet, Detective. It's a pleasure." Sheriff Toliver explained loudly enough for his deputies to hear him, "This kind gentleman cleared a homicide for us last year. Burned-to-shit body we found in a Rover. I owe you for that one, Detective. Kept my stats clean enough to get me reelected."

"Didn't you run unopposed?" Manseur asked, laughing.

"That helped, too. What we got going on out here? Must be a homicide."

"Homicide it is," Manseur said.

"I don't reckon I'm lucky enough it's somebody got themselves murdered in New Orleans and got brought over here as a corpse, like last time. What's the FBI got to do with it? Don't ever get the FBI out here."

"Corpse is connected to a kidnapping that went sour. Agent Keen here and my department have been working it jointly. One of the dead men is an ex–NOPD detective."

"I don't want to sound like an ass, but this *is* my parish." The sheriff looked at Alexa. "First I hear of this *joint* operation in my parish is that my deputies are called by Homicide detectives, and when they get here they're told to direct traffic for some helicopter. Naturally, I'm a mite curious."

"We were following a ransom delivery and it ended up over here," Alexa said.

"You want a piece of this, Sheriff?" Manseur asked.

Tolliver shook his head. "Well, if the FBI is going to handle the expenses of the lab work, the investigating, and all that, there won't be a whole lot left over for my people. And it doesn't affect my stats. One more murder doesn't mean a lot to NOPD, but it skews the hell out of my numbers."

Manseur told him, "But if you want a bite off a sour apple, I can give you a plug with the press."

"Naturally," Alexa added, "we'd both allow you

fair share of the credit for being instrumental in helping us with a very important, high-profile kidnapping case and murder."

Sheriff Tolliver lowered his voice. "And maybe I'd help you out best by standing back and letting you work the scene? You'll mention my boys can flag in hospital choppers?"

"If you don't mind," Manseur said. "Might be expeditious."

"Too many cooks ruin the stew," Bond offered.

"Truer words were never spoken." Buddy Lee Tolliver's bright eyes were like steady beams of light. "But lots of people can cook up a gumbo. Forget it. We got us a wild-ass category four hurricane coming tomorrow night, so most of my people need to be out informing our good citizens they have to leave."

"That's a coincidence," Manseur said. "We got one of those coming too."

"We tell those that say they're staying put, they have to write their names and socials on theirs and their kids' arms and torsos with markers we carry, and do it while we're there, so we can identify their bodies later on," Tolliver said, casting his eyes on Alexa. "It works better than you'd think. We also got us a couple of game wardens missing since this morning that we have to help the state boys look for. I hope they ran out of gas or their boat motor broke down. I'm stretched pretty thin about now. You just make sure you treat my department fair when the camera lights hit you, Manseur, and I'm content to leave this mess to y'all. You want, I can leave a cruiser in case you need anything."

"We can manage, Sheriff," Manseur said.

"Sheriff Tolliver, are you familiar with a ma[n] named Leland Ticholet?" Alexa asked.

"Agent, I'm as familiar with that individual as I eve[r] want to be," the sheriff replied, grinning. "Ticholet's i[n] on this? That old boy sure as hell doesn't strike me a[s] anybody would be tied into a ransom demand."

66

Alexa was content to let Manseur handle the evi-dence collection and the crime-scene investigation under the color of her authority. She would work ou[t] the details with her superiors later, and if there was [a] positive outcome, there'd be plenty of credit to g[o] around for the FBI, the New Orleans Police, and th[e] parish. Manseur ordered a van to remove Kenneth Decell's body. The New Orleans crime-lab techni-cians were more than competent to collect any evi-dence in and around the cabin.

If this case had gone sour, it could have devastate[d] her career, but every case had that potential. Her di-rector had told her to help the NOPD with this, us[e] her best judgment, and that was what she was doing. She didn't want an FBI team she wasn't familiar wit[h] walking in on the case at the present point. The[n] she'd have to go by the numbers. Anyway, at that mo-ment most of the local agents were either making sur[e] their families were out of the city, or battening dow[n] the offices before leaving themselves.

Alexa and Manseur were out behind the cabi[n]

down by the place where the boat had been tied up earlier.

"How badly did Casey hit the little guy?" Manseur asked her.

"She hit that valise and maybe those bonds slowed or stopped most of the rounds, but Casey shot him at least once. Maybe more when he turned to flee."

"She tell you she was armed before you got here?"

"She has a concealed carry permit for the .380, and she was certainly justified in her actions."

"So, the answer is no?"

"Of course she didn't. You can't blame her for carrying, though, can you? She handles a weapon better than I do."

"You mean she hung on to hers."

"Dry up, Manseur. Leland wants your gun, he'll take it. I gah-rhone-tee."

"I'll put out an alert to area doctors and hospitals. Maybe he'll show up for treatment if he's still among the living."

"Good," Alexa said. "Have your techs collect everything and we'll decide what needs to go to the FBI lab. I'll ask for expedited blood and DNA evidence on Doc Doe."

"If this case is still that hot up there. I have a feeling Evans might want to put us on banging on doors, now that West is going home."

"We still have to find Sibby Danielson."

"Yeah, I expect that's going to be right up there beside finding out where Hoffa's buried."

Alexa stepped back and felt something under her heel. She bent, parted the weeds, and, using her flashlight, saw that the object was a cell phone. "One of them must have dropped this," she said.

Manseur picked it up carefully by the antenna and dropped it into an evidence envelope. "With any luck we can trace it to one of them. Looks like it has blood on it."

"Hopefully it's a prepaid cell on our sheets. Michael, Leland called the guy Casey shot Doc. I think he's Grace's man friend. We need to get her picked up. The phone will connect her to Doc and to this. Doc—he could be a physician, dentist, chiropractor, maybe a Ph.D."

"Or a tree surgeon," Manseur said.

"LePointe might be upset since Decell gave up the bearer bonds, and he didn't get his notebook," Alexa said.

"He has to act happy, because he's got Gary West back, and he sure as hell can't ask us about the notebook. Be interesting to see who does ask."

"My money's on Jackson Evans. Christ! What the hell's wrong with me?"

She raced around to her Bucar, opened the passenger side door, reached in, pulled the computer out, and opened it on the hood of the car. "The tracker is still in the briefcase."

"The tracker is out of range now or got damaged by a round," Manseur said, after seeing there was no blinking dot on the screen.

"We could use a plane to locate the bug if it wasn't damaged. If they keep the bonds in the briefcase, and they don't discover the tracker, maybe we can find them."

"That I can handle," Manseur said.

"I hate to leave this in your lap, but I need to go to the hospital. I want to see how Gary and Casey are. Maybe you can send Kennedy by Smythe's address and pick up Grace. You get her in an interrogation room, call me."

Alexa got into her car, plugged the hospital's address into her GPS, and drove away. She was feeling light-headed from a lack of sleep. As soon as she made sure Casey was all right, she had some reading to do. After that, she was going to grab a cat nap.

67

When Alexa arrived at Tulane Medical Center, she spotted Dr. LePointe in the Emergency waiting room, talking with Superintendent of Police Jackson Evans, who wore his starched white uniform shirt, resplendent with gold and silver pins testifying to his importance. Casey was at the opposite end of the room, seated alone, head down, as though inspecting her hands in her lap. She looked up and smiled when she saw Alexa come in.

Passing LePointe and Evans, Alexa walked straight to Casey and sat beside her. "How's Gary?" she asked.

"They're trying to stabilize him. He's got some brain damage, and he's severely dehydrated, but other than that, they won't know until they get further along. You saved his life with that vest." She broke down. Alexa put a hand on her shoulder while she sobbed wretchedly.

Dr. LePointe strode over and stood silently above

them. His expression was impossible to read. Not that Alexa gave a damn.

"This is one hell of a mess, Agent Keen," he remarked, almost pleasantly.

"Yes, Dr. LePointe," Alexa told him. "It is definitely that."

"There will have to be an accounting."

Alexa felt the heat of anger rising inside her. "I'm glad you understand that. You know, if you had leveled with me about the note and whatever else you and Decell kept to yourselves, the outcome could have been vastly different."

"I acted in what I perceived was my niece's best interests, and I followed Ken Decell's suggestions to that end. This sort of thing is new to me."

"I bet." She thought it likely Decell's corpse would get the blame for everything.

"You are responsible for the fiasco tonight," Casey said, firmly.

Alexa knew LePointe was responsible for a lot more than the mess of that evening. The full scope of his involvement was something Alexa planned to discover. Then they'd see who got stuck for what.

"Kenneth Decell was a professional," LePointe said, looking away. "Perhaps I shouldn't have followed his advice in this matter. The fact remains, Agent Keen, that you put my niece in a very perilous position tonight."

"She did not! I'm an adult, and I made a decision to become involved! All of this is on your head. Dealing with abductions is what Alexa does, and she does it better than anybody else at the FBI. Decell got himself killed because you two decided to let him handle something Agent Keen should have been dealing with. Can you explain how you honestly imagined that a retired detective could handle getting my husband back home safely better than an honest-to-God expert at it?"

"I was trying to get Gary back for you. Everything I did was to that end. I didn't involve Agent Keen because Kenneth insisted he had everything under control and that when lots of people are involved, things can go badly. The instructions from the kidnappers were quite specific about not bringing in the police."

"Jesus, Unko! Have you forgotten that I read the letter? If you had followed those instructions, and delivered the bonds and not sent Decell, it might have worked out. Instead, two people are dead, and I may have killed a man. If I hadn't been there, Gary and Alexa would have been killed. You didn't do anything for anybody but yourself."

LePointe stiffened. "Superintendent Evans has everything in hand. He's going to investigate this. Legally speaking, I had every right to pay that ransom without involving the authorities. Can anybody say for certain that person didn't intend to kill Gary all along, no matter who brought the ransom? Professional advice was what I paid Decell for. It was his decision to deliver that briefcase. I wanted to do it."

Alexa thought it convenient that Decell—who was, in cop lingo, DBRD, or dead beyond a reasonable doubt—couldn't contradict his patron unless he did so through a medium. She wondered what LePointe would do if she whipped Fugate's notebook out of her purse and waved it under his nose.

No, when she confronted William LePointe, she

intended to have everything figured out, so no matter
how much money he had, or how many friends in
high places who might try to stop her, he'd answer for
everything he was guilty of doing. Whatever it ended
up costing her, he was not going to walk away from
this without a few scars.

68

Leland Ticholet wasn't thinking about what had happened at Doc's little house. He was on cloud nine, now
that he had finally earned the boat he was piloting
through the familiar system of waterways, heading for
his little home on the water. He hadn't cut and run
when that lady started shooting at Doc. He had actually helped Doc, who was shot up, get into the boat. If
he'd had the ownership papers already, though, he
wouldn't have risked his ass waiting around for Doc.
Anyway, the woman had just been trying to shoot
Doc, who deserved it. Probably he'd promised the
woman something he hadn't given her too.

Leland's attention shifted to the gas gauge and he
frowned. The boat was useless without gas for the big
outboard, so he headed to Moody's dock to fill up the
tanks so he could get an early start in the morning to
run his traps and see if he'd caught any gators.

Thirty minutes later, Leland cut the motor and
pulled into the dock near the gasoline pumps. He tied
the boat up and looked at Doc, who was slumped in
the rear seat, hugging his briefcase. Doc didn't look
good, and he was leaking his blood on the fiberglass

deck. His skin was even whiter than usual. His gloves were smeared crimson and he was sort of shaking all over.

"What're we doing here?" Doc asked, his voice barely above a whisper.

"Gassing up," Leland answered.

"I need immediate medical attention," Doc told him.

"They only got Band-Aids and alcohol here."

"Please, Leland."

"You want a soda, cheese nabs, something?"

"You have to bring a doctor to me. I can't go to a hospital."

"Where am I going to get one?"

Doc didn't answer. His head fell forward, his chin coming to rest on his chest.

"Sit tight, I'll be back directly," Leland said. He stepped onto the dock, took out the pump, and, after opening the cap on the first tank, put the nozzle into the hole and locked it open. After both tanks were filled to capacity, Leland replaced the nozzle on the pump and loped inside to pay.

69

Grub had seen Leland's fancy boat coming in and had hidden behind the live bait well. He didn't know if Leland was still angry with him, but he didn't want to get thrown into the water if he was. Of all the things Grub didn't like, getting wet was high up on the list. When he heard the store door open and close, he peeked around the well and saw that Leland had left someone sitting in the boat. Curious, he darted from his hiding place and scooted down the pier. He cautiously approached the vessel and looked down at the man sitting behind the center console. The guy looked like he was sleeping. Grub squatted and stared at the man, at the belt tied around his leg, and the blood puddle by his feet. He was hugging a briefcase to his chest.

"Hey," Grub said. "Was it Leland done that to your leg? He cut you or something? I wouldn't doubt he done that."

The man didn't respond.

Grub picked up a piece of oyster shell and tossed it into the boat, watched for a reaction, ready to spring off if the man looked up, but he didn't move. Grub drew closer for a better look. The briefcase. Checking over his shoulder in case Leland was coming, he slipped quickly into the boat, squatted before the man, and studied the briefcase in his hands, reaching out to touch the holes. He wondered if they were from bullets.

"You alive?" Grub asked him.

The man's head lolled, and his right eye opened slowly.

"Help . . . doctor."

"I can call one. Five dollars," Grub said, picking a nice number and holding out his grimy palm. "Cash."

70

The streets around the hotel were teeming with people who appeared to be going about the business of partying, despite the fact that Katrina was barreling toward their playground with winds approaching 195 miles per hour.

At the Marriott, the lobby was crowded with people who finally understood that it was time to set aside their go-cups and get the hell out of Dodge. Of course, now all the flights were overfilled, all available rental cars had long since left the city, and unless they could find some transportation, the luckless bastards were going to be huddled in the Superdome bleachers along with the city's poorest, sickest, and most unsavory citizens. For hard-core criminals, a city-destroying hurricane had to look like the career opportunity of a lifetime.

On her room's television set, a satellite picture showed Hurricane Katrina as a one-eyed saw blade of white-cloud fury that seemed to cover the entire Gulf of Mexico. Katrina's sustained winds were expected to rise to an unbelievable 210 miles per hour and, the newscaster said soberly, she was going to be the worst hurricane ever to make landfall on American soil.

Alexa, who considered herself beyond being surprised by anything, was stunned. Before, the hurricane had seemed like some abstraction, and she hadn't allowed herself to believe the storm was really out there, because of the tempest she'd been involved with that was already there. She had heard that people died in natural disasters because their minds couldn't grasp an approaching cataclysmic event—the fear zone in the human brain can simply refuse to consider something that seems impossible. People see a tidal wave in movies, but one unfolding before their eyes seems a film to be viewed with awe.

The weathercaster showed a graphic of the evacuation routes out of New Orleans and warned that anybody who was foolish enough to remain in the city might well be underwater when the levees—designed for a maximum category three hurricane—were breached by billions and billions of gallons of water pushed by two-hundred-mile-per-hour winds up the Mississippi River into Lake Pontchartrain and into the vast network of canals surrounding the city. This was the perfect storm the doomsday prophets had been warning residents about for the past forty years.

There were the now-stale scenes of store owners and residents covering glass with plywood or X's made of duct tape. There was footage of bumper-to-bumper traffic, of a fistfight at a gas station that was running dry, shots of fishing fleets tied up in harbors, and of cheering drunks in the Quarter, just around the corner from Alexa's hotel. The bleary-eyed, bald mayor of New Orleans was hoarse from issuing warnings. How many times could one man predict ten feet of water in the city without his words sounding like static?

Alexa turned her back on the video horror, sat on the bed, slipped on a pair of surgical gloves, and removed the folded notebook from her purse. It was just a typical spiral-bound notebook, like the ones sold to students. Alexa opened the cover and began reading.

ONE WOMAN'S LIFE
LIVED IN THE SERVICE OF GREATNESS
by Dorothy Mason Fugate, RN

The writing was in an almost adolescent cursive. The author dotted her i's and j's with tight circles.

I remember the day I first laid eyes on the most handsome young physician (never call him a doctor) I had ever seen. I had been an RN for less than two years at that point, and I was almost knocked off my feet when he spoke his first words to me. I have never considered myself beautiful, but when he looked at me, I felt like I was the most desirable woman on the planet. (He later swore I looked just like Marilyn Monroe.) I saw the desire in his handsome face and piercing blue eyes. His blood is noble, as I will explain, and the LePointe family goes all the way back to ancient France.

We had our first sexual relations a few days later, and although I was not a virgin, it was like it was my first time. When my dear William completed his psychiatric residency, he and his wife (more about that relationship, if you can call it such, later) returned to New Orleans. Knowing how some doctors tell lies to us nurses to get what they want, I must admit that I sort of thought he might not do what he said he would, about bringing me down there, but shortly after he started working at River Run, he secured a nursing position for me in that mental hospital for the criminally insane, where he was starting to do very,

very important work, even though he had a thriving private practice, listening to rich people whine. He wanted to deal with really sick people. Even though he was very, very wealthy, he always worked really hard, and as a result of his work many hundreds of sick people have been made better. And I'm talking very, very ill people.

Few men are blessed with greatness, and he is one in a billion. From the day I met him, I was his in every way. I have no regrets whatsoever that I have given my adult life in service to him. By serving, I made a contribution that has value far beyond what most humans, aside from Mother Teresa, ever find.

Alexa shook her head, and turned the page. On the seventh page, she found an entry highlighted with a marker. Flipping rapidly through the remaining pages, she discovered that there were a lot of highlighted sections of text. These she went back to and read carefully. Seeing no reason for the author to have defaced her all-important work that way, Alexa was certain that Doc, or Grace, had marked the most important sections—the most threatening to LePointe's reputation.

Alexa noticed something else too. The pages were bound by spiral wire, but they were scored so that a page could be removed without leaving tattered torn edges. By removing pages that way, a strip still connected to the wire by the tiny holes remained after the page was removed. Three consecutive pages had been removed at some point by someone, perhaps Dorothy herself. *Why? What could have been worse than what she had left in the book?*

When Alexa finally closed the notebook, she took a deep breath and exhaled slowly to lessen her tension, gather her thoughts. The illuminated entries made her feel sick. It seemed obvious that the nurse had never intended the book to be read by anybody else. These revelations of Dorothy Fugate, committed to paper for whatever reason, explained why LePointe had agreed to pay the ransom. The nurse's words had the power to turn not only LePointe's world upside down, but Casey's as well. Alexa's dilemma was in how to close the distance between her duty as a law enforcement officer and as a human being.

She jumped when her cell phone rang. She reached into her purse for it. It was Manseur. She looked at her watch. It was two A.M.

"Yes, Michael," she answered.

"I'm at Grace's house. I think you'd better come over here."

"Is she being cooperative?"

"At the moment she's being dead."

71

Grace Smythe lived Uptown in a small house, three blocks from St. Charles Avenue. Manseur's sedan was parked in the driveway. All of the interior lights in the rear unit were burning, and Alexa pulled up to the curb, parked, and as she approached the house, Manseur opened the front door. He handed her a pair of surgical gloves.

"Where is she?" Alexa asked.

"The lady of the house is presently in the bath."

"How did she die?"

"Appears for the world to be a suicide."

"Means?"

"Looks like she just slipped under the water. She'd be no less dead whether she started breathing water for the hell of it or took drugs and passed out. She didn't smother herself or choke on a pill bottle cap, because the whites of her eyes are clear. Well, except for blue contacts."

"Was she helped along?"

"I'm in Homicide, Alexa. No signs of a struggle. No water splashed on anything."

"Water dries. Bruises show up later. Maybe somebody killed her."

"Then it had to be some ghost that floated out through the walls. Windows are all locked from inside. Doors, the same thing. Clothes and mat on the floor were dry is all I do know. No noticeable bruising or marks of any kind on her body. Glove up and follow me."

In the bedroom, two suitcases open on the bed reminded Alexa of hungry clams.

Manseur said, "I tossed those."

Grace's bedroom walls were covered with framed pictures of Casey, or Casey with Grace Smythe, or Casey with Deana, or both women with Deana. Not one picture included Gary West. There were several of Casey's photo artworks, just as Grace said there would be, but all of them rested on the floor, leaning against the walls. "Jesus," Alexa murmured.

"Woman was a Caseyholic. You have any idea she was like that?"

"I got some odd vibes. This confirms it."

Manseur pushed open the bathroom door. Grace Smythe's nude body lay in the now-drained bathtub. Her hair was blond, as was her pubic hair. A wineglass, lying between her legs, contained some trapped bathwater. The gold ear studs were missing, and Alexa saw that there were no pierce holes where they'd been. Two black wigs were perched on foam heads standing on the back of the toilet. Beside the tub stood a nearly full wine bottle.

"Sure looks like she and Doc Doe were working together, and Ticholet was their worker bee." Alexa reached down and lifted Grace's arm to gauge the rigor. "How long, you think?" she asked. "Before or after the ransom drop?"

"Since the interior lights were off, I think this happened during daylight. Well before the drop. The medical examiner can nail it down. Think she did this out of remorse?"

Alexa shrugged. "Maybe she realized she couldn't get away with it."

"She left a trail Helen Keller could follow."

"Her cell phone here?"

"Come with me," Manseur said. He led Alexa to the kitchen. On the table Manseur had placed a series of evidence bags. "First we have a plane ticket to Paris in her name, and a second—Paris to Madrid, under the name Bridget Longwood. I found a passport in her purse in that name with her picture on it. Bridget the blonde."

"She'd probably been planning this a good while."

"I also thought this was interesting," Manseur said, pointing to several stacks of bills. "There's fifty thousand there in crisp new currency. Tossed into her suitcase. Enough to hold her until her boyfriend met her with the rest."

Alexa looked at the pristine bills, and reached for the cell phone on the table. She opened it.

"Last calls are from Casey, who kept getting Grace's recorded voice." Alexa hit the MESSAGES key and listened to Casey's voice on four messages, asking Grace to call her back as soon as she got back.

"And this I found in the garbage." Manseur opened a plastic grocery store bag and removed a stack of photocopied pages. Alexa recognized them as duplicates of the highlighted pages from Fugate's diary.

"You read them?" she asked.

"What do you think?" he said. "Are they from the notebook?"

Alexa nodded. "So, what are you going to do with them?"

Manseur's face showed surprise. "It's evidence. Turn them over, eventually."

"Why did Grace have a copy?" Alexa asked. "They're worthless without the original to authenticate them. Michael, if you place this into evidence now, what do you think the upside will be?"

"Aside from exposing LePointe for the sick sack of crab shells he is? He could do time for kidnapping, holding Sibby and torturing her, or at the least conspiracy to kidnap her."

"You really think he'll do time? Who is it who's always saying, 'This is New Orleans.' Evidence vanishes all the time in places that aren't New Orleans."

"Okay, I understand. You can take it federal."

"I could possibly make a case using Veronica Malouf's testimony. It isn't going to be my decision to prosecute, but they might file on it, and they might get a conviction in the federal courts. Of course, you realize they'd try him in federal court here in New Orleans. It's a long shot," Alexa said.

"And so you would do what? Let it go? Let the old son of a bitch walk?"

Alexa said, "Gary's found. He's free now, and he'll stay that way no matter what we do. LePointe would pay a fortune to get that notebook. Millions."

"So, he pays us or he pays somebody else?"

Alexa watched as Manseur's eyes narrowed, his face turning into solid rock. "Wait a minute," he growled.

Alexa put her hand up, palm out. "Relax, Michael. I needed to make sure you were willing to go to the wall."

"Tit for tat. Okay."

"The diary will certainly destroy LePointe's reputation, and Casey will hate him, but she has to find out the rest, even though she's already suffered more than anybody deserves to. I think we need to put some serious thought into this. I can't see where making a case on him will have any negative effect on me, but even disgraced, LePointe could still destroy your career. Might cost you your job."

"I'll just have to find another one," he said. "Somewhere else."

"Did Evans call you earlier tonight?"

"He wanted a briefing, so I told him what happened out there. He asked me what we found in the cabin."

"Did he mention the notebook?"

"He didn't mention it specifically. But he wanted

me to give him the list of items we found. After the first time I told him, he asked if that was all and if I was sure. Then he asked me for the list again."

"Did he talk to Kennedy?"

"Not that I know of. The perps had the notebook before Gary was taken, so why did they go to the trouble to kidnap him?" Manseur said. "There's something about this that doesn't quite add up."

"Grace obviously wanted Gary dead and out of her way."

Manseur reached into a small evidence envelope and took out a picture of Grace standing beside a short man with a neatly trimmed beard. "This was in the suitcase," he told her.

Alexa nodded. "Doc," she said.

Manseur lifted one last evidence bag and gave it to her. Inside was a receipt for a motel room.

72

Sibhon. Sibby. Sibhon.
Dark in my eyes.
Where I am.
Cut the fog.
Cut the fog.
I am Sibby.
Here I am in the dark.
Don't forget.
Never quit.
Tell the lies.
Find them where they hide.

Say the poems.
Say the poems.
Find the poems.

Stop saying I did it.
Tell a lie.
Stick a needle
In Sibby's eye.

Fucker man, fucker man.
Put the chopper in my hand.
Windy rain. Windy rain.
The stinky nurse is here again.

Lie bitch, lie bitch.
I know the trues.
I never lose.
I still can choose.

The baby comes, the liars go.
The smiling cop deserves a blow.

73

At 5:30 A.M., Manseur and Alexa arrived at the
Crescent Inn on Chef Mentaur Highway, a long line
of rooms with their doors painted fire-engine red to
match the plastic shutters that had been screwed into
the stucco beside the windows. The sad and shabby
place was an illustration of deferred maintenance and
a haven for crack whores on their way down.

At the sound of a buzzer activated by opening the door, the manager came out from the adjoining room. A rumpled daybed was visible through the partially open door. The middle-aged woman wore a crooked smile, which, thanks to the smeared lipstick, caused it to appear to be sliding off her face. Her red hair with inch-long brown roots was flat on one side and her eyes bleary from the alcohol—a rancid bourbon reek wafted from her—and the interrupted sleep. Before Manseur even raised his badge, the woman frowned in recognition of police authority.

"I don't know what all goes on in the rooms," she said automatically. "I just collect the money and hand out the keys."

"Room 113 occupied?" Manseur asked.

The manager made a show of opening a registration ledger and pointing to an entry. "Four days ago. A week paid in advance. Cash."

Manseur looked at the entry the woman's finger was resting on, reading it upside down before she turned the book to him. "John Hancock? Stands out among all the Smiths and Joneses," he quipped.

"You remember him?" Alexa asked.

"How could I forget an educated and polite young man such as he is? Quality individuals are not exactly in plentiful supply around here."

"Quality?"

"The vocabulary of a man of culture and breeding."

"Is this him?" Manseur showed her the photo of their John Doe standing with Grace Smythe.

"Don't tell me he's in trouble? Don't tell me. He some kind of what, grifter? They can fool you—the good ones. Thank God he paid in advance."

"Was he alone?"

"He had a woman in his truck. She didn't come in. I saw her through the window."

"Describe her," Alexa said.

"She's the one in that picture. I saw her pretty good, even though I didn't go out and visit with her. He paid cash in advance for ten days, and that's as far as my interest went into his business."

"When did you last see him?"

"Day before yesterday morning, I think."

"What was he driving?"

"An old green truck, which was not what you'd think he would drive. My father had one for his dry-cleaning business when I was a little girl."

"A panel truck?" Alexa asked.

"Dingy-looking. I figured he was planning to fix it up like people do with old shitty vehicles like that. They have the body fixed, you know, paint them, and it's no longer junkyard trash to a collector."

"I'll need the room key," Manseur said.

"I'm not gonna stop you. If anything kinky or illegal is going on in there, it's no skin off my butt."

Manseur and Alexa went to the door of room 113, Doc's lair, and stood on either side of it, guns drawn. The extortionist was wounded, but if he was in there, he'd be armed. Inside, the television was blaring hurricane warnings. Manseur slipped the key into the lock and turned it slowly, pushed the door open fast, and rushed in, with Alexa right behind him.

The overpowering stench of human excrement mixed with sweat and stale urine filled the airless room. Alexa hit the light switch and they stared at a large woman dressed in a nurse's uniform, lying motionless on the horribly soiled sheets. The uniform had been rolled up to expose her naked body from the waist down. Her wrists and ankles had been duct-taped together. Two bands of duct tape had been looped around her head to cover both her mouth and her eyes. Whoever had taped her eyes and mouth had also pinned her long white hair to her head in the process. Two cargo-securing straps had been looped around the bed, and the ratchets tightened to hold her bulk in place.

"Jesus Christ," Alexa murmured, shoving her Glock into her purse.

"I think it's more likely Sibby Danielson," Manseur contradicted flatly. "Why's she in that uniform?"

Frowning, Alexa moved around the bed and reached to feel for a pulse. The trussed woman jerked from her touch like she'd been touched with a live wire and began thrashing violently. Due to the duct tape over her mouth, her protestations were a steady humming.

"She's alive?" Manseur asked, surprised.

74

EMS arrived fifteen minutes later. Sibby Danielson had to be sedated before being freed by EMS and strapped to a gurney to be taken to Charity Hospital for a physical evaluation. Then she'd be relocated to the maximum-security mental ward to undergo observation.

The motel room held no obvious clues, and Alexa doubted the techs would find any meaningful fingerprints in the hundreds they would likely collect there.

It was clear the maids didn't bother to wipe the counters between hourly visitors.

The police plane that was using a receiver to search the lakes and swampy areas between New Orleans and Baton Rouge a grid at a time hadn't picked up the signal from the GPS by nine A.M.

Every available police officer in the region was pulling traffic duty, while the nonstop tourist-driven party on Bourbon Street was still going strong. Katrina wouldn't even notice that she was blowing intoxicated revelers into Mississippi.

From Charity Hospital, Alexa had followed Manseur back to headquarters and she'd collapsed immediately on the couch in his office and fallen into a fitful sleep. Her dreams were filled with Grace Smythe, Casey West, LePointe, and a menacing giant. When she awoke, two hours later, she was alone. She got up, found the restroom, used the toilet, and washed her hands and her face.

Back in Manseur's office, she poured a cup of coffee from the pot Manseur had made and stared at the stacks of phone logs they had left on the conference table the afternoon before. Manseur had highlighted the numbers of interest, and she flipped through them again, looking for something in them that would make everything fit together.

Had Grace and Doc's relationship been purely business? Lovers would probably have talked longer. She wondered how the two of them had met. It was most likely that Doc had instigated the plan to sell Fugate's notebook to LePointe, since Doc was directly connected by photographs to Fugate. But Alexa was troubled. Why had they kidnapped Gary West? Or had Casey been Grace's target? Grace clearly had an obsession with Casey. Whatever the motive, killing Gary should have worked. Now, with Grace dead, they might never know her true motive. Unlike Fugate, Grace hadn't left a diary to fill in Alexa. But had she left one in another form?

Did Grace, Doc, or Sibby kill Fugate to get their hands on the notebook, or had Leland Ticholet done it at their bidding? There was photographic evidence that Fugate had known Doc for most of his life. There was no doubt of the notebook's value as an instrument that would guarantee the payment of the ransom. Were the three missing pages enough on their own to hold in reserve in case more leverage was necessary? Or to allow them to go back to the well? Had Dorothy Fugate torn the pages out ages ago because she'd made a mistake? Or had she written something on them she felt the need to destroy?

Doc Doe—whoever he was—must have been connected to Ticholet through Fugate and her nursing position at River Run. He must have recruited the violent man for the job. What inducement did Doc offer him? What was a big payday to a fisherman/trapper? A few hundred? Drugs?

Manseur strode in and sat heavily behind his desk. "Brace yourself. Notebook's out of the bag. It—"

Jackson Evans walked in before Manseur finished his warning. He forced a smile at Alexa.

"Michael tells me you found a diary at the West crime scene."

Alexa was struck dumb by what appeared to be a betrayal. "I'm sorry?"

"I'll take charge of it and make sure it's handled properly."

"For safekeeping?" Alexa asked, sarcastically.

"It's evidence, Agent Keen. In a homicide."

"It's evidence taken from a crime scene *outside* your jurisdiction, but clearly *within* mine. It directly relates to a kidnapping, extortion, conspiracy to commit murder, and using the wires in furtherance of those crimes. You will get a look at that notebook only after it is fingerprinted by my lab and its authenticity is established."

"May I ask where it is now?"

"In the possession of the Federal Bureau of Investigation."

"I see. Fine," Evans said, clapping his hands together. He was seemingly nonplussed by the news. "All in all, I think this was a successful if somewhat unorthodox joint operation. I'll make sure your director knows you performed professionally and I'll send a letter of praise for your jacket. You have my personal thanks and I'm sure that of the Wests. I suppose you'll want to get packed and head back to Washington while the getting's still possible. If you can find a seat on a flight out." He looked at his watch.

"I'll do that. And I'll have a copy of the notebook sent to you as soon as we've fingerprinted it."

"The notebook's a moot point," Manseur said glumly.

"It is? Why?" Alexa asked.

"Because," Evans said, "despite the fact that *moot* actually means *arguable*, every TV station and newspaper already has it. Or will by noon. It's going to be all over the news very shortly."

"How?" Alexa asked, the heat of confusion rising within her.

"Copies were delivered to them."

"Delivered how?"

"In the morning's mail," Manseur said.

Alexa grabbed her purse. "I'm out of here."

"Where are you going?" Manseur asked.

"I have to get to Casey before she hears about the diary from a reporter. All they have are photocopies; it will take some footwork on their part to verify the pages are authentic. They'll learn the psychiatric-nurse author is dead and that Sibby has been found. They'll be cautious about confirming before they attack Dr. LePointe, but once they smell that he's vulnerable, it's too big a story not to run."

Alexa reached and picked up an evidence envelope from the table that contained the picture of Doc and Grace. She left the two men and made a beeline for the stairs.

Manseur caught up with her. "You thought I ratted you out," he said. "Before Evans told you about the deliveries to the press."

"It never crossed my mind, Michael. Well, just for a split second I was . . . Obviously the kidnappers were planning all along to take LePointe's money and kill Gary West and LePointe. And since the copies arrived in today's mail, the delivery mechanism was in motion *before* last night."

"But the notebook might never be authenticated if Doc had given LePointe the original."

"True. But it would have made LePointe squirm

nonetheless. And there's the missing pages. I don't think Dorothy took them out. They're consecutive pages. One event—or a couple of them that are worse for LePointe than what we have. The position of them datewise is crucial. I missed it at first. Those pages would have been written twenty-six years ago."

"I'll go with you."

Alexa's brain was racing as she went over avenues of investigation out loud. "Michael, we have to identify Doc. Maybe Doc visited the hospital with Fugate. He recruited Leland. That would take more than one or occasional visits. We know he was connected to Fugate and somehow to Grace. Casey told me she took pictures at River Run and that Grace flirted with an orderly. She's been seeing someone and Casey didn't meet him. Maybe Doc isn't a doctor. Maybe Doc is just a nickname. I think he was an orderly at River Run. It fits. Talk to Whitfield or Veronica, if you can find her, and see which orderly he could have been. Can you do that for me? And get an address for him."

Alexa left Manseur behind her on the stairwell. As she hurried to her car, she dialed Casey's cell phone. She had to contact Casey and tell her she was coming.

75

Traffic was light and Alexa saw no evidence of a door-to-door forced evacuation as she drove into Casey's neighborhood. No cops stopped Alexa's car to demand to know why she hadn't yet fled the endangered city. The guard Decell had stationed there was ignoring the reporters clustered outside Casey's gate. Several yelled at Alexa as she walked past them.

"Mrs. West is expecting me," she told the guard, who looked like a Midwestern college quarterback with perfect teeth.

"She's inside," the guard said.

The front door was opened by another guard, who accompanied Alexa back to the kitchen, where a woman in a white uniform was cooking lunch. Casey sat at the table holding her daughter in her lap.

"How's Gary?" Alexa asked as she placed her purse in one chair and sat down in the one beside it.

"He's going to pull through," Casey replied. "They won't know how much brain damage he has until he regains consciousness. Bad concussion, but thankfully not bad enough to be fatal. He was horribly dehydrated. They're very hopeful, though. He's being moved this afternoon by air ambulance to the Mayo Clinic because of the hurricane. They think he'll be stable enough in a few hours. We can't risk him being in a hospital here without power or water, and the best doctors are there."

"Casey, I need to tell you some things about all of this before you get blindsided. I'm not sure it's my place, but I thought it might be better coming from me than—"

"The reporters," Casey interrupted. "I've been getting calls, but I'm not taking any from numbers I don't recognize."

"Good idea."

"I can't get Grace on the phone to tell her we have Gary back. Have you spoken with her? Maybe she left with her parents, but she should have called."

Alexa looked at the cook, then back at Casey. "This is something I think you alone should hear."

Casey scooted back her chair. "Mary, could you finish feeding Deana? Coffee, Alexa?"

"No. Thank you."

Casey led Alexa to the den.

"Grace is dead," Alexa said bluntly.

"Oh, no! It can't be *true!* How? When?"

"Yesterday afternoon. She was in her bathtub."

"She fell?"

"No, she didn't fall. Coroner says suicide. There were no signs of foul play. She had bathwater in her lungs."

Casey stared at Alexa. "Not an accident?" she said in disbelief.

Alexa shook her head. "It looks like suicide."

"So, she *was* involved in Gary's kidnapping?"

"Yes, it appears she was."

"Was there a suicide note?"

"We didn't find one."

"Poor, poor Gracie!"

"Maybe she did it because, even though they might have gotten away with the ransom, she must have been sure we'd figure out her part in it. Or maybe she regretted her involvement. Couldn't live with the betrayal," Alexa said. "I believe her accomplice, the man you wounded, was connected to Dorothy Fugate, maybe even related to her. He killed Dorothy and then stole her diary to blackmail your uncle. It appears he and Grace took Sibby to a motel and tied her up. I have positive IDs on Grace and her accomplice."

"Why?"

"The diary Fugate kept might hold some answers. I don't know yet."

"So she kept a diary? Who gives a damn if Unko sleeps with a nurse? Was it because of Sibby and the hospital?"

"Yes, that was detailed in the diary pages. But I'm afraid there's more that is far worse than that. Casey, your uncle treated a young psychiatric patient. He got her pregnant."

Casey gnawed her lip, then shook her head. "He had an affair with a patient? And Fugate knew it?"

"She did. The baby was born in Fugate's house, and taken away from the girl. It was adopted. Your uncle had a judge friend handle the placement. Nobody knew the patient was pregnant. She had gone missing and her family was sure she was wandering the city, which she'd done before."

Casey shook her head dazedly. "Unko has an illegitimate child somewhere? He'd be a blood heir. That would explain why Unko wanted the diary so badly. The money is far more important to him than Gary ever was."

"Sibhon Danielson was the patient."

Casey's eyes were blank with disbelief. "I have an illegitimate cousin whose mother is an insane murderer? The woman who murdered my parents has a child who's related to me?" Her frown grew deeper. "You can't mean little Bill. He died. He *wasn't* Sarah's son?"

"It wasn't a boy. Your uncle gave her to a couple who desperately wanted a child but couldn't have one of their own. Someone in the family."

"In our family? Like a distant cousin? Who?"

"Your parents."

"But I'm the only daughter my parents . . ." Casey faltered, and the color drained from her face.

Alexa nodded.

Casey stood, stumbled, and collapsed.

76

"Sit here. I'll get you some water," Alexa said.

"It's impossible," Casey insisted. "I don't believe it. Fugate lied in her diary."

"I'm absolutely sure she didn't," Alexa told her.

"How can you be one hundred percent sure it's true?"

"I'm sure DNA will confirm it. According to Fugate's diary, your uncle spent a great deal of money to buy silence. Decell was first on the crime scene, and he freed you from Sibby. Fugate's diary says that Decell knew about Sibby being your mother, but not how he found out. Sibby could have told Decell that night or maybe he saw Dr. LePointe there. That secret explains his connection to your uncle, more than the fact that she attacked him when he interceded."

"Me? I'm . . . ?" Casey was totally stunned. "My uncle and that woman? Unko is *my* father? My birth mother is a schizophrenic psychopath?"

Alexa nodded.

"She killed my parents. Was she going to kill me?"

"I don't know for sure, but I don't think so."

"She was here to, what, take me back? Motherly instincts?"

"It's possible, I suppose."

"It's totally preposterous! Four years after I was born she just decided I was here and came here and murdered my parents. Don't you see, if it's true she knew I was here, then Dorothy Fugate must have been the one who told her."

"You may be right. That was twenty-six years ago, though, and I doubt we'll ever know." Again Alexa thought about those missing pages.

"After the murders, Sibby was committed to River Run, where your uncle was practicing. He and Fugate made sure Sibby never said a word about what had happened. The two of them conspired to keep her in a mental fog. Just in case she came out, your uncle performed a prefrontal lobotomy on her, which was not recorded. The doctors at Charity confirmed that by the scars."

"Where's the Fugate diary? I want to see it for myself."

"I have it in a safe place. I intend to use it to build a case against your uncle. I just wanted you to know what's in it before it becomes public knowledge."

"Where's Sibby now?"

"She's hospitalized for observation at Charity."

"What will happen to her?"

"She'll be going back to River Run, or someplace like it, I imagine. I don't know how dangerous she is now. They'll have to evaluate her and make that decision."

"I can't believe my mother is . . . that woman. And you think Grace knew it?"

Alexa nodded.

"How?"

"This is the man she called Doc." Alexa took out the picture of Doc standing with Grace and handed it to Casey. "He had a connection to Fugate and another inmate at River Run, who helped them kidnap Gary and kill Dorothy. Grace had a copy of the diary at her house."

"I've seen him before. Wait. He's that orderly at River Run. Just a minute. Is he the man I shot?"

"He may be a relative of Fugate's. She mentioned her nephew in the diary, but not by name. I think he targeted Grace and somehow enlisted her help."

"Grace was so alone that it probably wasn't hard. He probably seduced her, poor thing. What's his name?"

"Doc is the only name we have. That's what I heard Leland Ticholet call him."

"Grace is—*was* my closest friend. She was loyal."

"Maybe you were her friend, but it appears she wasn't yours. I'm sorry to have to tell you all this."

"You were suspicious all along." Casey shook her head. "You said I shouldn't tell her anything you told me. . . ." She put her head in her hands, ran her fingers through her hair. "My grandmother told me never to trust anybody. She said those closest to me would be the most envious of what I had. She didn't care for Grace, but allowed us to be friends because Grace was socially acceptable. My grandmother wasn't much fond of anybody." Slowly, Casey tucked her hair behind her ears. "Maybe you're wrong. Maybe Grace was framed and that man I shot killed her so we wouldn't know. It's possible, right?"

"The man you shot got away. I think he gave Grace the money they'd need to get away until they could cash the bonds. We found a plane ticket to Paris in her name and another to Spain, in her false name. Her suitcases were packed. Grace had dyed her hair and had colored contacts to alter her appearance. This was well planned."

"Grace always was organized."

"I think Grace and Doc sent out photocopies of the diary to the media. That's why they're calling you."

"Why would she do such a thing? This is all going to be made public? All of it? Why? And if this Doc had the diary, why did they bother to kidnap Gary?"

"I'm not sure, but I think that may have been Grace's idea, maybe a requirement for helping Doc. She had lots of pictures of you in the apartment."

"We've been friends for nearly twenty-five years. I have pictures of her in my house and studio."

"She had boxes filled with them. Covering the walls, in drawers. She was obsessed with you."

"You mean like stalker obsessed?"

Alexa nodded.

"Is it possible that Unko or Fugate told Sibby about my parents? So that she'd harm them? How awful!"

"The diary didn't say so."

"It wouldn't necessarily, would it? Who in their right mind would write *that* down? That they'd deliberately sent a madwoman into the home of two innocent people, to butcher them? Unko would never have had any control if my father had lived. Alexa, my family history is filled with the person in control being ousted by the person next in line. The strongest warrior in waiting defeats the king, and takes over. Alexa, it's true! I know that's what happened. Unko deliberately used her to murder my parents!"

"I'm sorry you had to hear all of this from me. Sorry you had to hear it at all."

"You're most sorry because it's true," Casey said, smiling for the first time since Alexa had mentioned the notebook. "You are a wonderful, kind person, Alexa Keen. We're alike, you and me. Orphans. It's true. Don't you see?"

Casey embraced Alexa. "You *are* the savior of the lost. If there's anything I can ever do for you, it's yours."

Alexa left the West house. She ignored the shouted questions of the members of the fourth estate, gathering like hungry crows.

77

Alexa tried to call Manseur to give him an update on her meeting with Casey, and to check the status of the search for the tracker that might lead them to Leland Ticholet and the wounded Doc Doe. The call went straight into his voice mail.

"Call me when you get this," Alexa said.

Ten minutes later, when her cell phone rang, she flipped it open.

"Keen," she answered.

"Alexa," Manseur said. "Where are you?"

"Almost back to the downtown."

"Have any blue jeans with you?" he asked her.

"At the hotel. Why?"

"Sneakers?"

"I have running shoes? Why?"

"Go to your room and change into them. We got a signal on the briefcase tracker in the swamp. I'm leaving the office. I can swing by and pick you up. Kennedy and Bond are getting some equipment and they'll meet us."

"Ten minutes," Alexa said. "I'll be out front waiting for you."

Twelve minutes later Alexa climbed into Manseur's car just as he was yawning. "I thought this might be better than a purse out there." Manseur handed her a high-rise belt holster for her Glock as well as a magazine holder with a pair of loaded magazines. "Those are your mags. The lab returned them."

"You are so thoughtful." Alexa went into her purse to give Manseur the one he'd loaned her.

"The cell phone you found in the grass was the mystery prepaid cell number," Manseur said. "The phone links Grace to the other perps."

"No surprise there. By the way, Casey confirmed that our Doc was the orderly from River Run that Grace was flirting with when she was taking pictures out there."

"Which reminds me. Doc's real name is Andy Tinsdale. Veronica gave me his last known address. Tinsdale was on the violent wards for three years. He left, under a dark cloud, about the time Fugate did. There were some unsavory accusations involving patient abuse and missing meds."

"Tinsdale. I remember the name from the list of staff. We need to have a look in his place."

"We will when we get back. I had patrol check the apartment and it's locked up tight. Neighbor said nobody's been in since day before yesterday. By the way, don't be surprised if there are sound trucks from a caravan behind us. The damned media is in a feeding frenzy, trying to slip this bombshell in to augment their hurricane coverage."

"Already? They don't know the diary's authentic yet."

"Yes, they do."

"How?"

"Casey West told them."

"Casey? You sure?"

"Saw her on the TV myself just before I called you. Announced that she's just learned about the diary from an FBI agent, who told her it was authentic. Said she's crushed by LePointe's actions, but says her uncle should have a chance to explain everything to her and to the public before he's judged. No matter how scandalous and despicable his actions were, or what actual crimes he committed, he has been a friend of this community, or some such happy crap. Woman threw the old goat to the wolves."

"Couldn't happen to a more deserving individual," Alexa said. She certainly couldn't blame Casey for reacting as she had, but she hadn't expected Casey to go public.

Usually people like the LePointes played things close to their vests and the public arena wasn't the place for washing their dirty laundry. But Casey had certainly earned the right to change the LePointe family handbook.

Alexa almost felt sorry for LePointe. Almost.

78

Alexa and Manseur listened in silence as the car's radio informed them that refugees from Katrina, using everything from motorcycles to bus-sized RVs, were leaving New Orleans. All of the lanes of the major roads leaving the city were handling one-way traffic only, and the vehicles on the main roads were leaving at a crawl. Vehicles of every description littered the sides of the roadways, some with hoods raised, their occupants waving desperately at passing cars. Even the back roads were bumper-to-bumper. Gasoline stations were mobbed by desperate motorists or people wanting gas for generators, or the stations had run out of fuel.

Mayor Ray Nagin's strong voice came over the airwaves, pleading. "*. . . believe that. People, the plain fact is that Hurricane Katrina is going to be the most powerful hurricane ever to make landfall in the history of the United States, and it is coming in right here this evening. The water surge, a wall of water twenty feet high, is going to be pushed by two-hundred-mile-per-hour winds up the Mississippi River into Lake Pontchartrain, and it is going overtop the levees. It is suicide to remain in the city, because your homes are going to be flooded. The police are going door to door with orders to forcefully remove everybody*

*found in any home or apartment, and those people
are going to be taken to the Superdome, which is
twenty feet above sea level. I urge you all to heed this
warning and get out of your homes and businesses
and remain out of the area until we give an all-clear to
return. The police and National Guard will deal with
any looters, using all necessary force. If you cannot
get out of the city, go to the Superdome now. This is
going to be the worst-possible-case scenario storm. I
can't say this any stronger. There are going to be bodies floating in the streets."*

The governor spoke about coordinating state and
federal agencies. But a new voice had been added to
the dire warnings. President George Bush talked
about which federal agencies he was sending and finished his message with *"I have just three words to say
to the people of New Orleans and the Mississippi
Gulf Coast. Get. Out. Now."*

"I guess he's made himself clear," Manseur said.

"It's mind-blowing that people think they can ride
this one out," Alexa said.

"This is New Orleans, Alexa. Where fantasy and
denial meet over drinks from sundown to sundown."

"We need a helicopter to get us around this,"
Alexa said.

"I tried to get one. There wasn't any to be had for
two hours."

"Maybe we should have waited."

"Look," Manseur said. "We caught up to Bond
and Kennedy's car." When Bond saw the blue lights
coming up behind his Crown Vic, he slowed and let
his ex-partner pass him. Seconds later Bond's car was
riding right behind Manseur's bumper.

With sirens blaring and blue lights flashing, it took an hour and a half of hard driving on rural highways and snaking parish back roads to get to their destination.

The two-car caravan got to Moody's landing, where Buddy Lee Tolliver's sheriff's department boat had just been unloaded from its trailer and now waited, moored to a dock beside a bait and tackle store. There was a cluster of small boats—a redneck armada—waiting their turn in the channel to be loaded onto trailers, one of which, behind a ratty pickup, was submerged to allow a young boy to drive his boat onto it. One of two deputies dressed in a brown-and-tan uniform stood at the vessel's center console. He waved at Manseur when he saw him.

"Must be our guide," Manseur explained to Alexa.

Larry Bond slid out of the other car, wearing hunting boots and camouflage pants like a deer hunter. Detective Kyler Kennedy was dressed the same way.

One of the deputies stood smoking a cigarette beside the truck that had pulled the boat's trailer, looking up at the fast-moving clouds above him—the early feeder-band edge of a doomsday, two-hundred-mile-per-hour grass-skinner. As he made his way over to the arriving Crown Vics, Alexa noticed the large deputy's shirt was darkly wet where it stuck to his torso.

"Detective Manseur?" the man asked, looking at the two detectives in camouflage at the second car.

"I'm Manseur."

The deputy turned to the source of the voice. "Sheriff sends his regards, sir. Kip Boudreaux is going to take you back in there. Kip's been fishing around here all his life. He's the sheriff's cousin by marriage. Going back in there without an experienced man is asking for trouble. Going in after Leland Ticholet anytime is looking hard for trouble. Sheriff said if you need any more men, he'll try to send a couple. But you know what it's like right now."

"How will they find us?" Manseur asked.

"Boudreaux is going to leave markers floating so we can find y'all in case you need us. He was in on arresting Leland a few years back, and he can advise you some on him. Only thing for sure is, he's one badass sombitch, and pepper spray don't bother him any more'n a cat fart would. Most people live back in here are tough customers or they don't make it, but people here go miles out of their way to avoid Leland."

The deputy reached into his back pocket for an envelope. "It's his mug shot. He's six three, weighs two-sixty and he ain't got a inch to pinch on him. If he decides to fight it out, I'd just go on and shoot him like a hog. Won't nobody miss him. Y'all best be back out before two o'clock with or without him. Wind is going to be picking up by then and the water is going to get choppy."

Alexa took the envelope, slipped out the picture, and studied the shirtless, wild-eyed young man with a full head of Medusa-like hair and a wild beard specked with twigs and a forehead marked with small criss-crossing scars. His chest and arm muscles looked like they'd been machined from surgical steel and covered with wet nylon. "His hair is short now," Alexa said, handing the picture to Manseur. "No beard."

"How's radio reception out there?" Manseur asked.

"Real good. There's repeater towers all over, and

you can use cell phones most everywhere in the parish these days. Most of that is on account of the oil companies."

"Okay, then we'll advise the sheriff when we make the arrest," Manseur said.

"I guess I could go along if you want extra help," the fat deputy offered.

"Thanks anyway. You've got your hands full with Katrina. I think we can handle this."

Alexa saw a flood of relief wash over the deputy's reddened baby-face. He waddled back over to the truck at twice the speed with which he had approached, lighting another cigarette as he went.

Manseur popped the trunk of his car, picked up a 12-gauge Mossberg shotgun. He loaded the magazine with 12-gauge buckshot rounds. He did the same with a second shotgun. Alexa took a ballistic vest from the trunk and slipped it on. Manseur put his on, then pulled on a black baseball cap with NOPD emblazoned in gold. He handed Alexa a plain dark blue ball cap and a windbreaker with POLICE in three-inch letters across the shoulders in the rear and the same word in smaller letters over the left breast.

Alexa looked down and noticed that Manseur was wearing his brown wingtips. "Don't you have any other shoes?"

"These are very comfortable," he said. "I don't own any Keds."

"Keds?" Alexa laughed. "Do they still sell Keds?"

A sudden hissing made Alexa turn. Bond was spraying his ankles with repellant from a green aerosol can. "Chiggers," he explained. He handed the can to

Alexa. "Spray yourself good. There's also mosquitoes, ticks—"

"I've had chigger bites before." Alexa accepted the can and sprayed herself liberally. "Nothing short of losing an arm in a machine could be worse than chigger bites."

Bond and Kennedy opened gun cases and removed high-powered rifles with telescopic sights and slings.

"The signal is coming from five miles west of here," Manseur said.

"There's a labyrinth of bayous and canals and you can't go anywhere back in there by straight lines. This is by far the closest road in any direction," Bond added.

Alexa looked toward the ramshackle store. She spotted an emaciated and hump-shouldered young man, whose nose was so long and sharp that— coupled with the shoots of blond hair radiating out from his head—he appeared as much bird as human. He leaned against the corner of the building watching the detectives through narrowed eye slits. When he saw that Alexa was looking at him, he averted his gaze and slipped around the corner like a starving but fearful dog.

"How many boat launches are there around here?" she asked.

"Not many," Bond offered. "One other within five miles."

"You're familiar with this place?" Alexa asked.

"I've fished some around here a few times. With a guide."

"We should ask inside if they know Leland," Alexa said. "This is likely where he buys fuel."

Manseur reached into his pocket and took out the picture of Grace and Doc, which he showed to Bond and Kennedy. "This other one is Andy Tinsdale. He's the guy that Casey West shot. Hasn't showed up in any clinics or hospitals and he isn't home. Hopefully, he's still with Leland."

Alexa accompanied Manseur into the store while Bond and Kennedy went to the boat to load their equipment and meet the pilot. There were people shopping inside. A couple of rough-looking fishermen in oily clothes were standing at the counter, and they moved back as Manseur and Alexa approached. The radio droned warnings. The shelves, made of unpainted lumber, were almost cleaned of canned foods. The square-headed man behind the counter was built on the order of a potbellied stove. The cap perched on his head was so grimy, it was impossible to read the logo. He blew his nose into a red and white bandanna and shoved it into his back pocket. Coils of black hair seemed to be growing from his shirt up his neck like wisteria vines, and covered his forearms and the backs of his hands like fur.

"I'm Allen Moody, the owner. Can I help you folks?" he asked, lighting a cigar that had probably been lit on several previous occasions.

Manseur flashed his badge. "You know this man?" he asked, showing a mug shot picture of Leland Ticholet.

Moody leaned forward to get a better look, taking a pair of reading glasses from the counter and putting them on. The fishermen strained to look, without moving in closer.

" 'At's Lelun," Moody said. "He's crazy as a rat in a milk pail."

"Tickerlay's his name," a young fisherman said, nodding. "Some call him Tickle."

"You wouldn't want him to catch you calling him Tickle," another fisherman added. "He ain't got a sense of humor. He's a lot like his daddy was in that respect. A sorrier sample of a man than that Jacklon never drew breath."

"He sure shit never drew a sober one," Moody said, chuckling.

The older fisherman nodded in agreement.

" 'At's a pure-dee fact," Moody agreed. "His red-bone second wife, Alice Fay, killed him."

"Red Bone?" Alexa asked.

"That's an Indian and nigger mix," the younger fisherman translated.

The older fisherman elbowed his younger buddy, who frowned, realizing he'd made a social faux pas. "I certainly didn't mean to insult you by that, miss," he mumbled.

"You get on Lelun's bad side and you can go missing. Like some done recently," the older fisherman said.

"What do you mean?" Alexa asked.

"Game warden name of Parnell was asking about Lelun a few days back, 'cause he was thinking Lelun bought that new boat he's been riding around in with alligator hide profits. Wanted to know where he stayed at," Moody said. "Now they're looking for Parnell and a lady warden that was with him yesterday. I wouldn't be surprised if they never found a trace of them."

"That Parnell's a pure-dee bastard," the older fisherman declared. "He probably checks his own licenses hoping he can write his own self a citation ticket."

The fishermen and Moody laughed. The sound was that of a donkey fighting with seals.

Manseur showed them the picture of the young man standing with Dorothy Fugate. "What about this one?"

"The woman, or him?" Moody asked.

"Him. Have you seen him before? Maybe with Ticholet?"

"Never seen anybody with Lelun. Well, this one time a few days back a man was with him, but I didn't get close enough for a look. Figured he was taking him fishing or something. You could ask Grub. He's right nosy."

"Grub?" Alexa asked.

"What'd Lee do this time?" one of the fishermen asked.

"He stole that boat," the store owner announced. "I knew he don't have that kind of money sitting around. That boat cost thirty thousand if it cost a nickel. He was driving a beat-to-shit aluminum fourteen flat-bottom with an old smoke-belching Johnson on it one day, the next he's in that new one, riding around like the king of the bayous."

"What did he say about the new boat?" Manseur asked.

"I asked him about it and he said it was payment for some jobs he was doing for a somebody, who he didn't name. I figured he was fulla shit and stole it somewhere. Maybe knocked some poor bastard in the head for it. I wouldn't want him taking a fancy to anything I had."

"When did you last see him?"

"Late last night he come by and fueled up."

"You think he done in them wardens?" the older fisherman asked.

"Was he alone?" Alexa asked.

"Have to ask Grub. He was around. He always is."

"Where is this Grub?" Alexa asked.

"He's the retard works outside," the younger fisherman said. "Wormy-lookin' kid."

Alexa decided she could talk to this Grub later.

"Any of y'all know where Leland's camp is?" Manseur asked.

The men fell silent, blinking at him like owls.

"Okay. We'll find it."

"You do and you might wish you hadn't," Allen Moody said, with certainty.

79

In the morning breeze, naked but for a pair of tattered cotton shorts, Leland Ticholet flipped the last of the nutria onto its back on the dock, lodged its spine between two thick planks. Opening its belly with his skinning knife, he scooped out the entrails with his gore-caked hand and tossed them off into the water for the crabs. He began to skin the four-pound animal expertly, using the wide blade with the precision of a scalpel. Few things felt as right to Leland as skinning swamp rats.

That morning before sunrise he had gone out to

check his catfish lines. The gator hooks he'd baited the day before hadn't attracted anything, but he knew they would when the meat turned. He'd checked his nutria traps and found four of them caught up. He'd popped the nutria between the eyes with his .22 before removing their limp bodies from the traps. Once upon a time he had just clubbed them to death, but he'd been bitten by one and almost lost a finger to the snapping rascal. Bullets were cheap when you measured them against fingers.

He was glad his business with Doc was all over. His only problem now was getting up enough gator skins for Moody to keep gas in his boat and buy the supplies he needed to get by. He looked into the boat and frowned at the thick brown bloodstain on the rear seat and on the floor just in front of the seat, where Doc had leaked out. He'd clean it up later.

He was enjoying the steady breeze and the overcast when he heard the unmistakable sound of a boat, a good distance off yet, but definitely coming in his direction. It wouldn't be a fisherman or trapper passing by, because the only channel into the area ended not far from Leland's cut-through, and most everybody knew to stay out of his territory.

As the boat drew closer, the sound of the motors grew louder. A flock of disturbed blackbirds rose into the sky approximately where the channel formed a Y, the left fork heading for the mouth of his inlet. Any boat coming in would effectively block him in. Leland went into his cabin in order to prepare a proper welcome if that boat happened to contain trespassers.

80

Alexa thought the swamp both surreal and eerily beautiful. Above them, pelicans, egrets, cranes, and other birds of unknown denominations flew north below the clouds. Deputy Kip Boudreaux explained that the birds felt the drop in pressure and knew that their normal habitat was going to be inhospitable in a few hours, and they were leaving. He commented that it was too bad the people living around here weren't a tenth as smart as birds.

Alexa sat beside Manseur on the bench in front of the console where Boudreaux, a pleasant young man wearing aviator sunglasses and a baseball cap, stood piloting the boat. Manseur had his windbreaker positioned like a photographer's hood, shielding the laptop's screen from the daylight so he could see it. As he pointed to the position of the blinking dot, Boudreaux translated the direction into turns.

It seemed to Alexa they had traveled miles into the maze of narrow waterways. Tall reeds, bushes, small trees, weeds, and grasses lined the banks. Often the channel they were using would open into a large body of water, usually with several possible channel exits to choose from. She saw cranes with their skinny legs in the water, turtles sliding off logs, and alligators slipping from the banks into the water, spooked by the intruding vessel.

Before they'd left the launch, Boudreaux told her that he had heard stories about Leland Ticholet and his moonshiner daddy for years, but he wasn't sure exactly where the Ticholet fishing camp was located, or even if it was still standing. The swamp, he explained, tended to lay claim to any building left uninhabited for long.

They passed by several small cabins built on poles, on floats, or constructed on barges. The deeper into the swamp they went, the fewer they saw, but more of the ones they did see were abandoned and in some progressive state of ruin.

Alexa wasn't accustomed to speedboats. The fast turns and tight banks made her feel like the boat would keep sliding sideways and end up on dry land, but she did her best to lean against the turns and tried not to close her eyes when she became alarmed. She had no choice but to trust that Deputy Boudreaux knew the limits of his craft, and would not lose control of it or slam it into a submerged log. Although the confident deputy seemed to know the lanes, Alexa couldn't imagine how anyone could differentiate one of the waterways from another.

"The Ticholets are barn-burners from way back," the deputy told them. Alexa knew the expression meant that they got even with people for slights. "Leland's grandfather was executed for murdering another fisherman in a bar, then Leland's daddy was killed in a shootout with his common-law wife about ten, twelve years ago. Hell, they shot at each other all the time. That particular fight lasted all morning, and she got hit several times before she put a fatal round into his heart. She lost her left hand and a leg below the knee. I see her some, riding around town in her scooter chair. Her place got burned to the waterline, and she claimed Leland did that. He was fifteen or sixteen at the time.

"I was in on arresting Leland a couple years back. He thinks and acts like a wild animal, in most respects. You sure can't reason with him. He isn't exactly stupid, just primitive."

Alexa, sitting with the Mossberg in her lap, found herself wishing they had brought along more manpower. She looked down, taking in the absurdity of Manseur's rolled-up suit pants, his exposed ankles sheathed in thin nylon dress socks, and the wingtips on his small feet. This Ticholet was a wanted fugitive fleeing from an assault and abduction, kidnapping, and if Tinsdale had died from Casey's bullets, a murder. And it sounded like he was a volatile and dangerous man under normal circumstances. She knew Manseur was a good detective, but she wasn't all that confident that the group in the boat constituted a SWAT team.

Alexa was an adequate handgun shot, but her shooting experience was on a range, punching holes in paper. She didn't know, but she hoped Kennedy and Bond were more experienced than she was. Sure, they were hunters, but deer didn't return fire. Boudreaux was an unknown element, because a sheriff's deputy might not have adequate training, or even could be with the department simply because a cousin was the sheriff. In Alexa's mind, they were all just investigators.

Leland Ticholet was completely at home in this inhospitable world, and she and the others were just passing through it.

Well, hopefully just passing through.

81

Deputy Boudreaux cut back his boat's motors as soon as Manseur's receiver registered that the tracker's location was within a few hundred yards, and they started looking for the channel that they thought would lead them to the briefcase's present location. Bond had dropped one of the floating markers at the last turn. Although nobody said so, it would allow any one of them to pilot the boat back out if Boudreaux wasn't able to navigate. It was always good to be practical.

A waving wall of cattails extended between two fingers of ground, breaking the water like quills. There was a wide-enough gap in the reeds to allow a boat to pass through. The deputy pulled to the bank and Bond and Kennedy climbed from the boat, their boots disappearing in the muck. They made their way slowly in the direction of the tracker, rifles slung on their backs.

As Boudreaux began to move the vessel, Alexa caught sight of a tin roof visible above a line of reeds. He cut the wheel hard to the left and gunned it, plunging into an inlet protected by a V of land covered with bushes, trees, and waist-high foliage. The listing cabin was hemmed into the back corner by a floating wood dock that was grounded on either side. A boat was tied to the dock, just to the left of the cabin.

Manseur had put on his windbreaker and stood at the bow, with the shotgun at port arms. Alexa scanned the area, watching for movement.

The small structure, with corrugated metal walls, was listing about ten degrees. The steel pontoons beneath it—which may have once been LP gas tanks—were rusting, and the one on the low side was three-quarters submerged. The edge of the roof was peeled up like some giant had lifted the corner to peer inside. It rose and fell with the breeze.

A large fish broke the choppy surface beside the boat, startling Alexa. She racked a shell into the chamber of her shotgun and fed another double-ought round into the gate at the bottom of the receiver. Alexa had never killed anyone, but if Leland Ticholet or Andy Tinsdale made it necessary, she would kill either of them, and she would do so without hesitation.

The deputy pulled back the power lever and allowed his boat to drift toward the cabin. When it was almost to the pier, Alexa and Manseur jumped onto it. With shotguns aimed at the building, they moved toward the door. As she passed Leland's boat, Alexa saw dried blood in the stern. She stepped over the carcasses of four skinless animals. Flies swarmed above their wet skins lying side by side on the weathered wood planks.

"Leland Ticholet! Police!" Manseur yelled out. "Come out with your hands up!" His command was answered only with the sounds of insects in the trees, a fish breaking the surface of the water.

Under the porch roof, chicken-wire crab traps served as tables for jugs with thick monofilament line wrapped around them, tiny spring-loaded jaw traps, and a jar filled with rusted fishhooks. Manseur nodded at her and, using his left hand, turned the knob. He pushed the door open and swept the dim interior with his shotgun.

The cabin's interior, illuminated by sunlight pouring in through the windows and open door, smelled of mildew and rot. A still form lay on an Army cot. With Alexa aiming her shotgun at the figure, Manseur moved to the cot and gazed down at the man lying there.

Andy Tinsdale—still dressed in the black running suit he'd been wearing the night before—stared back, his partly open eyes clouded and dry. From the underside of the cot, accumulated blood had dripped through the canvas, forming a dark puddle. Alexa spotted the briefcase on the table, decorated with five bullet holes that could have all been covered with a five-by-seven index card.

"What's up, Doc?" Manseur said.

"There's the briefcase," Alexa said, pointing the barrel of her borrowed Mossberg.

"It would be nice to find somebody still alive just once, so we could interrogate them. We seem to be spending all our effort collecting evidence and stacking corpses."

Alexa crossed to the table.

There was a great deal of dried blood smeared on the case's leather exterior. Carefully, she opened the briefcase and looked at the stack of bearer bonds, most having been penetrated through-and-through by Casey's .380 rounds. Alexa wasn't going to count the papers. Two of the holes in the front side of the case were duplicated on the back panel, but larger and not perfectly round, due to the expansion of the hollow points as they violated the stack of bonds. "Ransom's here."

Manseur lifted Doc's sweatshirt to examine the deceased man's entrance wounds. He was a homicide detective, and naturally he wanted to see exactly what had transferred Doc from life to death. Alexa wasn't nearly as curious about what exactly had killed Tinsdale as she was about where Leland Ticholet was. "Chest wounds have irregular margins," Manseur told her. "Bullets lost enough energy to prevent them from penetrating his lungs or heart," he said.

She watched Manseur roll Andy up by lifting his arm, so he could get a better look at his backside.

"The one in his liver did the trick," Manseur reported. "Another in his leg. He suffered before he died."

Alexa saw something shiny on the floor, and reached down to lift it by its edges.

"Michael," she said, holding the object out so he could see it. "Game and fish badge."

"Man alive," he said. "I guess we solved that mystery."

Alexa looked up to see Boudreaux, shotgun at the ready, peering inside.

"Tinsdale's dead in here," Manseur said. "No Ticholet."

"He heard us coming," Boudreaux said. "Probably a long time before we got here. Leland could be a quarter-mile away by now." He turned on the shotgun's attached flashlight to peer down through the jagged hole in the boards. "Jesus," he said.

"What?" Alexa asked.

"He's got some cottonmouths in a box under the floor. Looks like at some point some uninvited company got a big surprise." He reached down and flipped over a hinged sheet of plywood to cover the snake hole.

"Might have been one of those missing game wardens," Alexa said, showing him the badge she'd found.

"I'll radio it in," Boudreaux offered. "If Leland's on the run, we're done here. With luck, we'll find his bloated corpse after the hurricane's done with it. Unless the crabs beat us to him."

Manseur lifted his walkie-talkie and pressed the TALK button. "Bond, Kennedy, Tinsdale's DOA. Ticholet is out there somewhere. Based on the boat and some fresh nutria skins, he's close by. Use extreme caution."

"I can see the cabin's roof," Bond said. "We'll be in position to cover you in a minute."

Three sharp cracks, followed by something heavy falling on the deck, ended the transmission. Alexa moved to the door and looked out, to see Boudreaux sprawled on the dock.

"Boudreaux's down," Alexa said.

"That's a .22," Manseur said.

"We have to get him inside," she said.

"Damn it," Manseur said. He keyed his radio. "Boudreaux's down. You see Ticholet?"

There were two sharp cracks as rounds smacked into the outer wall of the cabin.

"Negative!" Bond yelled, excitedly. "We're in position. He's in his boat!"

Then a boat motor sprang to thundering life.

"Damn it, Bond, stop him!"

Stepping out, Alexa aimed her shotgun at the moving boat, whose bow was raised out of the water. She fired just as Manseur opened up beside her.

There was a swift succession of thunderous explosions as Kennedy and Bond fired high-powered rifles from the shore. The powerful outboard motor sputtered, but the boat was still gathering speed. Alexa looked out, aiming the shotgun at the boat. She couldn't see the person piloting it because he was crouched behind the pilot's backrest. She fired at the outboard. The motor seized, silenced by the shotgun and rifle rounds that had hit it. The boat turned sharply. As its bow ran onto the bank, Alexa had a bead on Ticholet, but when she squeezed the trigger, there was a dry snap. She had run the Mossberg dry.

Running, Leland leapt from the boat.

Mumbling curses, Alexa fed fresh rounds into the shotgun. Manseur fired in haste, missing the fast-moving target—who, armed with a .22 rifle, scrambled with remarkable speed and disappeared into the shadowy tree line.

As Alexa watched over the bead sight of her shotgun, there were four quick cracks from the .22, and she turned in time to see Kennedy collapse into the foliage. Ticholet was firing at the two detectives from cover. Bond returned fire.

She and Manseur moved to the deputy. Kip Boudreaux was dead. Blood pooled in his right eye socket—his aviator glasses, lenses shattered, lay six feet away, by his boot.

"If Ticholet gets away, we'll never find him out here," Alexa said.

Manseur keyed his radio. "Bond?"

"Kennedy's hit in the lower leg. Looks like it broke the shinbone. It's not bleeding too badly, but he isn't going to be walking anywhere."

"Deputy Boudreaux's dead. I'll radio it in."

"Ticholet may double back on you. Give me a

couple of minutes to tie off Kennedy's leg. I'll swing around your flank and cover you."

Manseur lifted Boudreaux's radio from his belt and keyed it. "Dispatch, this is Detective Michael Manseur. Patch me to Sheriff Tolliver."

Manseur spent the next few seconds with the radio against his forehead like an ice pack.

Alexa loaded their shotguns, then watched the tree line over her barrel.

"You got Leland in shackles yet?" Tolliver's voice asked.

Manseur lowered the radio and keyed it. "He killed Deputy Boudreaux and wounded one of my detectives. He's still active and armed. We need medical, ASAP, and some backup."

"We're coming, Manseur," Tolliver said, excitedly. "Just hold what you got."

Alexa caught something—a flash of movement where Leland had vanished into the dense foliage. "Michael," she said. "He's coming this way. I saw him."

Straightening, Alexa sprinted down the dock, hoping to cut Leland off before he moved inland from the point. Manseur was right behind her. Seconds later, they were kneeling side by side in the soft dirt, ten feet apart, watching the foliage from behind trees. Leland Ticholet would have to come by them. Alexa knelt beside a tree, her shotgun aimed toward the point. She glanced to her left at Manseur. He was aiming in the same direction.

Now they had him. He could still surrender and be taken into custody. If he chose to resist, Alexa was confident that one .22 was easily divisible by two twelves.

82

From the cover of a scrub patch, Leland had watched the trespassers roar into his private inlet. He knew from the pilot's brown uniform, and the shotguns, the man and woman with the gold words on the backs of their coats, that they were cops. The gal cop had light brown skin, but he could tell she had some nigra blood in her, only not nearly as much as the dead lady warden, who'd been as black as a deer's eyes. He remembered seeing the gal cop at the house where Doc got shot. He didn't know if they had come because of what happened at the little house the night before, or because they were looking to find the warden trespassers, but he sure couldn't imagine how they had found his camp.

He should have gotten rid of Doc's body like he did the wardens', let the alligators and varmints crap out the meat and scatter the bones. Maybe they had come to take his new boat. He didn't have the pink papers because he didn't know where Doc had put them. He tried to ask him, but Doc wasn't able to tell Leland anything. He had looked through Doc's pockets and in the briefcase, but there was no pink paper with a picture of a boat in there.

He'd watched the man and woman jump off the boat as it neared his dock. Leland aimed at them until they went inside. He could swim the bayou and go deeper into the swamp and wait until they left, but he couldn't allow them to take his boat. He wasn't of a mind to walk out and leave it behind.

The deputy tied up his police boat. Leland thought

that the deputy, a man he was sure he'd seen before, was their pilot, and had guided them to his camp. He was pretty sure the deputy had helped arrest him and send him to the crazy house. If he didn't do something, he might bring others another time, and Leland couldn't afford to let that happen.

From forty feet away, Leland aimed the rifle at the pilot's head, putting the sights on the man's eye as he raised his radio to talk. When Leland fired, the deputy's sunglasses fell off and his body froze for a split second, before falling backward to the planks. Now Leland would kill the other two and get rid of their boat, all the bodies, and then everything would be back to normal. Doc had told him a big storm was coming, and people would think they got killed by it. They might think he killed them, but they couldn't prove it without the bodies to show a judge.

He would take his boat out, and sneak back to finish up. Once they were sure he was gone, they'd be easy targets. He broke cover, ran to his boat, started it, firing at the cabin to keep them inside until he got going.

He crouched down behind the pilot's backrest so they couldn't see to shoot him while he started it and gunned the engines. It went just as he planned, until two men on the bank shot his motor dead. He had turned toward the left bank and run off the boat and clambered to shore and to safety, carrying his Remington Nylon 66 carbine, a gun he'd inherited from his father. It was a good thing getting it wet didn't keep it from working. That gun was one you didn't ever have to clean but for running a brush through the barrel sometimes and oiling it a tad a couple times a year.

So there were two cops armed with high-powered

rifles and two with shotguns. When Leland got on dry land, he looked back at where the shots had come from, and when he saw the men, he fired, hitting one in the leg. Everybody knew that cops wore bulletproof vests, so he had to make head shots on them—from closer range—or shoot them in their legs or arms to immobilize them. Wounded, the cop would be easier to finish off, after Leland dealt with the others.

Four wasn't so many. Leland had ten rounds in the rifle.

He listened hard to see if he could hear any boats approaching with more cops in it. When he didn't hear one, he smiled.

83

Waiting for Leland to break through the brush, Alexa was perspiring heavily beneath the vest, and her hands were clammy where they gripped the shotgun. She and the other detectives had firepower on their side, and even though they were unfamiliar with the place, she didn't see how Leland's knowledge of the immediate area was adequate to tip the balance to his advantage in the present situation.

Alexa could feel the positive weight of the Glock in its high-rise holster on her right side. To her left, she could see the wind-rough dark scummy water through the brush behind Manseur.

As far as she could tell, Leland had stopped coming toward them. Likely he was waiting for them to go to him. She was still looking at Manseur when some reeds in the water swayed suddenly. The surface of the water parted as Leland's head and shoulders broke above the waterline and, to her horror, she saw he was aiming the gun.

Leland fired twice as Manseur was turning his shotgun toward him, and the detective fell sideways. The instant Manseur was down, Leland shifted his gaze, saw her, and swung the gun toward Alexa. She had reflexively put the tree beside her between them, and heard the twenty-two rounds smack the bark. She swung the shotgun up, jerked the trigger, and the gun roared, the recoil jarring her. The pellets had churned the water, but Leland had vanished below the surface. She thought she must have hit him, but there was no evidence of it.

Maintaining her aim, she scrambled over to Manseur, who looked up at her with dazed and frightened eyes. Alexa saw immediately that he had been hit twice in the head. There was a small hole in his cheek and another just above his lip, under his nose. When he opened his mouth to speak, blood poured out. He coughed and spit. Along with the blood, Alexa saw that he had expelled broken teeth and what appeared to be bone chips.

Alexa helped him sit up against the tree, his back to the water. "Stay still," she told him. "Let me take a look at you. Can you open your mouth for me?"

Alexa was trained to evaluate gunshot wounds. While keeping the water in sight, Alexa laid the shotgun aside on the soft ground where she could grab it up quickly. She took a few seconds to hold Manseur's head still while she inspected the bullet wounds. She quickly decided that, despite the amount of blood in his mouth, neither wound should be fatal. He seemed alert, and, for the moment, not going into shock.

"Michael, the round through your cheek exited your jaw. You've got some broken teeth, maybe some damage to the gums, and some tissue damage where the jawbone is hinged. The second went through your lip, hit your upper gum, and is probably lodged in your upper pallet. You understand what I said?"

Manseur nodded, and pointed behind him.

"I fired at him, but I don't know if I hit him. I think I closed my eyes when I fired." Admitting that she had flinched when she fired would have been embarrassing normally, because she had fired pistols and shotguns more times than she could count, and she had been trained and drilled, and drilled again, to teach her not to close her eyes when she fired a weapon. *Watch the bullet hit your target. Don't fire wildly and empty the magazine. Two-one-two-one.* The firing range wasn't real life, and more or less a stress-free environment, which this certainly wasn't.

Manseur had been lucky. If Leland had used a larger caliber weapon, and had fired with the same degree of accuracy, the round placed under his nose would have penetrated his brain. He wouldn't die from the wounds, but she had to get him to a hospital for treatment. Then she noticed the blood on his upper arm. He had also been shot in his left shoulder.

She heard footsteps behind her, grabbed up the shotgun, and aimed. Carrying his rifle at the ready, Larry Bond moved beside her, knelt, and looked gravely at Manseur.

"You okay, Michael?"

Manseur nodded mutely. Alexa told Bond what

had happened, pointed to where Leland had sur-
faced, and told him she may or may not have hit him.

"I don't see him floating," Bond said.

"The sheriff's people are on the way out," Alexa
told him. "It's going to be a long wait, based on how
long it took us to get here. They'll have to launch
boats."

"We can't just sit and wait. If Ticholet isn't hurt
really badly, he'll pick us off before we get out of the
channel," Bond said grimly. "We have to kill him."

"I couldn't agree more," Alexa said. She had no
problem with killing Leland Ticholet.

84

Leland had shown himself moving so the cops would
think he was heading toward the cabin. He knew they
would move to ambush him as he came in from the
point. After moving back into the shadows, he had
dropped to the ground and slipped into the water on the
far side of the finger of land. He knew they wouldn't expect him to flank them underwater. Swimming submerged without disturbing the surface was never hard,
but with the wind rippling the surface, it was downright
easy. Animals in the swamp survived by knowing how
things that mattered worked, doing whatever it took to
live another day. Leland had not watched and hunted
critters without learning how they worked things.

Lying in the shallows like a gator, he had watched
the cops take up positions, marked the closest land-
mark to them—the cattails, which were roughly at a

ninety-degree angle from where the cops had set up. Shouldering the 66 underwater, he broke the surface, knowing the pair would be aiming in the wrong place, and Leland gave the barrel only enough time to clear itself of water to fire at the closest cop's head.

The woman had seen Leland come up, and he'd have had her nailed, too, but the man didn't fall out of the way fast enough. He'd hit the little bald cop in his stupid head. Leland had seen the red marks blossom as the bullets hit home. The gal cop's gun went off, but missed Leland by a mile. The woman had scrambled behind a tree and turned her shotgun on him, but she wasn't quick enough, so he was almost completely underwater before she shot.

He slipped out of the water well away from where he'd gone under, felt a sharp burn in his side, and realized she'd been luckier than he'd imagined. She'd got him. He was bleeding, but the pellets had done little more than cut a couple of shallow channels in him, maybe broken a rib or two. As he lay there, he saw one of the other cops, this one wearing camouflage like a hunter and carrying a rifle, pass within ten feet of where he lay. Leland wished he had a rifle like the one the cop had. Shooting through a motor like it had, it would be even better at shooting through those vests.

He felt a bulge under the skin lodged between his ribs and pushed it this way and that until the dislodged object just plopped out of the hole where another one had gone through. He looked at the little round piece of lead, which was warped out of round. He inhaled; it felt like somebody was jabbing a sharp stick into his side.

He took a scoop of mud and pressed it into a piece

of Spanish moss and stuck that to the wounds. He moved silently, going around his cabin, toting the 66. The more he thought about it, the more Leland really wanted one of those big rifles. He smiled, because he knew where to get one.

He could go deep into the swamps and evade any cops or searchers that showed up. But this was his place, and he wasn't going to allow these strangers to defile his place. When you have something worth having, you do what you have to in order to keep it.

85

Detective Kennedy's wounded leg throbbed to the rhythm of his heartbeats. It hurt like hell, but, he knew, not nearly as badly as it was going to. Bond had cut into his pant leg so he could see the tiny hole below his right knee that, thanks to the tourniquet, was merely oozing a trail of bright blood. Bond had raised Kyler's leg using two Y-shaped limbs, with their Y's acting as supports, their lengths forming a bipod. Kyler had set his Glock in his lap and laid the Winchester .270 by his side.

Shortly after Bond had left to circle around to where Agent Keen and Manseur had gone, hoping to head off Leland Ticholet's escape, several twenty-two rounds had sounded. They'd been instantly answered by two shotgun blasts.

Kyler had wanted to be a Homicide detective since joining the force, having moved up from patrol due to hard work and making the right connections.

The detective closed his eyes to better concentrate on sounds coming across the channel from the other bank. He didn't dare use his radio, because he could give away Bond's or Manseur's position to Leland Ticholet. He had faith that between Bond and Manseur, things would end for Leland shortly. He knew Alexa Keen's reputation for closing cases, but, as far as he knew, none of it involved dealing with this kind of violence.

Kyler felt a sting on his cheek and slapped the mosquito that was feeding there. He wondered why the little bloodsucker didn't land on his leg and drink without piercing the skin. He was probably lying in poison ivy or in chigger-infested brush, and if he were being attacked by the mite-sized parasites, he'd pay a terrible price later on.

He closed his eyes and felt the cool wind on his face, and the sweat gathering underneath his clothes.

He shifted and reached for the Winchester .270, but felt only the ground. He looked down and saw, to his horror, that his rifle had vanished. He smelled Leland Ticholet, and had the Glock in his hand a split second before the butt plate of his Winchester crashed into the side of his head, ending his panic.

86

Manseur was in excruciating pain. Kennedy was on the other point, separated from them by the inlet. Leland, who might or might not be wounded, could be anywhere. Bond and Alexa had to figure out some way to take Leland out of the picture. Bond tried to reach Kennedy by radio.

"He isn't answering," Bond reported. "Might have his unit turned off."

"I hope so, but I doubt it. Leland isn't someone to underestimate. He killed two game wardens and Deputy Boudreaux."

"He killed those wardens?" Bond asked.

"I found a Wildlife and Fisheries badge inside the cabin. They were on Leland's trail for selling alligators or something. They got this far, but I doubt they got out alive. We have to assume Leland flanked us and has Kennedy's weapons," Alexa said. "If he does, what are we facing?"

"Two-seventy rifle, shoots on the money to four hundred yards. The rounds will totally ignore these vests," Bond answered. "He had maybe forty rounds with him, minus what he used up. Plus his Glock .40 and three magazines."

Alexa said, "He can pick us off as he sees us. And we can also assume he's taken Kennedy's vest."

"Possible," Bond agreed. "We'll just shoot him in the head, or blow off one of his limbs."

"We have to see him first," Alexa reminded Bond. "Any ideas?"

"He's wired tightly, primitive emotionally. I'm going to really piss him off and see if he overreacts."

"How?" Bond wondered.

"Boys and their toys," Alexa replied, smiling grimly.

87

Leland put on the cop's vest. It was a tight fit even after he loosened the straps to let it out. Once he cinched it, the vest did an admirable job holding the compress in place. Leland rubbed mud on his face, head and neck, shoulders and legs. The breeze would dry it quickly. Putting aside the 66, he lifted the pistol and the Winchester and filled his mouth with rifle bullets. Leland watched the shore across the channel from cover, looking through the rifle's scope for movement that would give away the cops' positions.

He moved the scope to inspect the hull and transom of his boat for holes, and to see those in the motor's cowling. *Those sons of bitches. They'll pay dear for screwing with my boat.*

He knew he could swap out his motor with the game warden's, which he had hidden nearby under leaves and brush. He'd caulk the holes in the fiberglass hull. The vessel's bow was lodged on the muddy bank just enough to anchor it. As he watched, he was sure he saw the boat move. He watched it more closely, knowing there wasn't enough wind to shift the heavy vessel the way he had seen it move.

He cursed when he saw the woman cop's head for a split second before it vanished below the transom. He could shoot through the fiberglass, and he might hit her, but he didn't want to make any more holes in the hull. The rifle could even go through into the water and sink it. He could see a thin film of gasoline on the water, where it was leaking from the damaged motor. Probably a fuel line was ruptured.

As he watched, the woman stood, ran the length of the boat, and jumped onto the shore. He was wondering why she'd been on board, when the boat, and the gasoline he'd seen in the water, erupted in flame, light gray smoke billowing from his beloved boat. Fury seized him and he stood, aiming at where she'd gone off into the brush.

Seeing sudden movement in the shadows, he swung the gun and saw the other cop in camo—aiming straight at him. Leland put the scope's crosshairs on him, but the cop's rifle went off a split second before his did, and Leland felt a punch in his left arm so hard, his shot went wide because of it.

He fell to the ground. His wounded arm was useless, and he crawled backward into the shadows, leaking blood.

He could smell his boat burning, and that infuriated him, more even than the sound of the cop that had shot him laughing over across the inlet. The woman cop had managed to flush him out so the man could fire, and Leland cursed his luck. He looked at his wounded arm, and was worried a lot by what he saw. It looked as if someone had scooped most of the meat off of his biceps; the shattered arm bone was visible in the ruined meat. Blood flowed down his limp arm. He wanted to howl, but he didn't dare give that woman cop another shot at him.

From across the water, he heard the woman laughing melodiously. He fought the urge to howl in rage.

It began to rain, hardly more than a sprinkle. There were only two of them left, and they were going to die soon. He knew he should go back to first camo cop, get his belt, and make the bleeding stop, before he got swimmy-headed.

88

Luckily Larry Bond was a smoker. Alexa had borrowed his lighter and, crawling from the trees, slipped to the bank; using the boat for cover, she pulled herself on board. The rear of the boat had been slowly filling with gasoline since the bullet hit its motor. She opened the caps to the gas tanks and, using her knife, cut the sleeves from her shirt and stuffed them into the opening of the closest gas tank. When she was ready to light the first sleeve, she moved into view for a split second, hoping Leland would see her, and that he didn't see Bond. For this to work, Bond had to see Leland before he had a chance to fire at her.

Bracing to run, she lit the gas-soaked sleeve. It burst into flame. She ran the length of the boat, jumped to shore, and raced into the shadows, diving to the ground. Bond's thundering shot told her that Leland had shown himself. She was fairly sure there had been two shots, close together, but the second could have been an echo of the first.

Alexa crawled to Bond's position on her belly, just as the first gas tank erupted, engulfing the vessel in flames. The second tank exploded seconds later. The boat became an inferno, black smoke choking the air in the channel, blowing into the tree line across the water. Bond dropped to the ground and roared his laughter into the skies.

"I hit him," Bond said.

"Solid?"

"Good enough to have him thinking about it. We need to move while we have a smoke-screen cover."

Bond laughed again and Alexa joined him.

"Even if it wasn't a killing shot, the more angry he is, the more likely it is he'll make another mistake."

Even badly wounded, Alexa imagined Leland Ticholet would still be an extremely dangerous adversary.

They rushed to Manseur, who had managed to stand to lean against a tree, blood dripping from his mouth and jaw. With Bond at his side, Manseur's good arm over his friend's shoulder to support himself, Manseur managed to walk toward the cabin. Bond carried his 30-06 in his left hand, his right holding Manseur's belt to keep the injured man balanced.

Alexa carried her shotgun, gripping the stock, finger beside the trigger guard. Manseur's shotgun remained propped against the tree he'd been beside when he'd been shot.

"What'll we do now, Agent Keen?" Bond asked. "Burn the cabin?"

"I'm thinking," Alexa answered. And she was.

89

Leland Ticholet worked his way back toward the cabin. He wasn't frightened, but he was losing a lot of blood. He wasn't thinking about the fact that he needed medical attention. With his boat gone, all Leland could think about was punishing the people responsible.

He couldn't let the cops take the other boat and get away. He had to make sure they didn't get to it.

He was sure he had killed the short cop. He was sure of it because he'd shot him in the head twice. The other cop with the rifle and the woman cop with the shotgun were all that stood between him and returning to life as usual. *If they hadn't come here, everything would have been fine.*

He was feeling a little dizzy, and he knew he had to stop the bleeding. He removed his boxer shorts and twisted them into a tight rope. Using his teeth and his good hand, he tied a knot in the end and slipped the loop up his arm above the wound. By turning a stick he'd picked up, he tightened the tourniquet until the blood flow slowed. He pinned the stick between his arm and his side so could pick up the rifle. He slipped five of the large bullets between his teeth and walked slowly toward the cabin, totally focused.

90

Alexa and Bond agreed that they couldn't wait for Leland to make the next move. They didn't really know much about Leland and what drove him. Bond said Leland thought more like an animal that could only plan in the short term, and react to situations as they came, than a person. Alexa thought he was very possibly clinically insane, which as long as he was alone out here and unthreatened wasn't a big deal. He lacked social skills, might even be marginally retarded.

Whatever the reality was, he was no ordinary criminal, and Alexa and Bond knew they couldn't trust him to do what most people would in similar circumstances.

Leland might or might not know other cops were coming and that his time was running out. Neither of them believed he would cut and run. Unless he was so seriously wounded that he was lying in the brush dying, Leland would try to resolve the immediate problem. He'd come for them or wait in hiding for them to move into his field of fire. Either way, Alexa didn't think he would wait long, given his wound.

Alexa stayed with Manseur, watching Larry Bond as he started his wide circle around the rear of the cabin. She was twenty feet from the edge of the dock, kneeling beside Manseur, who slumped, eyes closed, with his back against a tree. Bond moved silently, a man who hunted deer by stalking them, and his camouflage helped him melt into the foliage. One second he was there, the next gone.

Alexa turned her radio up until it squealed and backed off until it was quiet. She wouldn't call Bond, but he would be able to call her when he found Leland, or got to Kennedy.

She hoped Leland was dead, but despite Bond's confidence in his shot, she couldn't relax. Leland was a large and powerful man, and he had Kennedy's rifle. If he was drawing a bead on her at that moment, she wouldn't ever know it. Given the speed of a .270 round, you'd never hear the shot that got you.

Alexa thought about Kennedy, who was likely dead, the young deputy lying lifeless on the dock, the dead kidnapper in the cabin, and the shot-up briefcase full of bonds. The missing diary pages also entered her thoughts, and she wondered if they were in the cabin. Hearing a twig snap, she pivoted to see Leland Ticholet, stark naked except for the ballistic vest. He stood not ten feet away, aiming Kennedy's rifle at her head. She froze. Leland's wild eyes were burning like coals. Silver shells with black heads and yellow plastic points radiated from his mouth like talons. Alexa could see his finger in the guard as he squeezed the trigger once, and then again. She read the sudden slacking of his facial muscles when nothing happened, and she realized that there was no shell in the chamber.

Howling, Leland threw the weapon at her like a spear, then darted past her, zigzagging through the brush. She raised the Mossberg and fired twice.

"Alexa!" Bond's voice called out from the radio's speaker.

Fingers trembling, she keyed her radio. "Larry. I'm okay."

"You get him?"

"I tried. He ran off. How's Kennedy?"

"Alive. Leland hit him good in the head, but he's got a strong pulse. I'm coming back now. Wait for me."

"Okay," she said.

Alexa looked at Manseur, whose eyes were open now. He had drawn his Glock and was aiming in the direction Leland had run. Leland had to be stopped.

"Wait for Kennedy," she told Manseur. He nodded, squeezing his eyes shut when the pain hit him. Reloading as she walked, Alexa took off after her quarry.

The detective with the rifle passed by where he was lying in the brush, and had moved into the foliage before Leland saw him, and by then it was too late to shoot him. Leland moved as soon as he could do so without the rifleman hearing him. He'd gone around through the cover behind the cabin, sneaking up easily on the woman cop. Surprisingly, the man he'd shot in the head was very much alive, but hurt bad enough not to be a threat.

Leland had moved in close to them and had aimed at the woman before she knew he was there. He'd deliberately stepped on the dry branch so she would turn and see it coming. Surprised, she hadn't immediately raised her shotgun, and he had her nailed. He pulled the trigger, and nothing. He couldn't believe he hadn't worked the bolt, but what with being hit, he'd forgotten all about it. And he had left the pistol he'd gotten off the cop behind. Now he was unarmed, and running like a wild animal.

He was halfway to the point where he would have to swim to get away when he ran right past something that stopped him. A pump-gun was propped against a tree. He grabbed it up. Resting the butt on his leg, he pushed back the slide. A spent shell popped out. Putting the stock between his feet to hold it, he pulled the slide forward, feeding a shell into the chamber. He knelt and aimed at the sound of the cop coming, right toward him. In his mind he saw exactly how her severed head would hit the ground before her corpse collapsed beside it.

Shotgun primed and at the ready, Alexa moved swiftly toward the point. She was almost to the tree where Manseur had been wounded, when sensing—rather than seeing—Leland, she stopped abruptly and dropped to her knees. Leland's shotgun exploded, and she saw the bright blast from the muzzle. She felt the windblast as the buckshot passed inches from her scalp.

Without hesitating, Alexa shouldered and pointed her shotgun at the kneeling figure now silhouetted against the water, exhaling to steady herself. As she aimed at him, Leland Ticholet's image morphed into that of a silhouette target—the only target Alexa had ever fired a round into. *I will kill him. I will kill him. I will. . . .*

Holding on to the slide, Leland stood, jerked the shotgun violently in one hand, feeding in another round, dropped the gun into the same hand so he was gripping it like a pistol, finger in the guard, barrel rising up from his waist.

Watch the pellets hit him!

Alexa's shotgun roared.

The recoil shoved her shoulder back sharply, the barrel rising so she couldn't see the buckshot hit Leland. He fell back, and impacted the ground like a tree falling. Jacking in a fresh round, she slid toward the mud-encrusted bottoms of his feet.

Leland's arms were outstretched, and the vest he was wearing was dotted with shiny lead pellets. His eyes were open. The fingers of his right hand moved as though he were beckoning a child. Trembling, Alexa aimed the barrel of her gun at his head.

Leland coughed and his eyes began to gain focus.

Without saying anything, Alexa kicked the shotgun away from him.

Leland stared up at her.

"Do it!" Larry Bond urged as he ran up.

She shook her head reluctantly.

"Then step aside," Bond told her. He was holding his rifle pointed at Leland's chest.

"No," Alexa said.

"Step aside. I'm going to send this murdering piece of shit to hog heaven."

"Cuff him," she said.

"He killed Boudreaux. He shot Michael. He caved in Kennedy's skull. He's not walking out of here."

Leland looked at Bond. He said hoarsely, "Fuck you, pussy-ass."

"Leland Ticholet, you are so under arrest," Alexa said.

"He'll go to a nuthouse," Bond growled. "He's nuts. He's got to go, here and now."

"It's not our call," Alexa said, moving between the two men, her shotgun aimed at Leland's head.

"Get out of the way!" Bond barked.

"If you kill this man, I'll make sure you go to jail. I don't think you're willing to kill me just so you can kill him, Larry."

Angrily, Bond shouldered the rifle by its sling and yanked out his handcuffs. He snapped one of the cuffs on Leland's right wrist, grabbed him by his ear, lifted him into a seated position, then cuffed his wrists together behind his back. Bond put his own hands under Leland's armpits and lifted him to his bare feet. Once Leland was upright, Bond retightened the tourniquet. "Keep this tight, you piece of shit, or you'll bleed to death."

"You shot me, but you can't shoot worth a piss, you dog pussy bitch," Leland told Bond.

"I may shoot you for keeps, you naked piece of shit," Bond roared.

"I doubt you can even hit me from there."

Bond said, "You have the right to remain silent and I suggest you do just that, you ignorant killer swamp monkey. You have the right to a poorly skilled attorney and to have the prick present during questioning. If you cannot afford one, which is as obvious as your limp dick, one will be appointed for you at no cost. Do you understand these rights, like I give a shit?"

"I understand you bastards owe me a new boat," Leland said. "You think you can come to a man's place and burn his boat, you're the limp dick."

Shaking her head slowly, Alexa picked up Manseur's shotgun. She carried it over her left shoulder as they made their way back to the cabin.

93

Alexa and Bond handcuffed Leland's good wrist to a galvanized pipe that fed water from the cistern to an outside faucet, then went to bring Kennedy back on a stretcher they crafted from a wool blanket and two saplings. Kennedy was still unconscious two hours after he'd been attacked. Leland Ticholet had fallen asleep and was snoring. Alexa couldn't believe his threshold for pain.

While they waited, Alexa and Bond searched the cabin. She looked around in the cluttered kitchen, if it could be called a kitchen, since all there was in the way of appliances was a Coleman portable stove, an ice chest containing water left from melted ice, and a half-gone package of sandwich ham with embedded olive slices that stared out through the plastic like dead eyes. There was a chest of drawers. She opened the first one and picked up a folded four-by-five photograph, a black-and-white Polaroid. It was the kind of print photographers used to check lighting and composition. She looked at it and folded it again. Alexa placed the picture in the briefcase and carried them outside. There was no sign of the diary's missing pages.

The wind had picked up noticeably when the armada carrying Sheriff Toliver, a dozen of his deputies—only three in uniform, the rest looking for the world like armed vigilantes—and a three-person EMS team thundered into Leland's inlet. The sheriff's first words were spoken to Leland Ticholet as he officially arrested him for murdering Deputy Boudreaux, and suspicion of murdering game wardens Elliot Parnell and Betty Crocker.

Leland yawned.

Alexa was relieved to turn the prisoner over to the men, who manhandled him into a diesel-powered amphibious monster made of steel, possibly a surplus relic from World War II.

The EMS trio worked on Manseur and Kennedy

to prepare them for the trip out, ignoring Leland, whose only reaction to their presence was to yawn every now and again.

Leland didn't speak until one of the EMS medics was bandaging his arm, which the medic told him he was going to lose.

"It's good it's not the one I favor. Who's going to pay for what she done to my boat?" Leland looked angrily at the boat, which was still smoking.

Tolliver told Alexa the fastest boat would rush Manseur and Kennedy back to Moody's landing. There, a life-flight helicopter would take them to Baton Rouge, since New Orleans was no longer accepting patients. Leland was going to be taken to the local parish hospital for medical attention. The sheriff wasn't about to let Ticholet leave his jurisdiction until he had him convicted and sentenced to lethal injection for murdering his deputy, his cousin by marriage. He told Alexa and Bond they could speed back with Manseur and Kennedy. Alexa said too would rather ride back with the prisoner, because she had seen the same look in the eyes of the deputies, she'd seen in Bond's. She didn't want Leland shot for attempting to escape.

"Who's going to pay me for my boat?" Leland asked her. "I have to have a boat to make a living, you know."

"The federal government," Alexa lied. "They have a fund for equipment we destroy. They'll replace it for you as soon as all of this is straightened out. I'm sure you'll be right back out here skinning those beavers in a few days."

Leland frowned. "Nutrias, you dumb ass. Beavers

has flat tails. Nutrias has round ones. Nutrias is weed cutters. Beavers cut little trees to make dams with."

"Nutrias," Alexa said, meekly.

"None of this would have happened if y'all hadn't come busting into my camp without permission. Trespassing is against the damned law."

"You were defending your home against an invasion," Alexa agreed sympathetically. "Man's got a right to defend his home. You tell them that in court, and I bet they'll send you right back here."

"How long will it take?"

"This afternoon. Tomorrow at the latest. Maybe a little longer, due to the hurricane."

"That hurricane Doc talked about? I can feel some pressures changing."

"There's a huge hurricane coming this way."

"I got traps to run. How soon I get another boat like the one you burned up?"

"No time at all. It was a nice boat. Where did you get it?"

For the first time, Leland looked directly at her. "At the gettin' place."

"It was an expensive boat. Where'd you get the money?"

Leland narrowed his eyes. He didn't say anything.

"Did the guy inside get it for you?"

"I done jobs for it. A lot of hard work too."

"What sort of jobs?"

"It ain't none of your business what work I done."

"Like killing two wardens?"

"Naw, I did that on account they was trespassers."

"Where are their bodies?"

"Me to know and you to find out. You can't put them back together."

"How about that nurse? Did you kill her too?"

"What nurse?"

"Dorothy Fugate from River Run. You remember her?"

Leland nodded. "I know her. Damned bitch, if you ask me. She say I hit her?"

"Did you?"

"Hell naw. I ain't laid eyes on her since I was in that place. And she say I did, she's a lying sow. I don't like her, but I ain't never hit her."

"Did you help take Sibby Danielson to that motel?"

"Simpy who?"

"The woman who was living with Nurse Fugate. Long gray hair. Doc took her in your truck."

"Doc drove my truck some, but I never heard of no gray-haired woman."

"Did you hit Gary West with a piece of pipe?"

"You mean that guy in the fancy car?"

Alexa nodded.

"Doc said I had to do that job for the boat. I didn't do it on my own account. I never saw the man before in my life."

"Just be sure and tell the judge that Doc told you to do it. I'm sure the judge will understand. Just tell him you did it for the boat."

"Until y'all shot the motor and you burned it up."

"Where did you meet Doc?"

"Where do you think? He was a Doc," Leland said, exasperated.

"A doctor?"

"Sure was."

"He was an orderly," Alexa said. "He wasn't a doctor. You knew him from River Run?"

"Lying bastard told me he was a doctor. Why do people tell lies like that? I did wonder why he didn't doctor his own self after he got shot." Leland nodded. "He was nice and give me gum for free. He helped me get out, you know. He said I could have the boat if I would do a few jobs. Turned out, it was a lot of jobs."

"What about the picture?" Alexa asked.

"What picture?"

"Of you."

"What one?"

"This one." Alexa reached into the briefcase and unfolded the print.

Leland smiled as he looked at it. "The picture gal give that to me. Only time I saw my own handsomeness on film paper."

"What does this picture gal look like?"

Leland looked at her in the sort of stunned disbelief a man shows when he's speaking to an idiot. "Like a man, but with teats."

"Tall, short? White? Black?"

"She wasn't any too skinny or a fat gal neither. Sort of pretty, I guess you could say."

"The girl who took the picture?"

"This other gal took the picture and the other 'un give it to me. I never had nobody take my picture before except the cops, but they don't let you have none. You won't steal it from me, will you?"

Alexa looked out at the smoldering hull of Leland's boat, and suddenly felt as empty as a shattered pitcher.

94

The activity of the gathering of cops had drawn a crowd of civilians. NOPD Superintendent Jackson Evans waited, standing before two television crews, making a statement. Several members of his staff watched from the sidelines. The police had arrived in two helicopters, visible in the gravel lot beside Moody's store. Alexa had intended to take Manseur's car back to New Orleans, but she saw two men she was certain were FBI agents, walking toward her from a parked Ford sedan.

Bond had called Manseur's wife to tell her about Michael's condition before she saw or heard it on the news. He had told her they were going to the trauma center in Baton Rouge, where Manseur would receive the best of care. She said she'd leave her daughters at her sister's and make her way there.

As the boats approached the dock, the news crews abandoned the superintendent. They scrambled to get footage of the wounded detectives as well as the covered bodies of Deputy Boudreaux and Andy Tinsdale. Leland smiled at the attention. Jackson Evans hurried to the dock, perhaps out of genuine concern as well as the fact that it would enable him to get in the frame. As the crews recorded, Jackson Evans shook the sheriff's hand briskly. Several still photographers painted the scene with their flashes. Alexa could see Leland talking to the cameras as he was being perp-walked to a waiting ambulance. She was pretty sure he was telling the world about how that black woman FBI cop had burned up his wonderful new boat—earned by the honest sweat of his brow.

Alexa used her anonymity and the general confusion to escape the media. Luckily, Jackson Evans was too busy basking in the spotlight to think to share it.

The agents approached as Alexa was striding from the dock. "Agent Keen," the older one said. "I'm Special Agent Moore and this is Special Agent Montgomery. We're here to assist you as necessary."

"I'm all done here," she told them. "I could sure use a ride back to my hotel."

"There's a Lojac in it to direct us. By the way, the director asked me to tell you that he would appreciate a call at your earliest convenience," Agent Moore told her. "He said to tell you, 'Job well done.' He will send in a plane if you'd like to fly out of here. You sure don't want to try to drive. The field office is closed down. We've evacuated personnel, computers, and files. We'll be relocating to Baton Rouge until all's clear."

"Sounds like an intelligent course," Alexa said.

"Did you recover the ransom?" he asked.

Alexa held up the briefcase. "The majority of the bearer bonds are in here. Make sure Dr. LePointe gets them back, will you. I need to get the briefcase processed."

"How much is there?"

"Two million, three hundred thousand. Twenty of the bonds are missing. Maybe NOPD will turn up the rest in their investigation."

"Two hundred thousand in bearer bonds turn up in an NOPD investigation?" Montgomery smiled. "Like that'll happen in our lifetimes."

Alexa studied him. "What is that supposed to mean? The detectives I worked with are one hundred percent professionals. Don't you dare question their integrity in front of me. If you knew them, you wouldn't say such a thing."

The agent's face reddened. "Sorry. I didn't mean anything about them. There are a few good eggs in the carton."

She watched as the wounded detectives were being fed into the life-flight helicopter. She waved at Manseur, who was walking with the help of a pair of deputies. He saw her and weakly waved back.

"This is New Orleans, Agent Keen," Moore reminded her.

"So they tell me," she said.

95

Grub watched the excitement on the dock through the store's window because he didn't want Leland to see him and think he was gloating. He was sure that Leland would be back, because he was too mean not to. Grub liked pissing him off, because it was such good sport that he couldn't help it, but there wasn't any future in pressing your luck too far when it came to old Leland.

Grub heard one of the deputies saying that a boat had gotten burned up and they could use the smoke to get a fix on the location. He heard one of them telling the fat deputy that Leland had killed the deputy that had gone out with the other cops and that he'd shot up two of the cops that came from New Orleans to arrest him. They also said Leland had killed two missing game and fish officers. Like that was a surprise. They were lucky they'd shot Leland before he'd killed all of them.

Grub waited until the TV people and the cops were about done loading up and the deputies had pulled the first of the boat trailers down to get their boats. They'd driven the amphibian up onto a flatbed eighteen-wheeler, so in a while they'd be gone and the dock would be back to normal. One good thing was that the cops had filled up all their boats with gas, and Moody was happy about that, plus on account of all the chips, sandwiches, and cold drinks he'd sold them. None of them had tipped Grub, because cops and TV people were all a bunch of stuck-up idiots. He decided that he wouldn't ever again watch their TV shows or talk to cops if he could help it. They were all dick-brain shit-heels anyway.

Grub walked slowly to his bus and climbed inside, slamming the door behind him.

It was funny how that shot-up man in Leland's boat had hung on to his briefcase when there weren't nothing in it but a bunch of ruined paper. Grub had taken some of it, and now he opened his footlocker and took out the stack to look at it. With the bullet holes in them, he couldn't even use them to draw on, but the paper felt nice to his fingers and the writing on it stuck out so you could sort of feel the words.

Grub took one of the big papers and held it up to the window and looked at the way the light went through it and showed a design that appeared to be stuck inside the piece of paper. He studied the edges for a seam, but there weren't any, so he couldn't figure out how they got the picture and words inside a skinny piece of paper. He didn't know what the words said or what they could be for.

Grub knew what they'd be good for after he got tired of looking at them. Rolled up and set afire with a match, they'd reach deep enough in the heater to light it.

96

Back in her hotel room, Alexa ran herself a hot bath. She soaked for almost an hour, running more hot water into the tub as it cooled. After draining the water and drying off, she lay across the bed and closed her eyes. The events of the afternoon in the swamp played in her mind like a slow-motion nightmare. At least, she decided, there was only room behind her eyes for one nightmare at a time.

In her short life there had been many terrors emblazoned in her brain. A thousand insecurities, pains, and insults had occurred, and each was cataloged in her mind's files. She wished that she could, as the local field office had, remove the files to a faraway place and leave them stored where she would never have to recover them should she choose not to do so. If only life were so simple to deal with.

She took the bundle of postcards out of her suitcase and, one by one, tore them into confetti. That done, she flushed them down the toilet, watching the shards of evil spiral down into sewer oblivion. Alexa smiled. Maybe her sister's venomous words would live in her memory, but maybe she could erase their impact, close the open wounds in her heart. She had gathered evidence on her sister by duplicitous means, had arrested her because it was the right thing to do—the only thing she could do and remain true to herself. It had obviously hurt her more than it had her sister. Antonia was a creature who had been maimed by her early years. Alexa had come out of similar experiences and had not allowed her history to shape her into a coldly manipulating thing. Antonia would never forgive Alexa, but Alexa was going to forgive herself and move on. From now on she would never read another postcard. Never again would Antonia make Alexa feel bad.

Alexa was sure she could sleep for a week, and would have drifted off, except the ringing phone invaded her silence, demanded her attention.

She lifted the receiver. "Alexa Keen."

"Please hold for the director," the pleasant voice instructed.

"Agent Keen. Good job! Gary West is alive and the perps have been rounded up. The LePointes should be quite pleased. As soon as you get back to Washington, you and I are going to have lunch and you can fill me in. Agent, I'm not a man who forgets the people who make me look good. See you next week, Agent Keen. By the way, our plane will be leaving from the Naval Air Station at nine o'clock tonight. It's over the river in Belle Chase. You weren't thinking of staying there, I hope."

"No, sir. I'll be at the field."

"Good," he said.

After she hung up, Alexa opened her eyes. Her attention fell onto the book of portraits that Casey had given her.

She picked up the book and thumbed through the pages. Each new image was as good or better than the one on the page before it. Then Alexa turned a page and stared at the image in disbelief. Her heart began beating like a drum.

2/3/04—Violence Ward Inmate / Louisiana State Facility for the Criminally Insane, the caption read.

The image was that of a bare-chested young man with the kind of sharply defined muscles you'd see on a racehorse, and eyes that seemed like pits filled with windblown coals. Scars crisscrossed his forehead like an elaborate tattoo worn by a South Seas warrior. The calloused fingers of his upraised hands shot out from his palms like rays from the sun. It was apparent that every fiber of his being was electrically charged with blind outrage, or madness. Alexa didn't know how many times Casey had photographed Leland Ticholet, but, due to the Polaroid that had been the man's prized possession, she knew it had been at least twice: once when he had the hair and beard, and sometime later—after he had shaved them both off.

With this discovery still thundering through her, Alexa went to her jacket and slipped out a snapshot that she had taken from Dorothy Fugate's house and stared at it for a very long time. She chewed her bottom lip as she ran her finger over the small face in a photograph taken years before by an anonymous photographer. A photographer she had no way of identifying.

Alexa dressed hurriedly, found her mini-recorder, and left the hotel.

97

At five o'clock, under fast-moving clouds, Alexa parked on the street in front of the Tulane Medical Center. As she climbed from the Bucar, a powerful gust of wind that peppered her face with dust also snatched the door from her grasp, slammed it, and, lifting her all-weather coat, flapped it behind her like a flag. A second later, just as abruptly as it had struck, the demon windblast was gone.

With so much on her mind, Alexa had not been monitoring the approaching hurricane. According to the last report she'd heard, it was still six or seven hours away. Now with the leading edges of the feeder bands ruling the skies, it was easy to believe the monster storm was coming.

Alexa knew that she'd better start making a serious effort to wind things up and get out of the city before Katrina came roaring up the Mississippi River. The idea of being trapped in a geographic bowl as it filled with dark water was a sobering thought.

Alexa entered the hospital room where a cleaned-up Sibby Danielson lay in a bed, her wrists and ankles secured with fleece-lined leather restraints. Her long gray hair had dried and had been combed. And she was smiling like a sleeping child.

A young doctor entered and hung a chart off the end of the bed. "She doesn't look like a killer," he remarked.

"No, she doesn't," Alexa said. "Did she say anything?"

"Talked total nonsense nonstop until we sedated her. Yakata, yakata, yakata. Took enough happy juice to knock out an elephant. She's built up quite a resistance to it."

You don't know the half of it. "What sort of nonsense?" Alexa asked him.

"Gibberish. Rhyming nonsense. A few choice vulgarities peppered in."

The doctor left the room and Alexa drew close to the bed and stared down at the woman, who looked like a heavier and older version of her daughter, one of New Orleans's wealthiest citizens. Alexa's heart went out to the woman who had spent the past three decades wrapped up in a cocoon of illness. She couldn't imagine the torture this creature had suffered at the hands of the powerful for one night's actions she hadn't been capable of preventing herself from doing. Sibby wasn't evil, but as pure a victim as there was. Alexa felt herself close to tears.

"Sleep, Sibby," Alexa said, close to tears. "You've earned it." She picked up her purse, and when she looked back at Sibby, the woman's eyes were open and searching the room wildly.

"Sibby?" Alexa said.

"Sibhon. Sibby. Sibhon." Her intonation was as flat as a tabletop.

"Sibhon." Alexa smiled down at her.

Sibby's eyes darted around as though she were looking for someone else, perhaps a point of reference.

Suddenly she fixed Alexa in her gaze. Her lips curled back from her yellowed teeth. "Sibhon. Remember. *Never forget.*"

Alexa nodded. "Are you comfortable?"

"Cut the cop. Cut the fog. Sibby. Sibby. Sibby. Here I am. Don't forget. Never quit. Tell the lies. Find them always where they hide. Say the poems. Say the poems. Find the poems."

"You know a poem?"

Sibby smiled and nodded rapidly. She closed her eyes. "Stop saying I did it. Tell a lie. Stick a needle in Sibby's eye. Fucker man, the fucker man. Put the chopper in my hand. Windy rain. Windy rain. The stinky nurse is here again. Lie bitch, lie bitch, I know the trues. I never lose if I still can choose. The baby comes, the liars go. The smiling cop deserves a blow. Tell the people what you know. Fucker man, the fucker man. Put the chopper in my hand."

"Sibby, what does that mean?" Alexa asked.

"God is love. Love is God. The Trinity. Heaven is the carrot on the stick. Hell is the bullwhip to keep you straight. The Mother Church is the name brand."

"Sibby, do you know who put you in the motel?"

"Stop saying she did it. Tell that lie. Stick a needle in Sibby's eye. Fucker man, the fucker man. Put the chopper in my hand. Windy rain. Windy rain. The stinky nurse is here again. Lie bitch, lie bitch, I know the trues. I never lose while I still can choose. The baby comes, the liars go. The smiling cop deserves a blow. Tell the people what you know."

"Do you remember Dr. LePointe and Nurse Fugate?"

Sibby closed her eyes. "Fucker man, fucker man . . ."

Alexa felt a surge of excitement shoot through her. She dug into her purse for the mini tape recorder.

98

Alexa raced across town. Nobody had checked out Andy "Doc" Tinsdale's place, and unless somebody did so tonight, the place might not still be there later. He was dead and it was a loose end that would bother her until she saw for herself what was there. She had no warrant and no way to get a warrant. Most of the judges who were smart enough to issue one had long ago left the city.

With her GPS lady's assistance, she arrived at 912 Fulton, her wipers barely able to keep the rain cleared. The hurricane was closing in. If the storm had ever seemed an abstraction to her, it was as real to her now as a section of lead pipe.

She ran through the driving rain to the darkened house and stood on the porch. She picked the lock and let herself inside, slipping on gloves as she did so.

The living room and kitchen held only a recliner, a floor lamp beside it, bookshelves, and a television set with rabbit ears, perched on a spindle-legged table. There was no dining table or chairs, only a TV tray leaned against the wall. The bookcase was comprised of cinder blocks and planks. The shelves held only paperback novels, alphabetized by author. There was not room for one more book on the planks.

The bedroom contained a mattress on box springs. Tinsdale's clothes were neatly folded and in stacks against a wall. A cheap Oriental carpet covered the floor.

The closet held a packed suitcase. Alexa took it to the bed and opened it. Inside, she found clothes, a wig, a passport in the name Douglas Winston, and a plane ticket to Madrid. There was also a brochure in Spanish that showed before-and-after examples of cosmetic surgery. *No wonder he didn't care if he was identified.*

Alexa ran her hands over the lining. Using her pocketknife, she cut the lining open and took out a manila envelope. She reached in and removed three sheets of notebook paper, filled front and back with cursive script she now knew well. The pages were the ones that had been removed from Fugate's spiral notebook.

Trembling with excitement, she sat on the edge of the mattress, and read the pages slowly, absorbing the words written by a woman who was stunningly candid, although completely deluded, and perhaps as insane as the people she had spent her career nursing. Alexa was amazed by the same brand of evil that had allowed the Nazis to commit their atrocities to paper and film.

Unbelievably, the entry was dated the night of the LePointe murders. It began, *It was a dark and stormy night. . . .*

Before she finished the first page, she understood

why Andy Tinsdale had torn these sheets from the diary.

These lone pages were worth many times what the notebook without them was. Anyone with half a brain would never have killed this golden goose.

Not in a million years.

99

At eight o'clock on Sunday evening, Alexa left her hotel for the last time, put her suitcase and valise in the Bucar's trunk, and made her way slowly up St. Charles Avenue. The street was not nearly as deserted as it should have been, with the storm's fury mere hours away. The streetcars were still running, packed with evacuees headed for the Superdome.

It was raining hard, and according to the radio, the wind was gusting to thirty-five miles per hour now. Alexa passed a lone television sound truck parked outside Dr. LePointe's home and pulled up to the gate in front of the mansion. The guard made a call before he opened the gate. Suddenly floodlights blasted her car as a cameraman aimed his camera at her. She ignored the shouted questions from the reporter wearing a raincoat with its storm hood up to protect her hair—a woman who looked like she just wanted to get the hell back to the safety of the TV station.

The Bentley was parked under the portico, aimed out for a fast exit. Alexa parked and strode to LePointe's front door. A solemn black man opened the door and let her inside. Two men in overalls walked the large Turner painting up the hall, turned in the foyer, and carried it upstairs. Alexa supposed they were figuring if New Orleans flooded, the waters couldn't reach the second floor.

"The doctor is in his study, miss. But he is leaving in a few minutes for the airport in Baton Rouge."

"Thank you," she told the servant before making for the office in the rear of the mansion. "I'll be brief."

Dr. LePointe looked up as she entered, closing the door behind her.

"The Bureau will be returning your bonds as soon as they process them," she told him. "We recovered all but twenty." She sat down without being invited.

"Twenty thousand?"

"Twenty bonds."

"What happened to those?"

"I have no idea," Alexa answered truthfully.

He said, "Not an excessive amount to pay, considering the results."

Alexa noticed the glass of amber liquid on the desk and realized that LePointe was drunk.

"I suppose you can write it off to the soaring cost of dirty business."

"You think I care about that money?" He waved his hand dismissively. "Inconsequential."

"What I think is, it's amazing you can keep from blowing your brains out."

LePointe smiled thinly and rocked back in his chair. "I suppose it's beyond your experience, and I don't want your understanding or forgiveness. I made misjudgments, but I assure you my intentions were to protect my niece from the ugly truth. Are you here to gloat?"

"I'm going to do everything I can to see that you go to jail."

"That's a good one. Take your best shot, Agent Keen."

"I intend to." Alexa took the recorder out of her purse, turned it on, and sat back to watch LePointe's face.

"*Stop saying I did it. Tell a lie. Stick a needle in Sibby's eye. Fucker man, the fucker man. Put the chopper in my hand. Windy rain. Windy rain. The stinky nurse is here again. Lie bitch, lie bitch, I know the trues. I never lose. I still can choose. The baby comes, the liars go. The smiling cop deserves a blow. Tell the people what you know.*"

"Do you remember Dr. LePointe?"

"*Fucker man, fucker man. Put a chopper in my hand.*"

"Sibby, who killed those people in the kitchen?"

"*Fucker man.*"

"Who brought you to that house where the dead people were?"

"*Windy rain.*"

"It was stormy that night. Who took you there?"

"*Stinky nurse.*"

"Nurse Fugate? . . . Note: Sibby is nodding." Alexa's voice was steady. "*Sibby, who chopped up the bodies?*"

"*Raincoat fucker man. Put the cleaver in my hand.*"

"He put the cleaver in your hand after he chopped them up?"

"Fucker man push Sibby down. Bloody blood. Who did it? You did it. Who did it? You did it. Who did it? You did it. No. Lie, lie, lie. Fucker man do. Not Sibby."

Alexa snapped the recorder off.

LePointe's face had lost its color. He took a drink, then shook his head.

"She's an extremely sick woman."

"She knows," Alexa said.

This surprised Dr. LePointe, but he managed to say, "Pure nonsense. Obviously Dorothy can't confirm your suspicion."

"That's why you and Dorothy kept her a prisoner and tried to destroy her mind. Sibby knew."

"Sibby heard voices. In fact, if I recall, this fucker man was a voice she listened to. One among many. The voice probably commanded her to kill Curry and Rebecca."

"Dorothy's pet name for you was Dr. Fuckerman. Even through the fog of her delusions, Sibby knew. Did you make Sibby call you by that name?"

LePointe laughed. "Jesus God. Take that obscene tape and put it in the nearest trash receptacle, where it belongs."

"I don't know why you killed your brother and his wife that night. Maybe you planned it or maybe you just snapped. There was a storm and the streets were empty. Maybe you killed Curry, and Rebecca came in and you thought you had no choice but to kill her too. Maybe you had Sibby out in the car with Dorothy, or maybe you had her bring Sibby there to you after the murder. It doesn't matter. I know you did it. You made sure Sibby was found there with the cleaver. Maybe Decell was already working for you, or maybe it began that night because he knew, or figured it out. I'm not sure, and it doesn't matter anymore."

"I don't have to sit here and listen to this."

"Stand and listen, then. Sibby will get stronger and healthier. She will become more and more lucid. Sibby is the sword of Damocles and she's hanging over your head by a thread. I've made sure she's beyond your reach and I think modern psychiatry can bring her back a little. When it does, her testimony, coupled with the diary and the missing pages I found tonight, will be enough to convince a prosecutor."

"I loved my brother. I was here that night. All night long, until the police woke me. There were witnesses. Good luck breaking my alibi."

"Witnesses like your mother? Casey's grandmother?"

"She was away. But my wife and the servants made statements proving I was here."

"Your witnesses are dead or long gone, I bet. Your wife is in no condition to testify. You're going down. One day very soon. I promise you that. The public is going to learn about it."

"One day soon." LePointe held up his glass in salute. "Unless you are arresting me today, I have a plane to catch, Agent Keen. Anyway, why are you here instead of celebrating with Casey?"

"She isn't gone?"

"She isn't leaving. She's perfectly safe."

"Celebrating what?"

"Ascension to the throne." He smiled at Alexa. "She's got everything she ever wanted."

"You can't accept that she can love so completely?"

"Love? You honestly believe she loves Gary West?" He laughed and took a swallow from the glass, a drop dribbling down his chin. "The boy served his purpose, which was as a sperm syringe. He's no more to her than a bull that's conveniently out to pasture."

"Casey is devastated." Alexa felt hot anger rising within her.

"She's devastated by joy at her wealth and power."

"Casey doesn't care about money or power."

LePointe's laughter was a sudden bark. "Don't feel too badly. She fooled me too, Agent Keen. Like Grace Smythe, another gold-digging bitch. Turns out my daughter is twice the LePointe I am. She's on par with my mother, with her father . . . uncle . . . Curry. I didn't have any idea until I saw her standing where you are with the trust's lawyer handy. They had the resignation paper for me to sign. God knows how long she's had it prepared. Hell, I didn't even know Casey was aware of the covenant. I have to hand it to her. Hoisted on my own petard. I'd have done the same thing in her place. Never would have imagined she had it in her."

"What covenant?"

"Ask her about it. Something my ancestors instituted to prevent any one person from throwing the family's fortunes away, and reputation is part and parcel of the whole shebang."

"In English?" Alexa said.

"A straightforward morality clause tucked into the family rules and regulations. According to the covenant that I, like all of my predecessors in the last fifty years, signed upon taking control of the family trusts, any LePointe heir loses any rights of participation in or control they have immediately upon doing anything that brings disgrace or casts a scandalous shadow on the family name. Financial irresponsibility that threatens the capital is also covered. Three-point-nine billion last count, give or take a hundred million. All privately held. No public participation or interference. That is *power*, Alexa Keen."

The amount stunned Alexa.

"I saw the glee in Casey's eyes tonight. And to think I could have paid for an abortion and made this impossible. Her eyes. They were as bright and as icy cold as my own dear mother's."

LePointe sat bolt upright. "You aren't recording this, are you?"

"No. I'm not."

"I'm going to tell you something, because you are so smug, you should know. Your poor little rich girl is a monster."

"I don't believe for one moment that Casey is anything but a victim." Alexa crossed her arms. "You're drunk."

"Hardly as intoxicated as I will be in an hour. A cleverly hidden time bomb, best I can figure. She was behind all of it. I can see her handiwork through all of this. That nasty conniving bitch from hell."

"Casey?"

"My mother. Well, my mother and Casey. My mother believed, as do you, that I had Sibby kill Curry in order to take his place."

"Didn't you?"

LePointe smiled at Alexa with an I-may-be-drunk-but-I'm-not-crazy look.

"I am of the opinion—and I do not know this for a fact—that Dorothy may have done what you have accused me of in order to help me be all that I could be." He smiled sourly. "Mother must have told Casey at some point, or left her a letter. My dear mother hated me as much as she loved Curry. And she saw Casey as Curry's daughter . . . complex biology issues aside."

"Your mother *knew* Casey was your daughter?"

"Of course she did. She put Casey in Curry and Rebecca's possession against my wishes. I had a constant reminder of my weakness right in my own home. Mother held the real power till the day she died. She told me on her deathbed that I would live to regret what I had done. I thought the old bitch meant God would see to it. She's probably ruling the seventh level of hell about now. She hated me with a passion. She tortured me like you wouldn't believe, but I thought after she was gone, that would be over."

"I suspect a lot of people hate you," Alexa said.

"Touché," he said, draining his glass. "Casey did it all in such a way that nobody can touch her. Brilliant! Perfection in breeding and environment. She didn't inherit her mother's illness, but that would have been better for all concerned."

He poured another drink from the decanter on his desk.

"No matter how deep you dig, Agent Keen—and she knows you of all people believe she was the victim, so you won't bother to look any deeper than you have. The local cops are way out of their league with her. And so, it appears, is the FBI. Hell, I certainly was. She is a master, and any evidence you find will point to others. Casey is as hard as her grandmother, and my mother was a stainless steel magnolia with a diamond-coated carbide heart."

"So you say."

Alexa thought about something. She reached into her purse. "Do you know this man? Andy Tinsdale. The blackmailer. He shot Decell."

"And Casey shot him. He was in on this? That makes everything fit," he said, shaking his head. "Of course. I never imagined he was capable of anything. But with her help . . ."

"Andy Tinsdale was an orderly at River Run. You knew him very well."

"I never cared to know him. Ask Casey about him. She knew him a lot better than I did. Show her the picture. You already did, didn't you? What did she tell you?"

"That doesn't matter."

"I think it does, based on your expression. Andy was a creepy little bastard. A sick little fool of the first order. When he was thirteen or so, my gardener caught him with his pants around his ankles masturbating in the tool shed with a pair of Casey's panties on his head."

"What did that have to do with Casey?"

"She was there watching. Egging him on. He swore she put him up to it. I believed her because she seemed so upset. An actress even then. She said he forced her to watch him. I forbade him ever coming here again, or being within ten miles of Casey. Now I know she put him up to it."

"How was Tinsdale connected to Dorothy?"

"He's Fugate's bastard. He was raised by Dorothy's brother as his son. Her brother may have been his real father, as far as I know. She gave the miserable creature a job as an orderly on the wards. He had to change his name to get the job, of course. Casey enjoyed his company, probably because she could get him to do anything she liked. I'm sure she hooked up with him recently."

"You're just trying to make trouble for Casey. You paid the ransom only to get that diary, not to get Gary back."

"She has him back. Think what you like. Don't you wonder at all why the diary was there for you to find, or why it was released to the media? Don't you at least think it odd that Casey ended up going out there with you, and that she just happened to have a gun with her? Haven't you wondered, if the diary was the reason I paid the ransom, why Gary was kidnapped in the first place? They could have brought the diary and I would have paid them off. Simple business transaction."

"I assume Gary's abduction was at Grace's request. She was in love with Casey and jealous of anybody near her."

"Casey and Grace. That's a dark and sticky web. Grace thought she and Casey were friends, maybe much more than friends. I'd wager Casey told Grace that Gary was a mere necessity—a baby maker. Casey probably intended that Gary and I both would die in that hellish hovel, but she didn't count on Decell being there. I imagine Tinsdale was supposed to kill me and be gone long before you arrived. Instead, you rush in. You're suddenly in peril, so Casey comes in, gun blazing, fills old Andy full of lead, snipping *that* loose end. The other loose end was her assistant, Grace Smythe."

"Grace committed suicide."

"Sure she did." LePointe shrugged. "I'm only a psychiatrist, not an FBI agent, but is a woman who is about to live happily ever after with a very wealthy woman a prime candidate for suicide? Maybe times have changed and people kill themselves because their wildest and wettest dreams are about to come to fruition. I know Casey had that idiotic little thing in her thrall, but I never suspected . . ." LePointe's focus dulled. "That's the beauty of planning things out five moves ahead, something we LePointes have mastered. Well, some of us obviously better than others. Casey makes sure she never leaves loose ends."

"Casey doesn't need your family's money," Alexa offered. "She has her own fortune. She told me she has more personal money than you do."

"Four times as much. Personal money is one thing, but that amount pales in comparison to the trusts. When is too much ever enough?" LePointe asked. "Casey's my own flesh and blood. And oddly, despite everything she has done, I am proud of her. I lost a game I wasn't aware I was playing, but I know I would have still lost even if I had known. Now she's one of the wealthiest and most powerful women alive. Shoot all the holes in it you want, but she's made sure believing her is the easiest course. The one thing I know is, she's played you like a flute and there's not one thing you or anybody else can do about it. She's not done with me yet. That's why I'm telling you this. Catch her if you can, and stop her. It's in my best interests."

"I don't believe a word you've said."

"I bet you didn't know that Casey can revoke the prenuptial she signed with Gary West. There is an escape clause in the fine print that if he were to be incapacitated at any point before the magical anniversary, it is null and void."

"Nobody is that good an actor," Alexa argued.

"Is she that talented? You tell me. Never mind. You just have." LePointe laughed loudly. He stood. "Now, please leave my house. I have an impending hurricane to flee from."

Alexa left the house, feeling sick to her stomach. She didn't want to believe that Casey was a sociopathic liar and cold-blooded killer. LePointe had surely twisted things around to make Casey look bad, to punish her because he was that sort of bastard. Casting the blame onto his daughter was the logical act of a twisted sociopathic mind seeking redemption. What he had told Alexa was a trial balloon, one he would no doubt spread to the public to clear his reputation.

Alexa prided herself on knowing a lie when she heard one, and she had never sensed the slightest deception in Casey West.

In the car, Alexa removed the picture from her pocket of the children at play and studied it under the map light. She knew who had taken it—the boy's proud mother, an ambitious nurse who had hopes in her heart that the children would be together for years to come. The girl's father would not have known his mistress had recorded it. Alexa's heart sank and she clenched her teeth, the anger rising so close to the surface, she could taste it.

The idea that William LePointe was being honest in his accusations was totally preposterous. If it was the truth, Alexa had never been so completely taken in by anyone in her life.

Am I being objective?

Alexa had a more troubling thought. If Casey West was indeed the cold-blooded, plotting monster her father claimed she was who was responsible for all those deaths, there probably wasn't anything she could do about it. And if that was the case, Casey West was laughing at her along with everybody else.

100

The wind buffeted the car mercilessly. The rain was being driven horizontally and the trees and bushes seemed to be trying their best to get their roots out of the earth and fly. It was impossible for her wipers—as often lifted by the wind as not—to do their job.

Alexa had gotten lost on several occasions because the GPS lady was no longer functioning, but since her cell phone was, she finally called Casey to get directions to her house. She wouldn't have been surprised to learn that the GPS satellite had been knocked out of the sky, but it was just as likely faulty FBI equipment.

When Alexa finally turned onto Casey's street, she was sure the Bucar would overturn. It was impossible to see twenty feet ahead of the car, but Casey's house was as easy to find as an Easter egg on white carpeting.

As Alexa fought her way to Casey's gate, the rain stung her skin like BB's. She was drenched before she even rang the bell, and was let inside the house by the guard.

Casey was standing at the entrance to the hallway, wearing a robe, holding Deana on her hip like an ornament. "I'm glad you called me," she said. "You'll be safe here with us until this passes. Here, you need a towel. I meant to call you as soon as I heard about your ordeal in the swamps, but as you might imagine, I've been . . ." She left the rest unsaid and a tear rolled down her cheek. "I'm glad you missed your flight, Alexa. Is that selfish of me?"

"Thanks for letting me come. It's a far more attractive refuge than the Superdome."

"You must stay with us. We missed our window to fly out. I suppose you're here because you've heard about Gary? My poor Gary."

"Gary?"

"Stroke during the flight to Mayo. We have to have faith that he will regain everything the assault and this stroke have taken from him. It will take years of rehabilitation, but it's obvious he'll never be the same. I'll fly to be with him tomorrow, if the plane is still in the hangar. Hell, if the hangar is still standing tomorrow."

"Dr. LePointe told me you were riding out the storm," Alexa said, not sure if she should call him Casey's uncle or her father.

Casey frowned. "Unko hates storms. I'm sure they

bring back unpleasant memories. What took you by Unko's?"

"I went by to let him know I'll be doing everything I can to put him in prison. He deserves to be in prison for life."

"I wish you all the success in the world. That's a terrible thing to say. But I mean it."

"Are you alone, Casey?"

"At the moment, except for the kitchen help and Edgar, my remaining security guard, we're alone. It will be nice having a friend here to huddle with."

Casey led Alexa to the kitchen. "Ahm not you fren," Deana said, sticking out her bottom lip at Alexa.

"Shouldn't you have gotten Deana out?"

"She's perfectly safe with me here. So are you. Deana, Alexa is your friend. She saved your father's life. She's Mommy's very best friend ever. Aren't you, Alexa?"

"I hope so," Alexa said.

Casey put her daughter in her high chair and handed the child three cookies to keep her occupied. Retrieving her abandoned martini, she turned to Alexa and asked, "Coffee? Or a stiff one?"

"Nothing for me," Alexa told her.

"Just a sec," Casey said, and went to the laundry room, returning with a pair of dry jeans. "These may be a bit large, but you can roll the cuffs."

"I'll change in a few minutes."

A maid entered the room, and busied herself preparing coffee.

"So tell me everything that happened," Casey urged. "I heard some of it from Chief Evans. It's terrible about those two detectives. I'm going to hire the very best doctors for them and we'll send them wherever they need to go to be made whole. After all they did for us, it's the least I can do. And I want to do something for you. Name something, Alexa, anything."

"You don't have anything I need."

Casey's smile vanished and she gave Alexa a hurt look. "Is it an insult to offer? It isn't like I'm trying to buy you, really. You've done so much for me. . . ."

"There is one thing."

"Name it."

"Talk to me. Now."

"I know we have a lot to talk about, but is now a good time?" She waved her hand absently at the storm outside. "We have all night."

"I'd feel better getting it out of the way now."

"You want me to hear what that woman had to say?"

"I think you should. Alone," Alexa said, turning her eyes toward the maid.

Casey tilted her head and studied Alexa thoughtfully. "Mary, watch Deana. Please, follow me," Casey told Alexa.

Alexa followed Casey down a long, glassed-in corridor with a view of a garden on either side. The limbs of the trees rocked violently. Leaves had long since flown from the branches, the flowers were all stripped of their petals. The corridor ended in a pool house, which would have made a wonderful home for a family of five. There, Alexa played the tape of Sibby's interview while Casey listened intently. After it was over, Alexa turned it off.

"Fucker man," Casey said, exhaling loudly. "So he . . ."

"He killed your parents. I believe Sibby. She's fought to remember it all these years."

"But she can't testify, can she?"

"No, not any time soon. There's some areas to explore, along the lines of corroboration from witnesses and sources, but I'm not sure about the fine points of law." Alexa told Casey about finding the missing diary pages. Taking the plastic-sleeved pages from her purse, she handed them to her to read.

"I don't want fingerprints on them, other than those that may be on them already."

After reading the pages twice, Casey handed them back to Alexa. "That's horrible. Beyond horrible. Did you play the tape for my uncle?"

"Yes, I did."

"You showed him these pages?"

"No. But he knows they exist."

"Did he admit anything?"

"He is under the illusion that Sibby's words are not going to hurt him."

"There's no justice," Casey said sadly.

"There is only setting things right. A lack of justice could work to your advantage."

"What do you mean?"

"Your uncle told me some disturbing things. I didn't want to believe them, but I've been doing a lot of thinking, and what he said makes a great deal of sense. Too much sense."

"Do explain."

Alexa felt the chill gathering in the room. "It's about an actress who's been playing a very challenging part—victim, sensitive artist, bereaved and loving wife. Perfect mother."

Casey stared at her, her expression unreadable.

"You really had me going, Casey. You really did. Trouble is, things don't really add up."

"You've been talking to Uncle William. He's a cagey and a professional-quality liar. He hates me."

"You told the press the diary was authentic. Is it true that the prenuptial you told me all about is void now because Gary is incapacitated? Did you force William out of his position and take his place today? I'm getting a disturbing picture, a nasty interpretation of events that looks like motive."

"Let's continue this talk in the sauna."

"The sauna?"

"It's more private."

"You think I'm wired?"

"Don't be silly, Alexa. We're dear friends. Leave your purse on the table." Casey opened a door, and Alexa could see into a room where a blond-wood bench held a neat stack of linens. Across the room, a tiled enclosure area had two showerheads and a drain in the floor. A wooden door with an opaque glass panel obviously led to the sauna.

"It helps me relax. Take off your clothes, wrap up in a bath sheet, and we'll talk. Unless we've talked enough."

Alexa said, "I'm here because I want to talk this out. Because you matter to me, and I think after all I've been through that I deserve to know."

"Fine. Why does it matter where we are when we talk?"

While Alexa undressed, Casey watched her with a serious expression, studying her bruises.

"You've had a rough couple of days."

"Comes with the job." Alexa took the top sheet and wrapped her body, tucking it above her breasts. Casey slipped out of her robe and Alexa was somewhat surprised to see that her hostess hadn't been wearing anything else.

Casey opened the door to the sauna. The walls, ceiling, and floor were tiled in limestone. A wide stone slab ran along three walls, forming a bench. Casey poured a dipper of water on the kiosk filled with heated stones, sat across from the door, pulled her feet up so her heels rested against her buttocks, and leaned back against the wall.

The light went out.

"We just lost power," Casey said in the pitch-blackness.

The light came back on before she'd finished saying it.

"We have a generator that runs on natural gas. Let's talk." She patted the bench beside her.

Alexa sat close enough to give the impression of intimacy, but far enough away so someone could have fit between them. If LePointe was right about Casey, Alexa felt she might talk about it because she had won, and there was nothing Alexa could present as evidence that could tie her into anything. Once Casey walked out the door, the conversation was her word against Alexa's, and Alexa knew she couldn't win in a battle against Casey West and her lawyers.

Alexa began, "Before I went to your uncle's earlier, everything fit neatly, but after I listened to his vitriolic diatribe, I had a problem. Until I learned about the covenant and your prenuptial escape clause, you were without any motive."

Casey sipped her martini. "I'm listening."

"I know you killed Grace, I just don't know how."

Casey raised her eyebrows. "But you said the coroner ruled she killed herself."

"So it appears."

"Take off your sheet," Casey said.

"You know I'm not wired, Casey."

"You want your pores to open, to get the full benefit."

"My pores are fine semiclosed," Alexa said.

"Humor me, Alexa. Don't tell me you're shy. I've already seen your body. It's a very nice one. You take very good care of yourself."

Why not? Alexa stood, undid the tuck above her breasts, and let the sheet slip to the floor.

"You have a very nice body," Casey repeated. "You hide it in those silly, off-the-rack business suits. The right tailoring would do wonders for you. I'll take you shopping soon. Just the two of us."

"Thanks. I have to stay in shape," Alexa said, sitting and raising her feet to mirror Casey's pose. "I like the suits I wear." The heat was making her drowsy because she hadn't slept in a very long time. "I guess I am guilty of liking you too much, of feeling we were close based on common experience. I wanted too much to believe you were what you seemed. It blinded me."

"We're a lot alike," Casey said. "Possibly more than either of us imagines."

Because you imagine that what I did to my sister was comparable to what you did to your father? That was different, very different.

"Do you have any illusions that this talk will lead to my arrest?"

Alexa shrugged. "Bringing charges would be very difficult, if not impossible. You were very smart. The witnesses are either dead or uninformed as to your involvement. There's no one left to testify against you. William won't because of the remote possibility you'll forgive him in the future."

"So he can destroy me," Casey said. "That will *never* happen."

"I doubt he has anything he can blackmail you with. Not yet anyway. He has a lot of possible directions. He thinks he's playing a chess game."

"You have old Willie Boy pegged. Can you make a case against him for what he did to my mother and father? What he did to Sibby?"

"I'm going to try. And if I do, he'll try to take you down with him. Anyway, you said it yourself—there is no justice."

"I really do like talking to you," Casey said, taking a sip and putting down the glass. "You have this way of making me want to be honest with you."

Alexa said, "Honesty is probably all but impossible for you, Casey. I do understand why, and my heart goes out to you. I think what you did is cold and horrible, and I hate what you did, but . . ."

"You empathize." Casey put her open hands to her chest. "Dahlin', that all means a lot more to little ole me than you can imagine. I've been alone all my life and you know better than anybody what my uncle did to my parents. You are the one who found the missing pages at Andy's."

"I didn't say I found the pages at Andy's apartment," Alexa said, leaning back casually.

"Of course you did. How else would I have known?"

"Beats me, since we haven't discussed Andy Tinsdale, or should I say Andy Fugate. You looked at his picture and said you only knew him as an orderly, which ensured I would find his apartment and the pages. It was a needless lie, Casey. You could have told me who he was and slammed that door closed, the way you did so many others. I would have found out you knew him anyway, which would have been worse."

"You can't plan everything perfectly." Casey took another sip of her martini. "Obviously I'm too tired to talk candidly. Or without an attorney present. I had a thought today. Decell's gone. It occurs to me that the LePointe trusts could use a security director with FBI experience. At a salary commensurate with the responsibility."

"You offering me a bribe?"

"Goodness, no. A job. You'd be perfect."

"That's tempting. But wouldn't I be under your thumb? Like Grace was?"

"That's not nice," Casey said. "The money would simply be commensurate with your law enforcement experience."

"I make all I need."

"Eighty-nine thousand, six hundred, and forty-one dollars last year before taxes. And you have almost a hundred thousand in your retirement accounts, another fifty in stocks and bonds. You live in a rented apartment all by your lonesome in Washington. You have no family to speak of, and workaholics make few friends. It must be awful. I could pay you five hundred thousand a year on a twenty-year contract. And you could have whatever perks and private entanglements you liked."

"That's tempting," Alexa said. "But there's Grace."

"Grace, Grace, Grace."

"You murdered her. You are the only one with the access to the money I found at her home. Who else could afford to walk away from it after it had served its purpose as a very clever prop?"

"Fifty thousand is a lot for anybody to walk away from."

"Not for you. You paid thirty grand for a boat for a lunatic psychopathic swamp dweller."

"I've never bought a boat in my life."

"Okay, you bought it through Andy."

"I barely knew the man."

"Unko told me about the garden-shed incident."

"He didn't tell you that!" Casey squealed. "That old bastard. Well, I did tell you about Dr. Fuckerman. Andy Fugate was a very accommodating man, with extremely limited prospects."

"Other than blackmail."

"No big deal. I suppose I paid him to look the other way—help me make a few portraits of people I didn't have releases from until he got them for me. He was not kind to the inmates, in ways you wouldn't believe. He was a truly despicable individual."

"Nurse Fugate didn't recognize Leland in your exhibition?"

"Dorothy never saw any of my work as far as I know. She certainly didn't attend the exhibition in Zurich where I showed that portrait, and she wouldn't have had access to the catalog. Unko wasn't there either. He'd have shit a brick. He treated Leland. So before we go any further, is this an interrogation or a job interview?"

Alexa said, "Just humor me. I just want to know how competent I am. We both know I can't make this case."

"This is between the two of us and the walls?" Casey said. "Andy was sometimes in town in the summers. More when we were younger. I think Dorothy wasn't fond of having him around, because he was a reminder of something she didn't like thinking about. He was a bastard in more ways than one. I couldn't stand the sight of him." Casey giggled. "He always wanted to play doctor, and guess who was the patient? He resented his mother since she treated him like a leper. Face it, they both imagined she would marry Unko after Sarah died and they'd win the blue-blood lottery.

"I suppose I tolerated Andy's company because he was virtually unlikable and I was fascinated by that. He was a repulsive know-it-all loser with delusions of importance. It seems sometimes that the world is filled to bursting with unlikable people."

"And Grace's cash—that was yours. Andy didn't have access to that kind of money."

"I told you, the fifty thousand could have come from someone else that was in on it."

"There it is again. I never said it was fifty thousand. Just like I never said I was in Andy's apartment."

"Next time I talk about it, I'll try to remember all these little traps."

"How did you get Grace to commit suicide?"

"This is growing tedious, Alexa. I never forced Grace Smythe to do anything, ever. You give me far too much credit—or too little. I'm not responsible for anything that woman did. Including her dalliance with Andy."

"Did Andy tell you Sibby Danielson was your mother?"

"I think it's more likely that Andy told Grace."

"Grace was in love with you. She'd have done whatever you wanted. That I had figured out already, from the shrine and how she looked at you. I just didn't know how you used that longing until tonight. We'll say, for the sake of argument, that Andy snooped and found the notebook. Maybe he saw Dorothy making entries and found her hiding place. He approached you, thinking . . . you'd want to know?"

"Imagining I'd help him blackmail my uncle because Unko murdered my parents would be a better theory," Casey said. "Andy could never have blackmailed me with information that I don't care to keep secret."

"Your grandmother had already told you about Sibby. But your uncle figured that out too late."

"If Andy killed his mother, it was probably because she caught him trying to get his hot little hands on her precious tell-all notebook. He wanted a lot of money—he always believed it could make his insignificant life worth living."

"We both know that isn't true," Alexa said, laughing. "You've always had more than enough for a hundred Andy Fugates."

"Money is a tool. Money is power."

"Power is a tricky thing, Casey. You have so much

of it, and yet you want more. Too much is never enough for you."

"It's human nature to want more of a very good thing," Casey said. "Can we cut to this story's ending?"

"Your grandmother figured out that Dr. LePointe sicced Sibby on his older brother so he could have control when she died. You simply wanted to pay him back. It's understandable. And to take away his power—the LePointe billions."

Laughing melodiously, Casey said, "Can you imagine him being disgraced professionally, with no fat grants to dangle over his contemporaries and with a mere two million or so a year to live on? He won't go hungry, but he'll die knowing that his little pecker brought him low. It's so *trailer park*. Gary would love it."

"You shot Andy because you were planning to kill him anyway, and it was a convenient setup for you. But he didn't die immediately. The briefcase slowed the bullets."

"A .357 would have been more appropriate than a .380. But there's the size and weight, and my jacket pocket was small."

"You didn't even shoot at Leland. I guess you figured Leland was too crazy to be believed even if he knew you were involved."

"Leland strikes me as being the way people were ten thousand years ago. So, did Andy write out a confession before he died, and do you have it put away someplace?"

Alexa smiled as if to confirm Casey's question. It was plausible enough. She wished she'd thought to fake one.

"It doesn't matter. Andy surely must have hated me enough for shooting him to make up something like that. Shooting him in order to save your life, I might add. He probably would have killed you."

"I know that, Casey." *And I appreciate that saving me was convenient.*

"Can't you forgive me the rest?"

"There's Grace."

"I hate to speak ill of a suicide. Grace had a thing for me. She was in love with me. I told her I didn't love her, and she couldn't take it. The fifty thousand was a year's severance. If she killed herself because I rejected her or because of her unfortunate involvement in this scheme, it isn't my fault."

Alexa said nothing.

"You were sexually abused in one or more of those Mississippi foster homes, weren't you, Alexa? I'm not an expert on such things, but I imagine an abused young girl could see a penis as a weapon of control and for inflicting pain and degradation. Do you sleep with men?"

"I mostly sleep alone."

"Right," Casey said, picking up the empty martini glass and gazing at it before setting it back down. "Then you must be really frustrated."

"I don't feel frustrated."

"I've seen the way you look at me." She put her hand on Alexa's shoulder, rested it on a bruise. Alexa winced. "I'm sorry. I wouldn't hurt you for anything . . . on purpose."

Casey held the fingers motionless for a few seconds, then traced her finger in the perspiration on Alexa's shoulder, down her arm, to her elbow, where there was another bruise. "A mistreated child could have easily grown up to hate men, or at least to distrust them. Such a child might prefer a woman's touch to a man's. It's just—"

"Basic psychology. Touch for touch's sake isn't something I seek out. Andy didn't kill Sibby. Is that so she'd take the blame for Dorothy? Or because you couldn't bear to kill your own mother?"

"Mother? That sad creature was an incubator at best, a vessel to hold William's sperm. I feel pity for her—how she was manipulated. I've never laid eyes on her, nor do I intend to. But my theory is that she was Andy's genetic proof to back up the notebook, and he put her away in case it was necessary." Casey said, "I want us to be able to be open with each other. I want this suspicion behind us."

"Why did you have them kidnap Gary, knowing they were going to kill him?"

Casey shrugged. "I'm no longer enjoying our talk. Can we change the subject?"

"I kept Gary from dying. That must have disappointed you."

"Gary would have given the money to some Indian tribe or charity, just to watch Unko's facial expression. That's Deana's future."

"I understand. You wanted to punish your uncle too. That's why you sent out photocopies of the diary."

Casey nodded warily. "My timing didn't take the hurricane into consideration, or the splash would have been far greater."

Casey put her hand on Alexa's chin and moved forward to kiss her. Alexa stopped her by turning her head, and standing.

"I don't think that's a good idea," she said.

"You don't think I'm attractive? I think you're very attractive, Alexa. Aren't you starved for attention from someone who adores you and accepts you as you are?"

"You're an extremely attractive woman, Casey. I mean that sincerely. But, despite your take on me, I'm not into women that way, and I don't think you are either."

"You sure about that?"

"I think you use sex as a tool. And even if I were open to a dalliance, your lovers don't exactly fare too well."

"Okay, on your terms." Casey sighed. "When can you start work? A month to tie up your affairs and submit your walking papers should be adequate. That work for you?"

"I'm not sure I could work for you," Alexa said.

"But you aren't refusing me? Will you at least consider my offer seriously?"

"That, I will do."

101

The two women showered side by side, under separate showerheads, without talking. When their eyes met, Alexa didn't avert her gaze and neither did Casey. Alexa knew Casey's mind was working as fast as her own, and wondered what she was thinking. Casey had been over-confident, since she had spent years planning this maneuver, which had been almost perfect—or as perfect as perfect gets, what with the nature of variables always being in flux and the complexities of the number of people involved. Casey was the most cunning and brilliant individual Alexa had ever met, and probably the most totally sociopathic, after Alexa's own sister, Antonia.

"Casey, I want to be totally honest with you. You did some terrible things, and I understand why you did what you did. But I believe in doing the right thing. You are a victim here and you were wronged terribly. You may not face judgment in a court of law, but punishing you that way wouldn't make things right. And you did just punish the guilty, for the most part."

"Those who sought to harm, who did harm, were themselves harmed."

"That's right. Let's say, for the moment, that what you have done is done, and it is forever in the past. Frankly, I'm amazed at how accurately you read and manipulated so many individuals. Your insight into people is astounding. You could have become a psychiatrist. With your intelligence and your instincts, you could have cured untold numbers of very ill people."

"Like my mother?"

"Yes. Maybe. Here's my thinking: You have a vast fortune in your hands, and a potential for decades of doing good and easing suffering."

"The trusts can work miracles if I apply the resources to that end," Casey agreed, smiling. "I've thought about that a lot."

"You could be one of the great benefactors of all time. You have a great talent that transcends art, you create beauty—more than beauty. Your portraits are the most powerful I've ever seen. The sensitivity of your vision is astounding."

"I'm blushing."

"I'll try to stay on point. Your attributes, even your manipulative skills, can be an asset. Casey, your potential is boundless. If you can turn over a new leaf, transcend the evil you've done, the pain you've caused, the revenge you've taken. Was the revenge really satisfying?"

"Yes, Alexa, it was satisfying. They deserved it, every one of them."

"You played evil against evil. But good people were hurt too. Michael Manseur and Kyler Kennedy didn't deserve what they got. Manseur's wife is suffering along with him. A young deputy sheriff was killed. He had a family. He was a good man doing his duty. And Gary loved you."

"I didn't intend for anybody who was innocent to be harmed. I intend to put all of it right. As right as possible. I can't bring that deputy back, but I'll take care of his family. And I will make it right with Gary. I promise I will.

"Alexa, I want to put this all behind me. While honestly I don't regret doing what I did, I'm done with it. I don't want Deana to ever feel the pain I've felt. I want to change the LePointe legacy, bury forever what this family became, what our fortune did to us. I intend to dedicate myself to showing my daughter what her wealth can mean in the lives of many people. We should see ourselves as caretakers of the fortune, use it to do positive things. William actually did good, despite himself, didn't he? His grants had some positive results. We can expand on that. And Gary will help me."

"That sounds promising," Alexa said.

"Let's dress and we'll drink a toast to it and watch the storm waste its time trying to get inside. I feel wonderful. Thank you, Alexa." She kissed her on the cheek. "And you'll help?"

"I'll watch from afar," Alexa said. "That's all the help I can give you." *And I* will *be watching*.

102

Alexa dressed slowly, thinking. Was it possible? Could good spring from evil? Casey West could do so much to help so many. There was no limit to what the interest from four billion dollars could do, no end to the possibilities. Casey could play megabenefactor for forty, maybe fifty years. And Deana could follow in her mother's footsteps for another fifty years. A golden age of the LePointes. The idea was as attractive as silk and as intoxicating to Alexa's mind as . . . heroin. It all seemed possible. As possible as a shattered child becoming as whole as Alexa had. Casey was a shattered child, too, and in that, she and Alexa had common ground. Casey had been a damaged child who had then been nurtured by corrupted and diseased people who had no regard for anyone but themselves. Alexa had been changed by unconditional love and acceptance by wonderful people, which had failed to save her sister, Antonia.

The reality was that Alexa didn't believe for a second it was true. Casey didn't have feelings; she imitated those she sensed and saw in others. Casey was the epitome of corruption made worse by power, and now she had more power than ever. But it would never be enough, and she would use that power to corrupt and harm. She had tempted Alexa with the manipulative insights of Satan. Even if Casey were totally sincere, knowing what she had done, could Alexa really let her go? No. The fact that Casey had done most of her damage to evil people didn't matter.

Alexa also knew instinctively that knowing what she did about Casey's true nature wasn't a major ingredient in a prescription for a long life.

Alexa slipped into her blouse and Casey's jeans, rolling up the legs. She went into the dining room of the pool house and stared out through the sliding glass doors at the increasing fury of the hurricane. Outside, the storm of the century raged; within Alexa Keen no smaller storm had calmed at last.

103

Casey West hurried down the corridor, scarcely noticing how the winds were decimating her gardens. Her house could certainly weather any storm that nature could put together and the elevation precluded any flood the levees admitted.

Casey had gotten a call from Baton Rouge from the copilot who flew the G-III. The plane had lifted off, carrying her real father, Aunt Sarah, and the nurse who tended to her, to New York. She would never go anywhere with them again. Soon the smug bastard would wish he'd been in Decell's shoes when Andy blew his brains out. Casey wasn't finished with him yet, and nothing Alexa said could change that.

Casey hadn't expected, nor believed, that Alexa could put things together, but she had certainly underestimated her, and misread her in crucial ways. Bringing the FBI agent into the plan at such a late date and knowing her so superficially had been a risk, but one she'd believed would put to bed any suspicion of her own involvement.

Andy was supposed to kill William, but she had factored in the fact that her uncle might live. If he survived, she'd had that covered with the covenant bombshell, and had mailed the notebook copies just in case he did survive.

Alexa Keen was no longer relevant. Casey had won her over for the moment, but Alexa would not remain bought with inexpensive and hollow promises. She was too good and too compassionate to be trusted. Besides, Casey wasn't about to have some half-breed guttersnipe watching over her shoulder.

Gary West was alive, but the contract was as good as voided. The jerk was just a vegetable now, one she could keep parked in some institution. He certainly wouldn't be able to taint Deana with his unfortunate and soft attitudes. No, the only remaining problem was Alexa Keen, and Casey was going to handle that one for good.

Casey ran upstairs and started dressing hurriedly in comfortable clothes, singing as she went. The door opened while she was still shirtless, and she looked up to see Edgar, the security guard. When he saw her breasts, he turned hastily away.

"Sorry, Mrs. West."

"It's okay, Edgar. You can look."

The young man turned and stared at her, his face reddening.

Casey tossed her top aside and approached him. She kissed him, placed his soft, strong hand on her breast. She felt him growing against her. He wanted her. They always wanted her. She reached down and stroked his penis through his jeans.

"I'm in a hurry at the moment. But in a little while, Edgar, I'm going to strip your clothes off and do wonderful things to your body. Do you want that, Edgar?"

"Yes, ma'am. I sure will . . . do."

"And you'll return the favor, won't you?"

"If you want me to," he said huskily.

She turned from him and pulled on her top, lifting her hair clear of the turtleneck and letting it drop.

"Is Keen here alone?" she asked.

"There's no cars on the street."

"Good boy, Edgar. You be a doll and go to the den. I'll call you if I need you."

"Yes, ma'am. I'll go to the den and wait." He turned.

"And Edgar," Casey said, checking herself in the mirror. "One more thing."

"Yes, ma'am?"

"Keep that thing of yours nice and hard for me."

104

In the wine room, Casey selected a '97 vintage, Nuits-Saint-Georges Grand Vin de Bourgogne. It was her last bottle of the Burgundy and, she decided, an excellent choice. It had been good enough to tempt Grace into drinking.

Carrying the dusty bottle, Casey went to the kitchen and took down two glasses. Before carrying them out to the pool house, she went into the bathroom with one of them, closed the door, and opened the secret wall vault behind the medicine chest. She pulled out the sole item in there—a small cobalt blue bottle she'd put in there two years before—opened it, and using an eyedropper, carefully moved the tip around the wineglass's inside edge, squeezing the bulb gently as she did so. There was a shine where the clear liquid coated the lip, so she blew on it gently until it dried.

She had only used it once before, the afternoon Grace died, and she knew the venom cocktail she'd paid six thousand dollars for was worth every penny. After making sure the wineglass was the one of the pair that had a small crack in the base, she replaced the blue bottle and went out to the kitchen, where she placed the wine bottle and glasses on a tray.

She lifted Deana to her hip. "Mary, I'll be right back. Make some coffee."

"Yes, ma'am."

Casey wanted Alexa to be at ease, so she decided that Deana's presence would be disarming and distracting. She lifted the tray, and started for the pool house.

"We're going to see Alexa, honey. And, sweetie, Alexa is not your friend. I'm your only friend. I'm the only friend you'll ever have."

105

Alexa removed the tape of Sibby's statement, dropped in a blank one, and pressed the RECORD button. She looked out at the storm, which was tearing bushes apart and blowing wrought-iron pool furniture across the courtyard. A sheared tree limb slammed into the soft earth of a flower bed, sticking upright like a diseased sapling.

When Casey returned, she had dressed in black jeans and a long-sleeved turtleneck. She had Deana on her left hip and carried a tray with two glasses and a bottle of wine. Casey handed Deana to Alexa and placed the tray on the table.

"I not you fren," Deana said. It seemed to Alexa that the little girl seldom said anything else. Deana stared up at Alexa, a smile on her cupid lips.

"Darling, be nice to Alexa."

"Poo-poo," Deana said.

Casey handed the wine bottle to Alexa. "Could you open this for us?"

She placed a glass in front of Alexa, then lifted it. "Oh, damn. The base has a crack in it. I'll go and get you a good one."

"This is fine," Alexa said. "I'm not drinking out of the base."

"You take mine. I'll use the damaged one."

"Don't be silly," Alexa said. "Should this sit before we drink it?"

"Let it breathe in our stomachs."

After Casey poured wine into each of the glasses, Casey took Deana and put her in a high chair.

"Cooteeee!" the little girl demanded.

Casey went to the kitchen cabinets and, after rummaging around, returned with three chocolate cookies.

Casey laughed. "She's a baby. She's happy with cookies. Why should I deny her? I was never denied and I turned out fine."

Alexa was silent, took a long sip of the wine, and was delighted by the rich flavor. "Tastes marvelous. What is it?"

"Burgundy. A very special wine I've been saving for a special occasion. This is certainly that. Today I'm closing the door on the past and bringing in a new day."

"I could grow accustomed to good wine," Alexa said, smiling.

"That's probably the best wine you'll ever drink." Casey looked at Alexa and smiled. "I have to say, I feel like a great burden is lifting off my shoulders."

Alexa took another swallow, then set the glass on the table. She wasn't going to get tipsy.

"I have a confession to make," Casey said.

"Yes?"

"When I came out earlier, I unloaded your gun

and took the magazines. I hope you can forgive me going into your purse without permission."

"Why?" *She intends to kill me.*

"I thought you might pull it on me since I admitted . . . you know, killing Andy. Killing Grace. How do you like the wine?"

"I suppose expensive wine is an acquired taste. I guess it's wasted on me. You took my bullets because you don't trust me. You don't intend to change, do you? You aren't capable of changing."

Casey picked up her glass and emptied it in three swallows. "You should have let me replace the glass for you."

"The wine?"

"It's laced with a little something that is decidedly lethal and highly unlikely to be detected. Since you wanted to know, it's what I used to put Grace down. She purchased the poison, so it will ultimately be traced to her. I'll say Grace gave me the wine, knowing I would drink it and die, but, horror of horrors, *you* drank it. After they know what to look for, your blood will show it. A flawless plan, I think. It works in only a few minutes. Do finish the wine. It won't make any difference, I assure you."

"Casey, why?" Alexa asked, setting down her half-empty glass. Terror blossomed inside her. A burning sensation grew in her chest and she found it hard to get her breath.

"I really do admire your abilities, Alexa. That makes this very difficult for me. I'm sorry to have to kill you, but you're a little too dangerous for my tastes. Nothing personal."

"You didn't—"

"You'll feel the paralysis starting any time now, Alexa. I was assured it's not at all painful. It simply paralyzes the lungs, stops the heart."

"You're drinking the wine too."

"I put the poison on the rim of your glass. I'll put some in the bottle later and say I was fortunate not to have had any before you collapsed."

"Casey, you need to listen to me. What is the poison? You have to tell me, so I can help you."

"Help me?"

"Tell me! What's the antidote!"

"There's no antidote, Alexa." Casey's smile was not one of regret or pity. It was the smile of victory and pleasure.

"You didn't poison me," Alexa told her. "I switched wineglasses when you were getting the cookies."

"What?"

Alexa stood and looked down at her would-be murderer. "You poured me more than you poured for yourself. I don't like red wine and I didn't want to drink too much. Please, tell me how to stop it!"

Casey's face was a luminous white. She looked at the wineglass in front of her in disbelief. "Alexa, what did you do?"

Casey stared at Alexa with an expression that morphed into one of unbridled hatred. "You? You! You bitch! I . . . can't die. I can't! You . . ." She stiffened suddenly in her chair, locked her eyes on Deana, then turned them back to Alexa. "I . . . can't . . . breee."

Casey fell sideways to the floor. Alexa rushed around the table, rolled Casey over onto her back, and started CPR compressions.

"Mary! Call 911!" she yelled.

Alexa pressed as hard as she could on Casey's chest as she counted the compressions. But as hard as she worked, as horrified as she was, she knew that Casey couldn't be brought back from where she was going. Casey shuddered violently, and then was still.

"Mommy nigh-nigh," Deana said, waving a partly eaten cookie in the air. "Ahm not your fren," Deana said, smiling down at Alexa coyly.

Alexa kept working, compressing and blowing into Casey's open mouth for ten minutes, then gave up. She realized that she was crying, and put her head in her hands. She heard the security guard talking to Mary, but she couldn't make out the words.

The wind howled, rattling the windows violently like a raging man trying to beat them in to save his children from a fire inside. The moaning and creaking sounded like a chorus of grief-stricken mothers.

As she knelt staring into Casey's fully dilated and clouded eyes, she was aware of an explosion as an oak tree gave up its grip on the earth, rolled over, and crashed into the long hallway, collapsing the roof and exploding the glass walls.

106

The J. Edgar Hoover Building
Washington, D.C.
March 2006

Alexa was aware of the ticking of the clock on her desk, of each second of precious time passing—the merciless race she was running. Her eyes were locked on a series of still photos depicting two dead body-guards, whose employer, an industrialist from Akron, had been abducted from his house by unsubs, who'd demanded fifteen million dollars for his safe return. Alexa was painfully aware that the man was going to die unless she and her team could find him before his abductors decided to end his life. The FBI hadn't been brought in by the local authorities until it was too late for Alexa to get on-site before the deadline had passed to pay the extortionists.

Her gut told her it wouldn't matter if she was there. She wasn't as convinced of her gut feelings being right as she once had been.

When her direct line rang, she reached for the receiver reflexively.

"Keen," she said, automatically.

"How you doing, Alexa?"

"Michael Manseur!" Alexa exclaimed, sitting back in her chair. "How are you?"

"Well, you know as well as I do. You were here for the worst part of the afterward."

Alexa had spent two days trying to help the city's residents who had remained in New Orleans and become trapped by the flooding. She would have stayed even longer, but her director had ordered her to return to duty in D.C. and had sent a helicopter specifically to take her out. She had refused to leave until the pilot agreed to take Sibby Danielson from flooded Charity Hospital to safety.

"How are you feeling, Michael?"

"I can't complain," Manseur said. "My jaw isn't wired shut now, and although my sinuses are giving me fits, I'm not drooling through a tube into a cup anymore. I'm back at work, up to my wide butt in alligators. Murders are way down, you know. City's more like Mayberry RFD these days, since we exported our worst offenders."

All of the evidence she and Manseur had collected had been destroyed by the floodwaters that had slammed into the NOPD's property and evidence rooms. NOPD had also lost all case files and records that weren't computerized. The same had happened to courthouse files, leaving a few hundred lucky criminals free—unless they continued their evil ways, which every cop knew most of them would, they'd never be brought to justice.

"Alligators." Alexa laughed. "Figuratively this time, I hope."

"We're seeing a lot of progress, given everything. Emily and the girls hope to be coming back in a few weeks. I've got mixed feelings about that. We don't know what all's in the soil and the water, but the water's been poison long as I can remember. No schools open yet, and the city is broke, like always. It's never going to be like it was, but it's where I live."

"I see Jackson Evans wound up in Detroit."

"Yeah, and good riddance. The new chief is all business, and he hates microphones and cameras."

There was a long silence.

"What can I do for you, Michael?"

"Did you get the tape I sent?"

"Yes, I did. I'm sorry, I haven't had time to watch it."

"No hurry. Reason I called, I thought I should catch you up on what's going on down here with you-know-who."

Alexa closed her eyes and rubbed them gently. "Yeah, I've been meaning to call you too. You know how it is. So, what's the latest?"

"Dr. LePointe hasn't been indicted yet. You know where that's at?"

"The federal prosecutor has offered Dr. LePointe a deal. I tried. I truly did. Interesting speculation, coincidences, circumstantial evidence, and the word of a lunatic, who is less than presentable to a jury against LePointe. Twenty-five years of heavy drugs—and a lobotomy, to boot. And after what Casey did, LePointe doesn't look so despicable."

"Sibby's in a nice facility in Virginia, I understand."

"Yes. I've been to visit her. Dr. LePointe set aside enough money to keep her wherever she likes. And he doesn't know where she is." *The bastard.* Since Alexa had recorded proof of what Casey had done, LePointe's lawyers had managed to cast the public's attention on Casey's bad deeds, and to blunt the truth of what he had done, who he really was. What he and Nurse Fugate had done to Sibby had become mostly what Nurse Fugate had done due to some misguided loyalty blended with a sickness that LePointe, a very busy and dedicated professional who only wished to help Sibby, had been unaware of. No witnesses came forth to dispute his assertion of his naïve innocence and misplaced trust in Fugate. It was disgusting, though hardly surprising.

"His wife, Sarah, passed away day before yesterday. If I were him, I'd take a long trip to Europe and never come back. He has nothing but time on his hands now—since the trusts are being run by a bunch of bankers and lawyers, and he's surrendered his license to practice at the request of the medical ethics board."

"He belongs in prison."

"You don't think what's happened to him is worse than jail? He's disgraced. He's lost everything he gives a damn about. The media's roasted him. People openly mock him. Despite the evidence, most people don't really believe Casey was the insane psychopath LePointe claims she was."

"Disgrace is temporary if you're rich enough. He's still very, very rich."

"He is. And poor Leland Ticholet is on death row. His lawyers are trying to have his conviction overturned and him committed because he's insane. Big surprise. He never denied any of it."

"He wasn't competent to stand trial," Alexa said. She had testified at his trial, and he'd had to be taken from the courtroom because he had spent the time she was testifying interrupting the proceedings to ask her when she was giving him a new boat, and to yell out that she'd lied to him. "He never understood that he was on trial for his life."

"The ME identified the poison that Casey used on Grace and herself. It was a mixture of jellyfish venom and something to get it in the bloodstream through the stomach wall. Very rare. Took a top lab to identify it. Iritableji or something. I have it written down here . . . E-ray-kon-ji. It's collected from a teensy little jellyfish by that name from Australia. Grace Smythe bought it from some research assistant she knew."

"And Gary?" Alexa asked.

"He's making progress. He's learning how to

walk, and he's saying a few words. I'm praying he gets it together real soon."

"So he'll be getting Deana back?"

"When he gets better, I suppose so. Casey's former lawyers are now working for Deana. They may not like the fact that Gary might be a threat to their jobs, but they don't like LePointe either. They're watching him like hawks."

"I hope Gary's better soon. I have a suspicion he'll be equal to the task."

"Sooner the better. We all hope that," Manseur said. "We all do. You doing okay, Alexa?" he asked.

"Michael, I appreciate your concern. Truth is, I have this case I'm working on that's had me running around like crazy. I haven't had any time to dwell on the tragedy yet. Maybe I'll have a breakdown when I do have time to think about it, but I'm okay for the moment."

"It's the job. Heartbreak is a constant, darlin'. You ever stop having your heart broke, you quit the job. You did good, real good. You have nothing to regret. You did what nobody else would or could have done. You hear me?"

"I hear you, Michael."

"Alexa, if you ever need to talk, I'm sitting right here. I mean that."

"Thanks. If I need to talk, I'll call you."

"Promise?"

"You take care of yourself," Alexa said.

"I'll do the best I can. This is New Orleans, you know," he said, hanging up.

And you can have it, she thought.

Opening her desk drawer, Alexa removed a photograph. In it, a boy named Andy and an orphaned girl tugged at a little red wagon. Alexa rested her finger on the girl's face—the spitting image of her own daughter, Deana. Alexa couldn't bear to toss the purloined print in the trash can. Maybe, she told herself, she would make sure Deana got it someday.

In the image, a delighted young girl did not yet reflect the razor-sharp beauty that would become her tool. The pain that would spawn an amazing talent was just a seed waiting in her to bloom, along with a sickness that would lead to deaths and self-destruction.

Alexa had lied to Manseur. She couldn't bring herself to admit that she had watched the videotape he'd sent—more times than she could count, just as she had pored over the book of photographs that Casey had given her. Maybe she was punishing herself for being so wrong about Casey. How she had missed for so long that such a talented and sensitive artist, a seemingly loving wife and mother, could have been a totally evil and psychopathic entity. Alexa wasn't sure she wanted to face any of the answers that could explain it.

The video was a compilation of the news coverage of the case, the notebook's stunning revelations, the shoot-out in the swamp, and the coverage of Leland Ticholet's trial. But the thirty seconds of footage at the end always made Alexa cry. The shot had been recorded by a news camera with a very long lens, near the LePointe family tomb in the city-sized cemetery in Metairie. It showed Casey LePointe West's body being buried beside those of her deceased ancestors. It wasn't the fact that she had seen Casey die, or that she blamed herself in any way for any of what had happened, that made her cry. Alexa had done her job to the best of her ability, and Casey West had been killed by her own devices.

And what made Alexa cry while watching the tape wasn't the sight of an old man with gray hair wearing sunglasses despite the overcast, who walked very slowly down a path toward a waiting black Bentley.

What devastated Alexa Keen was the fact that William LePointe's pace was slowed because of the angelic, towheaded, smiling grandchild who, hand clasping his, walked uncertainly beside him.

Get well soon, Gary West. That little girl desperately needs you to protect her from evil—to make sure she doesn't grow up to be a LePointe.

She put the snapshot away, closed the drawer, and took a deep breath.

Pausing just long enough to take a sip of lukewarm coffee, Alexa Keen bent forward in her chair to concentrate on the crime-scene photographs from the Akron field office. When she'd done that, she had to review the in-depth case file and search for any edge there might be that had been overlooked.

Alexa Keen had a lot of work to do because, unless she could pull off a miracle, time was extremely short for an abducted Ohio businessman.

About the Author

JOHN RAMSEY MILLER's career has included stints as a visual artist, advertising copywriter, and journalist. He is the author of the nationally best-selling *The Last Family*; of three Winter Massey thrillers: *Inside Out, Upside Down*, and *Side by Side*; and a stand-alone crime novel featuring FBI Special Agent Alexa Keen, *Too Far Gone*. *Upside Down* was nominated by the International Thriller Writers for the Best Paperback Original Award. He is at work on his next Winter Massey thriller, *Through & Through*, coming from Dell in 2007.

A native son of Mississippi, he now lives in North Carolina with his wife and writes full-time.

If you enjoyed John Ramsey Miller's
exciting new crime novel, TOO FAR
GONE, you won't want to miss any of
his bestselling thrillers. Look for them at
your favorite bookseller's.
And read on for an exciting early look
at the next electrifying thriller,

THROUGH
&
THROUGH

A Winter Massey Novel

Coming soon from Dell Books

Through & Through

by
John Ramsey Miller

Coming soon

1

The Mississippi Delta
South of Memphis
December

The hunter pulled off the gravel road, parked his vehicle among the trees and scrub brush made leafless by the season, and climbed out. There was a sharp bite in the cold predawn air.

His breath made thin fog that leaked from his nostrils and seemed to hang in the stillness.

Going around to the back of the SUV, he opened the rear door and took out his tools.

Dressed warmly against the cold, he slowly made his way through the woods on the damp leaves. Not that there was any danger here in this remote place, and no possible enemy seeking him out, just a target waiting for a well-placed, precision-loaded high-powered rifle round.

The hunter moved to the hide he had selected at the edge of the tree line—a thick sweet gum tree felled by winds. He knelt beside the tree, set the hard case he carried on the ground. Opening it, he lifted his Dakota T-76 Longbow rifle topped with a powerful Zeiss scope, which he had sighted in for the range of the shot he intended to make with it. At that range he could place a hand-loaded round—traveling at over 3,000 feet per second—through a ballistic vest or through a skull. For this shooter, shattering a porcelain saucer at the distance this shot called for was no more difficult than flipping a cigarette through a discarded tractor tire leaning against a barn five paces distant. He had done this before and knew that the .338 round would hollow out the organic shell, filling the air downrange for thirty feet with a vapor comprised of brain tissue, bone chips, fluid, and blood. Surviving such a cranial event would be impossible.

The hunter leaned his Dakota gently against the fallen tree's trunk so he didn't jar the scope. Reaching into the bag, the man pulled out a canvas sandbag and placed it on the tree. Using the back edge of his right hand he chopped a channel into the center of the bag before setting the gun's stock into the groove.

Opening a small container, he removed and rolled the ends of each of the foam earplugs into points, licked the tips, and slipped them into his ear canals. There was the familiar crackling sound as the plugs expanded to fill the spaces. He slipped on his wool watch cap to warm his ears. Reaching into the pocket of his jacket, he removed his thin leather shooting gloves and slipped them on.

Drawing back the gun's bolt and pressing it forward, the hunter watched as the brass case of the topmost shell slid from its home in the magazine and vanished from sight into the firing chamber. He engaged the safety, brought the butt firmly against his shoulder, lowered his cheek to the cold synthetic stock, and closed his left eye. The scope's lens surfaces were slightly fogged, but in a few short minutes the temperature differential between the case and the air would equalize and they would clear.

Ready now, the shooter, seated on the cold leaves behind the fallen tree, chewed on a toothpick, and waited patiently for the morning light to gather and for his target to come into sight. He yawned into his gloved hand and, as he rubbed his hands together briskly to generate heat, kept his eyes focused downrange on the killing zone.

What do you feel when you take a human life?
Recoil.

2

Winter Massey used his Surefire flashlight sparingly, as he led Faith Ann Porter along a logging road that had been cut through the hardwood forest decades before. Their footsteps were all but silenced by the dew-dampened leaves, and their warm breath created plumes of vaporlike smoke in the air.

Winter carried a rifle slung over each shoulder. On his right was a Tikka T-3 stainless in 30-06, and over his left he wore a .270 Browning A-bolt. Each gun was equipped with a telescopic sight. Faith Ann had fired the .270 on numerous occasions and Winter knew that the girl could put a shot within an inch of the target's center at 100 yards. The question was whether or not she could place her shot as accurately when she was firing at an actual living animal as opposed to a printed cross on paper.

Faith Ann, a thin-framed, fair-skinned thirteen-year-old with an elfin face featuring large blue eyes and soft red-blonde hair, stopped at the base of the steel ladder that was misted with a coating of dew. The rungs led up twelve feet to a platform with a wide padded bench. A shooting rail covered with padding designed to keep exposed water pipes from freezing surrounded the platform. Hung from the shooting rail was a burlap skirt that served to protect them from the wind, help hold in their scent, and prevent sharp-eyed prey from spotting their shapes and movements as they waited. The stand, positioned against a hickory tree, was secured to its trunk by nylon straps.

After Faith Ann climbed into the stand, Winter used the karabiner on the rope hanging from the stand to clip the carrying handle on the rucksack Faith Ann had worn to the stand. From the platform, she pulled the rucksack up into the stand the way they had practiced the day before, and she unhooked it quietly before lowering the rope so Winter could attach the karabiner to the sling on her unloaded Browning. Hoisting up her weapon, she unhooked it and again lowered the rope so Winter could attach his T-3. Climbing up to join her in the stand, he pulled his gun up.

After he was seated beside her and had closed the burlap skirt, Winter loaded both guns deliberately and silently. Chambering a round in each, and engaging the safeties, he propped the weapons against the rail—hers in front of her, his before him—and they settled in to wait. Inside the pack were additional hand warmers, face shields, energy bars, water in plastic bottles, and other accessories necessary for the long hours they might have to spend in the stand. Winter carried a custom drop-point hunting knife in a sheath.

The pair wore electronic earplugs designed to amplify ambient noise but to close when detecting sudden loud noise, like ear-damaging gun reports.

Faith Ann had completed the safety course required to obtain a hunting license and both her uncle, Hank Trammel, and Winter had spent time working with her to hone her shooting skills with the .270 until they were sure she could shoot accurately enough to take a deer. It had been a short course because she was a natural, and her groups at one and two hundred yards had been tighter than those of her teachers. Faith Ann could hit a deer in the vitals at two hundred yards or better, but as to whether or not she could actually shoot one was a question only opportunity would answer.

As the sun rose, the Mississippi woods around the field, and then the field itself, came slowly into focus. The bright green field, planted with rye, clover, and alfalfa, was a natural bowl bordered by two ridges that ran east to west. The thick woods on the slopes leading down from the ridges fed water down into the field when it rained, and filtered deer into the field in the evenings. There they would feed on the grasses planted for the single purpose of attracting game. At either end of the field were impenetrable thickets where deer bedded in safety.

At the edge of the plot directly across from the

stand, a line of tall bamboo formed a natural fence. In other places, the perimeter was laced with thick and thorny growth. The trees on the ridges grew close enough together to allow the animals a sense of security, but far enough apart so animals could be seen moving and to allow a hunter to make a killing shot between the trunks. The creek, less than a hundred yards away to the south, provided fresh water. The food plot was both a perfect habitat and an ambush point extraordinaire.

As light gathered, Winter could make out the black shapes of several grazing deer, and saw that none were bucks. Some of the animals were noticeably smaller than the others—yearlings the size of large dogs. Whitetail doe were social creatures, and their offspring often remained with them even though they were no longer suckling. A pair of button buck yearlings romped at one end of the food plot, butting heads and ramming each other playfully. Someday they would mature and the fighting would be in earnest—combat over does ready to breed. Mature males lived solitary lives in the safety of the thickets, feeding only at night except during the rut, which was now in full swing. During the winter ruts they chased after any doe in estrus. Normally male deer were wary, bedding down just before sunrise and rising just before sundown and moving as little as possible during daylight hours. Toward the end of the rut, as fewer doe remained in heat, the males ranged farther and wider to seek them out.

From the stand, it was seventy yards directly across to a major rub—a cypress sapling in the bamboo whose bark had been rasped off by a mature buck polishing the moss from his antlers—the ground before it was stripped bare by his large forehoofs and the tree bark impregnated by the musk transferred from the hairy, circular tarsal scent glands on the animal's hind legs. Scrapes were designed to attract does in heat. At this point in the rut, the animal who'd made this particular scrape might be miles away checking other of his scrapes, like a fisherman might change favored places on a lake. Deer hunting held no guarantees, but if a hundred things went right, a careless buck might make an appearance within the range of a well-placed bullet in the daylight hours—especially in this area of mostly private property, where there were relatively few hunters putting pressure on them.

According to the hoofprints near the scrape, the animal who tended it was huge, his hoofs measuring over three inches. The depth of the prints, too, revealed him to be a heavier than usual animal. Faith Ann had nicknamed the scrape maker Rudolph, and although they hadn't actually seen a large buck on their visit that autumn to check on the food plots scattered around the property, Winter was sure the placement of the stand was as perfect as possible to ambush the deer.

Faith Ann slowly turned her head and smiled warmly at him, her face pinkened by the chill and framed by the camouflage fleece hood. The mittens on her hands and the bottoms of her boots held chemical warmers to fight off the penetrating cold that could become unbearable as time passed.

In the distance a gunshot cracked like dull thunder. That shot was followed a few seconds later by a second. The grazing animals in the food plot did not seem to notice, but as daylight was building, they were moving toward the edges of the field, having satisfied their hunger and feeling a need to rest and digest in the thickets' cover.

Movement on the ridge to their right drew the two hunters' attention where four does were moving cautiously down the slope among the trees. Winter felt Faith Ann stiffen as she slowly lifted her rifle and turned the barrel toward the animals so she could evaluate each through the telescopic sight. As they watched the does, a buck came over the ridge and trotted warily after them, head up, ears flickering, nose sampling the air. Winter's heart quickened as he studied the eight-point.

A single anonymous gunshot boomed hollowly from the east signaling that a hunter on the adjoining property had decided to take an animal.

The buck stopped and lifted his head to sniff the still air, expelling a thick cloud of steam through his nostrils. In a loose pack, the four does trotted down toward the field, and several of the grazing deer that had remained in the plot spooked and darted into the cover. The button bucks, rightfully fearing any approaching buck, bounded off and vanished through the bamboo curtain. Fifty yards away, the eight-point moved broadside to the stand. Flicking his tail, he lowered his head, and Faith Ann, doing as Winter had instructed her, used this opportunity to fix the crosshairs of her scope on the area just behind his shoulder where the fist-sized heart pumped and the lungs filled and deflated.

While Winter was waiting for Faith Ann to make the shot, a rustle across the field caught his attention. He turned to see a second buck break from the bamboo wall. The massive deer's coat was dark, almost black, and the golden antlers growing from his skull looked like tree limbs. Like a stallion, he trotted straight into the middle of the field toward the does, now clustered nervously at the edge of the field.

"Hold up," Winter whispered. "Very slowly, look in the field to your left."

Faith Ann turned and saw the other buck.

Winter held his breath, his own hand closing around the stock of his rifle to lift it. If she missed or couldn't bring herself to shoot—which happened even to seasoned hunters faced with the prospect of taking such an animal—he would make the shot for her. If she missed, he would have a second or two before the animal bolted, and he would either fire before it took off or let it go. Winter would never fire at an animal in flight for fear of wounding without killing—something a conscientious hunter didn't do.

In all the hunts he had made during his lifetime, Winter had never witnessed bucks in combat over does, but he knew that was exactly what was unfolding before their eyes. He counted the points on the rack of the larger deer and came up with twelve. A second count turned up two more tips. Fourteen points with perfect symmetry was a rarity.

"What are they doing?" Faith Ann whispered.

"They both want the girls," Winter said.

Head erect, the eight-point marched into the field, placing himself between his harem and the mature interloper. Like gladiators, the two males faced off and circled each other, sizing up the opposition. Rudolph had perhaps three years and forty pounds on the eight-point. The beam distance between the outside edges of Rudolph's heavy rack was at least twenty-four inches, the eight point's maybe sixteen. Rudolph's muscles were better defined, his neck half again as thick. It was like a hound facing off with a Mastiff.

Rudolph moved first and the eight tried to sidestep at the last moment. The larger deer hit the smaller in the shoulder with his broad chest, knocking the smaller off balance and skidding him sideways in the soft earth. The smaller buck spun, lowered his head, and struck the larger animal head on, locking his antlers with his larger foe. Muscles tensed, both twisted their racks for advantage, like wrestlers. The head twisting and clicking of horns went on for a long minute until the smaller buck lost his footing and tumbled to the ground, expelling his breath in a rush.

The larger buck backed up and lowered his head. As he tensed for the rush, the smaller rolled, made it to his feet and shook his head.

Lurching, the eight rushed the fourteen and the sound of their antlers colliding was like a gunshot. Rudolph's weight sent the smaller deer sideways and he whirled and lowered his head again, but the larger buck hit him a raking blow down his length that opened the hide on his back leg like a razor. The smaller buck was breathing hard as Rudolph circled him carefully, seeking another vulnerable spot to ram.

Winter was watching the battle with such intensity that the unexpected clap of gun thunder raised him off the bench.

3

A peal of thunder ended a meandering dream that had taken a turn that had involved her mother. It took Sean Massey a second to orient herself to her surroundings, to realize the dream-killing noise was actually a rifle report. Morning light lit the closed curtains with a warm yellow glow. Sean yawned and looked at the toddler sleeping peacefully beside her. Winter had managed to get up, get dressed, and leave the motor home before dawn without waking her.

The land was owned by Billy Lyons, a high-school friend of Winter's. Billy was a lawyer who had missed the opening of the hunt because he was in the middle of a murder trial in Memphis. His other regular hunting buddy, the chief financial officer for a large securities firm, had pressing obligations that had him in London. Sean and Winter had decided to make it a family event and had rented the motor home to add a degree of comfort not afforded by the one-room wood-frame shack the three friends usually shared. The cabin was fine for a group of men, but between the wood-burning stove, mattresses that looked like they'd been salvaged from the side of the road, and the outhouse fifty feet from the back door, it didn't rise to the level of comfort Sean thought Faith Ann deserved. And Olivia Moment Massey, their child, was at the stage where she walked where she chose to go, wanted to do everything herself, and, when frustrated, was vocal at a disturbing volume. Enough said.

Sean slipped out of bed and dressed in a wool

shirt, jeans, and ankle-high muck boots. Closing the bedroom door gently behind her, she looked out into the galley where Rush Massey, her fourteen-year-old stepson, sat at the table dressed warmly for the day ahead. He had his fingertips on the page of an open book, the paper blank but for neatly ordered raised dots of braille. He inclined his head and his bright blue eyes seemed to focus on Sean.

From beneath the table at his master's feet, Nemo, Rush's Rhodesian ridgeback seeing-eye dog, lay with his chin on his forepaw. Without raising his head, he wagged his heavy tail at Sean.

"Morning, Sean," Rush said cheerfully. "You heard that shot?"

"I sure did."

"I bet you a quarter it was Daddy's ought-six. I bet Faith Ann couldn't shoot," Rush said. "I bet Daddy had to do it."

"You think that was them shooting?" Sean asked, taking a box of cereal off the counter and filling a bowl. "There are a lot of hunters around here."

"I know it was."

"And you think Faith Ann doesn't have what it takes?"

"She *is* a girl," he replied. "No offense. Girls don't shoot like men and they don't kill either."

Sean smiled. *If you only knew.* "None taken. You want me to cook you some breakfast? Eggs and bacon?"

"I ate some cereal right after they left," he replied. "I know it was them since the stand is that way and about six hundred yards off." He pointed over his shoulder.

Sean put her hand on Rush's head as she passed by him to take a seat across from him.

"You want a cup of coffee?" he asked.

"Would love one, dear son," she answered, pouring milk into her bowl.

Rush rose, opened the cabinet, got a cup, and, using his finger to gauge the level of the rising heated coffee, filled it to an inch from the lip. After replacing the pot, he set the cup on the table before Sean and took his seat across from her. She looked into his eyes, and if she hadn't known the orbs were painted acrylic, she would have sworn he was studying her.

Rush had lost his eyesight in a plane crash that had taken his mother's life. Eleanor, a flight instructor, had been giving her young son lessons when a Beech Baron had entered the landing pattern from above and behind the two-seat Cessna and swatted the smaller plane out of the sky. Eleanor had managed to maintain enough control to crash-land with enough forward speed so Rush wasn't killed. A section of the shattered windshield had sliced just deep enough into his skull to destroy both of his eyes without damaging his brain. Eleanor hadn't been as lucky. Only her brain stem had been functioning enough to let her body live long enough to be put on a life support until Winter, then a deputy U.S. marshal, had arrived to hold her for a little while before the machine was switched off. Per her wishes, the doctors had managed to harvest most of her organs, and Sean had seen the collection of letters written by grateful recipients.

Eleanor's heart had gone into an eighteen-year-old girl living in Oregon, who had since married and had delivered one child, whom she had named Eleanor.

Eleanor's liver had been sectioned and saved two recipients, both middle-aged men, and her undamaged kidney had been implanted in the wife of a car salesman who had three towheaded children and, according to the picture she'd included, a Siamese cat that wore a red collar—at least on picture day.

Sean finished her cereal and set down the bowl for Nemo, who rose and lapped the milk slowly. She gazed out the window beside her at the opening in the trees where the logging road entered the woods.

Nemo went to the door and stared at it, whining once—his signal for wanting to be let outdoors for a short walk.

Sean looked out the window again and saw something orange move at the edge of the woods. She smiled when she realized that it was Faith Ann, wearing a Day-Glo vest. The girl was alone, and she was without her backpack or her gun. As Sean watched the approaching child in mounting confusion, she saw the crimson lines on her cheek, like war paint made in what appeared to be blood. Then she saw that Faith Ann was crying.

Sean ran from the motor home.

As Sean approached, Faith Ann tilted her head, met her eyes, and stopped short.

"He's *dead*!" the girl yelled.